Audrey Reimann was brough[...] was educated at the Macclesfie[...] School for Girls. she now lives in Edinburgh.

She has three children and is the proud grandmother of seven small children. She has been variously a bank clerk, nurse, teacher of problem children and foster mother to twenty-five. But above all, Audrey Reimann is a storyteller. She is the author of four wonderful novels, *The Moses Child*, *Praise For The Morning, Alice Davenport* and *Wise Child*. The latter is also available from Piatkus.

Also by Audrey Reimann

Wise Child

The Weeping Tree

Audrey Reimann

PIATKUS

For more information on other books published
by Piatkus, visit our website at
www.piatkus.co.uk

First published in Great Britain in 1999 by
Judy Piatkus (Publishers) Ltd of
5 Windmill Street, London W1P 1HF

This edition published 1999
email: info@piatkus.co.uk

A catalogue record for this book is available from the British Library

ISBN 0 7499 3123 X

Set in Times by Action Publishing Technology Ltd, Gloucester

Printed and bound in Great Britain by
Mackays of Chatham plc, Chatham, Kent

To my husband David
With special thanks to cousins Max and Jean Reimann
of Bancroft, Ontario

Prologue

1961

It was a tranquil Scottish summer evening and the swans, gliding upriver in regal formation, seemed oblivious of the rotting body of a man that floated, grey and bloated, face down in the reeds.

Above the watershed where the River Esk gushes into the bay of the Firth of Forth, high tides bring flotsam, fishing nets and lobster pots upstream. A fisherman's lad who daily scavenged the banks was the first to spot the clothed corpse swirling slowly, one bare purple foot caught under a piece of driftwood.

His father said that there was a reward of £5 for a body found at sea. That would buy a transistor radio. He ran swiftly up the bank, over the ancient stone bridge and past the church until he reached the police station.

'I've found a dead body,' he gasped. 'My dad says it's five pounds.'

The sergeant leaned across the high wooden counter. 'Dead body? Where?'

'Under the Roman bridge.' The boy took a deep breath. 'I'm first, if there's a reward.'

Half an hour later the sergeant rang through to Edinburgh and demanded to be put through to Chief Inspector Andrew Stewart.

From the window of his office in Royal Terrace, Chief Inspector Andrew Stewart had a good view of the high craggy ridge of Arthur's Seat, the 1,000-foot extinct volcanic mountain that rises in Queen's Park in the centre of the city. The phone rang.

'Answer it, Jenny,' he said over his shoulder to his secretary. He continued to scan the park where tomorrow, on his day off, he'd run to the summit of the mountain and see the whole city laid out at his feet, the castle on its rock, and below it the little graveyard where still stood the weeping willow under which as a young man he'd plighted his troth.

From the top, on a clear day, he'd see the three giant iron cobwebs of the Forth Bridge, the foothills of the Trossachs and, turning full south, the border country. But today he was looking for anything unusual. He'd have to rid himself of this habit of looking for trouble if he were to leave the police force. He'd had fifteen good years and could retire in another five, but was starting to think that perhaps now was the time for a change of direction. He was forty-one; not too old to make a new start, to buy a few acres of fertile East Lothian coastal land, build a house, look for a wife and hope for children. He should wind down, limit himself to civil work, not get involved in anything exciting.

Behind him Jenny said, 'It's the sergeant at Musselburgh station.'

'All right.' He walked over to the desk and took the handset from her to hear the sergeant saying, 'Chief Inspector, sir? We've just pulled a body out of the Esk. I think it's your old commander.'

This was the last thing Andrew wanted – the frisson of excitement that came when the song in his ears was different from the tune being played in the investigative area of his mind. He often thought in musical metaphors, for he was a good singer and a fair pianist. He rumpled thick dark hair that was greying at the temples and said sharply into the mouthpiece, 'Who else could it be?' And after a few seconds, 'No. His wife must identify him. Is he in the mortuary?'

While he listened, Andrew glanced at his desk, where the lead story on the local paper read:

The sea search for Sir Gordon Campbell of Ingersley has been called off. Sir Gordon sailed out of North Berwick harbour at high tide on 15 June in perfect sailing conditions. His empty yacht drifted ashore the following day but there

2

have been no sightings and there is little hope now of finding the wartime naval captain alive.

Lady Campbell, well-known local figure, JP and school governor, told reporters that her husband was being treated for depression. He had never recovered from the loss at sea of his son Robert, who went missing, presumed drowned, off the coast of San Francisco three years ago. It is looking increasingly likely that our foremost local family has once again been struck by tragedy.

Andrew knew all about the misfortunes and tragedies of the Campbell family, for he had been born and brought up on the Campbells' Ingersley estate. The sergeant's words came faintly over the crackling line. 'He's in our mortuary. It looks as if he capsized and drowned.'

Sir Gordon Campbell had captained a county-class cruiser in the Mediterranean from 1940 throughout the war. How could he capsize a small yacht on a night when a child could have set a straight course over the Forth? Andrew said, 'The fiscal depute's been called? And the pathologist? Photography crew? This is a suspicious death.' He put down the phone.

Outside, his metallic gold Ford Zephyr was parked in front of the soot-blackened building. He liked this car. It was big enough to accommodate his long legs and fast enough to cover the twenty-five miles to Ingersley in under an hour. He would break the news to Lady Campbell before she heard it from anyone else. She must identify the body immediately – if she could; the facial features on a body that had been submerged for three weeks were usually unrecognisable. He turned the car towards Abbey Hill and took the low road, through Queen's Park, past Holyrood Palace towards Duddingston loch and out on to the highway, heading for his old home at Ingersley. And as he went his normally alert, watchful expression gave way to a wry smile. This was the first time in his life that he had volunteered for the job that all policemen try to avoid – breaking the news of a man's death to his wife. He wanted to see her immediate reaction, though he did not expect Lady Campbell to shed a single tear over the man to whom Andrew himself owed so much.

As a boy he had hero-worshipped Sir Gordon Campbell, the

3

master of Ingersley, though the young baronet represented everything Andrew's youthful heart rebelled against: the Scottish system of feudal land rights where a few aristocrats, dukes and lords, own vast estates. Land parcels are leased annually to tenant farmers who can never own, but only rent the land they work. He also hated the knee-bending and fore-lock tugging that went with privilege. But Sir Gordon, the most honourable man Andrew had ever known, was contemptuous of privilege and had inspired every young man whose life crossed his own.

Chapter One

August 1936

Sir Gordon Campbell, the youngest Justice of the Peace in the county, glanced through the window of Haddington courtroom as the boys were led in. It was a perfect day for sailing, with a light breeze ruffling the leaves on the aspen trees outside. He was thirty-seven, tall, sandy-haired, and had the keen, steady blue eyes of a seafaring man. And he hated the civic duties that had fallen to him three years ago on his father's death. Three years he had been away from the sea and his life as a commander in the Royal Navy; three years of trying to adjust to the duties of landowner and master of an estate that, since the catastrophic stock market crash of '33, was all but bankrupt.

He had spent a soul-destroying morning here, sending to reformatories juveniles who showed any spark, any inkling of hope for reform. He'd also sent to prison the likes of the boys who stood before him now: four street Arabs, the eldest of whom was fourteen, the youngest twelve; not related, all from big families yet none of them had a father present in court. And without a father to plead for them and accept responsibility for their good behaviour, there was nothing Gordon could do about it. Prison was the only punishment for robbery.

He had no children, and though even before her riding accident he had never reproached Elizabeth, had any one of the four boy children she had miscarried come to term, his son would now be growing up. He might almost have been the age of the boys who stood before him, dirty, frightened and hostile. Gordon said gravely, 'You leave me no other course but to sentence you to six months' detention.' The eldest boy would

5

go to prison; the others to a reformatory. 'Have you anything to say?'

'No!' said one.

The sheriff's officer barked, 'No? No what? How do you address the magistrate?'

With surly reluctance the boys said in unison, 'No, Your Honour,' before they were led away.

Gordon signed the order, passed it to the clerk and asked, 'How many more?'

Before he could answer there came from the waiting room next door the sound of a girl singing: *'Speed, bonny boat, like a bird on the wing. Onward! The sailors cry. Carry the lad that's born to be King. Over the sea, to Skye...'*

Her voice soared, high and sweet, only to be silenced by the sheriff's officer, who left the courtroom bursting with indignation. Gordon heard him roaring, 'Wheest, lass! Ye're here to be sentenced. Show some respect.'

The girl replied, 'There's nobody here. What harm is there...?'

'They can hear you in court.' The officer slammed the door.

There was silence again. Gordon repeated, 'How many more?'

'Just the girl, sir.'

Gordon nodded as the clerk gave him the papers to read before she was sent in. No doubt it would be another sorry tale of neglect and misfortune. If he dealt with her quickly he could be home in half an hour and by three o'clock out on the Forth estuary, with the wind carrying him fast over the water to Fife. He read. She was a twelve-year-old orphan, brought up by her grandmother on a small tenanted farm, close to his own Ingersley. Her mother had died giving birth to her, and her father shortly afterwards. Her name was Flora Macdonald. Here, at last, he smiled. Fancy giving a commoner's lass the name of one of Scotland's heroines. Did she know she bore the name of Lady Flora Macdonald who rowed Bonnie Prince Charlie over the sea to Skye? He remembered her sweet voice, *'Speed, bonny boat, like a bird on the wing...'*, and read on.

In the waiting room Flora sat very still, though inside she was shaking. She must not let the sheriff's officer see how afraid

6

she was. She had sung a few moments ago to try to give herself courage – to imagine how much more courage had been needed by her namesake. But Lady Flora Macdonald had had a chance of escape, and Flora had none.

She adjusted her navy-blue beret over blazing coppery hair that fell in soft curls to her shoulders. To calm herself she closed eyes that were the liquid green of a deep, troubled sea and fringed with dark lashes that were damp with held-back tears. Biting her trembling lip, she tried to summon up the courage that Gran had instilled in her, tried to remember Gran's advice, but all that came to her was the knowledge that her life had changed irrevocably on that February afternoon, five months ago.

It was almost dark at four o'clock and Gran was nowhere to be seen when she came home from school. The fire was blazing and Flora's stomach rumbled in anticipation as the aroma of simmering leek and lentil soup wafted from the back of the stove. The merry jiggling of the lid on the long-handled iron pot told her that Gran had made cloutie dumpling as a winter's treat.

Flora, wearing a knitted brown hat and herringbone tweed overcoat against the freezing February chill, went to the door and smiled at the sight before her. Gran, careless of the hard frozen ground and the foot-long spears of ice that hung inches above her head from the eaves of the old pig sties, had no coat on. She was wearing a voluminous brown corduroy skirt, patched and pocketed, that reached to her boot tops. Over it she wore a thick jumper knitted in random stripes and random thicknesses of wool spun from her own fleeces, while on her head she sported a crocheted purple bonnet.

Gran was stomping squarely towards the vegetable patch waving her stick at 'they drat sheep', as she called the twelve blackface ewes who escaped from their field practically every day.

'Gran, I'm coming.' Flora grabbed a walking stick from the porch and ran down the yard. She reached Gran as the little flock of twelve sheep bunched together, ready to run across the cabbages.

Gran shouted, 'Over yon...' her breath freezing into a white vapour cloud about her dear old face. Flora leaped to narrow the gap between the sheep and the cabbage patch. Sheep made for the widest opening. The secret was to keep closing in, narrowing the way you didn't want them to take. They worked the flock in harmony, Gran shouting instructions, Flora running like a sheepdog under the darkening sky. She jumped, gawky but agile as a young deer, over tall Brussels sprouts plants, the cold air hurting the back of her throat as she herded and urged the animals forward. Gran ran behind the flock until the leading sheep went, dashing for the gap in the hawthorn hedge.

'Go on by!' Gran shook her stick again as the last panicking ewe shoved through the hedge. Then she leaned, heavy and unsteady, on the loose fence post, getting her breath back.

'Shouldn't we put them in the barn, Gran?' Flora asked. 'They'll be coming in for lambing in a couple of weeks.'

'No. Best keep them oot o' doors till their time. They'll stop escaping then. They won't be running in a flock when they have lambs at foot.' Gran dived into her skirt pocket for twine and scissors and on her knees in the dead, frosty grass began to repair the wire netting whose rusty, weakened state was the reason for the sheep's daily excursions.

Flora said, 'I hope we don't lose any sheep this year.'

'But you like your pet lambs,' Gran said, smiling. Her breath was a white plume in the frosty air. 'You want to go on bottle-feeding them long after the others are weaned.'

'I feel as if I'm their mother,' Flora said. 'You'd think that if a ewe died, then another one who'd lost a lamb would take it on, wouldn't you?' Ewes whose lambs were born dead would bleat plaintively for days, and yet they would not foster a dead ewe's lamb but would kick out at and attack the orphan lambs who needed mother's milk.

'Aye. You'd think. But it's a rare female of any species that will adopt a suckling.' Gran pulled hard on the twine to bring two rusty squares together and tied them firmly. 'It's nature's way. It's all to do with the secretions they call hormones. It's the protective instinct and it comes with the birth. Same wi' women and their bairns. Women can be cruel to a bairn that's not their flesh and blood. I never knew a woman who loved an orphan like her ain.'

Flora said, 'You weren't cruel to me. I was an orphan lamb.'

8

Gran smiled her crooked old smile. 'Ye felt like me ain bairn. I liked the smell of ye. And the feel and the sound o' ye.'

Flora stood for a few seconds stamping her booted feet on the hard ground, banging her bare hands together before saying quietly, 'Some of them have already left, Gran. Gone on to half-time work; the girls into service, the lads in the fields. It'll be me come summer.'

'You want to stay on, don't you?' Gran's face was a picture of regret as she looked up at Flora.

'It's not school. I'll miss my singing lessons if I go into service.'

Gran's arthritic fingers were blue with cold as she tried to hold the twine that was catching on the stabbing spines of the hawthorn. 'It's a shame there was no money to buy a piano and have you taught.'

'I am being taught, Gran.' One term of ten piano lessons cost two guineas from Miss Whitehead in the village. One term was all they could afford, and without a piano there was no chance of practising, but Flora now knew the basics of notation, and instead of playing she sang operatic arias to Miss Whitehead's accompaniment.

So well did she sing that Miss Whitehead gave her an hour's free tutoring every week, firing her up with enthusiasm, saying, 'You've got the finest soprano voice I ever heard,' and promising that when she was eighteen she'd get her into a choir or an operatic society.

Flora said, 'I'll have to leave before I'm fourteen anyway. We can go part-time from thirteen. But I don't want to go into service. They keep you in. I hate being kept in.' In fact she had a horror of being shut in anywhere. She had told nobody about the suffocating panic that came over her in crowded places, the fear of closed doors and small spaces, and the wariness if other people stood between herself and the nearest way out. She said, 'I'd have to live in and I don't want to leave you.'

'Then dinnae.' Gran winced as a spine stabbed into her thumb. 'You never know what might happen, lass, if you keep in mind what it is you want. Do as I did. Have courage.' Gran sucked her thumb hard before going back to her task. Gran told tales on winter nights of her young life, for she'd been

9

brought up on one of the grand ducal estates where whole families served as housemaids, farm workers, ghillies, shoemakers, wheelwrights and skilled craftsmen. The large estates had their own schools and churches, and the practising faith of the landed family they served became the faith of the estate workers. Gran had seen it as a form of slavery. It was an enclosed life and servant families had little contact with the wider outside world. Gran, like Flora, had been a painfully shy child who was given to occasional outbursts of bravery or rebellion. 'Besides,' she once said in a rare attempt at explaining her own actions, 'we Scots dinnae forget old alliances and allegiance, nor oor enemies. The family I worked for was a branch of the Campbells and I'm a Macdonald.'

Flora had said, 'I think you were brave to run away.'

'Aye,' Gran went on. 'Watch your back when a Campbell comes offering friendship. I ran away at fifteen when I was told the history of the massacre at Glencoe.' She cackled with laughter. 'Sounds silly, I ken. But I had five years of working life on the estate behind me and I'd had enough.'

Gran had climbed the wall and run away to find work on a little hill farm where, later, she married the old farmer. After he died, leaving her with a son to rear, Gran carried on – as she was doing still, fifty years after her small rebellion.

'I want to help.' Flora squatted down and said, 'Let me do that.'

Gran waved her away. 'Don't dirty your school clothes, lass. I'm nearly done.'

Flora stood up. 'I've been a burden to you, haven't I?'

Gran said softly, 'You're my pride and joy. I lost my son and your mother. And I never want to lose you. My own flesh and blood.' Gran had never said anything like that before. What she usually said was that blood was thicker than water and families must cling together.

'I want to make your life easier,' Flora said. 'But if I don't earn money I can't help. And if I go into service I'll never be a singer. You only get Sunday afternoons off at the big house.'

Gran stopped twining the netting. 'There's plenty work for ye here. Ye'll be a help. No regular money, mind, but you can keep on with Miss Whitehead. Tell those teachers that they can't force you.'

'Can't they?'

Gran was breathless from her exertions. She stopped twining for a minute and looked at Flora, her eyes full of sadness. 'I worry about you, lass. You cannae go through life being obedient. There's plenty will tell ye what to do, give orders. You need courage to make your ain choices.' She went back to her task, saying, 'It's dark. Run back. Set the table. I'll be nae mair than ten minutes.'

Gran didn't come back. A sobbing Flora found her, lying still and cold, the twine in her clawed hand where she had clutched it to her chest in the last agonising throes of what the doctor said was a massive seizure.

And Gran's advice could not be taken. Flora had no choice. The few acres of farmland and their cottage were rented and she was too young to have charge of an agricultural tenancy. The land reverted to the master of the estate and after that the authorities took care of everything. They sold Gran's sheep and hens. They sold her furniture, they emptied her penny bank savings book, to pay for the burial. And then they sold Flora, or so she believed.

Here in the waiting room at the Haddington courtroom she could have cried thinking about what had become of her. She had never done wrong in her life until they – the authorities – had told her they had no choice but to place her with an ironmonger as part-time schoolgirl and maid-of-all-work.

No girl would have stayed with that disgusting old man, who demanded that she went to school only two days a week and on the other days worked in his shop from morning until night. One night he tried to creep into her bed, saying she should not have left her bedroom door ajar, in invitation. Where was the justice in being brought before the court for running away from such a man?

Gordon looked sternly at the girl in front of him. She'd be a real Scottish beauty one day; she had the height and colouring and a proud way of holding herself, standing before him with shoulders back and chin held high. He said, 'Do you know that vagrancy is a criminal offence? You were found sleeping on a park bench. We cannot have young people living rough on our streets. Why did you run away, Flora?'

11

The girl made no answer. She was fighting back tears, biting her full lower lip. He said, more gently this time, 'If you have anything to say in explanation, then you must do so now.' He waited a few seconds. Then, 'Are you prepared to return to your employer? I see that he is willing to take you back.'

'I'm not going back to that old devil...' she began agitatedly.

'Respect the rules of the court!' The court officer silenced her. 'Address your replies to "Your Honour".'

Gordon knew that if he were to speak to her in a fatherly way – and this course was open to him – the lass might tell him what had gone wrong. But even if he did, there was no alternative employment he could offer. She had no parents and no home. He must find a safe place for her. Didn't she know that there were dole queues at every labour exchange and that skilled men, too proud to sign on for help, walked miles from the villages to Leith Docks, desperate to get a few hours' work so they could feed their families. The girl was lucky to have employment and a roof over her head. Three years of administering justice to juveniles had taught him that no matter what one did with a girl who preferred life on the streets to respectable employment, once on the downward path, in no time at all she'd be in the gutter.

He said, 'You should be receiving an education. I think it is best that we send you to the industrial school.'

'Don't send me to the reformatory.'

Before she could be reprimanded again, Gordon said, 'Dr Guthrie's has a fine reputation for reclaiming wayward Christian souls. You will have daily lessons and be trained for a life in domestic service or laundry work. You'll be fed, clothed, housed and obliged to attend church. I am giving you a chance. Two years in Dr Guthrie's establishment will make an honest girl of you.'

Flora drew in breath very sharply, her shoulders sagged, and with tears streaming down her face and her self-control broken she said, 'I am honest. I've done nothing wrong. I can work. Don't lock me up, sir. Give me another chance. Please ... please ... Your Honour.'

Tears made Gordon feel inadequate. He could not deal with emotional women or girls and he never again wanted to pass

12

sentence on youngsters. Most of the children he had dealt with today would not be in court if they had good homes; fathers to guide and protect them. He looked kindly at the orphan girl who stood, terrified, before him, and said, 'I wish there were more I could do for you.' Then he nodded to the court officer, who took her by the arm and led her away.

At the Ingersley estate's South Lodge, Andrew Stewart, seventeen years old and built like a man twice his age, lay asleep in bed. He was six foot four, with laughing brown eyes, dark curly hair and a wide, firm mouth that broke into a smile as Ma came to his room to wake him before she went to work in the big kitchen.

'Five o'clock, Andrew.' She drew back the curtain and tripped over the Sherlock Holmes novel that was on the floor. 'What a laddie,' she laughed. 'Isn't farming enough? You don't still want to be a detective?'

Andrew put a tanned arm across his eyes to shut out the light. 'All right, Ma.' He'd have another five minutes. He didn't have to be at the field until six.

Ma said, 'If you want something hot, I'll be cooking for the men up at Ingersley. But there's bread and cheese and hard-boiled eggs.'

Andrew owed his strong body to three years' labouring and his robust constitution to Ma's cooking of the good, plentiful food that came from the estate farm, Ingersley Mains. The estate farms of the great houses in this part of Scotland traditionally took the name of the estate followed by 'Mains', just as their counterparts elsewhere would be known as 'Home Farm'. Andrew's ma was employed as cook for Ingersley House, not Ingersley Mains farm, which was run by a manager, but she helped out at hay-making and harvest, cooking for the hired men.

Now Andrew sat up and pulled a pained expression to make Ma smile. She was forty years old, the best little mother a lad could have, the widow of a fisherman Andrew hardly remembered – and here she was at five o'clock in the morning, her brown eyes clear and bright and her pretty face cheerful as if she hadn't a care in the world. Other women would be worn down with the amount of work Ma tackled, for she had only

13

two kitchen maids to help her cook for the Campbell family, visitors and staff.

He pulled the sheet up to cover his broad, hairy nakedness, because Ma thought it more seemly for a young man to wear a nightshirt. Then he grinned. 'You work too hard. The Campbells ought to get more staff.'

Ma would be doing all the cooking for the next weeks, while a gang of itinerant Irish reapers were crammed ten to a room in the nearly derelict Dower House. She was up at five o'clock, making breakfast for twenty hungry men and toiling to keep up the high standards of the dining room. And all for a pittance and the rent-free house. Andrew wanted an easier life for his ma.

Ma said, 'We manage, son. Their money's all gone. I don't mind any of it. I'm used to hard work.' She was still smiling as she added, 'Don't fall asleep again. I'm off.' He heard her going down the oak stairs, her shoes clattering on the tiles in the hallway.

Andrew wanted to get Ma out of here, wanted independence for them, but he'd never earn enough as a farm labourer. And he had a terrible pride in his own worth. If he worked himself to death it would not be as anyone's paid hand. It would be because the land he worked belonged to him. A man could raise a family and have a happy, satisfying life if he emigrated to Canada, where virgin land was being given away to those who were prepared to clear and work it. Ma would not do it. She said he'd marry, and why would a wife want her mother-in-law living with them? Besides, she said, she would not leave because 'I belong here. We have a roof over our heads and work to do. Many haven't. And since young Lady Campbell's accident, they need me.' Sir Gordon's wife had been thrown from her horse a few months ago.

Andrew pointed it out to her – he said, 'The Campbells give us work, and a roof over our heads, but they don't own us body and soul.'

'They own our time if they pay our wages. I never had much schooling. I wasn't trained for anything. If we didn't have the Campbells we'd have nothing.' Ma, exasperated when he talked this way, would add, 'Know your place, Andrew. Show respect.'

He'd answer, 'I have self-respect. I won't be subservient.'

Ma said, 'Nobody's subservient now. The old order went

with his father's death.' This was true. Gone with the loss of their wealth and the death of Sir Gordon's father was an army of servants and a whole way of life for many families who'd been employed on the estate. Ma would remind him, 'The Commander' – though he'd left the sea three years ago, Sir Gordon was still referred to by his naval title – 'says the workers are worthy of their hire. He said it when his father died. The Commander said, "My wife and I do not expect servitude. Respect, yes. You for us and we for you." That would never have been said by his father.'

'Aye! When they sacked the workers they had enough money to have gas and electricity brought here. That saved them a good few wages. No lamps to trim every day. A big gas cooking range.'

Ma ignored this. She said, 'And Lady Campbell – look what she's done for the servants. She gives us a full day off every week. And she's put a piano in the servants' hall.'

'Aye. An old one that's not been tuned for years and can only be played after nine o'clock at night if the work's all done.' All the same, he acknowledged, the new order, espoused by the Commander and Lady Campbell, had led to a relaxing of the old master-and-servant system. Lady Campbell, before the riding accident that had fractured her skull and nearly blinded her, had given hours of her time to teach Andrew chords and show him how to read music. But though Sir Gordon Campbell talked in naval terms of all hands on deck and pulling together, he, the Commander, was still master and Andrew and Ma were servants. The old order was that servants who didn't toe the line could be turfed off the estate, thrown out of their tied cottages. The three-year-old new order had not yet been tested by Andrew or Ma.

Ma never stepped out of line. Ma was dutiful and loyal, and when Lady Campbell's younger sister Ruth made ever more demands of her, she said no more to Andrew than, 'She has a right to ask.' And once, 'She's not as gentle and soft as her sister. Lady Campbell's a stricken woman. Ruth Bickerstaffe has determination. It's what her ladyship' needs.' Ruth Bickerstaffe, though only twenty-seven, was driven, Andrew sensed, by a thirst for power, not sisterly love. He had seen her whipping her horse. Andrew would not trust Ruth Bickerstaffe with an animal, let alone her invalid sister. But he would not upset Ma by giving his private opinion of their bosses.

It was half past five when he woke again. He threw himself out of bed, put on his vest and moleskin working trousers and tied the laces of his work boots tight about the trouser bottoms, so no seeds or tiny thunder-bugs could get inside his socks and irritate his feet.

Into his pockets he stuffed cheese and hard-boiled eggs and he ate his bread on the run. The labourers were not allowed to cut across the park but he would not be seen and it would save a few minutes. The sun warmed his face, the air was clean, cool and invigorating and the dewy grass squeaked under his boots as he ran swiftly and quietly around the great beeches, elms, oaks and ornamental trees of the parkland. It was good to be young and alive and have the blood singing through his veins on such a morning. So that nobody would know he'd overslept again, he would cut round the back of the dairy cottages and hop over the beech hedge on to the track. He might even arrive before the Irish gang came up after breakfast.

He was there. He slowed to a walk, hidden by the herd of Jersey cows that were lowing softly in the holding yard, waiting their turn to be milked. He crept past the milking parlours, bent double so the milkers wouldn't see him, and round behind the empty, swilled-out dairy where the milk would be brought in half an hour. Suddenly, to his alarm, he saw Mike Hamilton, the manager of Ingersley Mains, come out of the front door of his farmhouse, which faced the dairy buildings. Andrew had not been seen. He pressed his back against the wall until Mike Hamilton went into the dairy. He'd be checking that everything was in order, hoping to catch some poor beggars and dock their wages for an infringement of his endlessly revised rule book. Andrew himself could lose a morning's pay if he were late.

He flattened himself against the wall and sidled towards the open door. If he could get past Hamilton's gimlet eyes, he'd make a dash for it across the doorway to the beech hedge barely thirty yards away. He edged closer, and then he heard them – Hamilton and Lady Campbell's sister, Ruth.

It was cool and dark in the dairy with the shutters closed

against the early sunlight. Ruth Bickerstaffe waited, a few feet back from the door, her small hands clenched into fists in the pockets of the long brown cardigan she wore over a silk shirt that was tucked firmly into riding breeches. Her bobbed golden hair fell in soft waves across her heart-shaped face and the pupils of her round blue eyes dilated as they adjusted to the darkness. She was aware of her good looks and aware that her delicate appearance masked a steely determination. She saw it as her strength that she was seldom opposed. Most people eventually bent to her will; saw things her way. Today she was set on showing Mike Hamilton that he was no match for her.

She heard footsteps. They paused then started again, heavier this time, and in he came, quick and furtive before he stopped in his tracks, seeing her. Her pulse quickened, as it always did when she was near this dark, swarthy man of thirty-two. He had the brooding manner of intelligent, uneducated men, but the greater part of his attraction for Ruth was that he was a natural athlete – the sort of man you'd put on to a horse and he'd ride, or drop into the sea and he'd swim – confident in his mastery of his own body and, as Ruth knew, sure of his mastery of hers. But though their affair was only three months old, it was high time he knew that his power over her began and ended in the bedroom.

'What the devil?' he said. 'What are ye doing here at this hour? Surely Elizabeth needs you?'

A suffocating tide of jealousy swept over her. Elizabeth, Elizabeth. That was all she had heard all her life. Her beautiful, sweet-natured sister, Elizabeth. Her sister's looks and compliant nature had brought to her all of life's prizes, even marriage to the heir to a Scottish estate. Ruth had never come close to Elizabeth, not in anyone's eyes – their father's or their brothers' – even though she was prettier, cleverer and two years younger than her sister. In Cheshire, where their wealthy mill-owning father had bought a small estate and brought his family up in grand style, the Bickerstaffe girls had had no hope of marrying into the minor aristocracy. Father's unpolished manners and new-money tastes saw to that. Then, when Ruth was eighteen and Elizabeth twenty, a young naval officer, Gordon Campbell, a friend of a member of the hunt, arrived on the scene. He was handsome, rich and would inherit a title.

17

He was a landowner in Scotland, where social divisions were clearly defined: one was either serf or master, it appeared to Ruth. English affectations, the Cheshire county set behaviour, could have no significance in Scotland – in fact, they were despised.

An introduction to the Bickerstaffe girls at the Cheshire hunt ball – though Gordon was not a hunting man – and he was hooked. His every leave had been spent in Cheshire from that day on, and though he showed no preference, Ruth was sure he liked her best. However, he pretended an encompassing interest, inviting their father and eldest brother as well as Elizabeth and Ruth to Scotland. And never had Ruth schemed and plotted so tenaciously as she did when first she set her sights upon a title and the means of acquiring it: Gordon Campbell. The Ingersley estate had not then fallen into disrepair. It was a devastating blow when Gordon married Elizabeth a year after they met.

But today, Elizabeth was helpless and Gordon needed Ruth. He had begged her to stay and help Nanny Taylor look after Elizabeth. Ruth could not risk damage to her reputation. Mike Hamilton must be made aware of his place. She said, 'Where were you last night? Anyone could have seen me. You left me hanging around the stables like some little floozy.'

'I canna get awa' in the middle of harvest.' He made a move towards her and smiled. 'Anyway, there's nobody about on the estate at night. Nobody but you, looking to your horse. Nobody suspects. I'll see ye tonight, after dark.'

She side-stepped him and gave him an icy look. 'I'm not here to ask if you are cooling off, though I warn you – nobody takes me for a fool.' She put her head back and looked him in the eyes. 'I spent last night going through the wages book.'

Mike Hamilton's eyes blazed. 'You did? What the hell for? Ye're not the mistress of Ingersley.'

'I came to Ingersley to be my sister's companion,' she said. 'She cannot be left alone for a moment in case she has blackouts.' The riding accident had left Elizabeth epileptic and though Elizabeth pretended it was not so, she was slowly going blind.

'Blackouts? Give it its name, woman. Your sister has fits. Full-blown fits. I've seen her.'

'Fits, then. I'm not her keeper,' she answered sharply. 'Elizabeth has Nanny, a trained nurse, as well as myself.' Yesterday Elizabeth had confessed that though she could see faces, her close vision was going and she could not do the accounts which, since the estate could no longer employ a bookkeeper, had become a duty of the wife of the master of Ingersley. So Ruth had done them for her. Now she said, 'You are getting above yourself, Mike. Sir Gordon has asked me to take on some of Lady Campbell's duties.'

'Don't come your English airs and graces wi' me. Gordon Campbell and his wife dinnae use their titles.' His face was dark with fury. 'I've known Gordon all my life. We were next-door neighbours. We were never as rich as the Campbells, who could waste a hundred acres of their good arable land on park and pasture. But my father's still farming. And making a profit.'

'And you'll make your profit here. I know what you are up to,' she said in a controlled voice. 'You are drawing money for workers who don't exist. You want us to think that there are thirty casual workers.'

'Us? Speaking for the family, are you?' Hamilton said in a fury.

'I am making myself indispensable. Everyone on this estate will be here because I trust them.' Ruth felt a quick thrill of satisfaction at the prospect of being the chatelaine of Ingersley. 'I warn you, Mike. Make good that money or I'll have no choice but to tell.'

'You bitch!' Mike came close again and put his face so near to hers that Ruth had to flinch away. 'I do the extra work meself. Making a few bob this way is an accepted benefit of the manager,' he said. He was so close that she could smell the sweat that had broken out on him, feel the heat of his breath on her face. He said, 'And if I tell Gordon that you are not the good, church-going, upper-class girl he thinks you are? If I tell Gordon that his sister-in-law warms the factor's bed?'

Mike Hamilton was too sure of his power over her. The dangerous thought that he might tell made rage rise in her, concentrated her mind sharply and brought two high spots of colour burning on her cheeks. But she replied coolly, 'You dare threaten me?'

'I'm remindin' ye.' He almost spat the words out. 'Ye'll be back for more.' Then he grabbed her by both arms and pulled her up hard against him. His eyes narrowed. 'Ye'll come crawling,' he said. 'Ye'll be crying for me to hurt and bruise ye.' He forced her arms down to her sides then twisted them quickly until with one hand he held both wrists behind her back.

Ruth snorted her contempt of him and did not struggle. She enjoyed the rough handling, the callused hand that was dragging her thin blouse open. She enjoyed the feel of his unshaven chin scraping down her neck, his open mouth fastening over her breast and the pink nipple that was distended with anticipation.

Mike Hamilton was as needful as she. He had to have her. She delighted in her wild sexuality. Her riding master had whipped her into shape when she was fifteen and had introduced her to the new rubber protection – the Dutch cap – a few years ago. Their affair had continued until she was called to Ingersley. And she'd been at Ingersley barely a month when she'd singled out Mike, estate factor and farm manager, and introduced him to practices he had before only dreamed about. Now, delicious sensations were thrilling and spreading about her loins as she said in a low, throaty voice, 'If you make a mark on me, Mike Hamilton, I'll have you thrown out on your ear.'

He let her breast drop for a moment and a tight little smile came to play around the corners of his full, sensuous mouth. 'Ye canna do that. Ye dinnae have the power.' He tightened his grip on her wrists, making her gasp. The cold morning air was chill on her hot, attar-of-roses-scented skin as he brushed aside the silk, exposing the other breast, and slowly brought his mouth down again, hearing the in-drawing of her breath as she felt the increasing suction and his teeth biting into her soft flesh. He stopped, released her and said, 'Show that to Sir Gordon Campbell. And ye can tell him that his little angel of mercy is nae better than a bitch on heat.'

Before she could strike him, for sensation was only just tingling back into her hands, he was through the open doorway and out in the yard. She did not stop to pull the blouse around her exposed, reddened breasts. She followed him to the door and saw that he was heading for the milking shed. She called out, 'Pay that money back. Today. Or I'll...' She stopped. A

young man – the cook's son – was flattened against the wall.
Ruth saw his alarmed glance travelling to her breast then,
blushing, to her face as she pulled the cardigan about her. She
demanded, 'What are you doing?'

'Nothing, miss.' He straightened, pretending nonchalance.
'I'm going to the field.'

'Labourers are not allowed in the yard.'

'No, miss. I was late.'

'So you broke the rules.' She could not let it go. Suppose he
had heard it all? He most certainly had heard her own last
words. Andrew had come to her attention before as too clever
and proud to make a docile servant. 'We can't keep you after
this. I will report you.'

The boy had an insolent look. He put his head back, looked
down at her and said, 'If you will, you will,' then walked past
her to the beech hedge which, without even speeding his pace,
he vaulted as easily as a young colt.

Andrew, waist deep in the cornfield, pitched his fork under the
last cut on the end of the row and turned it expertly and gently
so as not to damage the ripe ears of golden wheat. A couple of
hours of this heat and breeze was needed to dry it, then the
casuals – women and girls from the town – would tie the
stooks. The corn would then be ready for the threshing
machine and this year's harvest would be safely home. His
tanned arms were aching and the muscles were stretched tight
at the back of his strong legs. Slowly he straightened and
called out to Shuggie, the village idiot lad who helped out
when the farm needed extra hands, 'Shug. Dinner. Finish that
row.'

'I didnae hear the whistle,' Shuggie said. 'Master said,
"Wait for whistle."'

Andrew pushed the curly dark hair back from his damp
forehead and shaded his eyes to look over towards the farm
buildings. The sun was high. They had been toiling since six
with nothing to sustain them but water from the carrier that
had been carted to the fields a few days ago. 'He's a bad
bugger,' Andrew said quietly of Mike Hamilton. The heat haze
made distances appear greater and he could only just make out
the long line of Irish reapers who were scything at the far end

of the next field. He could not see Mike Hamilton amongst them. But he ought to be here blowing his damned whistle. It was well past midday – time for their break.

He was hungry. Ma would have the food laid out on trestle tables in the barn – soup and bread, cheese, cold cuts of meat and a barrel of ale. Andrew scratched fiercely at his chest. He had taken off his vest earlier in the day and tiny harvest flies had irritated and bitten him in the damp places – the inside creases of elbows and knees and under the curly black hair on his chest. He'd have liked to take a picnic down to the beach – Ingersley's private beach, a half-mile of flat sand under the cliffs that sloped away to a little sheltered bay that could only be reached on horseback or on foot by someone who knew the trail through the buckthorn bushes as he did – but the beach was out of bounds to all the field and house servants, though this was another rule that Andrew liked to break. How could a family *own* a beach and prevent anyone from walking along the seashore?

He screwed up his eyes and looked towards the lane beyond the field gate to see if Hamilton were near. He was not. Andrew stuck his pitchfork into the ground and called out again to Shug. 'He must be busy. Leave your fork there.' He grinned. 'Are you hungry?'

Shuggie threw the pitchfork on to the ground and his uncontrolled features broke into a contorted grin. 'I'm goin' hame for dinner.' His old father, whom the lad loved, was crippled with arthritis from fifty years' work on the land. They depended upon Shuggie's money. 'Dad needs ma wages.' The farm hands were paid on Fridays, at midday. Shuggie earned fourpence an hour, and though he could neither read nor write he knew to the last halfpenny how much he was due. 'I get one pound four shillings today.'

Andrew grinned back. 'Don't leave your fork lying on the ground. You'll never find it again. Look.' He demonstrated as he did every time – pitching the two prongs into the hard ground – and when Shuggie had done the same they left the fields, Andrew striding, Shuggie stumbling beside him along the rutted, stony lane, the red dust from the clay soil powdering their boots and the string-tied ends of their trousers.

They were in sight of the barn when Andrew saw Mike

Hamilton approaching down the lane, loose-limbed, arms swinging at his sides. 'Where are you going?' Hamilton shouted. 'Who told you to stop work?'

Andrew stood and waited for him. 'You know where we're going,' he said. 'You should have blown your whistle half an hour ago.'

Shuggie hopped from one foot to the other. 'Where's my wages? My one pound four shillings? I get my wages today.'

'No pay for you,' Hamilton raged. 'Ye're no' worth it.'

Shuggie's jaw dropped and he began to pant and whimper like a beaten puppy. 'But I've worked all week. Twelve hours a day. Fourpence an hour. That's one pound four shillings.'

Hamilton came a step closer, raised his hand to Shuggie and spat out, 'Get off with ye! Don't answer back, ye stupid ...'

'Come off it!' Andrew would not stand for this even if Shuggie didn't defend himself. Cool excitement filled him as his fists closed and he stood up to Hamilton. 'You can't do that. The lad works twice as hard as anyone on the payroll. He'd earn six and six a day on a good estate.'

'It's none to do wi' you.' Hamilton turned on Andrew. 'Shut your mouth. I'm warning ye. Any more from you and ye'll be signing on the dole every day – wi' your daft friend.'

Hamilton was a good half-head shorter than Andrew, though more powerfully set. This morning Andrew had stood meek and apologetic while Ruth Bickerstaffe threatened him with dismissal over what he'd seen and heard. And Hamilton thought he could do the same, did he? Well, he could have another think. The Commander said they would all be treated honestly. Sir Gordon was a man of his word. And Andrew was a man of his. He would not stand for lies or unfair treatment of Shuggie, who knew nothing about the new order. He stepped back a pace, the better to swing his fist if need be. 'Be signing on, will I?'

'You've just lost a day's pay, Stewart,' Hamilton said, but he backed away.

Andrew's left hand shot out and grabbed Hamilton's shoulder. His muscles tensed as he held the brute at arm's length. Hamilton stood stock still, surprised into inaction. 'If we're going to lose our bloody wages, Shuggie,' Andrew said through clenched teeth to the weeping lad, 'watch this!' and he

23

brought his right fist up hard under Hamilton's jaw. There was a satisfying crack and a sharp pain in his knuckles as Hamilton fell to his knees, roaring, clutching his face, blood streaming from his mouth.

'Come on, Shug.' Andrew took hold of Shuggie's shirt and pushed him into a run. 'I'll see about your wages. You'll get paid.'

He hared off up the dusty lane, Shug stumbling, crying, behind him. And as he went, Andrew knew somehow that he had become a better man. He was not ashamed of himself. He didn't care if they gave him his books – his marching orders. He couldn't stand cheats and liars. And he couldn't stand by and watch a poor underdog getting beaten.

He ran up the lane, leaving Mike Hamilton holding his bloody face, and made straight for Ingersley House. He would test the new order. The kitchen was deserted. Ma would be down at the barn. There was nobody about in the servants' hall. Andrew untied the cords on his trouser bottoms, stamped his feet to get rid of the dust and wiped his boots on the damp floor cloth that hung on the waste pipe under the sink. Then he took a quick glance at himself in the looking-glass that hung near the green baize door, placed there under the old regime so the servants could check their appearance before waiting on the family.

He looked fierce. His brows were drawn together and his hair was curly and damp from his efforts. It was Lady Campbell he wanted to see – the sweet, gentle woman who had taught him to play the piano. He ran a hand over his hair to flatten it and at last gave a rueful smile.

There was a new electric lift which went from the top, attic floor down to the kitchen, with stops on every landing. It had been installed for Lady Campbell's benefit so she could get about the house in safety without the risk on the grand sweeping staircase of having what the servants called fits but they were told to call turns or blackouts.

Andrew would not dare to use either the lift or the main staircase, so he ran up the steep servants' stairs – a stone spiral in the west wing tower. He was breathless when he reached the drawing-room floor and stood for a moment, wondering whether he might knock at the drawing-room door or try the

24

study. Then he heard the lift coming down at the far end of the landing. It was Lady Campbell with the Commander's old nurse, Nanny Taylor.

Nanny Taylor was a strait-laced, straight-backed woman who had always looked old to Andrew. She had been only twenty-three when she first came to Ingersley as trained midwife, nurse and nanny to the baby Gordon. Over the years she had delivered all the babies on the estate – was even known to them all by the name of Nanny – as well as having sole charge of Gordon when his mother died when he was five years old. When he joined the Royal Navy, Nanny Taylor spent a few years with a sister in Canada, returning when Elizabeth and Gordon's first baby was expected. She was very sharp in her mind – though it was rumoured amongst the servants that she was a secret tippler.

Nanny, dressed as usual from head to toe in working grey, waited to close the lift gates after Lady Campbell. Lady Campbell, wearing a close-fitting dress of blue silk, was tall and stately, not as pretty as her sister Ruth but in Andrew's eyes a hundred times more attractive. She was approachable and took a personal interest in everyone who worked for her – and was so feminine that every man on the estate went weak at the knees in her company, though she was seldom seen about the estate since she was dependent on help. Nobody knew how little Lady Campbell could see. Her eyes looked normal as they went from speaker to speaker but today, Andrew knew, she had not seen him for she started to talk with indiscreet excitement. 'I'll wait for Gordon in the drawing room. Leave us alone when he arrives, Nanny. Gordon likes us to go to the bedroom after the court sessions. They are a terrible strain. He needs me.'

'Of course I'll leave you alone. I know better than to be a gooseberry...' Nanny stopped here, for she had seen Andrew. She put a finger to her lips to indicate that he must not let Lady Campbell know of his presence.

Andrew stepped back quietly into the shadows of the study doorway as Lady Campbell came down the landing, one hand placed on Nanny Taylor's arm, her feet as light as a dancer's, saying as she came, 'Did Gordon say what time he'd be home?' She passed within a yard of Andrew, without a flicker of recognition of his presence, a beautiful, scented woman who longed to be in her husband's arms.

Nanny Taylor looked at him and put her fingers to her lips again. She replied, 'I'll ask Ruth, dear,' as she led the way into the drawing room.

A heady French scent lingered in the air and Andrew wondered at Lady Campbell's not having noticed his own sweaty, cut-corn and earthy odour. He waited a couple of minutes before he heard Nanny say, 'Was that a knock at the door, Elizabeth?'

'Was it? I didn't hear.'

'Yes. It was. I'll go.' And the old nurse came to the door and said in a loud, surprised voice, 'Ah. One of the workers. Is there anything?'

Andrew squared his shoulders. 'It's important. Or I wouldn't ask.'

Nanny Taylor's quick smile flashed off before it could light up her face. She said, 'Come in. Lady Campbell will see you.'

Andrew found Lady Campbell seated by the centre one of three tall windows on the long wall, opposite a marble fireplace whose hearth was filled with jardinières containing ferns and aspidistras. The rooms were all spacious, with high ceilings and tall windows. From the front the house appeared to have four storeys, but because it was built on sloping ground, the garden floor which housed the servants' entrance and quarters had no windows on to the front and was two floors below the room where Lady Campbell now sat, waiting to hear Andrew.

Andrew was embarrassed by what he'd heard and irritated by this charade, but understood well enough that the nurse was colluding with Lady Campbell in her pretence of being able to see. She put out her hand and said in a soft, soothing voice, 'Please, sit down,' then whispered to Nanny Taylor, who had gone to stand behind her chair, 'Who is it?'

Andrew said, 'Andrew Stewart, ma'am. I won't sit.'

'Andrew, of course. What do you want, Andrew?'

'It's your farm manager. I've just hit him.'

Her blue eyes fixed on his face. 'You say you hit Mr Hamilton? Why?'

'He refused to pay Shuggie's wages. Sorry, Hugh's wages –

we call him Shuggie. Hugh has worked all week. He's a hard worker even though he's a simpleton. He has to be paid.'

'Can you send Hugh to me? I can deal with the wages.'

'And I've been given my books.'

'Oh dear. And you want me to explain to my husband that it was done in the heat of the moment? It won't happen again?'

It would happen again if Mike Hamilton bullied Shuggie, but Andrew could not tell this to Lady Campbell. He said, 'We need the jobs. Ma and I. I don't want Ma to suffer.' And he left her to the attentions of Nanny Taylor.

Chapter Two

Gordon drove the Armstrong Siddeley hard, picking up the coast road three miles from Haddington. He glanced sideways at the sea, rammed his foot down on the accelerator and wound the window down so the salt-laden air blew on to his face and through his sandy hair. Seven miles across the dazzling blue water the coast of Fife seemed to beckon, clear and bright as a painted backdrop. And try as he might to divert his thoughts from what he had done when he dealt with her, he heard the sound of the girl's voice singing in the waiting room of the county court: '*Speed, bonny boat, like a bird on the wing. Onward! The sailors cry. Carry the lad that's born to be King* ...' Her song was echoing in his ears as he covered the last few miles home.

Ingersley House, built in the seventeenth century and set in the middle of five hundred acres of East Lothian's fertile, rolling country, was once one of the finest houses in the district. Not any more, Gordon mused, as he drove in at the South Lodge entrance. In the old days a gatekeeper-cum-lock-smith would have looked after the gates. Now the cook and her son occupied the South Lodge and the great wrought-iron gates were fastened back against the high stone wall. For the quarter-mile drive to the house the car rumbled slowly uphill over weed-infested gravel until the sandstone edifice came into view at the top of the rise. It was imposing, symmetrical, five storeys high and, as Gordon used to say when he was a boy, eight windows wide. His mouth made a wry smile in spite of himself. Most of those windows needed urgent attention. The others were not in such a bad state of repair, but the

Campbells' money was gone, as was the old way of life for families like his. War was coming, he had no doubts about it – the old feudal systems all over Europe were being challenged and torn down; and rightly so. Gordon was not a man to cry over an unfair system of privilege and patronage.

He left the car parked awkwardly at the foot of the twenty stone steps that led up to the massive front door in the centre of the house. It was barely two o'clock. He would be out again by three, driving the half-mile from the South Gate to the harbour at North Berwick. First he wanted an hour alone with Elizabeth. They would make love and the tensions of this morning would be eased. Their marriage was a perfect union. Elizabeth's ardour was undimmed even after five miscarriages and still-births. Excitement built in him as he ran up the crumbling steps two at a time. He went through the oak doors and into the square panelled hall from where he could hear the chatter of the few servants they employed wafting up from their quarters on the lower floor. He crossed the hall and went up the flight of stairs to the drawing room. Elizabeth was not there.

He went to his study. She was not there either but there was a letter from the Admiralty. He pocketed it, then went back to the drawing room to press the button that would jangle a bell in the servants' hall.

Within a couple of minutes a housemaid was summoned. He said, 'Please tell Cook to make up my hamper.'

'Yes, sir.' The girl bobbed a little curtsey.

Gordon was momentarily irritated by her action. He had told the staff that neither he nor Elizabeth wanted this kind of ceremony from servants. Then he realised that it would be Ruth's doing. He would talk to her about it, tactfully. He would not upset Ruth, whose presence was making Elizabeth's life so much easier. He was enormously grateful to her. And as if in answer to his thoughts, at that moment the door opened and Ruth came in.

Gordon smiled, but she came close and offered her cheek for him to peck. He was unused to what he thought of as cock-tail-party manners but it pleased Ruth, so he bent and kissed her cheek, then said, 'Elizabeth? Is she resting?'

'Yes. I – we expected you home earlier, Nanny and I.'

'I told Elizabeth that I would see her before I went to the boat.' Gordon looked at his watch, then quickly at the clock over the fireplace, which showed the time as half past three. 'Who has put the clock on? I wound it last evening.'

'Oh dear! It must be Elizabeth. She has to touch the hands.' Ruth looked at him, alarmed. 'Nanny and I told her to lie down. She needs to rest to preserve her sight for as long as possible.' Ruth's own eyes suddenly brimmed with tears. 'You want me to disturb her?'

He could not bear to see a woman in tears. He was at a loss, just as he had been when young Flora Macdonald had cried an hour ago. He said hastily, 'No. Of course not. Will you tell her when she's rested that I'm taking the boat out? I'll be home before dark.' He was relieved to see that she had control of herself again.

Ruth really was a remarkable girl – practical and capable. He said, 'There's nothing the matter? Nothing I need attend to?' She dropped her eyes and he heard her catch her breath, as if she were perhaps a little afraid of him. He repeated, 'Is anything the matter, Ruth?'

'I don't like to trouble you,' she began, then after a few seconds she looked directly at him. 'But I'm afraid it isn't something I can deal with.'

'What?'

'It's the cook's boy. He'll have to go.'

'Young Andrew Stewart?' Gordon was surprised. 'He's one of our best.' He and Elizabeth had taken a special interest in Andrew, seeing in him a boy whose intelligence would take him far and who would be an asset to the family. He said, 'What has he done?'

'Struck the farm manager. We dismissed him instantly. His mother, the cook, wants to plead for him.' She began to rush her words. 'I told them that you could not intervene. The matter will be dealt with by us.'

'Us?'

'The problem is Mr Hamilton. I can't persuade him to take the boy back.'

He might be hopeless at dealing with women but Gordon knew what to do about a boy. He would not see his own estate workers – boys whom he had watched growing up – brought low like this, fighting – beyond control. He said sharply, 'No, I'll do it. I will speak to Hamilton. Where is Andrew?'

Ruth lifted her pretty, arched eyebrows and said, 'There's no need. I'll attend to it. Move the boy from the fields to the house if you wish.'

'I do not wish.' Since she was trying to be helpful he did not add that it was no concern of hers. He said brusquely, 'I'll deal with it.'

Downstairs in the stone-flagged kitchen, Andrew followed his mother from table to deep white sink, explaining. 'He wouldn't pay Shuggie.'

Ma elbowed him aside. 'We could lose our house and our jobs over this. You can't carry on like you did at school, aye gettin' into fights. Sticking up for them as won't fight their ain battles. You read too much. Grow up. Learn to take orders!'

He followed Ma back to the table, saying hotly, 'Not from Hamilton!' knowing Ma was going to say 'If your father were alive you'd have known your place.' Ma reminded him daily of a fisherman's need to obey orders without question.

Ma went to the dresser to gather the plates and tin mugs for the hamper. Then she stood by the table, her little hands on her wide hips, dark hair coming loose from the white cotton cap she wore in the kitchen. 'What will happen to us if we get thrown out? We were lucky to be kept on when the old master died.'

'Shot himself, you mean!'

'Hush! Don't,' Ma said quickly, looking towards the door.

'Well, it's true. He shot himself because he'd lost all his money.'

'It was accidental death, the coroner said.' Ma was defending them again. 'They had to sell two hundred acres of their best farmland to the corn farmers, the barley barons. Landed gentry never sell land. Nearly all the servants for the house and grounds, and their families, had to go. We were lucky. Now you do this! What's to become of you? You've had a good education. You got your school leaving certificate. And you don't use your brain when your fists will do.' Her dark eyes flashed and her round bosom heaved. 'You knocked his front teeth loose.'

'That should shut him up, then.' Andrew was not going to back down. He looked at his angry ma, wanting to pick her up

31

and hug her – and not daring to. 'I saw Lady Campbell. She knew nothing about it.'

Ma would not think twice about his having gone up to see Lady Campbell. The Commander had called the servants to a 'conference' when they lost everything. He said that he and Lady Campbell would give and be given respect but the old master-servant ways were gone. The servants would now be called the staff and every one of them had the right to a fair wage and a hearing.

Ma looked up at Andrew. 'I hope you're ashamed.' Then she began expertly to wrap cold chicken and roasted ham in sheets of greaseproof paper, folding linen napkins about them, slicing her thick crusty bread, packing that too with a little parcel of butter and a knife. She took small jars from a drawer and filled one with home-made mustard and another with strawberry jam. 'If they won't keep you there's nothing else round here. Millions on the dole. You'll have to work on the fishing boats. They'll take you on.' Then she took from the dresser a large jar with a screw-on lid which she filled from the barrel of nettle beer which stood under the table. 'But I don't think they'll get rid of me.'

Now Andrew knew she was going to say what she always did. 'The Commander says I must never leave him. Who else could make nettle beer like this?' She dipped in the scoop and ladled a measure of the clear amber drink into a pint glass for Andrew. 'Here. Have a drink. He won't mind.'

Andrew smiled apologetically between gulps of the beer, then they both jumped in guilty surprise, for at that moment Sir Gordon appeared in the doorway.

The new master was admired by young and old but nobody ever forgot his rank. And though there was no bowing and scraping, everyone behaved towards him, as he did to them, with the utmost respect. Ma's face went fiery and Andrew knew that his own neck was reddening in embarrassment when the Commander came into the kitchen.

'Ah! The hamper is ready.' Sir Gordon looked steadily at Andrew. 'Change into plimsolls or canvas shoes, put on a jersey and meet me at the harbour in twenty minutes. We must have a serious talk.'

*

Andrew's spirits were low as he ran down the hill to the harbour. Sir Gordon would have to sack him and there would be nothing for him but the boats, though it was typical of his hero that the Commander would do it kindly, not in front of everyone at Ingersley. There was a boathouse on the cliffs above the Ingersley private beach, with a wooden slipway to the launching place, but it was all but derelict now. The Commander had abandoned it in favour of the good, small harbour of North Berwick.

The harbour was busy, though the granary that ran along one side was closed. A Danish grain boat, tied up at the quay, would be ready to sail in an hour's time, judging by the activity on board. Half a dozen noisy fishwives were seated near the harbour entrance with their backs to the sparkling water of the Firth of Forth. They were baiting herring drift lines, their hands quick and deft as they reached into the baskets for pieces of fish bait and hooked them on to the lengths of line that would be trailed through the water. 'Andrew! Are ye goin' out wi' the men?' one of them called out.

He waved to them and to the men who, while the engines turned, were making ready the heavy wooden fishing boats that sat like two broad-beamed ducks in the brown water below. 'I'm helping Sir Gordon,' he called and ran around to the far side of the quay where, under the red sandstone harbour wall, *The Lizzie*, twenty-seven feet, a sloop-rigged yacht with a two-berth cabin, sat high in the water, her sails ready to hoist, Sir Gordon aboard.

He saw Andrew and said, 'Good. Here on time. Have you any experience?'

'I've put up a mizzen on a fishing boat to keep it from rolling when the engine stops. But I've never been under sail in anything fast,' Andrew said. He knew *The Lizzie* of course – and had often stood over by the harbourmaster's place and watched the Commander take her out.

So, he was going to be sacked and taken for a sail at the same time. That was all right by Andrew. He'd always wanted to feel the power of the wind taking a boat fast across the water. He'd been down to Leith Docks a couple of times, to see the great windjammers that occasionally came in, their many masts and the complicated rigging and clouds of canvas sails a marvel to him. Sir Gordon tossed a line that landed at Andrew's feet. 'Give me a pull.'

The Commander used a boat hook to push her away from the harbour wall. Andrew pulled. The boat heaved a little and inched slowly along the quay. 'She's moving,' he called.

'Keep going. Jump aboard when you reach the harbour entrance.'

A few moments later Andrew leapt into the boat and now there was no time to worry about getting the sack, for he had to pull the fenders on board. The deck was rocking gently, the loose sails were flapping and the boom was swinging as if *The Lizzie* herself were impatient to be off. Andrew was eager to do everything right. He had watched the procedure time and again so he knew what to do. With a mighty heave Sir Gordon hauled in the mainsail with the rope halyards, telling Andrew, 'Haul in the jib sheets!' and the boat began to pull away. They were moving under sail. Out of the shelter of the harbour, the boat rolled gently. Sir Gordon said, 'We're going close-hauled on starboard tack. Slacken off the leeward back stay.' The wind filled the sails. They were under way.

'Well done.' The Commander was at the helm, Andrew at the lee side of the cockpit, the wind on the starboard quarter as *The Lizzie* picked up speed. 'What do you want to do, Andrew?'

'You mean – do I want to go on working for the estate?'

'No. Mr Hamilton won't have you. No matter the rights and wrongs of the other boy's treatment, we can't have insubordination.'

The Lizzie was beating out towards the Fife coast. Andrew gripped the edge of the seat and placed his feet wide apart to steady himself. 'I'm not asking to be kept on, sir. I'll go on the boats.'

'You don't want to be a fisherman?'

'Not really. I'll do it if I have to. It's my duty to look after Ma.'

'You didn't think of that when you struck your superior?' the Commander said as *The Lizzie* went slicing through the water.

'No. I didn't. I'm sorry I let Ma down. Ingersley is her home. But I'm not sorry I hit Hamilton.'

'Mr Hamilton is a man of the land. A good farmer. He has an uncanny way with animals.'

He had an uncanny way with people, Andrew thought, but he would not sneak and repeat what he had heard this morning. The Commander would find out for himself, sooner or later.

'Get ready to move across.' Sir Gordon was at the helm, pushing the tiller. 'We're going on to the port tack.'

Andrew quickly changed over, tightening the port back stay, loosening the starboard as the Commander said, 'I asked what you wanted.'

Working together like this, it was too much to expect that Andrew would be able to keep up the bravado – the pretence of indifference. The sea and wind were in his blood now. It looked as if they were going to be out for a few hours. He'd speak his mind. He said, 'Farming's all right but I don't want to work on someone else's land. There's no future in being an estate worker.'

Sir Gordon Campbell, though apparently concentrating on holding the boat on a steady course, said, 'I agree. The days of a paternal system are over. The old ways are gone. We must adapt. But we all have to set individual courses. What is your aim in life? What do you want? Riches and fame?'

'I suppose I'm like everyone else, sir. Boys my age. First I want adventure. Then I'll need to make a bit of money to buy a few acres of land, find a wife and have half a dozen fine sons.'

'We can't get everything we want.' Sir Gordon's jaw tightened as his eyes grew wistful. 'I expect you think that a man in my position would not want the same blessings in life that you do.'

'No, sir. I didn't say I expect them. These are only my hopes.'

'I see. So you enjoy farming?'

'I do. But I want adventure first.'

Sir Gordon Campbell smiled. 'You are being vague, Andrew, saying, "I want adventure".'

'I just want adventure. But who will look after Ma?' he said. Ma could not apply for a better job, for, to her mortal shame, she could barely read and write and went to elaborate lengths to hide her semi-literacy.

'Your mother will always have a home with us. When she retires she will be given a cottage on the estate. Have no fears for her.'

Sir Gordon's eyes narrowed as he looked from Andrew to the coast ahead. 'Ease the jib sheets,' he ordered, and when Andrew had control, 'Once we're on a steady course, you can take the helm. You know the drill. The helmsman gives the orders. The crew obeys them promptly and efficiently. They must be "going about", not "messing about".'

The wind was blowing steadily. Andrew felt the pull of it in the jib. It was a thrill, sailing *The Lizzie*. The wind whipped through his hair, tasted salt on his tongue and brushed cool over his strong arms. They were heading towards the great Bass Rock; the basalt island that was home to one of the world's biggest colonies of gannets. Sir Gordon appeared to have come to a decision. He said, 'Have you considered the navy?'

'No, sir.'

'You should. There is going to be war.'

'You think so too, sir?' Andrew read the papers every day when they arrived in the servants' hall, two days old. The *Daily Mail* had come out flat-footed for Fascism when Hitler marched into the Rhineland. *The Scotsman* simply reported without opining and *The Times* had recently carried an advertisement that someone in the house had circled in pencil. It was an invitation to 'Gentlemen with Yachting Experience' to apply for commissions in the Royal Naval Volunteer Reserve.

Sir Gordon answered him gravely. 'I know so. British and American warships are in the Straits of Gibraltar. Spain is fighting a civil war and Germany is trying out her muscle. War is coming to us.'

As they drew nearer the rock Andrew saw the great white gannets with their six-foot wing-span diving, plummeting into the water from a great height, dropping too fast for his eyes to follow them. All the human eye could see was the thin water spout that shot upwards as the birds speared long and folded into the blue water. He was uncertain as to how he should answer the Commander, who had become very solemn at the prospect of war. So he said, 'And you, sir? Will you have to go back into the navy? Aren't you too old?'

Sir Gordon gave a hearty laugh. 'I have already been re-called. My orders came this morning. I will be given a command soon. You will be conscripted sooner or later and then you'll have no choice ... Here.' He reached out for the jib sheets. 'Take the helm. Keep the tiller steady. You have to learn the values of discipline, order and service, Andrew. I want you to join the Royal Navy.'

9th January, 1937

Not a great deal had happened at Ingersley in the six months Gordon had been away. Ruth, dressed for riding in jodhpurs and green jersey, was seated at the big desk in Gordon's study, directly above the front entrance, which had a splendid view over the park and driveway. She had spent an hour of her precious time contacting people to make up a small dinner party for Elizabeth's thirty-third birthday. Gordon would be here, since Elizabeth's birthday coincided with a five-day maintenance stop at the naval dockyards of Rosyth. He did not get back to Ingersley often, for his ship was based up north, at Invergordon on the Moray Firth. But he had promised to bring a couple of officers with him this evening, and the Misses Stevenson and the rector of the Episcopalian church and his wife had accepted last-minute invitations.

At last it was done and Ruth slammed down the telephone and surveyed the park. The drive curved down to the South Gate, flanked by evergreen ornamental firs and the pleasing monkey-puzzle trees. From here, on a clear day such as this, under a huge, blue-washed sky, you could see for miles beyond the bare oaks and elms that stood like dark guardians over the stiff white grass of the parkland.

Damn! she thought. She wanted it. She wanted it all. She would never leave this place. She stared out into the distance, barely noticing the navy blue of the river Forth, at its widest here on the estuary. Had she looked, every detail could be picked out on the coast of Fife, seven miles across the water, in the crystal-clear morning light. Flashes of sunlight – mirrored like the lighthouse beacon – glanced now and then from windows on the distant shore. Ruth saw none of it. It was Ingersley she wanted, not the view. She turned her attention to the ledgers. There was no longer any pretence of simply helping Elizabeth. In Ruth's opinion Elizabeth could not focus her mental energies on anything above trivial matters; fretting about the state of the world and Hitler's oppression of the Jews, as if worrying could do anything about it. She ought to be concerned about matters closer to home, like the figures that held Ruth's horrified attention. A year at the most, and the estate would be lost to the Campbells for ever.

'Damn it, why won't he see what any idiot can?' she breathed, angry at Gordon's refusal even to acknowledge the depth of financial trouble the estate was in. He didn't seem to care that she, Ruth, knew all about his finances when he would not even discuss such matters with his wife. Perhaps both Elizabeth and she were expected to believe that there were big investments elsewhere. Ruth knew it was not so. If he would only take Elizabeth's money – the generous marriage settlement – there would be no need to penny-pinch, to cut down on servants and maintenance. They could live as they used to do; entertain the grand families the county had by the score. There were ducal estates within spitting distance of Ingersley. There was the Duke of Buccleuch at Dalkeith, the Duke of Hamilton at Lennoxlove, the Earl of Wemyss at Gosforth. These circles might be difficult to break into, of course, but there were any number of landed gentry about the county.

If it were she, Ruth, whom he had married, she would have insisted that Gordon took her money. Since their father's farm and the mill would go to their four brothers, she and Elizabeth each had an endowment of thirty thousand pounds. Elizabeth's dowry had gone to her on her marriage. Ruth was living comfortably on the interest from hers. The capital sum would be hers when she married.

Damn again! Elizabeth's thirty thousand would solve only half of Gordon's problems. The house, gardens and park- land covered ten acres. The farm, Ingersley Mains, comprised five hundred acres of Grade A arable farmland with farm- house, cottages and a dairy herd. But the big money was to be made in grain, not in dairying, and this fertile land grew the best wheat and malting barley in the country. If Gordon would only see the wisdom of it, they could get rid of the dairy herd and all the workers that went with it, and go over completely to grain – or tell Hamilton to find £1,500 per annum in rent, which was three times as much as the profit he now showed. Since she had been doing the books, Mike had never again claimed wages for nonexistent workers, but there were a hundred and one ways to hide a profit that should come to the estate. There were forty cottages on and outside the estate and all paying next to nothing in rent. Gordon had given the choicest places to servants. Ivy Lodge, a small mansion house on the farthest reach of the estate, had been given to Nanny for her retirement home. She hardly used it. It could be sold for £3,000. The South Lodge – a fine small house worth at least £700, was occupied by the cook. And at even three shillings a week each, regularly collected, the cottages would be bringing in £300 a year. The way Gordon ran things, the income from them was less than it cost to collect the rents. Ruth knew the rental value of every farm and tenanted holding in East Lothian.

The clashing of the lift gates interrupted her. Elizabeth and Nanny were back from their morning visit to the kitchen and the servants' hall.

'Ruth? Are you there?' Elizabeth opened the door. She was dressed in an ankle-length camel-hair coat and a fetching brown hat, with a cashmere scarf about her slender neck. 'We have had such a nice walk, Nanny and I.'

'I'm here. I'll be with you in a minute.'

'We'll come and talk to you, won't we, Nanny?' Elizabeth hopped aside with an embarrassed giggle to let Nanny Taylor into the room.

The feebler Elizabeth grew, the sillier and more indiscreet she became, and this girlish behaviour was an irritation to Ruth, who now said, 'Put your coat over the back of my chair, darling. Sit down. I'll ring for coffee and biscuits.' Then, quickly, 'Or perhaps Nanny will send for them on her way out?' and smiled to herself as Nanny left the room. Ruth could not order Nanny about, for she was loved by Elizabeth and revered and respected by Gordon, who, not remembering his own mother, treated her like a dowager duchess. However, Ruth owed Nanny no favours. A few days of polite skirmishing when Ruth first came to Ingersley had made it clear in whose hands authority lay.

Now Ruth seated herself opposite Elizabeth by the hearth,

where a log fire blazed. 'I've been doing the books,' she said.

'Oh dear! Don't tell.' Then, frightened, 'Sorry. But I worry so.'

Worry could trigger an epileptic fit. Gordon demanded that they call the fits 'little spasms' and ordered that Elizabeth was not to be worried. Ruth was prepared to risk it. She said coldly, 'Ruin is staring the estate in the face. It could be spared if Gordon would use your settlement.'

'He won't take it. If we had children he'd want them to have an inheritance. Since we don't, we need leave nothing behind, he says.' Elizabeth was agitated. Her eyes darted up to the elaborate ceiling, down to the Persian carpet, over to the window and now to the door, which was opening as a maid entered and placed a tray of coffee and biscuits on the desk. 'Gordon says that war is coming and if anything should happen to him he wants to know that I have the security of my own money.'

Ruth poured coffee and said, 'Marriage settlements are not a wife's nest egg. You should insist on helping. Or why don't you make contacts and use them? Well-chosen friends could introduce you to people of influence – help you make money.'

'You don't know Gordon. He's as straight as a die and as inflexible. Total strength of character.' Loyalty and love shone from Elizabeth's unseeing eyes. 'And he's knowledgeable, Ruth. He says that all these old estates will have to be broken up and sold.' She waved an elegant arm around, vaguely. 'You can see empty ruins all over the place. The world has changed and there is no place now for gentlemen.'

'Elizabeth!' Ruth protested. 'If ever there was a gentleman in this world, it has to be Gordon.'

Elizabeth's mouth twitched. 'I meant gentlemen in the old-fashioned sense, dear. Gentlemen in the sense of men who do not have to work for a living. I know Gordon is the other kind of gentleman.' Here Elizabeth gave a sweet smile and added shyly, 'And no woman could have a more devoted, loving husband.'

Ruth gritted her teeth and grimaced. It was a blessing Elizabeth could not see. She said sweetly, 'And you, dear, in spite of all the debt ... you have made him happy?'

'Don't let's discuss money,' Elizabeth said.

Blunt speaking was a waste of time. Talk of love and marriage was the quickest route to encouraging Elizabeth's indiscretion. Ruth sighed wistfully. 'When I get married . . .'

Elizabeth was quick to pick up on this. 'You said *when*, not *if*. Oh, Ruth . . . have you met someone?'

'If I had, I should have no idea how to be a wife. I should have to come to you for advice.'

'What do you mean?'

'I mean, I'm twenty-nine, not an innocent, but. . .'

Elizabeth giggled. 'But we'd never get a husband if we waited for the man to take us by force, would we?'

'Elizabeth!' Ruth gave a shocked gasp then, as if becoming bolder, 'That's where I've gone wrong. I'm waiting. What do I do to entice a man?'

'So there is someone? Oh darling, I'm so glad. Anyone I know?' Elizabeth leaned forward, her manicured hands gripping the carved armrests, eager as a young girl to talk and listen. 'But I'm sure you will get him to the altar. Remember Daddy used to say, "Whatever Ruth desires, she shall have".'

'Actually what he said was, "What ruthless Ruth wants, she will get."' Ruth spoke flippantly, but it incensed her even after all these years that their father had always favoured Elizabeth over her. He had never had a good word to say about his younger daughter. 'He said it after Mother died. I was only twenty.'

'But Father doesn't hold you to blame. That's a preposterous suggestion. Mother had accidentally taken five times the proper dose of her sedative draught. The coroner gave an open verdict and said a troubled soul like Mother should never have been prescribed that stuff. It contained strychnine.'

Ruth corrected her. 'It contained the seeds of the nux vomica tree. Strychnine is a derivative. Mother must either have added strychnine to her sedative or drunk several bottles. Remember, she had taken to her bed,' Ruth reminded Elizabeth, 'as she always did when she could not cope with the family.' Ruth had always seen her mother as a pitiful creature who could not face trouble. 'Mother and I had had words – over my riding lessons. She threatened my instructor.' The recollection of her own fury brought blood rushing to Ruth's head, flaming her cheeks. She remembered how it was, she standing there, head bowed as if in penitence, while Mother raved, ranted and threatened. As she recalled it, Ruth's mind had split into two distinct sides: one half miserable and the other plotting revenge and triumph and wanting her mother dead. Now she took a deep breath and continued, 'Mother threatened him with dismissal, with prison – and worse, she said she would have to tell Father when he came home next morning.'

'Why on earth. . . ?' Elizabeth said.

'She'd spied on us. Overheard our talk about putting a mare to stud.'

'Mother knew nothing about horses,' Elizabeth said.

'Exactly. She assumed we were talking about – well, you know.' Ruth's face suffused with heat now, remembering.

'Oh my goodness. I didn't know.' Elizabeth put both hands to her face in horror. 'And this was on the very day she took the overdose?'

'Yes,' Ruth said. 'She never had the opportunity to carry out her threat.'

Elizabeth replied, 'The coroner gave an open verdict. It was not your doing. Anyway, dear, Mother left all her money to you.'

'Yes. But she felt you were secure, safely married and financially settled. It was when the will was read that Father said it: "Whatever ruthless Ruth wants, she will get."'

'But he didn't mean it in the way you imagine, you chump!' Elizabeth said. Then, with the assurance and ease with which she could always turn the talk to something more agreeable, 'I should not have mentioned it.' She waved an elegant hand towards the desk. 'Coffee? Will you pour?' And when she was sipping the coffee, 'Forgive me for bringing up a painful subject. You want to marry and have children?'

'God, no! No children for me. I hate them.'

'Don't, Ruth. . .'

'Sorry!' Ruth hoped she sounded at least a little contrite. Then, 'But you must be glad now you've had the operation. You won't have to go through all that again. And you could always adopt a child.'

Elizabeth was becoming agitated. 'I would. Gordon won't . . . it's painful.'

This was not the way Ruth had intended things to go. She gave a dry little laugh. 'Sorry. I didn't mean to upset you. What I really want to know is, how does a woman let the man know she's interested?'

'All men are different, I expect.' Elizabeth was making an effort to control herself by breathing slowly. 'But Gordon – he's very. . .'

'Passionate? Demanding?'

'Oh no. He never demands. Oh dear! I don't mean to sound disloyal. . .' Elizabeth blew her nose delicately.

'Tell me, dear. Between sisters?'

Elizabeth put away her handkerchief and seemed more at ease. 'I'm sure some men are demanding. But to tell the truth, I have to let him know I desire him. We have an unspoken code that has evolved. It's one of those secret messages wives and husbands send all the time.'

Ruth said, 'What do you do?'

'I put on a little perfume, wear something clinging – Gordon adores me in beige silk – and I simply take his hand and slide my fingers against his thumb. Oh, Ruth, I used to love to see the secret smile that came over his face when I did it in public – and then, when we are alone, and I still have to make the first move. Gordon is a gentleman. He needs to know that I consent. . .'

'So? What do you do?' Ruth repeated impatiently.

'I say, "Please, darling. Kiss me. I do so need to love you." Gordon tells me that a woman who is desperate for a man is irresistible.' She hesitated, but only for a second or two before her tongue loosened even further and she said, 'I shouldn't tell you this but . . . I need Gordon's love. I can't possibly obey the doctor on this.'

'What?' Ruth interrupted her.

Elizabeth fumbled again for the handkerchief. 'The doctor has told me that all marital relations should cease.'

'And Gordon ignores his advice?'

'I haven't told him. If Gordon didn't love me, I'd want to die.'

'Don't upset yourself.' Ruth touched Elizabeth's hand to show affection and understanding and felt the grateful return grip of her sister's fingers. 'I am sure the doctor is wrong. Let us go and find Nanny now, shall we? Before she starts on the tonic wine?'

Elizabeth crumpled the handkerchief and reached out for Ruth's hand again. 'It fortifies her. And she would hate for any of us to think she needed it, dear.' She took Ruth's arm as they left the study and crossed the landing to the drawing room, where Ruth expected to find Nanny nodding off in the corner chair. Elizabeth said, 'She's a treasure. Gordon looks upon her as his mother. I couldn't carry on without her.'

For once Nanny was not asleep. She was standing by the fireplace, waiting for Elizabeth. Ruth kissed her sister's cheek. 'I'll leave you now, Elizabeth. I'm going to exercise Heather.'

'Isn't the ground too hard?'

'No. I'll ride her on the beach. The sands are perfect.'

'Ask Mike to go with you. I know I'm a fusspot but since my own accident I worry when you are riding alone,' Elizabeth said.

'All right. I'll ask him.' Ruth spoke carelessly, suppressing a smile. Nanny might be old and a lover of tonic wine, but she had a rare talent for discerning hidden motives. She went back to the study for her tweed jacket, threw it on and ran down the main, wide marble staircase, sure-footed, skilfully avoiding the carpet's threadbare edges. She liked to feel her muscles working, feel the adrenalin-induced rush of blood to her vital organs. And the thought of the coming physical delight made her slam the oak door and take the twenty steps in a clattering of leather boots on stone in the frosty air.

Mike's farmhouse had its own cobbled yard at the back, enclosed with stables, coach house and the now empty grooms' cottages. Ruth went through the arched stone entrance to where Mike was waiting in front of the loose boxes. The horses were stamping impatiently, and he was scowling and shifting his weight from foot to foot. 'What kept you?'

'Elizabeth. She's getting worse.'

They mounted and turned the horses towards the lane that ran to the shore between ploughed fields of rich dark earth whose beech hedges were sprinkled with russet leaves amongst the dense branches. Over hedge tops the sea could be seen as they went slowly at a walk down the rutted, stone-strewn lane, the horses' breath blowing like white steam ahead of them. Mike asked, 'Did she have a fit?'

Ruth answered drily, 'No. I managed to avert one.'

'You are good for her,' he said. 'Is Gordon coming home today?'

'Tonight. He's bringing a couple of officers with him.'

His voice had an edge to it. 'For you? The officers?'

'Who knows?' Was Mike Hamilton afraid of losing her? They rode side by side as far as the bank of buckthorn bushes that grew thick, wild and in such random abandon that a walker could wander lost for hours, unable to get down to the beach below. But the horses knew their way through the maze, though there was space on the tracks for only one at a time.

'You go first,' Mike said, and they cautiously picked their way down to the beach.

He was not motivated by courtesy. He liked to watch her seat – liked the view, as he'd often said – liked to see the shape of her rear as she lifted out of the saddle. She was on the beach now, signalling to him with her riding crop, calling over her shoulder, 'Shall I kick her off? Race you to the old slipway?'

'I've told you a hundred times to warm her up slowly. She doesn't need the whip,' Mike said, though it was doubtful if she listened. He pulled up beside her. 'Ye've a cruel streak, Ruth.'

'Me? Cruel?' Their horses were stamping, impatient.

He said, 'When I declared meself, ye said the only creature you love is your horse.'

Ruth snorted a derisive laugh. Mike was wrong in thinking that animals needed a gentle hand. Horses, like humans, needed to be mastered.

Mike repeated, 'Warm her up slowly, I keep telling you.'

She gave him a bold look. 'Canter down and race back?'

He shrugged. 'Aye. Off ye go.'

Ruth urged Heather into a trot, then kicked in her heels hard to send her into a canter, the easiest pace, the steadiest movement. The mare moved like silk under her, responding to her every command. She was in control, and how good it felt! She heard the creaking saddle and rasping breath of Mike on Major behind her and laughed out loud, knowing that the strenuous ride and her rear view would inflame Mike. She stood in the stirrups, the weight in her heels, no contact with the saddle, knees out, the searing cold air against her glowing face blowing back her thick blonde hair. The scent and salt of the sea was on her tongue and her lover was riding close behind her, obeying her siren call. It was as near to control of another human being as she could wish for.

Last night, instead of going to his cold bed, Mike had taken her, stripped bare, over the saddle stand in the heat of the ammonia-scented stables, with the horses snorting their interest behind the iron grating of their stalls. He had been wild last night, demanding, forcing himself roughly on her. But he knew her needs so well; knew that she needed his strong hands to hold her down when she writhed and twisted in her throes. He knew she liked him to suck hard on her – to make marks in hidden places, to bruise her so that her daily activities were a secret, painful and exciting reminder and foretaste of the pleasures of the night.

Even now as she rode she could feel the ache in her wrists and ankles. Last night when Mike had released his own first need, she told him to shackle her at the ankles, wide apart like a mare at stud. When she was immobilised he tied her wrists to an iron wall ring so that her only support was her feet and her elbows against the rough wall, then he teased her, at first lightly with a riding crop and afterwards firmly and slowly with his fingers until she cried out for him and he entered her hard and violently from behind while he grasped her breasts in a clenching tight grip.

They had reached the rotten boards of the slipway under the cliff, and Ruth yanked Heather's head round and brought her to a halt. She saw Mike wince at her action as he pulled up beside her without any visible signal to Major. She was breathless. 'Race back?'

'If ye're entertaining tonight, then how about this afternoon?' he said. 'Stables or bed – wherever.'

'We'll see,' she said. It was good to make him wait. She was the leader in this game. 'I have to make a phone call this afternoon. I'm going to invite the doctor to the dinner party.' But that was for later. She leaned forward over Heather's neck, gave a fast, sharp flick of the reins, shouted, 'Go on!' and they were away, racing down the beach, sand flying under pounding hooves, the horses' necks stretched. The ride was thrilling – she could think of nothing else.

Chapter Three

Summer 1938

The reformatory, Dr Guthrie's School for Girls, as it was called, loomed large and forbidding above the houses and shops on Liberton Brae that warm summer night. Flora, grown tall and well developed after nearly two years in the institution, sat on the windowsill of the dormitory, where girls slept ten to a room. Outside the birds sang, and on the street behind the high wall that enclosed Guthrie's, people were strolling just as they pleased. Young children played in the fields and ran free as air in the enchanting Edinburgh evening light. It would not start to grow dusk until 9.30, yet the Guthrie girls had to be in their nightgowns by nine. There was no arguing with it; the excuse of fear of locked places could not be made. They would be locked inside – and Flora's stomach tightened into a knot of fear. But she dared not let it show. To say you were afraid was to ask for trouble.

She eased herself to sit upright, and spread the voluminous flower-sprigged nightdress wide over the sill to conceal her actions, whilst behind her back she felt with nervous fingers for the screwdriver she had taken from the tool drawer in the sewing room. There was one last screw that held the retaining bar. She was going to steal her papers, at night, from the headmaster's study before escaping over the wall.

Across the room the others were gathered round Cissie Kerr, who was wearing outdoor clothes. She had absconded a month ago and tonight had been brought back by the police. Cissie undressed while the girls questioned her.

'Where d'ye get tae, Cissie?'

'No' far. Leith.'

'Why didn't ye go home?'

'I'd rather be here than hame.' Cissie stepped out of her underslip and pulled the regulation nightgown over her head.

Flora didn't trust any one of them, nor did she believe that a girl, even one as hard as Cissie, would prefer to live in Guthrie's than with her own family. But she had to pretend. 'Where in Leith?' she asked.

Flora was the tallest girl in Guthrie's, and because of this, though she was one of the youngest, she looked older, more mature than the girls who encircled Cissie. They couldn't know that her insides were shivering jelly even as she gritted her teeth and felt the blade at last get purchase on the rusty screw head. 'Did you find Jessie? Did you say I'm asking after her?'

Cissie gave Flora a cold stare. 'I found her. She says to tell you she'll find ye work when you're oot.'

Jessie Fairbairn had been a good friend to Flora. Sentenced to a year in Guthrie's for living rough and stealing food, she had redeemed herself and found a place with a watchmaker's family. The screwdriver slipped into the soft cushion of Flora's thumb. She caught her breath, ignored the pain and, looking blankly at the girls, said, 'I'll be out soon.'

'How long did you get?' someone shouted to Flora.

'Two years,' she said. 'I've nearly done it.'

'Miss McNair says ye'll go to hell. She says ye canna be trusted. Ye've run away once too often, Flora Macdonald.'

She had run away from Guthrie's twice – trying to be brave, like Gran. Twice she'd tried to get back to the place she belonged, but each time she'd been caught and had a few extra weeks added to her sentence, the first time by the very same magistrate who'd sent her here. Next time, he'd warned her, she'd be old enough to go to prison. It would not happen again. She had it planned. She was going to find work and save money so she could make her own choices.

'Miss McNair's a fat old cow,' one of the girls was saying as the screwdriver engaged at last in the rusty slot. Miss McNair was a tall, skinny woman with not an ounce of fat on her, but Flora nodded her agreement while giving the screwdriver a quick snatching twist. Her fingers were slippery with sweat but she felt the screw loosen.

'Aye, So she is. A fat old cow.'

'I hate her an' all.'

'And me.'

'She's got her knife into Flora. Flora never gets into cookery. She's aye toilin' in the laundry.' The girl who said this added, 'You didnae want laundry work, did ye, Flora? An' it's only the ones Miss McNair hates that she puts in the laundry.'

'I despise the way they treat us in this place,' Flora said. In fact she was scared stiff. It was her looks, carriage and the quiet manner she had developed to cover her shyness that saved her from being treated like a down-and-out offender, in the way the weaker girls were.

'Despise? Think you're clever?' Cissie spat the word out.

'I've done nothing wrong,' Flora said quietly. And teachers such as Miss McNair knew it too – knew she had done nothing wrong. They resented it, wanting her to be grateful for her very life; wanting her to bow and scrape, to apologise for being in need. Flora quickly turned the screw with her fingers. It came out. She pushed it and the screwdriver into the corner of the sill. Then she slid to the bed to lie on her blanket.

'Then why were you sent to Guthrie's?' Cissie started across the room towards Flora's bed but stopped at the sound of the door being unlocked by the night duty woman, who shouted, 'Close the curtains. Into bed.' She came in. 'Anyone out of bed in five minutes' time will get an order mark. No talking.'

Flora pulled the curtains behind her before anyone else could do it, then slipped down again under her sheet, her huge liquid eyes with their opalescent whites glancing from bed to bed and back to the door. The duty woman slammed the door and turned the key, and the frightened, sick feeling that a locked door always brought swept over Flora. She had to fight with herself to control these fears. The others were silent – afraid that the woman would burst in, find them talking and put them on orders. Orders were severe. A girl who fell foul of the staff might have all privileges taken away; home visits, if she had a home, would be stopped for a month. In Flora's case, having no access to the outside world, if she were on punishment, the three evenings on which they were allowed to play the wind-up gramophone and have singsongs would be spent in solitary silence, reading and memorising improving works.

She lay still and watchful for two hours until the night staff had done their rounds and gone down to their quarters. In the dormitory, now, the only sounds were the deep breathing and light snoring of the girls. Flora heaved herself up to look through the window. The moon was full and the silvery light lit up her side of the building as clear as day. If anyone were watching Guthrie's windows she'd be caught before she had a chance, but there were no lights showing in the houses opposite. The temptation that came from weakness and fear was to leave it for another night, but *Do it now or you'll never escape,* she told herself. *It's a perfect night.*

She crawled on to the sill and closed the curtain silently behind her, then, kneeling, began to work the lower sash, inching it upwards. She had been rubbing a candle end over the sash ropes so that when the time came the window would slide easily. Sweat broke on her forehead as she worked. It was so slow ... so slow ... Suddenly the sash shot upwards with a groaning sound and a blast of cool night air rushed in.

'Oh God!' she whispered. With trembling hands she eased the curtains back and peered into the dormitory. They slept on. *Go on!* she urged herself. *You can do it.* The wrought-iron side support of the sewing-room balcony was only four feet below the window. There was a hiding place between the railing and a huge potted plant. The second part of her plan was to hide her papers and belongings there, ready for her escape.

She was out on the sill, sliding a bare foot over the edge, turning, sliding the other foot and now hanging and finding that her arms were not strong enough to hold her and slipping with the roughcast harling tearing against her shins, knees, thighs and inner arms until with a sickening, painful jolt she landed crumpled and winded on the balcony. She bit her lip to stop herself crying out, got to her knees and then to her torn feet, flexing her legs, Nothing was broken.

The sewing-room window slid upwards silent and easily and she was in, padding to the door; the tearing sound of her bloodied soles, sticky across the linoleum, and the rapid beating of her heart sounded to her like thunder in the silence. Her hair, dark burnished copper, clung damp with sweat to the back of her neck as she opened the sewing-room door. The headmaster's study was three doors away. She reached it in two terrifying seconds, turned the door knob and slipped inside, and in the ghostly moonlight went straight to the fourth drawer down of the wooden drawer cabinet. It slid open under her shaking hands and she began feverishly to search the brown cardboard folders for her papers – the court orders and her birth and Gran's death certificates. Here it was. Flora Macdonald. She took out the papers, pushed the folder back into place and, with her heart thumping in her chest like a wild animal, ran back to the sewing room.

She climbed on to the balcony rail, found purchase for her foot and hauled herself on to the dormitory windowsill. Slipping her hands under the gap, she felt the window slide up easily.

She crawled in. They were all still asleep. She had done it. She slid the papers under her mattress and then lay in bed, heart hammering, the metallic taste in her mouth turned to sweetness, legs, feet and arms stinging, but she was proud of herself. 'I'm making my ain choices, Gran,' she whispered.

There was no hope of sleep for the rest of the night. Dawn was breaking and Flora lay alternating between fear and hope as she made her plans. The next stage was to offer to sweep the sewing room after the lesson and conceal on the balcony her belongings, which she would have to wrap in brown paper. In case it rained she would slip her papers into the pocket of her mackintosh and turn it inside out. Then, when the time was right, on a quiet black night she'd go through the window again on to the sewing balcony, only this time she'd have to leap out the six feet on to the wall. Then she'd run as fast and as far as she could – not to Haddington and the old home ground, but towards the city and anonymity.

Grand Harbour, Valetta, Malta 1938

At eight o'clock in the morning, with a subtropical climate outside, Stoker Mechanic Andrew Stewart was hotter than he'd ever been in his life. Sweat ran down his broad, muscular back under his boiler suit as he crouched, cramped, in front of one of the eight oil-fired boilers that drove HMS *Rutland,* a 10,000-ton, three-funnel cruiser. The hairs on the back of his neck were rising in anticipation of his superior's arrival. Stoker Petty Officer Pearce had come through the steel door from the deck down the iron steps, to make his inspection in the second engine room. He was an ugly devil, with leery, bloodshot eyes and a misshapen nose that had been broken in a fight. Andrew had become used to receiving a clout across the ears in training and to the rough justice of life on board, and he was not unduly bothered by physical violence, but Pearce was mean and nasty. From Andrew's first day he had found fault with everything he did. Pearce was now standing behind him. 'Show me the burners. If they aren't clean there'll be no shore leave for you, sailor.'

Stopping shore leave was beyond Pearce's powers but he could hold them back for hours with these tactics. Andrew had only just cleaned and replaced the heavy steel burners but he removed the first one from its housing and held it out. Pearce took it to the bench, inspected it minutely, turned and said, 'Take them out. All of them. Clean them. Or I'll put you on a charge.'

'I've just done them, Petty Officer.'

'Do them again.'

Andrew bit back a reply as his dark eyebrows drew together. Not only could Pearce make a stoker's life a misery but he could also bring a charge of dumb insolence. Behind Andrew, his oppo, Greg, a boy from Edinburgh who had joined up and been with Andrew from the start, went white with anger as Pearce turned on him, saying, 'You too. You won't get a run ashore until those burners are clean.'

Greg gave Pearce a murderous look. It would take them three hours to clean all eight burners and replace them.

But four hours later they sauntered, smart in number sixes, bell-bottom whites, under the blazing heat of the Maltese afternoon. If they had gone ashore in shorts they'd have to be back on board by sunset and they had no mind to do that. They were going towards the harbour bars, following three sailors from the *Devonshire* which had docked ahead of them.

'I'll have to find a girl,' Greg said. 'Haul my ashes. It's been weeks. . .'

Greg was ahead of Andrew in experience but Andrew

wanted to appear a man of the world, so, referring to the
'goobers' – the rubber protection that sailors were ordered to
use against the punishable offence of catching a disease – he
said, 'Did you ask for your free issue?'

'Aye,' said Greg, 'You ought to ask for them. You never
know. . .'

Andrew grinned. He did know. He'd never go the whole hog
with a girl – not until he was married. It wasn't religious scruples that held him back, or the worry of disease. It was Ma.
He'd never let Ma down.

Greg was his mate though. And they had a plan of action.
When one of them found a girl and thought she looked promising, he would say to the other, 'Look at the time. You'll be late
for your date . . .' But now Andrew could not wipe the smile
off his face, for they were approaching Straight Street, the
dark, narrow street known to sailors as The Gut, famous for its
brothels and dives.

'Let's start here.' Greg jerked his head towards the first
seedy bar they came to. 'We'll have a quick one, then try the
others. Order two Blues.' Blues were the local beer. Already
they were learning the lingo.

The Gut, seven feet wide and five hundred yards long, was
noisy and bustling. Music, a dozen different tunes, came
jangling and discordant from the bars that lined the street. A
sailor, already drunk, lurched towards them, waving his arms
and singing. Andrew stepped aside as he passed and the lad
fell to the deck, knocking his hat askew, still singing.

It was not until they had drunk eight pints between them and
eaten a good dinner that they reached the halfway mark and
entered the Golden Hind. The noise was deafening. Well oiled
by now, Greg called out, 'This is more like it!'

The tables were crammed close together to leave a small
area for dancing, but there was no space to dance for the floor
was filled almost to bursting with sailors and girls.

'Shame about you. . .' Andrew was happy, not drunk.
'Shame you're too drunk to apprecie. . . You know what I
mean?'

'Speak for yourself.' Greg elbowed his way to the bar
counter and ordered. He turned to Andrew. 'Wanna rum?'

Andrew said, 'My turn.' Then, as he looked back, he saw

53

the prettiest girl he'd ever clapped eyes upon. Her scarlet dress was pulled tight across big, beautiful breasts. She was smiling at him. Her hair was shiny black, long and curling over her shoulders. Big brown eyes fixed on him and her lips, glossy with scarlet lipstick, were parted in invitation.

He felt a familiar tightening as he spoke. 'Care for a drink, miss?'

'My name is Anita,' she said in English. She came closer until the scent she wore filled the air around her.

'Here—' Greg turned with the drinks and handed the rum to Andrew. 'Hey.' He tried to slip an arm about Anita's shoulder.

She shrugged free. 'Not you. I like him,' she said, and slid her hand across Andrew's back.

Andrew grinned at Greg. 'Sorry, Greg. I thought you had a date ...' Then, *sotto voce*, 'Find your own.' He put his free hand possessively on Anita's arm and looked down, he hoped winningly, at the girl. She came only to his shoulder.

'She's a—' Greg started to say, but thought better of it. Instead he said, 'She'll fleece you. She gets commission on everything you order.'

The girl pressed closer. Andrew squeezed her shoulder. 'Want a drink?'

'Champagne.'

'Bloody hell!' Greg was looking towards the door. 'Bloody Pearce.'

Pearce elbowed his way through the crush towards the bar and came to a stop within feet of Andrew. He saw Anita and leered, showing brown-stained teeth. 'Anita, my lovely.'

He was stinking, rotten drunk. Anita shrank back for a second then stuck out her chin. 'I won't go with you. I've told you before.'

Andrew kept a firm hold of her to protect her. 'You heard what she said, Pearce. Sling your hook!'

Pearce swayed, his mouth slack, eyes bleary, voice thick as he said, 'Bloody Stoker Mechanic Stewart, is it? She's mine.' His left hand shot out, fastened on the girl's forearm and gripped tight, making Anita squeal.

'There's other bars,' Greg urged. 'She's not worth it. Let's get out.'

'Like hell we will.' Fury boiled inside Andrew. 'Take your

bloody hands off her,' he snarled and gave Pearce's wrist a sharp chop with the side of his hand.

As his hand fell Pearce muttered, 'I'll get you for this, Stewart. Striking a senior...' but his voice was slurring.

Quickly Andrew shoved the girl towards Greg. 'Watch her,' he ordered. He had seen that Pearce's left hand was low, weakened by the chop and in a poor starting point for a return blow, but he did not see Pearce's right fist arriving with a mighty crack, square on to his ear. He staggered back against the wall of sailors, who pushed him upright again and, laughing and spoiling for a fight, urged him on: 'Go for him!'

Only Greg had the sense to urge, 'Leave him. Let's get out!'

Andrew shook his head. Pearce was coming at him, his arms swinging wildly, teeth bared. It was an automatic reaction for Andrew to put his own fists up, to aim accurately. He felt the painful jarring contact of his knuckles under Pearce's chin, saw Pearce shake his head as if to wake himself up, then totter backwards against the bar.

Greg yelled, 'That's enough! You're even now. Pack it in!' as Pearce, still leaning on the bar, grabbed wildly for the brass rail. His hand fastened on to a beer bottle.

Andrew came forward, fists curled, 'Stand up, Pearce, you bastard!'

Pearce stood, swaying drunkenly, spittle dripping from his lower lip as he hit the bottle against the brass rail. It bounced off. The music stopped. The crush moved back. There was nothing, no shouting, just air being drawn in and exhaled fast and greedily by the sailors at the front of the crowd. Andrew lunged with his right fist, caught Pearce a glancing blow on the jaw and felt the sharp stab in his wrist. And now the little crowd was starting to shift, to join in, calling out here and there, 'Go on, sailor! Give it to him...'

He heard the splintering sound at Pearce's second attempt to break the bottle but he did not feel the jagged broken glass lacerating his neck and throat. He was wild with anger, unaware of the blood that was pouring down his neck and chest. He landed another right hook under Pearce's jaw and heard, behind him, shouts of encouragement. There was a coppery taste of blood in his mouth. Sweat, or tears, blinded him as he landed another hook under Pearce's jaw and felt another shock go juddering down his arm.

Pearce was short of breath, his face purple and red, mouth hanging open with saliva dripping from his loose lips. He growled like an old bear every time he received one of Andrew's blows. But Andrew knew he had youth and strength and stamina on his side, and he had drunk only enough to make himself merry, not drunk like the steaming, sweating Pearce. Andrew moved in fast, landing another blow on Pearce's jaw. The crowd moved back. Someone, probably the barman, called out, 'Send for the police. They're fighting like ruddy tigers!'

Andrew heard all this commotion at the same moment he felt the low thud in his stomach. His breath was being punched out of his lungs and he tottered, slipping on the bloody, wet dance floor. He did not feel Pearce's boot cracking into the back of his head; he did not see Greg and half a dozen other sailors tackling his opponent to the deck before Pearce could land the second kick that probably would have killed him. What he next knew was white light spinning in blackness and gradually, fuzzily, his eyes focused on the faces above him and he heard, 'Call an ambulance. Take him to the Royal Naval hospital...'

'Get him back to the ship—' Pearce's voice – 'before the provost marshal police get here. He's not hurt.'

Then Greg: 'You'll be court-martialled, Pearce. If he dies...'

'He won't die. But if he squeals, he's as good as dead.'

Andrew came to on the operating table of the *Rutland*. His throat was tight. His neck was a ring of pain and the medical officer, a surgeon lieutenant, annoyed that his own first leave in weeks had been held back while he stitched up a brawling stoker's wounds, was impatient. 'Sit up!' he ordered.

'Aye aye, sir.' Andrew heaved himself awkwardly into a sitting position. The tiny room circled around him. He grabbed the edge of the table and held fast. He put his hand to his bandaged neck and said, 'What happened?'

'You fought. That's what happened. You'll be charged. Drunk and disorderly. Causing an affray. Stand up.'

Andrew stood to attention. On the floor was his blood-soaked tunic. His white bell-bottoms were splashed and streaked red. The medical officer said, 'Get yourself cleaned up. The duty regulating petty officer will escort you to the captain.'

'Aye aye, sir,' Andrew said as he was gripped and steered towards the door, his head heavy, hot and bursting with pain even as a cold chill ran down his back. The captain was Sir Gordon Campbell.

In his cabin, Captain Sir Gordon Campbell read the hastily written charge sheet. Andrew, the boy both he and Elizabeth had helped, would have to be punished. No excuses could be made for bar fighting with the local Maltese, using broken bottles. Andrew Stewart knew the ropes. He had been in the service for a year and a half.

While he contemplated Andrew's punishment it gave him a shock to realise that two years had passed since the day he had taken the young lad out on to the Forth. He glanced at the silver-framed picture of Elizabeth that was attached to the wall and thought of how his own life had changed so drastically since that afternoon. He remembered the night of her birthday in January 1937, when he had gone home to Ingersley from Rosyth, the river Forth base in Fife.

After a successful tour of protection duty in the Med, where General Franco had ordered the shelling of a British steamer off the coast of northern Spain, Gordon had been given his first command: the *Rutland*, a bigger ship than he had ever commanded – a three-funnelled county-class vessel with Pearson General turbines and four propeller shafts. He had never had charge of so fast a ship and felt that he needed more briefing on their powerful engines. That week, his cabin was being refitted and he could take a few days' leave.

He was anxious for Elizabeth, who seemed to be losing confidence in herself as her sight worsened. She had said, the last time they made love, 'If you ever find a healthier, more desirable woman, I should not want to live.' He'd been astonished and hurt, and back on board he knew he needed to reassure her of his love by seeing as much as he could of her. He rang home and spoke to Ruth, who naturally assumed he knew that a party was being arranged for Elizabeth's birthday.

57

'Can you bring some officers home with you, Gordon?' she said. 'The balance of guests is wrong.'

Gordon, though not contemptuous of hierarchy and ranking, did not follow the strict social rules of naval protocol. As well as the young lieutenant-commander, he would invite the chief engineer, a non-commissioned officer who held petty officer rank. Chiefie, as the chief engineer was affectionately called, could explain the ship's mechanics to them both.

When they arrived at Ingersley his worries vanished, for Elizabeth was her old self. Wearing a mauve crêpe de Chine dress that clung to her slender, graceful figure she greeted them at the door, shaking hands with his junior officers, accepting their birthday good wishes, smiling into their faces as if she could see as well as once she had. Her beautiful face and bubbling charm had his junior officers bowled over in seconds. She took his hand and climbed the stairs ahead of the others, her voice low and soft as she said, 'Darling, I hope you don't mind. Ruth asked if she might invite the doctor and his wife as well as the minister and the two Miss Stevensons. Poor Ruth doesn't get many opportunities to shine socially.'

She slid her fingers gently against his thumb as she spoke. The scent of Chanel perfume drifted in the air about her and he felt the quick rising of desire for her. He forced his mind on to the waiting guests to avert embarrassment even as he returned the pressure of her fingers and whispered, 'Later, darling...'

In the drawing room Ruth was obviously in good form, pink-cheeked, speaking earnestly to the doctor one moment, the next relaxing and acting the part of the lady of the manor. Ruth had social ambitions and he asked himself if he and Elizabeth were being fair to her sister, who ought to have a wider circle of friends than they could provide. He smiled to himself. The lieutenant-commander was a bachelor. Gordon took Elizabeth across the room to be near to Ruth then, since they no longer kept a butler, took upon himself the pleasant and now entertaining duty of serving drinks from a rather elaborate trolley that Ruth had given them at Christmas.

The guests were mingling well and the confident small talk and tinkling laughter of the ladies gave every indication of a pleasant evening ahead, yet Dr Scott was standing a little apart from the rest, by one of the windows where the curtains were not drawn, looking out over the frosty white park. It was as if he wanted to be out of earshot. Gordon went towards him. 'What will you have? Whisky? Sherry?' Then the doctor's solemn look made him say, 'How do you think Elizabeth is?'

The doctor gave a thin smile. 'Whisky. I have to talk to you.'

'About Elizabeth?'

'Yes. Could you come to my consulting room in the morning?'

Gordon poured whisky into a crystal glass and handed it to the doctor. 'I'm afraid not. But – look here – after dinner we can talk in my study for ten minutes. It's the room directly opposite the drawing room.'

The cook had excelled herself. With the help only of the two housemaids, who also had to wait at table, Mrs Stewart had prepared a delicious game soup, which was followed by fish caught that very morning – whiting in a tangy sauce made from cream and capers. Next came Gordon's favourite, roast rib of beef with vegetables from their own fields and the rich gravy that only Mrs Stewart, in all his experience, could make so well. Scotch trifle was the dessert – another of his favourites. He would go downstairs to thank her before she left for the South Lodge.

Elizabeth sat at the opposite end of the table and, watching her, Gordon knew a return of his earlier anxiety. She was overexcited, overreacting to the conversation, which had turned from the inconsequential bits of news of other families and church affairs in the little harbour town of North Berwick to highly charged talk about the Duke and Duchess of Windsor's being welcomed by Hitler to Berlin. Elizabeth saw this as treachery. The Misses Stevenson saw it as peace-making. The doctor too was worried, for his eyes went frequently to Elizabeth down the long mahogany table.

It was nine o'clock before Elizabeth, with dear, devoted Ruth beside her, calmed down. His fears subsiding, Gordon nodded to the doctor and slipped away to the study. There he poured two brandies and waited for the doctor to speak.

The doctor accepted the drink and, unsmiling, came straight to the point. 'Your wife is deteriorating,' he said. 'You may not be aware of it, but Elizabeth's fits are increasing in severity and frequency. I have to advise you that marital relations should cease.'

Gordon stared at the reflected light that shimmered, golden, in the brandy goblet. He did not look at the doctor. Later, he'd recall every word, every inflection in the doctor's voice as he continued: 'Your wife will not tell you. She is naturally very afraid of losing your affection. She asked that I observe the code of confidentiality.'

Gordon kept his eyes on the glass, head averted as he said, 'I see. You believe that the fits are aggravated—?'

'Absolutely. The brain's electrical balance is disturbed by the act.'

Gordon took a deep breath, looked directly at the young man and said quietly, 'Thank you for telling me. I will respect your confidence. My wife will not be told that you have broken yours to her.' He opened the door for the doctor.

When he was alone, he sat at his desk in a state of appalled disbelief. How was he going to do this? If he told Elizabeth that he had sought independent medical advice she would see it as a betrayal. She herself would never speak about their married love to anyone but himself. And how could he turn away her offers of love without explanation? He must make his poor darling understand that it would be as great a sacrifice for him as for her. But he could not do it tonight, with so many people in the house. He would speak to her before he left Ingersley in the morning. He drained the last of his brandy, opened the study door and saw that Ruth was speaking to Nanny at the far end of the landing. He beckoned her. She nodded acknowledgement, dismissed Nanny and came into the study.

'Ruth, my dear. Has Nanny gone to her own quarters?'

'Yes. I didn't think Elizabeth would want her – with you here.'

'Sit down, Ruth. I have to ask yet another kindness of you.'

'Anything at all.' An expression of cool calculation seemed to lurk at the back of Ruth's wide blue eyes even as she said, hesitantly and tenderly, 'What can I do, Gordon dear?'

Gordon glanced at the clock. It was almost ten. Everyone would understand if Elizabeth retired early – and in any case the guests were starting to shift a little, as if waiting for a signal that it was time to go. He said, 'Take Elizabeth to bed. Tell her not to wait up for me. The officers and I have a lot to talk about. I will sleep in my own room.'

'You want me to sleep with Elizabeth?'

'If you will.'

'In Nanny's bed?' Nanny always slept in Elizabeth's dressing room when Gordon was away, in case she had an epileptic fit.

'Yes.' He had no intention of telling Ruth any more than this and he saw with gratitude that it was not necessary. She patted his arm and said, 'There is no need for Elizabeth to come downstairs to see the guests off. I'll take her up to bed. And tell her that you and your officers will be talking all night. All right?'

'Ruth?'

She turned at the door. 'Yes?'

'Gently does it. Tell her – I'm sorry...'

'I understand, Gordon. I'll give her some sedative medicine. She may need it after all the excitement.'

'Thank you, dear.' He watched Ruth go to Elizabeth, take her sister's arm and incline her head, smiling as she bade good night to their guests. His wife gave the sweetest smile as if she understood perfectly and all was well.

Gordon saw Dr Scott and his wife, the rector and the Misses Stevenson to their cars in a flurry of thanks and polite handshakes and a crunching of tyres on frost-white gravel under the black bowl of a still night that was brilliant with thousands of stars. He'd give anything to have Elizabeth on his arm, her sight restored, sharing with him the wonder of the night sky. He remained a few minutes, gazing at the constellations – Orion, Ursa Major and Cassiopeia – that had inspired the legends of gods, poets and peasants, thinkers and dreamers, since man had first pondered the universe and his own part in it. He reflected too on the fact that even today, with the wonders of modern science, sailors still navigated under the same skies that early man had regarded.

Indoors, his officers drew up chairs in front of the drawing-room fire, where the chief engineer made a splendid furnace of the logs that crackled and sparkled and threw shadows across the elaborate plaster ceiling. They talked long into the night in the otherwise silent house. It was three in the morning before the officers went to their rooms and Gordon to his old childhood bedroom that connected to his study.

He was sound asleep when Ruth came in, white and terrified, shaking him by the shoulder, whispering, 'Gordon! Elizabeth has gone...'

He sat up with a start. 'Gone? What are you talking about?'

'I don't know. I heard something. I looked. Her bed is empty. I can't find her. Oh, Gordon, I'm afraid...'

He shook his head, the better to clear his thoughts and waken his sensibilities, then, 'She must have gone to the bathroom. Have you—?'

'I have looked everywhere.'

He got out of bed, found his dressing gown, hastily tied it about himself and went ahead of Ruth to search the house. Elizabeth did not have the confidence to venture outside alone. A cold dread came upon him as they went first to Elizabeth's bedroom, to check that Ruth was not mistaken, then to every room on the bedroom landing.

There was no sign of Elizabeth. They went carefully down the unlit staircase to the drawing room, where the electric light switches were located. They flooded the second floor with light and searched with more fear and urgency. There was nothing to be seen. Down the staircase they went again, this time joined by the officers, whom they had awakened.

Gordon was sick with apprehension. Elizabeth was not an impulsive, eccentric person who might, upon a whim, do anything. Foreboding was heavy on him now, contracting the muscles in his stomach, fogging his mind with dread as the search of this last floor proved fruitless. Elizabeth would not have gone down to the servants' quarters. She had never done so unaccompanied. She would have to have taken the lift and fumbled her way.

It was when he began logically to second-guess Elizabeth's movements that he thought again of the lift. He ran back to the bedroom floor, found the outer gate open and lift descended. If Elizabeth had fallen, she could be unconscious, lying on top of the cage at the foot of the shaft. 'Call the police,' he cried. 'Tell them we need a mechanical engineer with an understanding of hydraulics.'

The chief engineer said, 'I'll check the lift shaft.' And it was he who found the broken body of the love of Gordon's life. Elizabeth had fallen to her death.

Now, here in his cabin, Gordon recalled all that had followed. The police at first were not satisfied that the death was accidental. Everyone was questioned: he first, and by his distraught state they were convinced of his devotion to Elizabeth; Nanny Taylor, who had spent a restless night and was adamant that, even from two rooms away, she had heard Elizabeth sobbing; Ruth who had given Elizabeth a sedative so as not to risk one of her fits. Ruth said that Elizabeth was asleep when she left her side for half an hour to do her nightly tour of the stables. Ruth never, ever used the lift. She did not even know how to operate the gates.

The police were dogged in their questioning. They asked if Elizabeth had ever threatened to take her own life; Gordon said absolutely not. Ruth recalled occasions when Elizabeth had said she would rather be dead than go on living without all she held dear, but this was not held to be significant. Then they enquired who had prescribed sedative medicine, and when told that it was a common remedy that could be made up and sold by any chemist they asked, 'What would be the effect of an overdose?' They were informed that a large overdose would make the patient disorientated. A massive overdose would be fatal but no patient could have swallowed such an amount of the bitter medicine and Elizabeth's post-mortem showed no trace in her blood of the strychnine agent which one would expect to find in an overdose. They turned their attention to the lift.

'Were the gates always fastened?' they asked. 'Who, other than Lady Campbell and Nanny, used the lift?' For the first time since the lift was installed, the outer gates on the bedroom floor had been left open. If Elizabeth had stumbled by accident into the shaft then the gates must have been opened by somebody on that floor who then went to the ground floor and called the cage down.

The only servant who used the lift was the cook, Mrs Stewart, who sent food up to the dining-room floor on a laden trolley. Lady Campbell or Nanny invariably called the lift to take them to the top bedroom floor at night and there it stayed until it was called to the kitchen for breakfast.

The whole household had undergone two days of police questioning before the procurator fiscal's office decided that there was no case to make and the matter was closed. As far as the police were concerned, however, the case was unsatisfactory.

As for Gordon, it had changed his life. And now he was being reminded of Ingersley by the need to discipline one of her sons. But it would not do to go over it again and again. It was time to stop mourning. Gordon took down the photograph of Elizabeth and put it away. That done, he went to the ward-room on the quarter-deck and called for the stoker mechanic to enter.

Andrew stood to atention in front of his hero. His head was still light from the whiff of gas the doctor had given him but not so light that he couldn't grasp everything that was coming to him.

The captain spoke coldly, without signalling acknowledgement of their past connection. 'You are charged with common assault. Have you anything to say?'

'No, sir.' The captain was not asking for an explanation. All Andrew could do was to accept his punishment, which could be as severe as fourteen days on number eleven's, the cells, or twenty-one days detention in the military prison in Valetta.

'You are charged with being drunk and disorderly. You are also charged with causing an affray. Have you anything to say?'

'No, sir.' So, Pearce had claimed that he, Andrew, had attacked him. Pearce had got him on three charges.

Sir Gordon Campbell glanced at the record sheet. 'I see that you make an allotment of ten shillings a week to your mother.'

'Yes, sir.'

'And your own pay is four shillings and sixpence a day.'

'Yes, sir.'

'You will lose all leave this tour and will forfeit seven days' pay. I am letting you off lightly since this is your first offence.'

'Thank you, sir.' Andrew saluted and left the captain's presence.

Sir Gordon had let him off lightly. He would not get a single day's leave until they returned home in three weeks' time. But when they did – he would get his own back. Pearce would

64

cross the Forth by rail or ferry to spend every drunken night at the Black Bull, the sailors' bar in Edinburgh's Leith Walk. Andrew would find him when they were outside the jurisdiction of the Royal Navy.

Andrew walked up to the South Lodge from the station at North Berwick, his navy bell-bottoms swinging about his ankles, kit bag slung across his shoulder, a fitter, harder lad than had left the estate. Far beyond the wall on his right, Irish reapers were scything wheat. He could hear them, distant and faint, calling to one another in singsong voices. Two years had passed since he'd worked in the fields, and now that he was here, he realised he missed it; missed the raw scent of turned earth in the spring and the summer sounds that were drifting across the fields to him. But he did not miss working as a labourer.

Before he turned in at the gate he had to move aside to let Ruth Bickerstaffe and Mike Hamilton ride through on their horses. Hamilton ignored him but Ruth stared down her nose directly at him. Then she tossed her head and looked away, pretending she had not seen him. Andrew knew she had; he recognised the startled look in her eyes. He'd seen it before – a long time ago, when he'd stumbled upon their tryst in the dairy. Now he smiled, wondering if they saw him as a threat.

Ma was in the big house kitchen. She beamed with pleasure at the sight of him, and at the sight of the kitchen maids' interest in him. 'Aye,' she said when he took her arm and escorted her back to the South Lodge, 'ye're a son to be proud of. So you are.'

When they were inside the lodge and she'd followed him up to his room to help him unpack she suddenly cried out, 'My heavens! What's those great ugly marks on your neck?'

'It was an accident, Ma. In the boiler room. Looks worse than it is. It was my own fault.' He would not tell Ma that he had been charged by the Commander. He changed the subject. 'I want to take you out – Portobello funfair, a day on the beach, tea at Crawford's if you like.'

'I can't take a day off,' Ma said. 'The Commander's bringing half a dozen officers home next week. And the harvest's in full swing too.'

'Aye, but they have a tractor. Haven't they cut down on workers?'

'There's still as many men to cook for at reaping time.'

'I see Ruth Bickerstaffe's still here,' Andrew said.

'He can't do without her. She runs the estate. They'd have to close the house and let everything go if she went back home,' Ma replied. Then, in a hushed whisper, 'It's not a happy house. The staff don't like her – she's very hard on everyone. Only happy and smiling when she's on that horse. Rides it every single day, she does – rain or shine.'

Was he, Andrew, the only person at Ingersley who knew what was going on between Hamilton and Ruth Bickerstaffe? It was possible. She'd been swift and ruthless in getting rid of him once he'd rumbled them. There were five hundred acres to get lost in, and many hiding places. It amused him to think that her nightly trips to the stables had only confirmed in others' minds Ruth Bickerstaffe's concern for her horse.

But seeing Ma taken in by the woman Andrew knew as a dangerous, scheming bitch, he put his arm about her. 'Why don't you pack it in?'

His lovely little ma smiled. 'I'll never leave Ingersley. The Commander will never be a man of the land. Without Ruth Bickerstaffe the place would go to pot. We'd none of us have work.'

'I don't know. There's work to be had in town.' Since Hitler had marched into Austria, the whole country had been re-arming. Andrew said, 'There's houses to rent all over the place. The factories have gone over to making munitions. They're crying out for workers.'

'Factory work's for the young,' Ma said. 'Nobody would leave here.'

'Course they would. These big estates will never get people back into service once they've been independent – once they've made a go of it without a lord and master controlling everything.'

'Oh! Dinnae talk like that, Andrew. We've a good home here. I've got fifty pounds in the bank. It's all thanks to you, son.'

'I'll look after you, Ma.' He put an arm about her.' 'But I'm going to spend the last week with Greg,' he said. 'You won't mind?'

'I don't mind. But, don't go into those Edinburgh sailors' bars...'

Greg's noisy family lived above their baker's shop on Liberton Brae, and his three younger sisters chattered incessantly as they followed Andrew up to the room he would share with Greg.

'What's that place?' Andrew asked, looking out from the dormer window over the high wall opposite.

'It's the industrial school. Girls' reformatory,' Greg said, then, turning to his sisters to shoo them away, 'If you don't leave us alone you'll be sent to Guthrie's.' The girls went gigling down the stairs and Greg came to stand beside Andrew.

'What do they do to get locked up in there?' Andrew asked.

'Bugger all! They lock up lasses who've done no harm to anyone as far as I can tell,' Greg said. 'Lasses can't get away with high spirits. They can't retaliate when they're bullied.'

'Not like us, eh?' Andrew said. 'Let's go down the town in our uniforms this afternoon. We stand a better chance of finding girls that way.'

'We'll be charged if we're in uniform when we do Pearce,' Greg said.

'We'll deal with Pearce tonight.' Andrew unfastened his shirt and stiff collar, pulled his tunic over his head and felt the scar – the purple gash that went from his left ear and across his throat and would mark him for life. And as he thought about it, his mouth tightened into a determined line. Pearce had it coming to him.

Chapter Four

Flora had been working in the laundry for three weeks, banned from sewing for the impertinence of singing, and banned from the kitchen work she enjoyed for cutting the bread too thinly and spreading the margarine too thickly. Today, in the midday summer heat, ten girls stooped over tubs, benches and sinks, but Flora's attention was not on the hard labour of scrubbing, wringing and rinsing by hand clothes from the never-reducing heaps of dirty linen. Sweat poured down her face as she glanced up through the steamy window of the stone-flagged cellar to the sewing-room balcony where her belongings were stowed. Every day she wondered that nobody else had seen the brown paper parcel, so clearly not a part of the plant pot that hid it. She felt sick inside, seeing them there.

If her belongings were discovered before she could escape, all would be lost. She'd be charged with theft and sent to prison. There was no hope of going through the window again. The day after she'd stolen her records the dormitory windows had been fitted with iron bars. No explanation was given. She could only guess that someone outside thought they saw something on that night. The rules in the laundry room had been tightened up. They were not allowed to talk, except in answer to Miss McNair, the vicious-tongued laundry mistress, who stalked the room looking for misdemeanours to punish.

All the same it was noisy. Mangle rollers thudded, iron gearing clanked, girls grunted and sighed in the steamy air heavy with the vapours from washing soda and bleach which caught the back of Flora's throat.

She straightened up and with her free hand swept the red

hair from her damp forehead, where it had escaped from the length of tape that held it back. She rested the scrubbing brush for a moment on a stiff pink corset and looked beyond the wet slatted wooden bench and the dripping tiled walls, through the open window to the fifteen-yard stretch of grass and the sky above the boundary wall. It helped just to look at that wall and the sky when the panic that came from being enclosed, surrounded, came upon her. To take her mind off her fears and the sick feeling of dread she had lived with for three weeks, she began to hum 'The Skye Boat Song'.

'Flora Macdonald, stop that noise. Get back to your work!' Miss McNair's harsh voice barked.

Flora cast her eyes down and returned to the scrubbing.

'Look at me girl, when I speak to ye.' The laundry mistress had come to stand between Flora and the window. 'What did I say?'

Flora made herself answer quietly and calmly, 'I'm to work harder.' Inside, she was churning with protest.

'And faster. Ye'll be nae use to man nor beast. Ye'll never find a place.' Miss McNair's thin lip curled up in scorn. 'And who do you think you are, that you can sing as if you haven't a care? Wouldn't we all like to sing? Oh, yes! But we have to learn that we cannae please ourselves. Who wants a singing laundry maid? Who'll take you into service if you show no respect?'

Flora was almost at breaking point. She threw down the pink corset and the scrubbing brush, and in doing so accidentally knocked the bar of coarse yellow soap to the floor. Miss McNair drew breath sharply. Flora protested, 'I don't have to scrub and serve. My gran said I was to refuse...' Blood rushed to her cheeks. The room fell silent; scrubbing and mangling stopped as the girls waited for Miss McNair to explode.

'Your grandmother's dead, girl. Time ye took stock of yer situation.'

'My gran wanted better for me.' Flora spoke in a whisper, but the outbreak of rebellion that had been simmering rose up in her.

'Aye. She must have had grand ideas. Was it she gave you your name?' Miss McNair made the sarcastic smile that never reached her eyes. 'Flora Macdonald, indeed! And nae bonny prince to save. Ye'll come to nothing, lass.' She looked past Flora at the other girls, who laughed to get on the right side of her.

Hearing their sniggers, Flora turned, fiery, tearful and furious, on them. 'I'll show you! I'm better than you lot. You bunch of yellow-bellies. Cowards!' They had all, all the girls, claimed they hated Guthrie's and Miss McNair, yet not one had said a word in Flora's defence.

'Right!' Miss McNair spat as she snapped the word. 'I'm no' havin' this in my laundry.' She pointed to the oldest. 'You're in charge while I take this wicked girl to the headmaster.'

A stream of sweat trickled slowly down between Flora's shoulder blades. She ran a clammy finger inside the harsh linen neck of the grey laundry dress. She braced her shoulders. Adrenalin was pumping into her blood, making her finely muscled body ready for fight – or flight.

'Did ye year?' The thin, wiry woman's eyes were steely. 'I said come with me.'

Flora would make a break for it. If she were taken to the headmaster the next step would be prison, for certain. Her mouth was dry but she licked her lips before replying in a slow, deliberately surly voice, 'Why? I've done nothing wrong.'

'Nothing wrang, is it?' Miss McNair said, loudly, so all would hear. 'Then why d'ye imagine they sent you here to have your character reformed? Nobody gets sent to Guthrie's for nothing wrang.'

'I ran away. That's all,' Flora said. 'And so would you have.'

There were a few seconds of silence while Miss McNair's thin mouth hardened into a contemptuous line and she indicated with a bony index finger the wet floor. 'On your knees. Pick up your brush. And the soap,' she ordered.

If Flora never disobeyed another order in her life she would not get down on her knees for Miss McNair. This was her last chance. A metallic taste was in her mouth and her legs were shaking but she bent double as if to reach for the soap that had fallen at Miss McNair's feet. Then, in a flash, she ducked under the bench and came up on the other side, face to face with the furious laundry mistress, who had to back away quickly, saying, 'What do you think you're doing, girl?'

Where her agility and her nerve came from, Flora would never know. She put her right hand on the windowsill and smacked her left into Miss McNair's face, sending the woman shrieking and reeling back to land heavily on the slippery wet flagstones. Then Flora was on the sill and squeezing feet first through the sash opening at the top.

She landed badly but got to her feet and hared across the fifteen yards of lawn to hurl herself up the wall, clawing for a handhold on top of the coping stones. It was as if she had wings. Her legs flailed madly for the few seconds it took to find a toe grip until, knees grazed and her inner thighs torn and bleeding, she was over and dangling by her hands. Below, laughing up at her, was a dark-haired sailor lad who had come running towards her as soon as she appeared on the wall. He was shouting. 'Greg! Help the lass!'

She fell in a gawky, heavy, noisy and squirming tangle of long limbs and red hair and near hysteria and struggled to get away from the lad, who held her tight.

'What's all this?' he said as he put her down on her feet. 'You nearly broke my neck.'

'Oh! Help me, please ... Help me...'

She was in a state. She'd never known such terror. Her hair was wet with sweat and fear, it straggled all about her face and neck. She couldn't stop shaking, crying and trying not to scream as she pulled away from the lad, who held her even tighter, pinning her arms to her sides.

He said, 'Steady on! I'll help you. What happened?'

'I hit her. They'll send me to prison. Oh ... help me...' Even her words were coming out all shaky now, on stuttering breaths. 'Don't let them get me.'

The sailor loosened his hold but held her hand. 'Come on then,' he said. 'Run.'

'My belongings ...' She was rooted to the spot, shaking all over – legs, arms, head – and in a voice cracking on the edge of hysteria and with tears streaming down her wet face, she said, 'They're on the balcony ... a parcel...'

'The balcony facing the wall?' the other sailor said. 'I'll get 'em. You two run ahead. I'll catch you up.' He swung himself on to the wall and disappeared from view.

71

The dark one held fast to her hand. There was devilment in his eyes. 'Come on then! Before they send for the police—'

Fear must have given her wings, for suddenly she found herself running like the wind, zigzagging from one side of the road to the other at the lad's orders, turning to look over her shoulder as if expecting a posse in pursuit.

They rounded the corner and finally were out of sight of Guthrie's. The sailor pulled her in beside him to lean against a high stone wall. Heart thumping, Flora dragged air into her lungs noisily, clinging for dear life on to his hand until the other sailor came tearing round the corner and ran straight past them. Her sailor, as she now thought of him, laughed and whistled. He had dark curly hair and a wide, generous mouth with strong white teeth, and he was laughing uproariously now because his friend, Greg, was twenty-five yards down the street.

Greg stopped in his tracks and looked back. Then he came bounding up the hill to stuff the parcel into Flora's hands, saying, 'That was good. An old woman was on the grass, squealing like a banshee.'

'Miss McNair,' she said. 'Did anyone follow you?'

'No. They were all going wild. The old woman was yelling to stop the girls going over the wall after you.'

She'd let go of the sailor's hand and he grinned as he took in her appearance. He said, 'If they send the police after you, they'll spot you a mile off in that garb. Haven't you anything else to wear?'

'In here.' She held up the parcel. 'Not a lot. I didn't want to steal anything I'd made with their cloth,' she rushed on. 'I've got a black skirt and a white cotton blouse, a mackintosh and a pair of shoes.'

'If they're looking for a girl with two sailors...' Greg began.

'Over the road.' Her sailor was a fast thinker. 'Behind that hedge. It's a big house. Nobody will see you in the bushes.' He took her arm and steered her across the deserted road. He said, 'I'll keep watch. Change your clothes. Stuff that grey dress in the hedge. Have you a comb?'

She shook her head and, with great politeness, he handed his own comb to her. Flora knew then that he would not harm her. She took the comb and ran across the road and deep into the dark green shrubbery.

Once she was out of sight, Greg asked, 'What are we going to do with her?'

'If you can run at that speed,' said Andrew, 'you can cut behind the houses and over the fields to your house. Bring my civvies. I'll change and you can take my uniform back.'

'Then I get lost?' Greg grinned. 'And you get the girl?'

Andrew was annoyed by Greg's assumption. 'I don't want the lass caught and taken back there. I've no designs on her.'

'What about Pearce?'

'We'll get him later. I'll be back before five.'

'Right. Watch this for gold medalist, Jesse Owens.' Greg thumped Andrew's arm, then ran, streaking up the road, crossing into the fields close to the hedge at a speed Andrew was sure could have beaten the Olympic runner.

'Where's he gone?' The lass was beside him, neatly dressed, hair combed and loose; under her arm a rolled mackintosh about her belongings. She looked a treat but her eyes held the fear of a hunted animal. 'Are you going to leave me?'

'Greg is. He's got a date but he's bringing my civvies. Hide behind the hedge while I change, then we'll catch a tram at the foot of the brae. I'm taking you to Portobello, to the beach and the funfair. Nobody will find you there and you can tell me all about it.'

Twenty minutes later, with the girl sitting beside him on a rattling tram crammed with holidaymakers, Andrew asked, 'What's your name?'

'Don't laugh?'

'I won't.'

'Flora Macdonald.' She looked at him quickly then away again as if expecting him to respond with a laugh and a cruel joke. She was pretty though – even when her face had been tearful and sweaty with effort and her hair clung damply to her neck and brow. She had enormous eyes of aquamarine that you felt you could drown in, and now Andrew saw a blush come poppy red into her cheeks. He took her hand and above the whining noise of the dynamo said, 'Then we're meant for each other. My name's Andrew Charles Stewart.'

Her eyes sparkled with laughter. She leaned over and whispered, 'I was singing "Over the Sea to Skye" when the laundry woman went for me.'

'And you hit her?' Andrew grinned.

She smiled back. 'Aye. I'm not sorry.'

'Sometimes you have to do it,' he said.

Then, subdued and with those beautiful eyes suddenly distant, she said, 'If they catch me, I'll go to prison.'

He took her hand again, held it fast and felt it relax, small and warm, and rough-textured from all the scrubbing. 'Over my dead body,' he said softly.

She let him hold her hand, turning her head to give him a shy smile every so often, and he felt all at once very protective of her. A happy, warm bubble seemed to fill to bursting inside where his heart lay. But he knew nothing about her. He squeezed her hand and turned to look at her again. 'How old are you?'

Flora squeezed in return. She liked the feeling of her hand being held, though she couldn't remember it ever having happened before. But then she had never in her life met anyone she'd taken to so fast. She didn't want to deceive him, but what if, when he found out how young she was – not yet fifteen – he didn't want anything more to do with her?

He repeated, 'How old are you?'

She couldn't look him in the eye and lie, so she looked through the window where the clamour of Princes Street was a distraction. She said, 'Seventeen. How old are you?'

'Nineteen.' He was smiling broadly, as if pleased she was old enough for him. 'Where's your mother and father?'

'There's nobody. I belong on a little farm down the coast.' And saying this, her heart sank. Would she ever belong to anyone or any place? A lump of self-pity came into her throat but she said, 'I can't go back there. I'll have to find a job and somewhere to live. There's a girl I know. Jessie Fairbairn. In Leith. She said she'd find me work.'

'Leith? You can't go to Leith.'

'Why not?'

'It's a rough place. Full o' thieves and drunks – and loose women.' His brows had drawn together until they met in the middle.

'Well. Temporary. So I don't have to sleep rough again.'

74

He held her hand tight. 'How much money have you?'

'Five and sixpence.' But five and six wouldn't last much more than a week, even sleeping rough.

'There's plenty of rooms to let in Portobello,' he said with conviction. 'I'll stop with you until you're fixed up.'

'Thanks.' She stole admiring glances at him as they rode in silence on the whirring, clanging, noisy tram. He was very handsome and tall and he had a long straight nose that he'd touch now and again with a hand that was broad and strong. She could see the hairs on his arms when the sleeves moved up. 'Sure you don't mind?'

He smiled, showing his straight white teeth. 'I'll enjoy it.'

The tram came to a halt at the working man's playground of Portobello, on the widest part of the bay of the Firth of Forth. There they found an empty bench on the esplanade, overlooking the sands. The beach was packed solid with families, children playing noisily, their parents relaxing in deckchairs, barely a foot apart from strangers. Andrew claimed the wooden bench seat. 'Keep me a place. I'll get us a bag of fish and chips.'

They ate hungrily from the paper parcels, talking fast, telling little details of their lives as if they were catching up after a separation. It was two o'clock before Andrew ate the last scrap and screwed the paper into a greasy ball ready to drop into one of the litter baskets. 'Right. Let's get cracking. What do you want to do? Find a living-in job in one of the boarding houses?'

She got to her feet. 'As long as I'm not shut up in a factory – but I'd rather that than be shut up in Guthrie's. Are you coming with me?'

'Where shall we start?'

'We'll start at the other end of the Esplanade.'

It turned out that casual work was easily picked up. Most of the boarding houses needed help, and Flora found herself a job as a morning chambermaid at one end of the Esplanade, and afternoon and evening work as cook's help and serving girl a few doors away. But there was not a spare bed to be had, not even where there was a 'Vacancy' sign in a window. Andrew was doing the asking – he said it would look better, coming from a man, but they were dealt with very brusquely when he said,

'Have you a room free?'

By six Flora was weary. The crowds had gone and only a few local children ran, shrieking, along the water's edge. 'I'll sleep on the beach – or a bench in the park,' she said.

'You will not!' Andrew was horrified at the suggestion.

She did not tell him that she'd done it before, not wanting him to know she'd once been a vagrant. 'I didn't really mean it.'

Andrew smiled at her, fondly. 'It won't come to that. I'll stay with you till you find somewhere.'

'You have to meet Greg. You have an appointment.'

Andrew laughed. 'He won't mind. I was going to beat up Pearce.'

'Don't!' she said quickly. Andrew had told her how he'd got the scars on his neck. 'It will make trouble.'

'That's the idea. Only this time it's Pearce who'll be in trouble.'

'But two on to one? It's not fair. It's cowardly.'

Andrew's upper lip tightened as it did when he was opposed. 'Greg won't hurt him. This is my fight.'

'Please. Don't get into trouble. Don't fight.' He'd told her all about the Commander, who was responsible for his being a sailor instead of a simple farm lad. He'd told her that he wanted promotion – to justify the Commander's good opinion of him. She said, 'If you won't do it for me – refuse to fight – do it for the Commander. He's been like a father to you. He'll want to see you get promotion. Don't let him down.' Then, 'Funny. The Commander's a Campbell and I'm a Macdonald, and here I am telling a Stewart how to behave with my old mortal enemy.'

Andrew went quiet and she saw that he was thinking on what she'd said. She tried not to move or blink until she saw a little smile replace the tight-lipped look. He said, 'If you'll be my girl, I'll leave Pearce alone.'

'You mean, your sweetheart?' she asked, then blushed, since it sounded as if she were being forward.

'Yes. Will you write? And put kisses and a sign, like SWALK, on the envelope flap – so the others will see? You don't mind, do you?'

Flora was flattered that he thought her grown-up enough to write love letters to him. She said, 'I will. I've never had a real boyfriend...'

76

'And I've never had a real girlfriend.' He laughed as he said it. 'Come on. Let's get cracking and try to find a room for you.'

Their luck changed. The first house they came to without a 'Bed and Breakfast' sign hanging from the gatepost had a card in the window that read 'Room to Let'. A brass plate beside the bell bore the inscription 'John Davidson LRAM ATCL Teacher of Pianoforte'. A piano was being played in the front room. Flora indicated to Andrew that they would not ring the bell for a few minutes so as not to interrupt the lively playing of 'With catlike tread ... Upon our way we steal...' from *The Pirates of Penzance*. Finally they rang. After a few seconds there was a noise of bolts being drawn, before the door was opened by a severe-looking middle-aged man whose first words were, 'Who is it?' He was blind.

'I'm sorry,' Flora said, embarrassed now. Then, realising that she should not have apologised for his blindness, she felt her face growing red. 'I was looking for lodgings. I want something permanent. I've been searching all day.'

Andrew said, 'Was that you, playing the piano?' as bold as brass.

'Yes. I used to give recitals. Now I give lessons.' A smile crossed his face. It made him look less severe and he seemed in no hurry to close the door in their faces. He said, 'Are you married?'

Andrew reddened as it came to him in a flash that of course all those others must have thought they wanted a bed together. He glanced at Flora, whose cheeks were glowing. He said, lying so as to secure a chance for her, 'Oh no. Nothing like that. Flora is my sister.' He felt Flora's hand slip into his with a little squeeze of gratitude. He said, 'I'm a sailor – Andrew Stewart. We must find lodging for her before I go back to sea.'

Mr Davidson turned his face towards Flora. 'Your parents?'

'I'm an orphan.' Then her cheeks blazed that amazing poppy red because of the mistake, and she added quickly, 'So is Andrew.'

'Come in,' said the blind man.

He took to them quickly. Ever since his mother died he'd been unable to manage the house, he told Flora. He was looking for a good, honest and God-fearing lodger – one who would uphold his good reputation and would take him to the nearby church three times on Sundays, so that he could continue as organist. Could she cook? For he could not.

Andrew said, 'My sister is looking for work as well as lodgings. She has been offered two part-time jobs, but a job with accommodation would be better.'

Then, said the good man, if Flora would do what he requested and look after him, cleaning and cooking for both of them, she could have the whole upstairs of the house. She would also earn a small wage, from which he would deduct two shillings a week for piano lessons.

Chapter Five

April 1939
The wind was roaring, lashing sleet before it, howling through the trees, sending branches cracking to the ground, alarming the horse from whose back Ruth had watched the Armstrong Siddeley turn in at the South Lodge gate. One of the few conditions Gordon had ever made was that, to keep the grass clean, the horses were not exercised in the park. He had come to rely on her to keep everything working smoothly in his absence. She was in control of everything on the estate: the farm and cottage rents, the servants' wages. Though there was no money for repairs and maintenance, the estate was at last viable now that Elizabeth's legacy had come to the rescue. And things ran more smoothly with Gordon away than here.

But Gordon must not learn that she flouted the few rules he insisted upon. He did not allow smoking in the house, and that was one rule she kept. She smoked occasionally, when riding. The rule that the park be kept free of animals was regularly broken, but always when Gordon was away. 'Go on!' she shouted over the wind as she dug her heels hard into Heather's flanks and headed for the stable. The animal leaped forward. They would easily outrun the motor car. Gordon wouldn't see her. He had only returned to his ship a couple of weeks ago. Why was he home again so soon? Preparations for war were in hand. The government had built more weapons factories and army camps, but that and the Czechoslovakia problem – Hitler had marched into Prague – could have no bearing on the British Royal Navy, surely?

The cold wind raked her cheeks as she glanced back and

saw Gordon pull up at the front of the house, but the roar of the wind would mask the sound of hooves and Heather's snorting, so she sat back in the saddle and tightened the reins to slow the horse down from a canter as they came into the yard.

'What the hell do you think ye're doing?' Mike roared over the wind that was lifting the corrugated-iron roof sheets and crashing them on to the timbers as if they were cardboard. 'I told ye not to take her oot.'

'She needed exercising,' Ruth shouted. She slid down, landed with practised ease and gave him the reins. 'Will you see to her? I have to get back to the house.'

'No. Ye'll damned well look after your ain horse. You treat this thoroughbred like a carter's beast.' The mare was frothing at the mouth, drenched with sweat and rain, as he took the reins and led her into the big box. He held the door open so Ruth would follow, then in the relative quiet of the loose box he bolted the half-door and said, 'Why do you have to go back?'

'Mothers' Union meeting.' Her mind was not on the lie that tripped so readily from her lips. She knew that Gordon would be fretting about the estate, worrying about every little difficulty, implying that it didn't matter if cottage tenants fell into arrears since the cottages lacked modern conveniences. She must assure him that the estate was safe.

'Christ! Ye go to church. Pray on your knees. Entertain the Mothers' Union. And ye're not even a mother.' Mike handed the reins to her to loop through the wall ring while he unfastened the girth strap. His anger cooled as he looked at her and said through tight lips, 'Ye could be a mother. As soon as ye say the word.'

'I've never wanted children.' Ruth adroitly turned away from the implied question. 'Elizabeth let the Mothers' Union use the house.'

Mike lifted the saddle and the horse's sides slackened in relief. He said, 'I don't care if we have no children. I want ye for my wife.' Then, 'Here, take this.' Ruth placed the saddle over the wooden saddle horse and obeyed when Mike ordered, 'Take her bridle off, for heaven's sake.' He took the towel, threw it over the horse's back and dried the animal down with smooth, practised strokes. 'I asked, when will ye do it?'

'We can't marry yet,' she said.

'Why not?'

She thought quickly. 'The Territorial Army has been doubled. You could be called up.'

'Ye'll have to think of a better excuse. There aren't enough farmers. We're a protected occupation. The government's paying two pounds an acre to plough up pastures and grow crops. You know all about it. You do the books. I'll have my work cut out here.' His voice was harsh as he added darkly, 'Don't take me for a fool.'

'I don't.'

'Well? When?'

'Give me until June.'

'What the hell for? You know I'm in love with you. And you wi' me. There's nobody else, is there?'

'No.'

'You wouldn't lose any status, if that's why you're hesitating. You'd still be in charge ...'

He didn't finish, for Ruth sent the bridle clattering on to the saddle horse and then gave Heather's neck a quick, sharp pat. 'I have to go,' she said lightly. She tightened the belt of her riding mac, turned up the collar and dragged on her gloves. Then, eyeing the filthy weather outside, 'What a bloody climate!'

'Back this afternoon?' Mike asked.

'No. Tonight if I can,' she flung at him as she opened the stable door, put her head down and bolted first for the shelter of the farmhouse and then, running like the devil, for the trees of the park. She tripped over a tree root, almost fell, righted herself and ran faster.

She was there. She went in at the back door to leave her outdoor things in the boot room beyond the kitchen, where one of the maids would attend to them. She grabbed a towel, dried her hair quickly, shook her head to settle it and went to the kitchen, where Cook was preparing lunch. 'Everything all right, Mrs Stewart?' she asked.

'Yes. The Commander's home.'

'Really? I didn't know.'

'He's only got a few days.' Mrs Stewart's cheeks were glowing. 'He said, "Can you make one of your delicious steak pies for supper, Mrs Stewart?"'

'And your son?' Ruth asked, out of politeness, not interest. She would not get too friendly, but on the other hand a loyal staff worked harder.

'The Commander got to know the truth about some bit of bother. He made Andrew up—' Mrs Stewart's face lit up – 'to leading stoker. Next step, petty officer.'

Ruth put on the cold, impersonal expression that stopped servants from becoming too cosy. She left the kitchen and took the lift to her room so she could wash and change before Gordon saw her looking a mess. Reaching the top floor, she closed the gates carefully and quietly, then jumped, seeing Nanny, who had come silently from her room at even so small a sound.

'I wondered who it could be,' Nanny said. 'Gordon's home.' Then, 'You don't normally use the lift, do you, dear?'

'Thank you, Nanny.' Ruth brushed past her. 'I'll be down in twenty minutes.'

'You don't normally take lunch, do you, dear?' Nanny said.

From his bedroom, Gordon watched the storm wreak havoc in the park. The damage would be enormous by the time the gale was blown out. Howling westerlies had broken limbs off the creaking and groaning oaks. Branches and twigs, smashed to pieces were being hurled over the grass. He turned away. He felt no affection for his home. Since Elizabeth had died, he could hardly bear the place. She had been the rock, the anchor of his life. He couldn't go on like this – could not come home to this emptiness. Everything in this room – the rose silk of the spread on the bed they had shared; the scent bottles whose lingering perfume brought memories back faster than thoughts, the memory of her soft skin and her delight in his every touch – everything reminded him of Elizabeth. At sea he could put it out of his mind. Not here.

Something must be done. Ingersley was too much for him. Landowners were being urged to plough up grazing pastures since less than a third of the country's food was home-grown. Soon farmers would be directed, not requested, to grow what was needed. In a matter of months they would be at war. He could not serve his country, grow crops and run the estate.

He had come to a decision and must break the news to Ruth

and dear old Nanny. Fastening his uniform jacket, he brushed his hand over the three gold rings to give himself courage. He had no qualms or hesitation in ordering men, but women were another matter. He adjusted his tie, ran a comb through his thick sandy hair and went down to the dining room, where he found the table laid for three and Nanny waiting.

Impulsively, he kissed Nanny on the cheek. She flushed with pleasure and said, 'Ruth will be down in five minutes, dear. Normally she doesn't take lunch.'

'Then we'll wait.' He went to the sideboard. 'Sherry, Nanny?'

'Just a small one, dear.'

He tried to keep his face straight as he poured a generous sherry for the woman he loved as his mother. Nanny had remained in residence at Ingersley instead of at her own Ivy Lodge so that Ruth would not be living in an otherwise empty house. He had already told Nanny that it would be better for her to get away – back to safety with her sister in Ontario. He would be able to pull a few strings, get her a passage to Canada any time, but far better if she did it soon.

He poured a good tot of whisky for himself and drank it fast. The fiery heat of the rough brand he preferred hit the back of his tongue then slid down, warm and welcome. He said, 'I want to talk to you and Ruth this afternoon. I hope you have made no arrangements?'

'No. No, I have nothing,' she replied as she sipped the sherry. 'And Ruth has not much to occupy her time with Elizabeth gone.'

The door opened. Gordon turned quickly and started. It was Ruth – Ruth looking so like Elizabeth it was uncanny. She had grown her heavy blonde hair to shoulder length. She said, 'What a marvellous surprise. How long will you be with us?'

'Only a few days.' He spoke fast, to regain his composure. Then a little sharply, 'I want to talk to you both this afternoon. Not doing anything down at the stables, are you, Ruth?' She looked up quickly. 'Unless you would like to talk over lunch?'

'You make it sound ominous,' she answered. 'We'll hear it now.'

When they were at table, Ruth ladled lentil soup on to their plates, seated herself and said, 'Now, Gordon? What is it we have to know?'

He had not wanted to say it so soon, but since Ruth had raised the subject he said, 'You must be aware that soon we will be at war. There are five or six airfields, civil and military, within a seven-mile radius of Ingersley and fighter pilots and bomber crews in training in the area. There is not much time. I realise that I have been imposing on you both. You, Nanny, ought to have been enjoying retirement in Ivy Lodge.'

'I love being around you young ones,' Nanny said in a vague, faraway voice which owed less to sentiment than to the sherry and the large glass of wine she had already finished. Gordon refilled her glass. Nanny took a quick little sip, then, 'But anything you say, dear,' she said, and returned her attention to the soup.

Gordon was a little more confident. He turned to Ruth, who had not touched her wine and was toying with her soup. 'I have allowed you, Ruth, to carry the whole weight of administrative work. I apologise.'

She put down her spoon and spoke very fast. 'Oh, please, Gordon. It's a pleasure, not an imposition. Believe me, I wouldn't have continued otherwise—'

'Thank you,' he said quickly. 'I intend to close the house. There is still time for Nanny to get away to Canada and for you, Ruth, to return to your family in Cheshire. I want you to go home.'

The silence that followed his announcement seemed to go on for minutes, though it could only have taken seconds before Ruth said in a voice high with protest, 'Close the house? Who will do the books – pay the farm wages—?' The familiar calculating expression flickered at the back of her pretty blue eyes whilst at the same time the knuckles on her left hand closed into a fist so tight that her bread roll was reduced to crumbs.

He was not answerable to her, but since she had taken it hard he tried to tell her patiently, 'An agent will administer a much reduced estate. The park will be ploughed and Hamilton will have control of all the arable land. The staff – there are few enough – will be put at Hamilton's disposal, or retired.'

'But this is dreadful. The house could be commandeered if nobody lives here.' Her voice was shrill with outrage.

If he were dealing with a junior officer Gordon would have charged him with insubordination. He was not handling this well. He said calmly, to defuse the argument, 'It may be requisitioned by one of the ministries anyway, regardless of who is living here.'

Ruth's cheeks were flushed. She got to her feet, scraping the chair across the parquet. 'You'd let the estate go to ruin? There is no place for me? After all I have done for you!' Furiously she threw her napkin on the table and faced Gordon. 'I have never been treated like this! Never. I won't be threatened.' She rushed from the room.

Gordon made to go after her, but Nanny stopped him with a firmness he'd forgotten she had. 'Sit down, dear,' she ordered. 'Ruth is a very passionate girl. Self-willed. When she thinks she is under threat she reacts badly. Let her cool down. She is bound to see the sense of it.'

'It was not a threat, Nanny,' he said in his own defence. 'I have not done this well, have I? I find it simpler standing my ground against the Admiralty.'

Nanny said, 'I have seen Ruth like this before. But she will recover, my dear. It will be a very different Ruth who comes down to dinner tonight.'

Gordon managed a smile. 'I hope so, Nanny,' he said, but he had lost his appetite for lunch. Unless Ruth recovered he would have no appetite for either dinner or her company.

But six hours later, when he went downstairs for dinner, Nanny was proved right. It was a very different Ruth who waited for him in the drawing room. Again, he was startled at the sight of her. She wore a short dress of ivory silk that clung to her slender, athletic body. And again she looked so like Elizabeth that he was taken aback. She came forward to kiss him on the cheek, saying, 'Gordon. I'm sorry about my behaviour earlier, dear...' and he could smell her perfume – not quite Elizabeth's but so very near it. '... I know you are doing your best for us all,' she continued, and she touched his arm gently and let her hand linger there for a little longer than was necessary.

Struggling to regain the high ground, he pulled his arm away quickly, as if her hand were red-hot. 'Where's Nanny?'

'She has a headache,' Ruth said. 'Brought on by the prospect of having to live with her teetotal sister in Canada, perhaps?' She laughed softly – there was no malice in her open, starry-eyed face. She had acknowledged the cause of Nanny's indisposition with poise and discretion, just as Elizabeth used to do. 'I suggested she had her meal served in her room.'

Relief flooded through him. He must make her see that he was closing the house because he was concerned for her and Nanny.

'Whisky?' he asked, and went to the monstrous trolley to pour drinks for them both. Then he smiled, seeing the grimace she made as she took a delicate sip before placing the glass down and going to the window. She closed the long wooden shutters and pulled the tapestry curtains to shut out sight and sound of the storm that still blew.

It was then that he saw that her legs were bare, and he found himself shocked yet excited by the thoughts that the smooth sheen of her shapely calves brought. He'd been taught that only low women went without stockings. He pulled himself together and said, 'What have you been doing with yourself while I've been away?'

Ruth looked over her shoulder at him. 'I'm on a few church committees.' Then, after a small hesitation, 'Everyone at church thinks highly of you, Gordon.'

'They approve?' He relaxed and his eyes twinkled.

She came back to the fireside and lifted her glass. 'If we have only a few days left, I'd like to spend them in your company.'

Again he was reminded of Elizabeth as a small, familiar thrill came tightening in him. Ashamed of this physical reaction and not wanting to seem churlish, he gave his attention to the drinks trolley, saying, 'Of course,' in a purposeful way. He refilled his whisky glass, drank it in a quick gulp and felt the neat, fiery spirit warming, lighting up inside him.

'Then put a few logs on the fire. We'll...' Ruth laughed, '... we'll repair to the drawing room after dinner, shall we? As we did when Elizabeth ... Oh, sorry...'

It never upset him to talk about Elizabeth. He said, 'You can mention her name, you know. When Elizabeth was alive?'

She nodded and came to stand close to him, so that he had to step back a little to give her elbow room to sip again at her whisky. She swirled the glass until shards of amber light came glinting through the crystal to dance on her small, pretty hands. She did not look at him as she said in a low, throaty voice, 'You miss her dreadfully, don't you?'

'Yes.' He downed the last of his own drink and put the empty glass on the marble overmantel. 'But I don't want to talk about my loss tonight.' He smiled at her. 'You need not finish the whisky. Let's go into the dining room.'

Long afterwards he would realise that he had never been a match for a determined woman. Possibly it was innate chivalry – but once his initial reserve was broken, he found himself responding to Ruth, enjoying her company, her talk, her pretty, animated face and the scent of her. He was excited by the closeness of those bare legs that were within inches of his own, for she had set her place next to his at one end of the long oak table. She had chosen two wines – normally one bottle was enough for three – and had chosen well.

Mrs Stewart sent up potted trout with thin-sliced brown bread and butter to start the meal. For this course Ruth had chosen a fine white Burgundy, and she filled his glass again and again, saying, 'I do so want you to enjoy this evening, Gordon.'

'Why this evening in particular?' He found himself responding in the same slightly flirtatious manner.

'I will tell you later.' She laughed and touched his hand for a second – a feather-light brush of her fingers across his that made goose bumps rise on his forearms. To bring himself down to earth, he tried to think of his ship, the crew and the tour of duty in the North Sea that was their destination next week, and he concentrated on the food, the light-as-air golden pastry that flaked around rich brown gravy and tender braised steak. But already he was weakening.

Ruth insisted on his testing the claret before she poured it. It was smooth and full and rich and it shone ruby red in the bowl of his wine glass. He turned to Ruth and said, 'This is a fine vintage...' and then he stopped, because she looked exactly like Elizabeth and the candlelight from the silver candelabra shimmered upon the ivory silk dress that followed every curve of her body. Even her eyes had lost their hard expression and were soft and melting – and he was in danger of forgetting himself and his duty to his dead wife's little sister.

Later, feeling mellow and completely at ease, they sat by the blazing hearth where a log fire burned. The only light came from the fire and the few table lamps at the far side of the drawing room. Gordon watched the reflection of the flames flickering across Ruth's now serious face. He asked, 'Would you like brandy, my dear?' and she jumped to her feet to serve him. He smiled, for he was used to being served with alacrity and solemn discretion in the ward room and captain's cabin and it amused him to have this attention from Ruth. He allowed her to pour a measure of cognac and bring it to him, and as he watched her coming slowly, swaying her hips as she moved towards him, not a wrinkle showed through the ivory silk; not a line of elastic; not a slip strap. She was wearing nothing under the dress. She stopped, the bare legs only half an inch now from his knees, holding the glass out like a child, making him reach for it.

His strong hands felt the touch of her small, light fingers and this time her hand stayed on his as, with a nervous little laugh, she dropped gracefully to sit at his feet. She had not noticed that the dress had ridden up to her thighs, revealing a shocking length of smooth bare thigh. Gordon was disconcerted and embarrassed by his own body's response to the sight. Ruth came closer. 'You don't mind if I sit close to you, do you?' she asked.

And Gordon knew even as he hesitantly answered, 'I don't mind...' that everything was changing. She smiled up at him before resting her head against his leg, and he could no longer hold his body back from arousal by the pressure of a soft cheek on his thigh.

He put down his brandy glass on the side table. Believing that his actions were prompted by affection and gratitude, he let his hand brush against her hair. And he was lost. Ruth immediately slid her arm up, reached for his hand and pressed it to her lips. With an almost electric shock and the excitement that had been simmering all night, he felt the tip of her tongue gently moving in the centre of his open palm.

'Ruth!' he pleaded. 'Don't do anything you may regret, my dear...' But she pulled herself up and knelt in front of him, making him open his legs so that she could come in close, and the brandy fumes billowed inside his head and the scent of her, the sweet, heavy scent, blotted out his reason.

'I don't want to go, Gordon,' she whispered. 'Don't cast me out.'

'Ruth!' He placed his hands gently on her shoulders, but he could feel her fine bones through the silk and her warm body trembled under the pressure. 'I'm not casting you out, my dear. You will be safe in Cheshire.'

'Don't! Please don't talk that way, Gordon. Not tonight.' Her round blue eyes locked on to his, her hair was a thousand shades of tawny gold and her voice was low and husky. 'You must know, darling, that I have always loved you.'

He tried to pull back but his will was gone. He said softly, 'I didn't know.' But he was hard and hot in blood and breath and her fingers were undoing the buttons of his uniform jacket so she could press her face close to his chest. He was pulsing and heat was growing in him even as he tried desperately not to respond to her and to say, 'Ruth ... Dear ... Please ... don't let us ...' But his voice was thickening and his heart was thundering behind his ribs. Her pretty face was inches from his own, her eyes were half closed, just as Elizabeth's ...

'Gordon ... love me ... Oh, Gordon ... I want you ...' she whispered. 'Please? Please, darling ... I need you...'

Then his mouth was on hers, locked into hers while he got to his feet and she rose with him to move close to the fire. His hands tore the ivory dress down from her shoulders. Her full breasts with their round and rigid pink nipples were thrusting forward for him as she arched her back and pressed her hips into the hard, urgent, throbbing and painful ... 'Oh God! Ruth...' was all he could say.

She leaned back a little and let him take her breast into his mouth, the nipple like rubber against his tongue as she made the exciting throaty sounds of a woman aroused and her hips moved sinuously away and back into him. Her hands were unfastening him, releasing him, and now she drew his trousers gently down his legs, her hands firm against his thighs. His head was light and reeling and all thoughts were gone, only sensation remained as she knelt before him, lowered her head on to him and took him in her mouth. He felt her tongue stroking around and along the length of him. Before he lost control completely he lifted her to her feet and removed the ivory silk dress so that her beautiful, slender body was revealed. He pulled her to him, sank to his knees and buried his face in her triangle of reddish hair, smelling the warm musk odour that drove every last rational thought from his distracted mind. Then she slid down to the Persian rug and reflections of the flames were dancing red and gold over the body that waited, trembling, eager and ready for him. He knelt between her thighs and pushed himself hard into her as she moaned and moved and grasped inside, fast and rhythmically, squeezing with muscles he never knew a woman had, crying out in delight even as he went first slowly to savour the pleasure, then in a fierce, thunderous release that he knew she shared.

Afterwards he lay, spent, his head on her belly while her hands stroked his hair and she whispered, 'Come to my bed...?'

'Yes.'

'I don't want to lose you now.'

'Nor I.'

Then she seemed to come back to reality with a speed that alarmed him. 'I might be pregnant. We must marry. Tomorrow. By special licence...'

Chapter Six

Under the hot showers at Rosyth Naval Dockyard, Andrew scrubbed his soot-encrusted arms until the skin glowed pink through the black hair. Cleaning out the boilers with wire brushes had taken three days and it was hard, hot work. The weather too was unseasonably hot, that Saturday 2 September of 1939. Over the hiss of water and the smell of coal tar he called to Greg in the next cubicle, 'Going ashore, Greg?' Greg was no longer his oppo, for Andrew had been promoted to leading stoker.

The firebox would be lit and brought up to pressure tomorrow. The engine room artificer – a good bloke, ten times better than Pearce who had been dishonourably discharged – had passed their work and the stokers had twenty-four hours' shore leave until 10 a.m. on Sunday, when they would hear the announcement that war was declared. Nobody believed it would not happen. Two eight-inch and two secondary four-and-a-half-inch guns were ready, along with twelve two-pounders and eight torpedo tubes. Both the North Sea, which they patrolled, and the Atlantic were infested with German U-boats waiting for the signal to fire.

'If you are,' came Greg's laughing reply. 'Going to see Flora?'

'Aye!' Andrew turned the hot tap off and watched the grimy foam sluice away while the fierce cold jet stung his skin, making him aware of every nerve ending and every hair down the length of his body. 'Oooh!' He groaned with pleasure and lifted his arms to prolong the shock to his skin. 'What are you going to do?'

'Ask for a free issue,' Greg said. 'See if I can find a girl.'

Andrew turned off the taps, emerged from the cubicle, found his towel and started to dry himself vigorously in the relative spaciousness of the washroom. On board, their quarters were cramped – thirty men to a mess that held two twenty-foot tables with hammocks slung above – but there was a good bit of space here. He'd brought his best uniform from his locker and laid it out on the wooden seat.

Greg came out of his cubicle. 'How will she know?'

'I'll ring her from the dock.'

'Telephone, eh? Posh!' Greg laughed.

'It's the blind man. He needs it. But it's ruddy useful.' Andrew pulled on his bell-bottoms and tunic then swiftly tied his shoes. 'I'll wait for you by the gate. Don't be long.' He ran a comb through his hair and put it in his pocket beside his wallet and travel pass.

Under a cloudless sky he ran down the quay, ignoring the men who were bringing supplies aboard, glancing only briefly at the deck crew of the *Rutland* who were scrubbing down the armour-plated decks. They were preparing for a long stretch at sea, judging by the stack of crates to be loaded. Andrew went to the office, found an empty phone box and within seconds the operator had put him through.

'Flora?'

'Andrew. Where are you?' Her voice was sweet and musical. She was his beautiful, graceful and gentle girl and as always his heart felt as if it were going to burst with love for her.

'I'm still in Rosyth. Take the day off.' He spoke fast and loud so she'd hear and he could get everything said before his twopence ran out. 'I've got twenty-four hours' shore leave but I have to leave Edinburth at midnight. So we've got precisely—' he looked at his watch; it was 10.30 – 'thirteen and a half hours. I'm taking you to Ingersley to meet Ma.'

'Oh, Andrew!'

'I'll be there in an hour.' Andrew looked through the glass door to see if Greg was about. 'And Flora?'

'Yes.'

'Can I tell Ma we're getting married?' He heard her catch her breath. His heart stopped for the few seconds it took her to say, 'Yes ... but...' and he took her hesitation for the shyness he loved her for. He'd settle all her fears about marrying him, but not from a call box. And she was full of fears. It could have already been done – they could have married in a registry office today – if she had gone for the forms when he'd asked her, weeks ago. He whispered over the line, 'I love you, sweetheart. I'll be there in an hour,' then blew a kiss and hung up.

Outside he saw Greg running towards him, being passed on the roadway by Captain Sir Gordon Campbell, who was behind the wheel of the Armstrong Siddeley, looking serious, making speed for the gates and Ingersley. Senior officers could take leave when the ship was in dock but Sir Gordon, though he left the ship for a few hours every day, returned to his command at night. It made him a heroic figure and a fine example to crew and officers.

Sir Gordon would know where they were being sent tomorrow. But it was all classified information and just as well, Andrew thought grimly. He hoped he'd acquit himself well under fire, but stronger than that hope was the hope that the war would be won in a few months.

Flora put down the phone and went to Mr Davidson's sitting-room door. She rapped hard because the radio was on. Mr Davidson left it on for long periods, without thought for conserving the battery. He did not like silences; besides which, he said, there was a chance that the Germans would retreat.

'Enter,' he called out in his educated Scots voice at the same time as he turned down the sound.

'That was Andrew,' Flora said as soon as she closed the door. She had become so sensitive to his blindness that she instinctively spoke as she moved towards him. He never had to turn his head this way and that, as he did in church, to locate the speaker. She said, 'He's got twenty-four-hours' leave.'

'Then invite your brother for supper and a musical evening, Miss Stewart,' he said. 'If that's what you'd like.'

Flora's stomach went into a quivering spasm again. How could she tell this kind, God-fearing man that Andrew was not her brother? How could she tell Andrew that she was not yet sixteen and was too young to marry? How could she go on lying to both of them? But she said, 'He's taking me to North Berwick.' She hesitated, seeing disappointment cloud Mr

93

Davidson's face, then went on to say, 'I made a bacon and egg pie. I'll leave you a slice with salad and ham. There's scones and bread as well. Is that all right?'

'That's very kind of you, my dear,' he said.

'We won't be back in time for supper.'

'Don't worry about me. You haven't forgotten that you are singing in church tomorrow, Flora?'

'I've remembered.' She sang in her powerful soprano in the choir and at church concerts. And tomorrow, she was to sing solo a verse of the anthem. 'I've been practising,' she said shyly. Then, with a little laugh, 'It's a wonder you haven't heard me. The woman next door banged on the wall to tell me to quieten down, then stopped me in the street and said I was a noisy lass.'

'Whatever next?' Mr Davidson looked cross. 'She's an awful gabby woman. A terrible gossip. I do wish she'd keep her nose out of my business.'

Flora answered, 'It's all right. I'm always polite. I said it won't happen again. I'll sing quieter songs – and sing them when she's out.' She would not dare tell Mr Davidson the downright wicked questioning the woman had subjected her to: 'Where do you come from?' and 'How old are you? You look awfu' young to be a housekeeper.' and once, 'I hope there's no funny business going on. It's not right for a young lass to be in a man's employ.'

Mr Davidson said he wanted her to go and enjoy her day out with Andrew, and now she ran upstairs to wash at the wash-stand placed to one side of the deep bay window that had thick net curtains for privacy. Anyone who had a view of the Forth as she had from here in her little sitting room could see that the wide river seaway had far more armoured ships than the cargo and fishing boats it was once home to. She was afraid. Andrew's ship was ready for battle operations and the men awaiting orders were on tenterhooks.

With shaking hands she soaped her neck and arms. In an hour's time, when she and Andrew arrived by train at North Berwick station, she'd be taken to meet the mother he talked about, wrote about and was so proud and protective of. Andrew was going to tell his ma that they were to be married as soon as possible. Suppose his ma didn't like her? Then, as if meeting her were not enough, Flora would also meet the Commander, who always came down to the kitchen after dinner to thank them all. Andrew would introduce her as 'the girl I'm going to marry'.

She dried herself on a snowy-white towel, put on clean underwear and checked for the umpteenth time that she looked neat and tidy. She was going to wear a maroon spotted dress with puffed short sleeves and white pique Peter Pan collar and cuffs. She had made it herself on the Singer treadle machine that had been Mr Davidson's mother's. The whiteness of the cuffs made her pale arms look less peely-wally than normal, for she could not take a tan but had to sit in the shade or freckles would cover her translucent fine skin. She was thinner than when she had come here a year ago, but losing her puppy fat was all to the good if she were to go on pretending.

Wearing only her underclothes, she sat down with a thump on the bedroom chair as she thought on the truth of it all again. She was a month off sixteen. And she was sure the police were after her.

She dodged into a doorway or turned about-face whenever she saw their blue uniforms. There was a police station only yards from her lodgings and the policemen stared at her more than they did the other girls who worked in the area. They were trained to spot spies and impostors. They could pick her up any time on suspicion of her being Flora Macdonald who had never finished her sentence at Guthrie's.

Six months ago she'd taken the tram to Leith and found Jessie Fairbairn. Jessie told her, 'It goes on your record, Flora. You'll have a record, ye ken. They'll take you back to Guthrie's or clap you in prison.'

'But I told you – I stole my records. Stole everything: the court order, my school report, birth certificate – everything.'

'They'll have copies. Stealing makes it worse agin ye.'

'But I nearly did my two years – all but for a week or two.'

'Disnae matter. There's girls of seventeen in Guthrie's. And girls of thirteen in prison.'

'You'll never tell anyone, will you, Jessie? Never tell anyone how old – how young – I am?'

'I won't tell. I'd never do that.'

'They maybe will stop looking. I've got money now. I've

saved four pounds. I'm not destitute like before. I'm not a vagrant.'

'Four pounds is nothing, to them.'

'When will they stop looking for me, do you think?'

'Never,' Jessie replied firmly. 'Not till you get married. They canna put a man's wife in prison.'

Flora was almost in tears. 'Are you sure?'

'Good grief! I should be. I'm married. Nobody is after me now.'

But even though she was not convinced of Jessie's legal knowledge, Flora went sick to the stomach thinking about it; she wanted to faint whenever she saw a policeman walking on the beat.

'Five minutes. We have to leave for church in five minutes,' Gordon said in the cold tone of voice he once used only on men for whom he had no time and less respect. He increasingly used it now on Ruth.

He watched her in the dressing-table mirror as slowly she ran a comb through her hair, turning it over her hand and curling it under into the page-boy style she favoured. He watched her – and he wondered why he should think that marriage to Ruth was a mistake. She had taken up the duties of Lady Campbell of Ingersley with alacrity, and her civic duties with a great deal less enthusiasm. He believed that she was more interested in feathering her own nest than in doing her duty when war came. Two weeks ago the government had passed the Emergency Powers (Defence) Act, giving themselves sweeping powers to requisition property and to take any steps deemed necessary in the defence of the realm. Poor women would be drafted into factory work. Already most ladies had volunteered for unpaid work. And all Ruth could say was that she was determined not to be pushed around when war came, but to be one of the civilian order-givers and to this end she would offer her services only where she would have the most influence. As far as she was concerned that meant that she would decide how the empty properties at Ingersley were distributed. She would be on the board of trustees and governors, should Ingersley, the estate and farm, be requisitioned.

Already she was prepared. When war was declared tomorrow, mothers and children and expectant mothers would be evacuated from Edinburgh into East Lothian. Ruth was in charge of billeting.

Against the fact that titled women were rolling up their sleeves to help the war effort in any way they could, it was only a minor vexation that Ruth had set about re-establishing the use of titles, expecting servitude and not service from staff she could not hope to keep. Now, the look on her face was one of utter vanity. His own expression could not be hard to read but she had not noticed, for she said in her sharpest voice, 'Why on earth – with only two days' notice – did you offer to give a wedding reception for an employee? And why here?'

'You know very well. There are hundreds of young couples marrying this weekend, before war comes to separate them.' He adjusted his tie and reached for his uniform jacket. 'Mike Hamilton is not just an employee. He is my neighbour and friend. He needs a wife. He has made a good choice in Lucy.' His eyes were steely.

'Lucy McNab's a simpering fool.' Satisfied with her reflection, Ruth set her hat over her shining gold-blonde hair. The wide brim framed her heart-shaped face and the ice-blue velour set off her eyes. 'She is older than him, you know. She will bring a large dowry, I expect.' She added, 'But for Mike Hamilton to choose a time like this? A hasty marriage in a registry office would have been best.'

His eyebrow lifted in amusement. 'Are you suggesting that Lucy is with child?' he said. Perhaps he misjudged Ruth. It would be hard for her to accept her own infertility if Mike Hamilton's wife produced child after child. In truth, though, Ruth was not solely to blame for their childless state. Their marriage bed was not a loving place. He was so much the gentleman that he needed to know that his wife consented before he would make a move, and Ruth initiated lovemaking only when she saw coldness and distance in him. As now, when he'd answered her remark about the hasty marriage by suggesting that Lucy might already be with child.

Ruth faced him and lifted her skirt high above the knees like a common harlot. She pursed her lips and said in the voice she thought provocative, 'Women like Lucy don't allow a man even a glimpse until they are married.' Then she dropped the hem of her skirt and bent down to fasten her corsage to her handbag so as not to ruin the lapels of her dress.

'How very different from you, Ruth,' he said. But he was angry with himself for speaking this way to his wife with what he saw as cheap and unworthy distrust of her, even though he felt the familiar thrill of arousal at her behaviour. It was as if he hated her, instead of himself, for his having been so easy to seduce in the first place. Why would a man feel that he had been used when the woman had offered the very sexual comfort he'd wanted? Why would he despise himself and think himself weak because, for all their differences, she need only crook her little finger for his body's response to override his common sense? And why did he always agree – why did he say, 'If you must, Ruth,' to her every suggestion of lovemaking in the bizarre places and positions that she seemed to need?

Ruth straightened up, looked herself over for a final time and said, 'I'm ready. Let's go.'

She waited for Gordon to go striding ahead before she closed the bedroom door and followed in his wake along the landing, under the iron and glass cupola that gave light to the central sweeping staircase. Tension mounted in her at every step that drew her nearer to witnessing Mike Hamilton's spiteful marriage. For she was certain that Mike was marrying to spite her. After all, she was in charge of every inch of the land he farmed, as well as the Ingersley estate. It was all under her control and, should anything happen to Gordon, the very title deeds to the estate would be hers. In fact she had everything she'd ever wanted. She had land, her own money, a handsome husband who adored her. She had everything – except Mike Hamilton's devotion to her wilder needs.

In the entrance hall the servants were lined up beside the front door to see them in their finery. Gordon and Ruth made a handsome couple; he resplendent in uniform and she in the blue silk grosgrain costume that showed off her tiny waist, slender hips and long shapely legs. They would far outshine the bride and groom – as she intended they should. There were gasps of pleasure at the sight of them, and though Ruth might only have nodded in recognition, Gordon shook hands with all the servants before giving last-minute instructions to Mrs Stewart.

Then they were in the Armstrong Siddeley and heading for the church in North Berwick, Gordon silent and evidently preoccupied with thoughts of war. He did not even remember that the last time they had made a wedding journey together, six months ago, she had returned to Ingersley as Lady Campbell.

Six months ago, with her marriage four days old and Gordon returned to his ship; and though she was dreading the confrontation, Ruth went to the stables to find Mike Hamilton. She walked towards him across the cobbled yard and saw that his dark eyes were cold with contempt. He sneered, 'Lady Campbell?'

Ruth made for Heather's loose box and stroked her horse's neck. She spoke calmly but avoided Mike's eyes. 'I did it for you as well as myself. Gordon wanted to sell the farm and send me back to Cheshire.'

'Gordon would not sell the land without telling me.' He came to stand behind her. He spat the words out. 'No, madam. Ye didnae do it for me. Ye did it for yerself.'

She turned around and, knowing that it excited him, moved closer and bent her knee so that their legs touched. She kept her eyes down, adopting a contrite, subservient pose, then looked up at him and said, 'Mike. We can still be lovers. You are the only man who can satisfy...'

She got no further. Mike's jaw clenched and his hot eyes flashed with rage as his hand smacked across her face with a sound like the crack of a whip. 'Ye're a cold, calculating bitch. And I'll have nae mair of ye.'

She'd thought he would be back, that he could not keep away from her, but eight weeks later she'd had neither sight nor sound of him. There were ten Land Army girls living on the estate, working in the fields and the dairy. She had put in the application herself as soon as she'd heard of the scheme; she'd picked them for their plain sturdiness and lack of feminine wiles, housing them in the Dower House and in the grooms' cottages across the cobbled yard from Mike's farmhouse. This labour force should have given Mike more time for leisure, for Ruth, but always there was someone with him when he came to the house on farm business. The nearest entrance to the farmhouse was the North Gate and he used that in preference to the South Gate, which was closer to Ingersley House, so she could not waylay him. And she never saw him around the stables so was obliged to groom and exercise her horse alone.

One hot July evening, when the hay was in, Ruth, who was always at her wildest on the long midsummer nights, went down to the stables to let Heather into the adjacent paddock to graze. Mike was alone in the barn, the Land Army girls having returned to their billets. He was stripped to the waist, moving the sweet-smelling hay bales so as to leave a space between them to lessen the risk of spontaneous combustion sending the wooden barn up in flames. Ruth had on a slip of a dress – a printed crêpe de Chine in apricot and blue. She wore nothing underneath, knowing that, standing in the doorway in the dim light of the barn, her body would be outlined against the pearly-pink July sky.

'Can't we be friends?' she said.

'No.' Refusing to glance her way, he carried on working. His bare back, hairy on the shoulders, was turned away from her. 'Ye're no' looking for company, Ruth. It's your pleasure you want.'

'And you don't?'

He did not reply immediately but after a few moments came to stand before her. She could smell his sweat. Beads of it glistened on his brow. 'Och aye. I want it too. But not half as much as you.'

'Then what's stopping us?' she asked, glancing upwards.

'Ye really don't know?' He was standing so close now she could feel the heat off his body. 'Ye dinnae give a tinker's cuss for your marriage vows?'

'Gordon doesn't want for anything,' she said in a small, cajoling voice, as if she were surprised he thought badly of her.

'Except children and a faithful wife,' he said bitterly.

'Don't be angry with me.' She went closer, ran her fingers down his bare chest and put on the pleading voice that used to excite him. 'Unless Gordon does better, I'll never have children. Does that tell you what's wrong?'

He grabbed her hands and thrust her away, a look of mocking speculation in his eyes. 'Go down to my house. Wait in the kitchen.'

She went, shivering in excitement like a filly at stud, towards the farmhouse. It was not *his* house. She was the mistress of Ingersley. The farm belonged to her. She controlled everything and could have Mike replaced as factor if she so chose. He didn't know how precarious was his position. But tonight was not the time to remind him of it.

She went in by the front door since it was not overlooked, then down the dark passageway to the kitchen, where she waited, not daring to light a lamp that might be seen from the cottages across the yard. She noticed that there was an airy, fresh smell and his house was neat and clean, as if a woman's hand had been at work. A jar of wild flowers stood on the slate window ledge under a muslin half-curtain that was starched and white as snow. A sour taste came into her mouth at the thought of another woman in his life – but she dismissed the thought. Rumour quickly spread and there had been no talk on the estate.

He came in, ducked his head under the low door frame, shot the iron bolt on the door and stood before her. Then, without a single gesture of affection, he held her at arm's length, looked into her face and in a hard and bitter voice said, 'I once thought you loved me.'

'I do,' she said in a small whisper, to soften him. 'There's no one else who . . .' But he was not listening. He did not wash himself at the sink first, but with callused and dirty hands tore the dress from her shoulders and began ripping away his own clothes. But he did not bend to suck on her breasts or tease the reddish hair on her pubic mound as before. Instead, with his eyes averted, he tightened his grip on her shoulders and pressed his thumbs under her collar bone until she cried out.

She pulled back and said, 'Not here! Upstairs. We'll be seen.'

'I don't give a fart in the wind who sees you.' He was sweating lightly and the acrid odour of unwashed maleness was overpowering.

She had never seen him like this – teeth gritted, lips drawn back, eyes flicking over her with an expression of pure hatred. She tried to back away, to push him off, but she was imprisoned between the table at her back and the heavy, hard body that was pressing the very air out of her so that she could not

101

cry out but could only gasp, 'Stop. You are too rough. You're hurting me. I don't want you to ...'

'Yes, you damned well do.' He lifted her and threw her on to the clean, scrubbed deal table and pulled her arms high, holding her wrists together in a fierce grip while with the other hand he opened the table drawer and took out a towel. He bound the cloth about her wrists and tied it tightly, then threw her face down over the table with her tied wrists coming to settle in front of her throat.

'You are hurting me!' Panic made her voice high and pleading. Her cheek was close up against the smooth coldness of the table and the force of his arm was hard across her back. She cried, 'Stop. I'll have you thrown off my land...'

'Your land? I dinnae think so...' A harsh, ironic laugh came blasting. 'This is Scotland. There's nothin' ye can do, woman, without your husband's approval. It's your husband's land. He'll throw you off before me, I'll see to that.' His weight came down on top of her and his voice was thick and hoarse. 'You like it rough, don't you, lady?' he said as he pulled her legs apart and forced her knees up on to the edge of the table.

Her back was breaking. She wanted to scream but dared not attract outside attention. 'What are you doing ...?' But her cries were muffled by the weight on her shoulders. She could not move her arms. The pain in her knees was excruciating.

His fingers were working inside her, groping for the Dutch cap. 'Ha! You made ready for this, didn't you? Bear down!' he ordered, and hooked his finger over the rim and drew it out of her. 'Gordon probably thinks ye want a son as much as he does. Ye'll no' be needing this, now ye're a married woman,' he said, and he threw it on to the stone slab floor and ground it under his heel.

'Please ... Mike ... please...' But she could not stop him from taking his own pleasure with violence and animal sounds and her legs forced wide and pulled down until she felt the cold stone under the soles of her bare feet.

'Ye'll conceive tonight, woman. Then what will ye do?' he said in time with his grunting and thrusting hard into her, again and again, slamming her hips into the edge of the wooden table. Going on until at last, in spite of herself, she was tightening and flowing and crying out in a sustained wail of hurting, release and delight at the feel of his coming high and hard into her.

'Enjoyed that, did you?' he said when finally she went limp and he helped her up. He said, 'Lie on your back. On the table.'

She held up her bound hands. 'Untie me,' she begged.

'No. You used to order me to tie you up. You like your men violent.' He pulled her right up to the edge of the table with her knees bent so he could take her hard and roughly again. He said, 'I'll make sure ye're well and truly in foal. And ye'll be slung out – for with your husband at sea there's no possibility of his having fathered your bairn.'

This time she did not respond but fought against him. But, bound tight, aching across her drawn-back shoulders, she was helpless as he took his pleasure of her, ignoring her cries for him to stop. When he had done, he released her bonds and, still naked himself, watched her try to dress herself with shaking hands. She said in a frightened voice, 'You won't get away with this. Never – never again will I allow you ...'

He laughed. 'Oh, but you will, Ruth. Your husband will cast you out and ye'll come crawling back to me. Until that happens, it's me that wilnae. I'm still looking for a wife, remember?'

She ran, crying, from his house, dodging into shadows in case she were seen. She saw nobody. Later still she sat in a hot bath for two hours, trying to soak away all visible traces of her ordeal and praying that she had not been impregnated. Her prayers were answered. A week later she knew that she was not with child. She had a spare Dutch cap. Before long Mike Hamilton would come crawling back to her.

Now, sitting beside Gordon in the car, Ruth watched the hired car ahead and saw Mike Hamilton turn his head sideways so that when he spoke to his bride his glance would slide across the twenty or so yards of road that separated them to try to engage her eyes, to gloat. She said to Gordon, 'The service was over quickly. Mercifully short, wasn't it?'

'Mercifully?' Gordon said in a cold voice. 'They made their vows before God. In church. A registry office ceremony is a poor substitute.'

'You think we ought to have married in church?'

'I think our marriage got off to a poor start.'

Surprised, she turned her head away from the window and the view of the coast to look at him and say, 'Why do you say that?' Then, before he could answer, 'I want you to make love to me tonight. Do you have to go back to the blasted ship? The announcement is not due until eleven a.m. tomorrow.'

'It is my ship, my duty. And I am serving my country.' His hands tightened on the wheel and Ruth saw his knuckles whiten, belying the calm expression on his handsome face. He said, 'You cannot be so crass, Ruth.'

'So crass as to what?'

'So crass as to expect me to abandon my responsibilities, for the sake of ten minutes in bed with you.'

'I was not thinking of bed, dear.' She saw the pink flush of excitement under his eyes and knew that he would have to struggle against arousal as she said, 'I thought on top of your desk – or in the bath—'

He took a deep breath. 'In the bath – if you must,' he said. They were driving in at the South Lodge gates, passing guests, mostly farmers and townspeople, dressed in their Sunday best, who were walking up to the house. A few moments later they pulled up behind the bridal car that had halted before the entrance, where six happy Land Army girls formed a guard of honour. Mike and Lucy were being greeted at the top of the stone steps by the hired butler and watched by cheering waiting-on staff, all locals who knew the bridal pair. Lucy, carrying a bouquet of white roses, wore a suit of cream linen, with an emerald-green picture hat that gave definition to her round face.

Gordon relaxed, smiled and said to Ruth, 'Look at that welcome. They are going to be a popular couple. An asset to Ingersley.'

Ruth made no reply, and no reference to her invitation to Gordon to share her bath before he returned to the ship. Her eyes were cold but that was due perhaps to tiredness and worry about tomorrow's declaration. They ought to be loving and good to one another. This bickering was unworthy of them both. He said, 'I know it's been a lot of work for you, dear. Mrs Stewart will come up trumps. She always does.'

He took Ruth's arm. 'Come! We have our duty to do.'

The programme was that they would first be served with champagne and wedding cake while the speeches were made, then would go down to the garden for photographs while the cold buffet food was brought up to the dining room. After the meal, the bridal pair would be waved off for their honeymoon which, Gordon suspected, was to be spent at the farmhouse.

Twenty minutes later, in the drawing room with the windows open and welcome breaths of cool air wafting in, Gordon indicated to the house servants that the guests' champagne glasses be topped up in preparation for the speeches. When this was done and the servants had gone back to stand in the doorway – more so as not to miss any of the action than to attend the guests – Gordon called for quiet.

'Mr and Mrs Hamilton,' he began, to smiles and giggles. 'Before I propose a toast to the bride and groom I would like to say a few words about my own personal pleasure in witnessing the marriage of, if not one of my oldest friends—' there was a burst of laughter here – 'then certainly a man whose friendship I have treasured for much of my life.'

He looked at the bridegroom as he spoke and saw that he had embarrassed Mike, whose eyes were misting even as his jaw clenched. He continued, 'But I am not here today to make sentimental declarations. The hours between peace and war are fast slipping away and this is no time to face the struggle ahead single-handed. Mr and Mrs Hamilton will need each other's support in the trials to come. I am delighted that they have both chosen so well. Lucy is a farmer's daughter and will be a loving wife and companion to a man I am proud to call my friend.'

There was a little burst of applause. The expression on Mike's face was almost shamefaced, as if, Gordon thought, his farm factor was surprised to hear how highly esteemed he was. Gordon would bring the speech to an end now with the news he had saved until last. He held up his hand for quiet again and continued, 'But before I sit down and let others do the talking, I wish to announce to you all that as from yesterday Mr Hamilton is no longer in my employ as factor. Instead, he and Lucy are the new leaseholders of the farmland of Ingersley.' The room had fallen silent. 'I have seen my lawyer and have signed over my interest in the land for the next five years.

105

After that time, and depending upon both the Hamilton and the Campbell family circumstances, the lease will either be renewed or the Ingersley estate and land will be offered for sale to its new tenant farmers – Mr and Mrs Michael Hamilton.'

He saw Ruth's face go white, then red. His decision had angered her instead of relieving her of the responsibility for all this land. But he had made the best decision, in the best interests of all of them. Mike Hamilton was now free to run the farm as he wanted to – and Ruth could go back to Cheshire, where she'd be safe. If he were killed then the proceeds of the sale would be Ruth's security. If he survived, when the war was over – and if their marriage was still viable – they might start again, somewhere peaceful, somewhere else.

He waited until the applause died down before saying, 'Please raise your glasses to the future joy and prosperity of the happy couple.'

The toast was replied to, 'The happy couple!' then in an explosion of excitement everyone was talking, congratulating the couple and discussing the new circumstances and rank of the delighted bride and groom. Gordon glanced across at Ruth and to his alarm saw that she was as white as death, holding on to the back of a chair as if she were about to faint.

'Get help. Quickly,' he said in a low voice to one of the servants before he went to Ruth's side.

Downstairs, in the kitchen, Andrew's ma was coming to the end of her tether. Her face was pink and shiny and her eyes darted from one to another of the ten or more people crowded in there. She called out, 'Take the sal volatile upstairs at once, Bessie. In the cupboard over the sink, girl!' then, louder, 'The smelling salts. Lady Campbell has fainted.'

Someone said, 'I'm not surprised. She won't have any more say in the running of the estate now the Commander's signed it over.'

'He's what?' came the reply.

'Tell us later,' Ma ordered. 'It can wait.' She wiped the back of her hand across her forehead with a smile and a pretence of weariness before turning to Flora and saying, 'Sorry, lass. What a day to come and meet me. But we'll have a right wee blether when the wedding's over.' Then she gave her attention once again to the kitchen sides – the bunkers, Ma called them – which were laden with trays of food. There were tiny triangular sandwiches and sliced brown bread and butter. On an enormous silver platter lay a salmon mousse, moulded into a fish shape, decorated with lemon and lime slices and surrounded with a creamy mayonnaise. There was tender cold roast beef, the thin pink slices overlapped on a bed of shredded lettuce laid out on ashets – the Scottish name for the huge china serving plates that were dotted about the kitchen. There was an ashet of cold roast ham with dressed sweet apple slices, there were ashets of sausage rolls and sliced ham. Green salads and cold potato salad filled great glass bowls and all were being carried by hired staff. They scurried, loading food on to trolleys under Ma's watchful eyes, putting the trolleys in the lift, sending them up to the waiting-on staff who had earlier laid out tables for twenty people in the dining room.

Flora said tentatively, 'Can I help you, Mrs Stewart?' her cheeks flaming as they did when she was self-conscious. They had not had a chance to be alone yet. Ma still did not know that Andrew had proposed to her.

'It's all right, lass,' Ma said before turning away again and calling out, 'Don't take the trifles and fruit compotes up yet,' to one of the kitchen maids – and back again to say to Andrew, 'Take Flora outside. They'll be going down to the garden for photographs, the Commander told me.' She smiled, took Flora's hand in hers and passed her over to Andrew. 'Don't get in the way outside. Stand well back.'

Andrew led Flora outside to find a sheltered spot out of the blazing sun, which would be ideal for photographs and torture to her. He said, 'What a devil not being able to tell Ma.' Then, 'This wedding is a big surprise to me.' He took her hand and led her to a shady corner by the servants' side door where a rose tree, rampant with yellow blooms, clambered all over the porch. He said, 'Remember I told you about them? You could have knocked me down with a feather! Ruth Bickerstaffe marrying the Commander only days after I saw her and Mike Hamilton riding out, ignoring everyone.'

'Maybe you were mistaken,' she said. Andrew had told her that he thought the woman who was now Lady Campbell was no better than a whore. 'Best to think that anyway.'

'Why?'

'Because your ma still works here.'

'You are like Ma, you know.' He slid an arm about her waist and pulled her close. 'I've never heard you say a bad word about anyone.'

Flora said, 'I like your ma, Andrew. Will she take to me?'

'She already has, I can tell,' Andrew replied with absolute confidence. He knew Ma's every facial expression. She was going to love Flora as much as he did. 'You'll have a chance to talk to her when this wedding breakfast's over.'

It was two o'clock. Andrew said, 'Kiss me. Before they come out and catch us,' and she did, pressing her soft lips on his, quick and light like the brush of petals. He held her tight for a few moments, whispering in her ear, 'I love you, Flora. Let's go – be on our own somewhere, as soon as we've told Ma we're getting married.'

She pushed him away gently, for she was afraid that someone would see them. 'Let's keep it a secret,' she said. 'If we tell them, we'll never get away on our own.' Then, seeing his crestfallen face, 'I love you, Andrew. I want to be your wife.' No girl had ever loved a boy as much as she. Then a chilling premonition that these were their last hours together came sweeping over her, just as she knew it would for the dozens of young couples today who were marrying at registry offices and churches all over the land. She thought about the evenings of songs and music round Mr Davidson's piano – Andrew playing the popular songs, Mr Davidson the traditional airs, and she singing her heart out, delighting them. Would there be any more such times? She clutched his hand. 'I'm afraid for you – for where you'll be sent, tomorrow.'

'I'll be all right, love. We've got the best captain in the navy, and the best ship.' He gave her the smile that made her head spin. He had beautiful teeth, white and even in his wide, generous mouth. Flora thought he looked like Clark Gable, only younger, more manly and handsome. She stood on tiptoe and kissed him again, quickly because she could hear the kitchen staff, noisy in the passageway behind the door. On the lawn a photographer was setting up his tripod, looking through the little viewing window then going to set small stones and sticks where the groups would pose.

Andrew pulled her aside, clear of the doorway. Ma came out and said in a voice high with excitement, 'I'll stand here with you two. Then I can point them all out to Flora,' as the guests came round from the front entrance to gather in little knots around the photographer. The bride and groom appeared and Flora, catching Ma's excitement, said, 'Isn't she just beautiful – and he's good-looking.'

Hearing Andrew's chuckle, Ma said, 'Wait till you see the Commander and Lady Campbell – they are like film stars.' She ignored Andrew and said to Flora, 'Give me a hand up, love. I'll have to stand on the wee stone wall to see properly.'

Flora eagerly gave Ma both hands. Ma didn't let go but pointed excitedly with her free hand while she gripped Flora's and said, 'Here they come! The Commander and Lady Campbell!'

Flora looked – and the smile left her face, a metallic taste came into her mouth, her face drained of colour and her knees buckled. The Commander was the man – the magistrate – who had put her away in Guthrie's – twice.

Andrew caught her before she could hit the ground. Ma wanted to watch the wedding party, so he made light of her anxious offer to help get Flora inside. 'It's the heat,' he said. 'She'll be better out of the sun. I'll do it,' and he half carried his fainting darling through the door and into the dark, cool kitchen, where he pulled out a chair and made her sit.

She was shaking violently – as violently as when she'd dropped into his arms a year ago. He rinsed a cloth under the tap and held the cold drench of it to her forehead, but she grabbed his hand and started to cry. 'Take me away, Andrew. I've got to go back. I can't stop here...'

'All right. But what's up?'

'I'll tell you. Not here. Please ... please ... Andrew?'

It was as if she had been struck dumb, for she could not speak at all on the way from Ingersley to the station at North Berwick. It took her two hours to quieten and tell him what was wrong and even then she could not tell him everything, for he'd never understand why she had lied to him for all this time.

109

Now, at five o'clock, with only seven hours left, they strolled the beach at Portobello, barefoot and hand-in-hand. Andrew put his arm about her waist and made her come closer so that he could feel her hips moving in harmony with the swing of his left leg, her head resting against his shoulder as they went. He said, 'I don't think the Commander would have recognised you, love. You are eighteen now. You were fifteen when he sent you to Guthrie's, and that was only because your gran was dead and you had nowhere to go.'

She smiled up at him, and love for her came stabbing through him like a physical thrust that was as exciting as it was painful.

'They wouldn't be able to send you back to Guthrie's if we were married.' He wanted desperately now to be married to her, to be with her, to love her and know her body. He stopped. They were too far down the beach. 'Let's go back,' he said.

They turned to retrace their steps and she slipped her arm through his. He could feel, through the thin stuff of her dress, her firm round breast pressing against his arm. She said, 'Jessie Fairbairn says a girl can legally call herself married in Scotland without going to church.'

'How?'

'By habit and repute. You have to live with your man and use his name. Then, after a time you announce before witnesses that you are his legal wife – by habit and repute. It's how Jessie married.'

'I didn't know.' He stood stock still. 'What difference can a registrar or a preacher make, anyway? We'll legalise it on my next leave.' He took her in his arms and, not caring a whit if anyone saw them, kissed her long and hard until his head was reeling with the honey taste of her mouth and the sweet, urgent response in the body that was pressed so close he had to stop before he embarrassed himself and her. He asked, 'Does spending every minute of my time with you – wanting to spend every day of my life with you – count as living together?'

'It must do.'

'And you call yourself Flora Stewart?' he said. She had stuck to the Stewart name ever since he'd lied to Mr Davidson, saying she was his sister.

'Yes.'

'Then we're married.' He kissed her again. 'Come on, love,' he said. 'We'll have our own wedding feast. I'll buy you fish and chips on Portobello High Street.'

She laughed and clung to him. 'What about the ring?'

'There's a jeweller's shop near the café. Let's run ...'

He grabbed her hand and ran with her across the soft sand until they reached the esplanade, where they put on their shoes. Then, arm-in-arm and sedately, they went to the jeweller's shop. Andrew bought twin plain gold bands and demanded that the jeweller engrave them while they waited: *Flora Stewart. Married Andrew. 2.9.39,* and on his, *Andrew Stewart. Married Flora. 2.9.39.* The jeweller said that usually people bought the rings well before their wedding day and chose to inscribe a message of love not a matter of fact. But he said it affectionately and shook their hands and wished them a long and happy marriage.

Andrew put the rings into his pocket and they crossed to the noisy café, where he bought plaice and chips with peas, bread and butter and tea; the most expensive fish supper on the menu. There they toasted the marriage with cups of tea and whispered endearments over the laden enamel-topped table. 'We'll put the rings on at Waverley Station, before I go,' he said.

Flora's eyes brimmed with tears – love and fear for him mingling unbearably. 'How much longer have we got?' she asked.

'Three hours.'

'Let's go quickly then.'

An hour later, on a station jam-packed with soldiers, sailors and civilians, couples clung together, backs to the crowd, whispering farewells and last-minute declarations of love, and in their midst Andrew could not find a seat anywhere.

'We have to find a quiet place,' he said, and took her out of the station on to the bridge that faced the steep-sided valley that was once a loch. They went hand in hand through the Saturday crush in Princes Street Gardens across the road from the famous shopping boulevard. They walked beneath the shadow of the two-hundred-foot Scott monument that resembled the spire of a Gothic church, and hurried through the

111

people who were strolling past the classical National Gallery and, further on, the bronze trooper on horseback that faced the castle and the medieval Old Town – a maze of steep cobbled streets, steps and alleys that clung to the ridge of the Royal Mile which dropped steeply from the castle at the top to the Palace of Holyrood House at the foot. They were searching for a quiet corner of the gardens where they could exchange rings and seal their solemn promises with kisses.

It was not until they reached the West End of the city that Andrew found the place he was looking for. Under the shadow of the castle that loomed on its rock high above them, and in the dark hollow behind St Cuthbert's church, a place that saw sunlight for only a few hours each day, was a graveyard surrounded by an eight-foot wall. The gate was unlatched and he led Flora through it, closing it carefully behind him, into the tree-filled green gloom and dank dampness that was cool and welcome after the heat of the day.

The silence was astonishing. On two sides of the little graveyard trams, motor cars and buses were rattling by, yet inside, under the wall where the sound was muffled by the overhanging trees, nothing stirred.

Flora dropped Andrew's hand to study the tombstones, though the sun was going down behind the castle and long shadows slanted across the hollow where the graveyard lay. He could only just make out the names on the sandstone obelisk and memorial stones. Flora turned to him and said, 'This is the place we learned about in school. The graveyard where the grave robbers ...'

'... carried out their gruesome trade,' Andrew added. 'The Resurrectionists – the men who dug up the dead to sell the corpses to the anatomy students at the medical school.' He put his arms about her and held her tight. 'You're not scared, are you?'

'No,' she whispered. 'I'm on holy ground with you. I'm safe.'

He had lost the light-hearted air of this afternoon and now she could feel his tension – a kind of desperation in the bones and sinews of his strong arms. He stopped kissing her and said, 'I'm not interested in history or the dead beneath our feet. I want us to make our vows and put the rings on.'

She whispered, 'Andrew, I want to be married properly. I want you to love me,' for her head was light with longing, and love and desire was flaming in her.

There was a weeping willow whose branches touched the ground, making a cave, a secluded vaulted area around the trunk. 'We won't be seen under the weeping tree,' Andrew said. He bent double and took Flora into the dappled darkness of the den of leaves and branches, there to sit on the dry grass with his arms about her.

'I wonder what this tree has seen,' he said. 'Do you think it was weeping in the eighteenth century when the bodies were being snatched?'

She laid her cheek in the clefted hollow between his neck and shoulder. 'It's not going to witness weeping and wailing today.'

Andrew unwound her hair, let it fall and fanned it out about her shoulders. She said softly, 'It's as good as a proper wedding, isn't it?'

'Every bit,' he breathed. 'Lovers marry over an anvil at Gretna Green. A weeping tree is more fitting for a wedding than a blacksmith's shop.' He buried his nose in her hair and smelled the sweet cleanness of it. He said, 'Do you know the words of the marriage service?'

'Yes.'

'Have you been to a wedding?'

She said, 'Dozens. I've sung at choral weddings at St Philip's.'

He pulled her up into the kneeling position he had taken. Then he leaned forward briefly and said, 'You say them. I'll follow.' He slipped his hand into his pocket, brought out the rings and laid them on the sandy space between their knees. 'I'm ready.'

He was deadly serious and a tremor went through Flora as she faced him and clasped his right hand. The scent of dry grass and the soft brush of the willow leaves was making her feel solemn yet faint as she said, 'Do you, Andrew Stewart, take me, Flora Macdonald, to your lawful wedded wife?' A lump in her throat made the words strangled.

He held her hand steady. 'I do.' And, not letting go, 'Do you, Flora Macdonald, take me, Andrew Stewart, to your lawful wedded husband?'

'I do,' she whispered. 'Will you promise to love me and keep me only unto thee, forsaking all others, as long as we both shall live?'

'I will.' Andrew nodded solemnly to her.

'And I promise to love and honour and obey you, my lawful wedded husband, until death us do part.'

He picked up the smaller ring. 'Give me your finger.'

She put out her left hand and he slipped on the ring, then held out his left hand for her to do the same, and Flora said, 'Now say after me. With this ring I thee wed. With my body I thee worship and with all my worldly goods I thee endow.'

He said the words slowly and deliberately and then he put his arms about her there, under the weeping tree, and felt desire burning through her in the lips that clung to his own and the arms that were winding about his neck and the soft hands that were threading through his hair.

He was trembling as he took off his tunic to make a pillow for her head, and shaking violently when she pulled him down on top of her. She waited, lips parted, eyes gone misty with tears and love and longing. He said gently, 'I want you so much, Flora. Would you believe me if I told you I want you so much I'm in pain from wanting?'

'And me,' she murmured. 'I want to do it before you go.'

'What if you have a baby?'

'Jessie Fairbairn says you can't get a baby the first time—' But his mouth was down on hers and there was nobody to see them in the dark little cave that the weeping tree made for them.

He unfastened her dress, spread it open and tenderly caressed the soft creamy skin of her breasts. She was his, his wife, and he loved her to distraction. He was dazzled by the beauty of her body that seemed to absorb and reflect the last of the light that came glancing over the tree, piercing the leaves and throwing light and shade over her. His love was a stabbing pain in him and yet he felt humbled that she had chosen him.

He was hard and hot and needful and she was helping him out of his clothes and he could not hold himself back. His mouth locked on to hers, tasting the sweetness of her, while he slid his hand along her slender white thighs and slipped his finger into the hot, slippery, tight little depths of her and felt her opening for him, moaning softly. It was happening so fast, for her as well as himself. He had never dreamed it would feel this way – that he would be on fire for her, desperate for her as he lowered himself in against the quick resistance of her virginal state.

But the pain that made her cry out was over quickly and she was moving under him, now wrapping her long legs around him and pulling him in higher and tighter and faster until in the sweet madness of love they came together, softly crying the other's name until they subsided, sated, and could lie content, side by side, their arms about one another.

Every so often they kissed without passion, then each would kiss the other's ring, the symbol of unending love. They lay until it was dark, awed with wonder at what they had done. Andrew said, 'We belong to one another for ever now. We made the big promise. The one we can never break.'

A nearby clock struck. Andrew counted eleven chimes, then took her back through the dark summer gardens, stopping every few paces to hold her in his arms.

It was eleven o'clock and Flora must catch the last tram to Portobello, and they must be brave because tonight thousands of lovers would be parting. Andrew held on to her hand as the tram came trundling towards the stop. He said, 'Promise me if you need anything you'll go to Ingersley and find Ma.'

'I will.' She kissed him for the last time as the tram pulled up, then climbed aboard, blinded by tears.

Chapter Seven

January 1940

Andrew's oil-soaked boiler suit made him clumsy as he heaved himself up the steel ladder to the washroom area beside the stokers' mess deck at the end of his watch. The *Rutland* was ploughing through atrocious Atlantic seas late on a wild January afternoon. The strain of the last four hours had been felt by everyone from the chief engineer down. They had been detached from station in the North Sea to see off the U-boat attacks on the Atlantic convoys. The convoys, endlessly zigzagging to confuse the enemy, but always at the speed of the slowest, a sluggardly six and a half knots, were a slow-moving target. All the convoys were having a desperate time of it, but this one had at its centre one of the Empress Line ships which had carried evacuees to Canada. Now it was returning with Canadian troops to Liverpool and Greenock. A corvette and two merchant ships had been sunk in the last attack.

Though Andrew's action station was the engine room, he'd been on deck after the action and seen ships blazing furiously; seen men by the dozens covered in burning oil, some dead, some soon to die, all half drowned, being pulled from the sea into the corvettes that were the outriders of a convoy so mauled it felt as if they were bleeding to death.

The *Rutland* was built for speed, and the slowness of her progress as she searched for U-boats on the outer edge of the convoy was taking its toll. On Andrew's watch a pipe had ruptured. Steam under pressure had scalded his hands even through the heavy gloves he'd worn to turn off the valve, replace the pipe and see the engine getting back up to pressure. Now the fear was that strain on the bearings could affect the propeller. The *Rutland* would be an easy target if she had to stop.

It would be simpler to wash all this grease off himself in the tub, he thought, and it was there in the hot water that tiredness set in. His hands were raw and painful while he cleaned himself. Here, in the midship bowels, the decks rose and sank, the water slopped from side to side of the tub that was barely larger than a dustbin. He had never suffered from sea-sickness, so that could not be the reason for the weariness that assailed him as, done with washing himself, he stood, took his bar of hard soap and pasted it all over the boiler suit, stamping on the hard cloth to wash and rinse it. He could be put on a charge for washing his boiler suit here but he was too tired to care.

Then, wearing only a towel, and with the blisters on his hands broken, he twisted and wrung his boiler suit then hung it over the pipes and made his way to the mess where Greg and five ratings waited for the blower to call them to night defence stations.

The mess, as always, was crowded and smelled of the unwashed bodies of thirty stokers – a smell that had become familiar to him; familiar and strangely comforting. Off duty men slept, their hammocks slung so close together that he had to bend his head to reach his own, which, since he was a leading stoker, he had chosen at the end of the line, nearest the door. One of the stokers said, 'Anyone know where we're going next?'

'Christ! They never tell you where we're going. All it takes is one drunken sailor in a bar and we're up Shit Creek,' Greg said. 'I'll make a guess about where we're heading next. Up the Clyde.'

Andrew put on clean underclothes then ate his meal from the hot plate where it lay, saved for him from midday. They saw how his hands were, and one of the stokers helped him treat and bandage them then made him a cup of cocoa, breaking off chunks from the block of raw chocolate, pouring on boiling water, stirring and adding dollops of thick, sweet condensed milk. He ate and drank quickly, then went to his locker and took out his letters, three of them Flora's and one from Ma. He'd read them all, over and over, the letters being all he had to remind him.

He slung his hammock, unfolded his blanket and, with his boots and tunic made into a pillow and the snoring man next to him quiet for once, took out Flora's letters. The throb of the engines, and the ever-present hum of motors fanning hot stale air from one compartment to another, was familiar and steady.

30 October

Dear Andrew,
It doesn't matter that you can't change your allowance. Your ma needs it and I never thought the navy would treat us as married. It's not the same as having wedding lines that are official no matter what Jessie says so I wear my wedding ring round my neck on a chain I bought from Woolworth's. I found part-time work in a munitions factory. The pay's quite good 25/- week and I can look after Mr Davidson and save for our house as well. There's been a lot of air attacks on the Forth. Four German bombers were shot down, one at Port Seton, and they even had two dead German airmen lying in St Philip's church. They had policemen standing watch over the coffins draped with German flags which upset a lot of people, me too, seeing those swastikas. On the coffins, not the police. We are getting identity cards. I'm worried (because of Guthrie's as you know why) but it's no use worrying and too late to send me back.
Love, Flora

She used to put SWALK, for 'Sealed with a Loving Kiss', over the sealed flap of the envelope. Since September she'd drawn a picture of a weeping tree in the corner. He hadn't told her how much this secret sign meant to him, nor had he told anybody about their private wedding under the weeping tree. He took out the letter dated 30 December and read:

Dearest Andrew,
I have only had two letters from you the last one in November. I hope you are getting mine ...

Andrew smiled yet again reading this. She perhaps didn't know why they were delayed – that all their letters were read and censored before they could be sent. Even then delays were inevitable, for the ships had to be in a home port for the mail to be posted. The last letter he'd writen to her might get back before he did if their mail had been put on to one of the Liverpool-bound ships.

I got my identity card in the name of Flora Macdonald. I didn't want them to ask too many questions. And they just gave it to me. Good job Mr Davidson can't look at it. Every day we hear of ships being sunk. Even neutral ships with women and children on board. I'm glad you get good food and plenty of it. Better than us surely. I am not feeling too good but I expect it's because of rationing. Butter 4 oz a week each. Sugar 12 oz a week each. Bacon or ham 4 oz. It's not much but I can make do for me and Mr Davidson. Potatoes, bread and vegetables are not rationed. We have a chicken for Hogmanay. I don't think the widow woman next door will first-foot us. She really hates me. I love you so much. I can't wait to see you again.
Love from Flora.

PS I still sing at church and Mr Davidson plays the organ. The church is filled every Sunday now there are Canadian troops billeted all over the place.

That letter had worried Andrew. The Canadians would be looking for girls, and with their men away, women would fall for their flattery. In her last letter Flora did not mention the Canadians but sounded less cheerful than before.

Dearest Andrew,
I still have not been to see your ma. The trams and buses are all to pot and the trains don't always run. It's called an exclusion zone round Ingersley so they stop you and ask where you are going and why and look at your papers so it takes hours to get anywhere. I don't like being out in the dark when there are no lights and air-raid wardens shout, 'Put that light out!' if you show even a chink. You can be fined £100. These winter days are too short. It is very cold here. It said on the wireless that the Thames is freezing over. You know how Mr Davidson likes his wireless. I'm

119

working longer hours, 8 till 5, but it means more money and I like that. I am tired because I have to do the housework as well. It's not like me to be tired but there is a flu epidemic and I think I'm sickening. I'm off my food. I'm sure you are writing to me but maybe the letters have been washed overboard. I have only had that one from you where you said it was best if we didn't tell anyone about our secret but to wait till your next leave and have a proper wedding. I love you so much.
Love from Flora

At the bottom of the page she had drawn the weeping tree again.

There was a letter from Ma too, painstakingly written. He knew it would have taken her hours.

Dear son,
I pray for you. The *Royal Oak* was sunk in Scapa Flo. 100s drownd. I ken you'r alrite. Lady Campbell would say if enything hapened to the Cmandar. Ingersley is turning in to a Hostpital. Ill do even more if they ast me. I dident see Flora not getting time of nor will she but on your next leeve.
Love from Mother.

Andrew read the letters through twice though his eyes were closing. He was drifting into sleep when the klaxon went. 'Action stations! Action stations!' he heard someone yell – as if it were necessary. He fell out of his hammock and in thirty seconds was piling down the steel ladder to his No.2 engine room action station. It was like the tropics in there – even the steel walkways above the pipes were hot, the handrails too. He squeezed past the stokers on the top level, and descended two more ladders at speed until he was right down on the floor, the iron plates hot and greasy underfoot. He looked up and saw men above him attending, adjusting the valves, concentrating on the orders of the stoker petty officers.

The chief engineer could be seen through the treads of the ladder, and no sooner had Andrew reached the bottom than Chiefie beckoned to him while he spoke to the bridge on the voice tube. Andrew ran up to stand beside him and heard him saying, 'Sir! One of the prop shafts has seized. She'll handle badly. I'll go in myself.' He put back the speaker and turned to address the boiler room. 'We are going after a surfaced U-boat. Its wireless message back to base was intercepted. We're on its tail and it hasn't seen us yet.' He gave a wry smile. 'Let's hope he's spent all his ammo.'

U-boats carried fourteen torpedoes and a deck gun. Its deck gun could do little damage to the *Rutland* – it would scarcely scratch the paint on the armour-plating – but torpedoes could, and U-boats made night surface attacks as a matter of tactics, coming up when the big ships were silhouetted against the sky. Tonight it was a wild, black night out there and the *Rutland* was charging straight ahead – no zigzagging. If she came to a stop she would be a sitting target, and if the U-boat spotted them and submerged they would all be in grave danger. It was the chief engineer's absolute responsibility to keep the ship running at the fastest speed during battle conditions, so things must be serious for him to have to give the order he now did: 'Close down engine four.' He turned to Andrew and said, 'Come with me.'

Chiefie went down the ladder slowly and confidently, as if there was nothing to worry about – and a smile flashed around the crew, one after the other. He was the best chief engineer in the Royal Navy, they all believed.

Down at the bottom he said to Andrew, 'Lift the grating.' When Andrew had lifted the heavy iron cover to the propeller shaft that lay over the bilges, Chiefie dropped into the square tunnel and said, 'Stand by the manhole. Hand me my tools. Torch, ring spanner and hammer!

It was pitch black down there. Andrew shone his own torch on to Chiefie's hand as he reached for the tools that should enable him to tighten the joint where the bearings had loosened. Andrew crouched and watched him crawling, inching his way along in the blackness, the flashing torchlight ahead of him all that gave away his movements as he swept every inch of the prop shaft with the beam. The second engineer and the third, along with four petty officers, would be working flat out to keep up the pressure on the remaining boilers. And over the noise of the engines, the throbbing of the three remaining prop shafts and the roaring of the burners, they could now hear the ship's guns firing and feel her shuddering right down through to the bilges. Her medium and light guns from all along the ship were being brought to bear on the lone U-boat raider whose commander would not risk submerging when he could do seventeen and a half knots on the surface against only eight submerged, running on batteries.

The chief was hammering. Andrew could hear his confident striking of metal upon metal.

Then, and it happened without warning of any kind, the *Rutland* was struck, right in the centre of the engine room area. It was not a torpedo – a torpedo hitting them there would have wiped them out. They had been rammed – probably by a badly handled merchant ship that was in the way. The *Rutland* lurched violently. Men were thrown against the engines or over the steel scaffolding walkways. The midships was pitched into blackness. The sound of bodies hitting valves, pipes rupturing, escaping steam was terrifying. Andrew had automatically obeyed the Commander's instructions from their sailing trips when the yacht was being hurled around in a storm: 'Take no chances. You don't want to be hurt. Hang on to something even if you are only taking a couple of steps.'

Men were shouting; someone screeched, 'Emergency lights!' and the huge glass face of the lights came on as the ship steadied again. Andrew was still holding on to the deck grating.

He could hear the other engines working. Two petty officers were lying, twisted, on the deck behind him – fallen to their deaths from above. Half a dozen men only were left standing; the others lay sprawled along and over the steel separating partitions, bleeding, dazed and groaning.

Andrew was the most senior man left. He must act quickly. He yelled out his orders to the six able-bodied men. The fourth engine was still out of action but the pressure must be restored and quickly.

The damage-control lieutenant dived into the compartment, shouting, 'What's the situation on number four? Chief still down there?'

'I'm going into the shaft, sir,' Andrew shouted back. He turned back to the shaft and with a quick appreciation of the new danger saw water – water where no water should be – rising in the prop shaft.

The lieutenant came flying down the ladders, crossed the walkways and down to where Andrew stood. He looked into the tunnel where water was seeping in, saw the water level and said, 'Five minutes. Then the watertight doors to the engine area will close automatically.'

Andrew knew this. His hands were sweating and his heart was pumping like the devil. He must move as fast as possible. While the lieutenant held back the grating, Andrew lowered himself into the cold water of the tunnel and crawled along, knee deep in a filthy mix of freezing water and fuel oil, calling, 'Are you all right, sir?'

There was no reply, but he saw Chiefie's flashlight bobbing ahead. Andrew flashed his own torch and saw at once what the trouble was. The impact had sprung one of the plates. The framework was collapsed under the sheared joint of the prop shaft. Painfully, and aware all the time of the rising water level, Andrew forced his way forward, bent double, dreading to find the chief sliced in half. He discovered him lying awkwardly but alive, half under the prop shaft, gritting his teeth, trying not to moan in pain.

Relief and fear flooded through Andrew, who dared not show either. 'You'll be OK, sir. I'll get you out.'

'Get out yourself. The water's rising,' the chief groaned. Andrew shone his light and saw that Chiefie's arm, high up at the shoulder, was trapped between the protruding handle of the spanner and the buckled frame. He said, 'Hang on! Keep your head up!' for the water was already up to the chief's shoulder. Another couple of inches and it would cover his face. Andrew had to keep calm for Chiefie's sake while he scrabbled frantically for the hammer in the black water. It was not there. It must be under his body. He reached over and lifted the chief's head. 'Don't close your eyes! I'll free you.' Then, knowing how little time he had, he backed down the tunnel, through the foul stinking water, to the grating, where he yelled, 'Wrench, crowbar, hammer!'

The guns were still firing. Colossal vibrations racked the boiler room as the tools were handed down to him by the second lieutenant, who said 'Is Chiefie alive?'

'Aye,' Andrew called back without wasting breath on formalities of rank. He inched forward again while the waters rose inexorably. Three minutes was all they had before the watertight doors would seal them both alive in this dark, stinking tomb.

Overhead the guns blasted; the icy water was up to the chief's chin and slithering like an oily, stinking stream over his trapped shoulder and the handles of the spanner. Andrew's progress was slow but steady. He could only move with knees bent and his back doubled. He was there. He had to get it right. There would be no second chance if he muffed this.

He felt for the handles of the ring spanner, dragged the wrench into place, fixed it over one handle, levered it against the second handle and tightened it. Then, with his face only inches from the water, he put both hands over the wrench's shaft and turned it fast until it locked. He braced his body. His back was hard up against the metal plate. In that tiny space and working underwater, he pushed the crowbar between the wrench and the buckled frame and tried to lever all his weight against it. The water was touching the tip of his chin. Sweat broke out on his face. His hands were icy cold and going numb but he held his breath and put every last ounce of strength into the effort. There was no movement for a few seconds, then, with painful slowness, he felt it shift. He eased off for a second and, putting his head back, took in as much of the foul air as he could, then, with a strength that could only have come from God, he would later believe, he found some extra power and the damned handle moved. It moved – it was over.

The chief's body slumped lower as the ship juddered again under the barrage of its firing guns. His face was under the water. Andrew pulled off the wrench, eased the chief's shoulder free and pulled on the arm that had dropped. The foul air was choking him but the body was sliding towards him. He lifted Chiefie's head clear of the oily water, gave it a hard shake, heard him cough and splutter – and then at speed dragged him the last few yards to the iron grating and the hands that were reaching down for them, pulling them to safety barely five seconds before the heavy steel door with its rubber and canvas flanges slid into place, sealing the shaft.

He lay gasping for air as the chief was carried to the lieutenant

124

surgeon. And it was then that they heard it – the guns roaring overhead, followed by a shout that went round the ship's company like greased lightning: 'We got it! We sank the bastard! Bloody marvellous!'

An hour later, after the urgent cases had been attended to, Andrew was seen by the lieutenant surgeon, who gave him a dose of a powerful expectorant that he said would bring up anything on his lungs. They stripped him and washed him clean of the oil and bandaged his hands. Then he was dismissed and sent back to his mess without a sight of the chief.

Though it was probably a couple of hours, it seemed that no sooner had he climbed into his hammock than one of the petty officers came into the mess to order him to go at once to the master-at-arms, who would take him to the captain.

'Aye aye, sir!' Andrew almost fell out of his hammock. His mind raced back over events. He ran to the heads and splashed cold water on his face with reddened fingertips that protruded from the bandages. Had anything gone wrong? The chief was going to recover, wasn't he?

He dressed as fast as he could, put on oilskins and fought his way back up to the bridge, clinging to the ropes of the storm rigging under a screaming wind with needles of ice stabbing into his face. It was pitch black. Giant seas were curling and breaking over the armour-plated decks that heaved under his boots. The master-at-arms shouted above the storm, 'On the wardroom flat, Leading Stoker.' This was aft of the ship, below the quarter-deck. Andrew went back down the ladder.

He discarded his oilskins and waited in line until his name was called. Flanked by the master-at-arms, he marched smartly ten paces forward, placed his cap under his arm and snapped to attention in front of the captain, his bandaged hands held rigidly down, heedless of the pain as the master-at-arms ordered, 'Stand at ease!'

'Stand easy.' Captain Sir Gordon Campbell said when the master-at-arms stepped back. 'You acted with courage and initiative in the boiler room, Leading Stoker. Your divisional officer has recommended your accelerated advance. You are being advanced immediately to acting petty officer.'

Andrew could not hold back the smile that came to his cold,

cracked lips. As soon as confirmation came through he'd put aside the square rig – the bell-bottoms and round cap – to wear the fore and aft peaked cap. He'd be moved up to the petty officers' mess at once – and his midday tot of rum would be neat, not two to one with water. Relief and pride brought a flush to his face. 'Thank you, sir,' he said.

The captain, who would have been briefed on wounds, looked at Andrew's bandaged hands and said, 'I'll be proud to shake your hand when the bandages are off. For the moment I salute you as a brave man.' Andrew did not even feel the pain in his hands. He could not stop the smile that came spreading across his face as the captain smiled back and said, 'The Royal Navy is looking for men who can make decisions. As soon as your promotion is approved you will be given the rank of upper yardman.'

Andrew smiled broadly now. He was on his way up. He was not stopping at petty officer level then. Upper yardman was the route to becoming a fully commissioned oficer, moving from there to acting sub-lieutenant through sub-lieutenant to lieutenant and lieutenant-commander. Ma and Flora would be proud of him.

Sir Gordon Campbell said, 'The officer training course in peacetime lasts six months. I believe it is much shorter now. You could be sent to Portsmouth. I'm not certain what the arrangements will be.'

'Thank you, sir,' Andrew repeated, still unable to erase the grin. 'I take it we are heading for port somewhere?'

Sir Gordon clasped his left hand on Andrew's shoulder. 'Well done, Andrew,' he said. 'We will be in Invergordon in about ten days' time, barring trouble. Your orders will come through as soon as I hear from the Admiralty. Don't bank on having more than twenty-four hours' leave before you are sent on the course.'

Flora, wearing navy-blue overalls and with her shoulder-length red hair tied up under a turban, stood at the bench where she worked a lathe, cutting a groove in brass shell cases. It was Monday afternoon. The girls' faces were beaded with sweat and the noise was so bad that Flora had stuffed her ears with cotton wool. She was overwhelmed with tiredness. The pain in her back got worse every day. She had made an appointment with the medical people at the end of her shift. Her stomach churned as the smell of hot metal assailed her. She looked at the clock. Four o'clock. Only another half-hour.

Over the noise of the lathes, Betty, the girl opposite, caught her attention. 'Come on, Flora! Sing!' she yelled, for the wireless was turned up full blast. They said it improved production.

Despite the ear plugs Flora could hear it all, even the bad language of the men who called out 'How about a kiss, darling?' and worse. Some of the women, bold as brass, would make replies that could make the men blush. Still only sixteen, she had got the job by declaring herself to be eighteen, and to make herself look older wore a theatrical shade of Tangee lipstick that tasted of marigolds and made her white face even paler than normal. However, Mr Davidson couldn't see it and the only person it offended was the widow woman next door, whose eyebrows lifted to heaven at the sight of Mr Davidson taking Flora's arm to church or choir practice.

Betty yelled again, 'Flora! You've got a good voice. Sing!' They were all singing now to *Music While You Work*, and Flora smiled, pulled the cotton plug from her right ear and joined in: 'We're going to hang out the washing on the Siegfried Line .. Have you any dirty washing, Mother dear ...?' Last night in church she had sung 'I know that My Redeemer Liveth'. It struck her as incongruous, and now she laughed with the others when next they broke into 'Run rabbit, run rabbit, run, run, run ...' It was true that music made you work faster. Four songs later, the rafters nearly lifting in the roar of voices, it was time to down tools.

Slowly she edged her way between the crowded, noisy benches to the cloakroom where, night and morning for the last few weeks, she had been sick, bringing up a gush of the brown, acid contents of her stomach. She went slowly, for if she walked too fast a hot streak of pain shot down her left leg. She scrubbed her hands and nails until every black speck was gone, but the inevitable could not be postponed, and she took a few deep breaths before awkwardly climbing the stairs to the room they called the clinic. She was the only worker there and, relieved, waited to be called; leaning against the wall of the

127

dusty room, looking at the posters that urged her to Buy War Bonds and Dig for Victory. She was waiting to be told. But she already knew. She had missed four periods.

They called her into a little room which smelled of carbolic, where a stout, severe nurse told her to go behind the screen, take off her clothes and lie on the thin white sheet that covered the black rubber examination couch. Shivering with nerves, she did so.

The doctor was a white-whiskered old man brought out of retirement since the young doctors were in the forces. He pulled back the curtain and came to stand over her. He looked from her medical examination request slip to her ringless finger, and said, with distaste, 'You have missed four periods?' His breath was foul. He handed the cards to the nurse.

'Yes.' Flora flinched when he put his bony, ice-cold hands on her stomach, then ran them down lower and began to press painfully above her pubic bone. She cried out and drew up her knees as pain radiated from her spine.

He took his hands away, but slowly. 'Only four months? Are you certain?'

Another blast of his cheesy breath made her stomach turn in protest as she replied, 'Yes.' What sort of girl did he think she was that she might not know when it had happened?

'Lie on your side. Pull your knees up as far as you can,' he ordered.

She shivered, then slowly brought her knees up, closed her eyes tight and gritted her teeth while he put a rubber-gloved finger inside her and pushed hard, making her cry out. 'You are hurting me. My back ...!'

He took off the glove, dropped it into an enamel dish and said, 'All right. Get dressed,' and left the cubicle.

It took her some minutes to dress. She could not bend easily to reach her chilblained feet, nor could she disguise the worry lines that were etched into her white face when at last she sat opposite him.

'Four months.' He cast a cold eye over her. 'There is pressure on your sciatic nerve. This will get worse until the baby is born – and I can give you nothing for it.' He picked up her works record, then said, 'Identity card, please!' She put it on the desk. He peered at it closely. 'You are only sixteen? And unmarried?' Sticky white stuff had gathererd at the tight corners of his mouth.

Her voice trembled. 'Not officially. We are promised.'

'You are not married.' He was contemptuous. 'You expect him to marry you?'

'Yes. But he's at sea.' She could feel tears welling and a hard, painful lump at the back of her throat.

'Get your father to contact his senior officer. Demand that he's given compassionate leave.'

She was cold. And she was hungry. 'I can't. He's on active service.' Surely they wouldn't call Andrew up in front of the Commander. His chances of promotion would be ruined. She began to cry. 'He wouldn't want his captain to know. I'll wait till he's home.'

'Will your parents allow you to stay at home – bringing shame and disgrace on the family?'

'I'm an orphan ...' Flora took out her handkerchief and blew her nose hard.

Exasperated, he looked at the stony-faced nurse. 'I've heard this story so often,' he said. 'This week I have seen four women who have got themselves into the same mess. Two of them with Canadian troopers – and one of them married to one of our own serving men. Why do women and silly girls behave like this?' He turned back to Flora. 'You'll never see the boy again, you realise? You must give up work immediately. This is no place for a pregnant woman. Go to your doctor. See what arrangements he can make for you.'

She did not have a doctor. She couldn't afford to pay three and six for a visit. In fact she had only been seen by a doctor twice in her life. She'd had a routine medical examination at Guthrie's, and now this one. 'Wh ... wh ... what arrangements?' she managed to ask, between sobs.

'Tell her, Nurse.' He walked out of the room.

The nurse said, slow and disapproving, as if talking to a naughty child, 'You will be sent away to a workhouse or a home for unmarried mothers, where the baby will be born. If you have any sense and any real love for your baby, you'll have it adopted at birth. They will find it a good home. If you don't give it up, it will go to a Dr Barnardo's or one of the Children's Society homes, where you will be allowed to visit by appointment – and you will make a contribution to its keep. I take it you don't have money or a home?'

She had nothing. A cold fear clutched at her heart. 'No. But when can I get my baby back?'

'When you have a proper home to offer to a child.'

'Or I get married?' Andrew would be home. He'd marry her properly. They would find a house. Even a single-end or a but and ben – anything.

'*If* you get married.' She added, in a cynical voice, 'Girls in your position have them adopted and then they keep their mouths shut. Not many men will marry a girl who's had another man's child.'

Flora left the clinic and went downstairs out on to the dark January street, behind a string of people who were going home. It was like playing follow-my-leader in the pitch black. She prayed with every step, 'Please God, send Andrew home soon,' until they came to where the pale moonlight reflected on the cold, choppy waters of the Forth and she could find her way to the house on the esplanade.

In the morning, shaking with cold and fright and with the fatigue of a sleepless night dragging her down, she dressed in her warmest things – a brown woolly dress and matching brown cardigan which she had knitted herself. Her bedroom was freezing – so cold that ice glazed and crazed the inside of her window and would not thaw out from one day to the next. Carefully she rolled on her best lisle stockings over her numb feet, jumping at the sharp nip of the chilblains that had spread right along the side of her feet as well as to the knuckles of every toe. She fastened the tight suspender belt that cut red weals into her flesh, desperate to get downstairs where there was a small cloakroom with a lavatory and washbasin right beside the front door. Every morning for the last month she had been sick first thing, quietly because Mr Davidson had sharp ears.

She kept a torch at her bedside, for there was no light on the landing. Flashing the weak beam on to the steps, she made her way downstairs and looked for the post. There was nothing for her – no letter from Andrew. Where was he? There might be one in the midday delivery, but her heart sank as it had done every day for the last two months. She retched painfully, vomited, wiped her ashen face over with an ice-crackled face cloth and made her way down the cheerless hallway to the still dark kitchen, where she switched on the light.

The kitchen had a rank smell of damp and escaped gas that would not disappear until the room was warm and aired. Her insides were painful, caving in from need of food, but before she could eat the dry biscuit she took with hot water, she must first pull the blackout blind and open the window an inch or two. Outside, in the stone-walled yard, a freezing white mist hung over the icy black flagstones. No fresh air would breeze through the kitchen today. Putting a match to the fire in the range, she chafed her hands together as it blazed and caught while her mind jumped from one alarming thought to another. She must say nothing to Mr Davidson about leaving her job.

There was a pot of oatmeal soaking and now she struck another match and turned the gas ring on to bring the porridge to the boil, then left it to simmer while she sipped her hot water and bit into a biscuit. Shudders of fear came in waves down her back as she cut bread for toast and placed the margarine, marmalade and cups and saucers in exactly the right spots on the enamel-topped table. There was nothing for it but to see Andrew's ma and tell her everything.

She cut more bread, opened a pot of fish paste and made sandwiches for Mr Davidson's lunch, then arranged them on a plate and covered them with an upturned pie dish to keep them fresh.

The kitchen was warm and welcoming and smelled of hot toast by the time Mr Davidson came down and sat in his place. 'Good morning, Flora,' he said, 'I trust you slept well.' Only in the last few weeks had he stopped using the formal 'Miss Stewart' and had begun to use her Christian name – and that only because the woman next door had told him that Flora was not, as he'd imagined, a grown woman but an attractive young girl whose presence under his roof was causing much gossip and speculation.

'Yes. Thank you,' she answered, surprised that her voice sounded normal while a hundred nervous butterflies twitched at her eyelids and pulled the corners of her mouth down. 'I'll leave your sandwiches and a glass of milk on the desk,' she said. 'Would you like haggis for supper tonight, Mr

Davidson?' She would queue at the butcher's before she got the train to North Berwick and take the haggis with her to Ingersley in her shopping bag.

'That would suit me well,' he said. 'Do you know what I'm going to do today?'

'What?' Her lips were dry. She placed his porridge before him.

'I am going to take a dish of tea with the lady next door.' He chuckled as he sprinkled salt on it. 'She says that we are going to become good neighbours and get to know one another.' He stirred his porridge. 'I expect that when she has found out all she wants to know, she will invite the ladies of the Esplanade round and they can exchange stories.'

Mr Davidson evidently thought the neighbour was harmless. Flora licked her dry lips and shuddered. If they discovered that she was having a baby, Mr Davidson's good name would be ruined. They would naturally think – Oh God! What would they say? She sat down heavily, jolting her back and making Mr Davidson jump. He said, 'Have you eaten already?'

'Yes ...' she said. 'It's ten to eight. Will you leave everything until I get back? Don't wash the dishes or anything.'

She struggled into her coat, pulled on her hat, wrapped a scarf around her neck and left the house.

At nine o'clock that same morning, at Ingersley House, Ruth was in bed, opening the letter which the housemaid had placed on her morning tea tray. She slit it open and withdrew the two pages written in Gordon's strong, sloping hand. The letter had been posted in Liverpool a week ago. Why had he not come home? Surely he would get a few days' leave? He used to ring Elizabeth as soon as he docked.

'*Dear Ruth* ...' He wrote as if she were nothing more than an employee on the estate. Not 'darling' or even 'wife'. He obviously didn't care any more. He probably regretted marrying her.

I have received two letters from you so the mail is getting through to the ship but I can't be sure that outgoing mail reaches its destination.

I am sorry that you are inconvenienced by the house being

132

requisitioned for a convalescent hospital. However, they tell me that they have made a good job of moving the house furniture upstairs and that the top, nursery floor is put to good use as bedroom accommodation. You still have two upper floors and only yourself and Nanny in occupation. We must be thankful that our injured servicemen and women . . .

As is she cared two hoots. The government measures requisitioning properties were excessive. Beside, there were dozens of large houses in the area that could have been requisitioned before Ingersley. It was not as if she hadn't done her bit. She had filled all the cottages accessible to the road with evacuees – mothers and babies, expectant mothers with young children – though at least she was compensated for that. A government grant per head of placement gave a much better return than the rents of tied cottages. There were no worries either about repairing the properties or the tenants falling behind with the rent. The government gave the money directly to her for this stream of endlessly shifting people.

But Gordon ought to have demanded that Ingersley be excluded from requisitioning, or at least that she be consulted. She sipped her tea and snapped a biscuit in half. How dare those awful Ministry men walk in and decide how her house should be run?

She ate half a biscuit, flicked the crumbs off the sheet and refilled her tea cup. There had been one small victory. She had won a battle of wills with the dreadful Wilkins from the Ministry when she demanded that they convert the room above Gordon's study into a kitchenette preserved for her privacy – and the workmen had made a speedy and good job of it.

Ruth got out of bed, slipped off her silk nightgown and quickly pulled on the fine wool vest and knickers which had been wrapped around a hot-water bottle. Then she took a bottle of Atkinson's lavender water from the dressing table, unscrewed the silver lid and splashed the cool, fresh scent over the insides of her wrists to calm herself and soothe her nerves before she could return to the bed and her tea. How dare Gordon say, *I am sorry that you are inconvenienced*? Inconvenience was a massive understatement. She was worn to a shadow with it all. If he were here, he'd see for himself.

Mrs Stewart was taking up one of the beds at the hospital at this moment, struck down with influenza a week ago. And with her out of action, Maud and Bessie – mother and daughter – the two remaining servants, who lived rent-free in one of the cottages, were having to do the cooking as well as the cleaning. Bessie would be making breakfast in the kitchenette instead of getting on with cleaning the drawing room and lighting fires. It was too bad of Mrs Stewart. She could not expect to be off work for much longer. She was needed here.

I am certain that you will be called upon to assist when the injured start to arrive. And then you will not feel so helpless, as you put it.

She had meant, by saying that she felt helpless, that she was managing without help. Nanny was no use at all. In fact she was becoming very managerial since she had opened two bedrooms at Ivy Lodge for mothers who could not be delivered in their own homes. So far Ivy Lodge had not been needed as a maternity home and Nanny found it more convenient to remain at Ingersley, especially as Lucy Hamilton was pregnant and had asked Nanny to attend her and deliver the baby. Not only that, but Nanny, who had driven an ambulance in the Great War, had volunteered to help both with the hospital and the District Nursing Service. They had taken up her offer with alacrity. Today she was to have driving instruction at some Ministry department or other. Ruth had no doubt at all that they would use her at the most inconvenient times.

She finished the tea and left the second biscuit uneaten. Still, if Nanny learned to drive properly it could be an advantage. Ruth had purchased a licence long before mandatory driving tests were introduced, but she detested driving. Nothing but a dire emergency would induce her to get behind the wheel of a car. Nanny would be able to chauffeur her around in the Armstrong Siddeley, which had been spared the ignominy of being requisitioned for the police or fire brigade by Nanny's District Nursing work. Nanny was sixty-one, and indefatigable.

Gordon's letter went on:

Yes, I do think about our future. As soon as I can, I will offer Ingersley either to the Ministry or to Hamilton. We will buy something more manageable. It would be different, I agree, if we had children. But we do not.

As curt as that. How did he know she was not already pregnant? The last time they had made love was four months ago, on Mike Hamilton's wedding day, before Gordon returned to the ship. If she had become pregnant after that encounter it could not have been confirmed before now. A lady simply did not speak of such things, even to her own doctor, until she was sure, around the fourth month. But Ruth was not pregnant, and had been distraught to find that she was not. The only way she'd keep Ingersley, and probably her marriage to Gordon, was by giving him children, preferably a son. It had come to that. It was now vital that she had a child. She read the line again: *It would be different, I agree, if we had children. But we do not.* There was no shadow of doubt. Unless she bore him a child Gordon would sell the estate. She needed a baby. Now.

She crumpled the letter and pitched it into the waste basket, then retrieved it, flattened it out and read it again. Gordon must come home. She would telephone the base in Liverpool tonight and tell him he was wanted here.

She dressed quickly. She'd give Heather a good ride out on the beach this morning. Road riding on the lanes as she'd had to do for the last months was no good for either of them, and a good gallop on the freezing cold beach would cool her temper. She pulled on jodhpurs and a heavy jumper and went down to what had been their bedroom floor and was now the living area.

Standing in the doorway of the new kitchen, she gave instructions to Bessie who was preparing breakfast for herself and Nanny. 'I won't be taking breakfast this morning. There's only Nanny.'

The maid raised a hand in weary acknowledgement. Ruth went over to her. 'You all right?' she asked. Bessie's normally florid face this morning was pale.

'I don't feel too good, Lady Campbell. I think I'm getting the flu or a cold,' she answered. 'I'll have to go home.'

This was the last straw. If the woman went down with

influenza then Mrs Stewart must get out of bed and help run the household. Ruth said, 'Oh dear. I hope it isn't infectious. Before you go, prepare a light lunch for me and Nanny. A sandwich or two and some soup.' She added, 'Your mother will be here to serve it and to make a simple meal this evening, won't she?'

Ruth left the kitchen, slung her hacking jacket across her shoulders and ran downstairs. The lift had been commandeered along with the house and she never used it, not wanting to have contact with those terribly common hospital people who talked incessantly in frightful voices. Nanny and she used the main stairs instead. Since Ruth had insisted that the front door entrance – their entrance – was not to be used by hospital visitors or employees, she could get by with a brief nod in the direction of the occasional over-familiar hospital staff whom she might have to pass on the stairs.

There were some advantageous spin-offs, though. The tradesman's entrance at the back of the house had been enlarged and fitted with smart double swing doors of bomb-proof reinforced glass, and the small patch of weedy gravel in front of the servants' door had been transformed into a wide area covered in concrete. It gave plenty of room for ambulances to turn in – and would be useful when this damned war was over. The roof, too, had been repaired, and painted in camouflage colours which she would insist was returned to normal when the war was over.

Outside, the bitter cold nipped into her fingers and nose. She wrapped her scarf about her head and across her mouth and pulled on her lined-leather gloves. When the South Lodge's iron gates were requisitioned for scrap metal, Ruth had insisted on having solid wooden gates made to close the entrance. There was now no way in from the road, as the gates were bolted from the inside. The price of her privacy was thus a serious inconvenience to herself, for she now had to use the North Gate, the drive to which passed right in front of the Hamilton's farmhouse. But closing the entrance had prevented every Tom, Dick and Harry of the hospital staff from using the front drive, which remained blissfully, her own.

On her way to the stables she passed Land Army girls cutting back the beech hedges and raking gravel. They had long ago learned to ignore her and did not acknowledge her presence. Ruth never wasted time gossiping. On reaching the yard she was greeted by Lucy Hamilton, who popped her cheery pink face out from behind the wash-house door, waved and called out, 'Morning, Lady Campbell.'

The sight of Lucy in the floral smock that advertised her otherwise unnoticeable condition brought a surge of sick, impotent jealousy to Ruth. Why should this enemy – this thorn in Ruth's flesh, this simpering woman – have everything that Ruth herself wanted? Lucy was to bear a child and, like the lowest of working women, didn't try to hide the fact. It was disgusting. If she continued as she was going, Lucy Hamilton could soon be the owner of Ingersley estate. If only Ruth had known that Gordon meant to sell the estate to him, she would have married Mike Hamilton herself.

Lucy was rich in her own right. She did not need to go to such miserly lengths as to do her own washing. There was a good laundry service in the town and the farm had all these Land Army girls idling about. It was quite plain that she revelled in both pregnancy and domesticity. There were chickens scratching about on the cobbles and in the straw of the unused loose boxes. In an hour's time the stable yard would be festooned with washing lines full of sheets and tablecloths and everything calculated to frighten the horses. If Ruth were in charge she would forbid it, but now she fought down her rage and said politely, 'Lucy? Did you pass on my message? Is Heather ready for me?'

'No. Mike said you might like to . . .' Her voice trailed off.

Ruth attempted a little irony, though it would be wasted. 'He said I might enjoy grooming and saddling my own animal? Is that it?' Fuming, she collected the saddle, bit and bridle from the tack room, then let herself in to Heather's loose box. The mare snickered in anticipation as Ruth lit a cigarette, tacked up and talked to her. 'We'll have a good ride out today, Heather – strengthen those hocks. . .' With the Gold Flake in her mouth and her eyes narrowed against the smoke, she lifted the horse's feet one by one. 'Perfect. You won't need shoeing for a while.'

A shadow fell across the sunlit straw and Mike Hamilton's voice boomed out: 'Don't smoke in here. Your mare will be taken to the smiddy next week and fitted with heavy shoes.' Ruth felt the old familiar thrill of being close to him, but she shot him a contemptuous look as she took the cigarette out of her mouth and through clenched teeth said, 'Who the hell do you think you are to tell me what I may do with my own horse?'

'Your horse is needed for farm work,' Mike said curtly before stepping aside to open the door for her to lead Heather out.

'I don't think so.' Ruth put her left foot in the stirrup and mounted, quick and lithe though Heather stamped impatiently. She looked down on him. 'My light hunter is quite useless for your purposes.' Mike was behaving as if he were already master of the estate instead of a simple tenant farmer. 'Take your hands off the bridle.'

The confidence of a man who knew he was within his rights was in his sly smile as he dropped his hands. 'Well, it's no' for ye to decide, woman. The ministry is putting tight restrictions and regulations on animals. We cannae afford to feed an animal that's nae use. Major's pulling a plough. Your mare will be hitched to the milk trap from next Saturday. Take it or leave it.'

She would not deign to reply. Mike Hamilton would lose control first. He would saddle up Major and follow her down to the sands and at last have the showdown she hoped would lead to a revival of their affair.

The frozen cobblestones rang under Heather's hooves as they left the yard. She glanced back as she turned on to the lane leading to the beach. Mike Hamilton, red-faced, was waving his arms madly, signalling her to stop. She laughed and urged Heather into a trot.

Ten minutes later, with the sea sparkling on her right and the frosty buckthorn bushes glittering in the sun, she was exhilarated. She let Heather have her head. A gentle, salt-laden breeze blew into Ruth's open mouth as she put her weight in her heels, lifted her seat out of the saddle, leaned over Heather's silky mane and urged, 'Go on!' They pounded down the flat sand to the old slipway, where she turned the mare, eased her left leg out, brought her right in and pressed into Heather's quarters to make the horse loop into the turn to race along the white fringes of foam. Hooves pounded wet sand. Sea water splashed up between the horses legs, soaking Ruth's jodhpurs as they raced along the water's edge.

Then she saw him again, Mike Hamilton, waving his arms like a man demented. She pretended not to notice and, head down over the horse's neck, drove Heather on into the sparkling, curling foam for the quarter-mile return, but they had not ridden this way for months and Ruth knew enough not to strain the heart of an unfit horse. She sat back in the saddle and slowed Heather down to a trot before they reached the sheltered, secluded bay area with its backdrop of buckthorn and jagged rocks above the waterline, and table-top basalt rocks which the sea had made smooth below. She brought the horse's head round and slowed to a walk as Heather picked her way between the rocks to the path that wound through the buckthorn.

He was here again, dark and angry, blocking her path. She pulled Heather up. 'What is it?' she demanded, a smile of satisfaction spreading across her face.

'Get off that horse!' He grabbed the bridle with one hand and the back of her jacket with the other and dragged her out of the saddle to the ground. She lost her balance and fell at his feet, put her hand out to save herself and wrenched her wrist. 'This beach is mined!' he shrieked. 'Can't you read? *Danger. Keep Out!* Ye've ridden past at least four o' the bloody things. You could have been killed.'

Then he pulled her to her feet and held her arms and the harshness had gone from his voice. 'Ye could have been bloody well killed...'

'And is that not what you want?' She looked up at him in the old inviting way. 'You have avoided me. Been rude to me. And now you ...' She moved so that she was hard up against him and his smell – horses and leather and sweating, angry maleness – brought a sense of triumph she must not let him see. He was excited. She could feel the hardness of him through all these layers of clothes. He could never resist her. 'You want me ... don't you?'

'Aye. But I'm not going to take ye. Because your man is fighting a war. And I have too much respect for him – and he for me.'

'Respect was always pretty low on your scale of feelings, Mike.'

'Aye.' His eyes narrowed. 'I've come a long way in the last

four months. I've aye wanted a son. I have a mighty store of respect and love now – for the woman who's carrying my child.' He released her abruptly. 'Ye'll have to find another if your man's nae use to you.' Then he turned and walked away.

She mounted the snorting Heather and swore under her breath at the pain that was shooting through her arm from wrist to shoulder. What a day this was proving to be. One damned thing after another. All her plans were crumbling. Her servants were dropping like flies. Gordon was going to sell Ingersley. And if he could not impregnate her when he came home, then her only hope of having a child – through Mike Hamilton's need of her – had been dashed.

How fickle men were. Six months ago Mike had been disconsolate because she, Ruth, would not marry him. Now he was like a solan goose, strutting and posturing, guarding his broody gander on the nest.

She reached the yard and heard Lucy singing and sloshing around, happy with her tubs of soapy water. She remained in the saddle and called out impatiently, 'Lucy! Come and help me down, will you?'

'You all right?' Lucy came out, a frown of worry on her face.

'I've had a fall. Help me down.' She leaned forward, kicked off the stirrups and swung her legs over so that she need not use her wrist. Lucy put a hand out to steady her at the elbow and she was down safely. 'You'll have to water, feed and unsaddle for me. I'm hurt.'

'Oh dear. Nanny need not come to me today. You need her.'

Ruth clenched her teeth to hold back from shouting in pain, but managed to say, 'Nanny is learning to drive an ambulance this morning.'

'That's nice for her.' Lucy took the reins and led the horse away then stopped and turned back. 'There's a girl wandering around the estate, looking for Mrs Stewart. She came to the farmhouse. Lost her way, I expect, now the South Gate's closed.'

Ruth said, 'It'll be one of the workers – or a patient's visitor.'

'Well, she definitely said Mrs Stewart,' Lucy answered. 'I sent her up to the house not ten minutes ago.'

Chapter Eight

'Damn!' Ruth uttered under her breath. Every step she took down the frosty gravel drive jolted her wrist. She must telephone the doctor. She would not go down to the hospital to ask for help. 'Double damn!'

There was a girl limping towards her, a pretty girl, dressed sensibly in a brown tweed coat and pull-on hat that could not hide the flaming red hair cascading about her neck and shoulders. She could have no business on this side of the house. Ruth put her hand gently into her pocket to support it. The girl stopped at the corner of the house. In a piercing, imperious voice Ruth asked, 'What are you doing here?'

The girl was tall, very young, and a blush came poppy red into her pale cheeks as she said nervously, 'I'm looking for Mrs Stewart. The cook.'

'Well, you won't find her. Not even if you go round to the tradesmen's entrance.' Ruth tried to indicate the way she should have taken but caught her breath with the pain in her hand. 'What do you want with her?' She looked harder at the girl. Though her clothes were not of the best quality, she was not a rough type. In her manner, dress and speech she gave the impression of being well brought up. But the blush had faded and left her white and drawn as if she too were in great pain. Ruth demanded, 'How far have you come? How did you get here?'

'I walked up from the station. I couldn't find the entrance. So I walked round the wall till I came to the gates.' The girl looked all in. She began to cry, soft tears rolling down her pinched cheeks. 'I have to see Mrs Stewart.'

Ruth's hand was swelling, her fingers were numb and for the first time in her life she did not know what to do. She couldn't leave this weeping girl, who was on the brink of collapse, to find her way out again and down to North Berwick station. 'I can't stand around in the cold waiting for you to explain,' she said. 'Stop snivelling. Come back to the house with me. Tell me what you want with Mrs Stewart.' She brought her hand carefully from her pocket and showed the girl the swollen fingers and the bruising that was spreading up from the wrist. 'Can you bandage? Have you ever bound a sprained wrist?' She looked at her closely again. 'Have I seen you before? What's your name?'

'Flora Macdonald.' The girl was trying to wipe her tears away with the back of her gloved right hand. 'I can bandage.' Then, 'I know you are Lady Campbell. I saw you on the lawn at the wedding.'

'The Hamilton wedding? Were you a guest?'

'No. Andrew brought me here to meet his ma. You see, we—' She caught her breath and clapped a hand to her back as if in pain. She staggered back a few steps and leaned against the wall.

'All right,' Ruth said sharply. 'Follow me,' and went swiftly to the house, with the girl, like an injured puppy, dragging along behind. She ran up the stone steps and stood back, watching the girl climb painfully slowly. Ruth indicated that she should go ahead and open the great oak door, and when she had closed it behind them said, 'Upstairs. Follow me.'

The girl made a neat job of bandaging her wrist, then asked to use the bathroom. 'Yes. Then come to the dining room. Across the hall.' Ruth went to the new drawing room to telephone Dr Russell and ask him to call in an hour's time. The rooms on this, the old bedroom floor were almost identical in size to those on the floor below. The dining room and drawing room looked much as they had before, apart from the floral wallpaper, but it rankled with Ruth that her old drawing and dining rooms were filled with iron-framed beds and all the paraphernalia of a hospital.

The girl returned. Ruth's wrist was easier for the firm bandaging. She was grateful; she would listen to the girl's story. She said, 'There will be enough food for two. Tell me

142

all about it over lunch,' before jangling the little hand bell to summon the maid.

Over lunch, which the girl hardly touched, Ruth began to question her, drawing out her story with a kind, concerned air whilst asking herself why she was allowing another aggravation into her day. All the same she prided herself on her sixth sense; the part of her mind that became instantly alert at times of crisis. She soothed the girl now. 'So Andrew helped you run away from Guthrie's, where the Commander – of all people – had put you, and this when you were only fourteen?'

'Yes. I told him I was seventeen.'

'And he found you a job as housekeeper to the blind Mr Davidson who lives on the Esplanade?' Ruth said, her voice warm with sympathy and encouragement.

'Yes,' Flora whispered, eyes downcast as she struggled to spoon up the leek and potato soup that Ruth had placed before her.

Ruth wanted to shake her. But if she spoke severely she might frighten the child. 'Come on! Nobody's going to hurt you.'

The girl put her spoon down. Deep, gasping sobs were shaking her shoulders as tears splashed into her soup.

Ruth repeated, 'What has this to do with Mrs Stewart?'

'It's about Andrew and me.' She mopped her face with the table napkin. 'I'm sorry. We're married.'

How could they be? Ruth would have known. 'Married?'

'Yes. On the day of the wedding. By habit and repute. I was only fifteen. I couldn't marry and I couldn't tell Andrew why—' All this between great gulps of tears. 'So Andrew bought the rings—' here the girl pulled on a ribbon from under the neckline of her dress and brought out a cheap wedding ring – 'and now—' She was overcome with the dreadful snivelling again.

Ruth was temporarily shocked into silence. Then realisation dawned. Her mind started to focus sharply as it did when something momentous was afoot. It was uncanny the way so often she could spot an opportunity – or rather, she thought, an opening, an answer to her own dilemma – in others' troubles. 'You are having a baby?' she said.

'Yes.'

'And Andrew Stewart is the father?'

'Yes.'

'And he told you to get in touch with his mother if you had a problem?'

'Yes.' The girl was breathing deeply into the napkin she was holding to her face.

Ruth needed a few moments to order the thoughts and possibilities that were crowding into her mind. So – it had happened on the very day that she herself had hoped to become pregnant. This girl had been sent to her. No girl *wanted* a child out of wedlock. Her mind raced down the bright, shining path of imagined possibilities. If you showed a troubled person a way out they would often take the required action for themselves. All one need do was to show the way, leave the gates open. How fortunate for herself that the girl had not found Mrs Stewart. A dependent mother and baby – the shame of knowing her son was responsible – was the last thing on earth the cook would want. 'You are sure of the date of conception?' she asked softly, gently. She was the girl's only hope.

'The second of September. The day of the wedding.' The girl twisted the napkin into a rope.

Ruth touched her arm. 'Take your time. Try to eat something.' There was a pot of coffee on the heated stand on the sideboard and Ruth went to pour for them. 'What did you say your name was, dear?'

'Flora Macdonald. Only I'm known to Mr Davidson as Flora Stewart – because, you see ...' and the girl went on to tell her, between snatches of tears and sips of coffee, about the search for work.

When Flora had finished, Ruth said, quietly and deliberately, 'You deceived both Andrew and your employer then, did you?' The girl was sixteen now, so it would make no legal difference – but Flora obviously thought it would.

'I had to ... I was afraid to tell the truth after the first lie.'

A girl of sixteen was no match for Ruth. 'You do realise that Andrew could have gone to jail?'

Flora unwound the napkin and blew her nose vigorously into it. Then she caught her breath and eased her back. Ruth took the napkin from her and handed her a handkerchief and her own, clean table napkin. The girl looked up, whey-faced and terrified. 'Yes.'

'Quite. And now you tell me that this – this common-law marriage was consummated in St Cuthbert's churchyard on the second of September when you were still only fifteen?' It crossed Ruth's mind to wonder how many more babies were conceived on that night, but she fought back the urge to be cruel and said in a soft, admonitory whisper, 'That was very, very wrong of you, Flora. You have put Andrew into the position of committing two criminal acts. Once in helping you escape from Dr Guthrie's and secondly in marrying a minor.'

'I know. I just kept getting in deeper ...' Flora was weeping again, ignoring the handkerchief, mopping her eyes with her table napkin. 'I had nobody.'

So nobody knew, except herself and Flora. Ruth asked, 'You are telling the truth – Andrew does not know about the baby?'

'I haven't told him.'

'And nobody knows you have come here?'

'Only some officials on North Berwick station. They wrote down the names of everyone who got off the train. They were all looking for billets and I didn't know what ...'

'Yes, yes. That's nothing. That's not what I meant,' Ruth said. 'You realise that any scandal would put an end to Andrew's chances of advancement – particularly with the Commander, who has helped him so much?' She paused for a moment, then, 'You know that the Royal Navy has prison cells on board ship? You know that these are very serious charges? If a sailor commits a civil criminal act it is far worse for him to be tried by court-martial.' Ruth knew very well that a civil case would never be heard in a military court – but Flora could not know it.

'I didn't know ... I didn't know ... I don't know any more.'

'You know what happens to girls who have babies out of wedlock?'

Flora buried her face in the napkin. 'They put you in the workhouse. And they take the baby away ...'

Ruth reached across and patted her hand. 'I'm trying to help you. Dry your eyes.'

After a few moments Flora lifted her face. She was as pale as death, flinching every now and again in pain. She choked on her words as she said, 'I have to tell Andrew's mother.'

'Mrs Stewart is very ill with flu,' Ruth said firmly. 'She is not allowed visitors. She is being nursed in isolation. I'm afraid this news would be too much for her to bear.'

Flora repeated, 'Andrew said I was to see his ma ...'

Ruth said, 'I have to tell you, Flora, that Andrew Stewart has given no end of trouble to his mother, and to me and the Commander.'

Flora's face was paler than ever. She put her hand into the small of her back, clearly in a lot of pain even as Ruth said, 'Andrew will have to be told – but in view of the punishment and the loss of his promotion, don't be surprised if he denies everything.'

It was too much. Flora clutched the table's edge wildly with her free hand, gave a cry of pain and crashed to the floor.

Flora came to in a strange, dimly lit bedroom where a fire burned brightly in an iron and tile fireplace on the far wall from the bed. Shadows flickered and dimmed over the beamed ceiling above her. She tried to sit up, but the pain that earlier had shot through her with such heat and force was now a dull numbness that had spread to her muscles, and she was not able to raise herself. She fell back against the lacy white pillows on the big, deep bed. Her head was thick and fuzzy and very, very heavy. She called for help.

The door opened, a light was turned on and now she saw that it was a big room with a sloping ceiling, filled with old-fashioned, ornate mahogany furniture. In the wardrobe mirror she saw Lady Campbell approach, pull up a chair and sit down. 'You have injured your back, Flora. My doctor has seen you. He says you are not to be moved.'

'I feel peculiar.'

'The doctor gave you an injection of morphine,' she replied. 'I don't want you to worry about a thing.'

'But – the baby—?'

Lady Campbell put her finger to her lips and looked towards the door. 'It is all right. Please. Don't mention your condition to anyone. Not until I've had a chance to speak to Mrs Stewart. Understand?'

'Yes. Yes.' Flora struggled again to rise but could not. She was too weak. She caught her breath and fell back once more. 'Mr Davidson ... I have to look after him.'

'It's done. Nanny Taylor has been to Portobello. I told her to tell Mr Davidson that you have fallen and injured your back. You have to rest.'

'I can't just leave.'

'There can be no going back. Mr Davidson needs reliable help. I rang the Institute for the Blind. They will send help to him tomorrow.'

'Mrs Stewart—?' Flora said.

'I will see her this evening. If she's well enough I'll tell her. Tomorrow you will write to Andrew.'

'I don't want to get him into trouble.'

'You must tell him about the baby. Tell him you are at Ingersley and he must come for you and marry you. Give the letter to me. I will post it,' Lady Campbell said. 'Can you lift your head just a little, so I can give you your medicine?'

She was holding a small glass of purple liquid. Flora hesitated, then, 'What is it?' she asked.

'A sedative plus tonic. Good for you. It doesn't taste nice, but will help you to rest.' Lady Campbell smiled. 'I have a boiled sweet for you to suck to take away the taste.'

Flora drank the dose and reached up for the sweet before the foul-tasting medicine could turn her stomach, make her sick. But such was her relief that she did not have to get out of bed that she closed her eyes for a few luxuriously drowsy seconds. Then she opened them again. 'Why are you doing this for me?'

'Andrew Stewart has been very much the Commander's protégé. He was brought up on the estate. His mother is an old family retainer. I'm speaking for my husband as well as myself when I tell you that we both feel responsible for any wrongdoing of Andrew's.'

'Andrew hasn't done wrong,' Flora said quietly. 'He wouldn't let the Commander or his mother down.'

'Then consider that you are being offered a helping hand.' Lady Campbell put a gentle hand on the counterpane but did not meet Flora's eyes. Instead she stared into the distance as she said, 'You do see that Mrs Stewart must be told first. She would not wish to be the subject of servants' gossip.'

Flora whispered, 'Please – tell her – I'm sorry ...'

147

'Then you tell nobody about the pregnancy, especially Nanny Taylor, who will look after you. Not yet.' Lady Campbell smoothed the sheet. 'And whatever you do, don't try to get out of bed. The medicine will make you unsteady.'

When Lady Campbell had left the room, Flora lay back against the pillows as warm tears rolled down her face and under her chin to soak into the cotton nightdress someone had put on her. All she could remember was falling, then Lady Campbell ringing for help and the woman who had served lunch lifting her on to a sofa – then nothing. Her limbs were heavy, the pain was less but she could not stop the tears that continued their relentless rolling down her cheeks. She had never been one for crying. Lately, everything brought her to the brink of tears and she could not help herself. Last week, in church, they had sung 'Eternal Father Strong to Save' and she'd blubbed into a handkerchief throughout the whole service, thinking of Andrew in peril on the sea. Everything scared her. The very word – 'pregnant' – terrified her. It was an ugly word. She didn't want to be pregnant. But she was – and she must tell Andrew. She'd write:

Dearest Andrew

I am at Ingersley. Please come and save me. Help me. I am expecting our baby. It was conceived under the weeping tree on the night we were married. I went to find your mother like you told me to do but she is in hospital. She has the flu and I have this terrible pain in my back. I collapsed outside. Lady Campbell is going to tell your mother about the baby. Please, please, Andrew you have got to come and get me. They will send me to a workhouse and the baby will be taken away. Nobody should do that to a girl – take her baby away.

Please. Help. I have nobody but you. I love you.

Flora.

The *Rutland* docked late at night under a magnificent sky, lit from the horizon to the zenith by the waving curtain, pearly green, amber and red, of the aurora borealis. With the engines closed down, the ship's company had been at the rails or standing on the dock, marvelling at the calm, the quiet, the lights and the sheer relief of a safe harbour after months of war. Gordon left the bridge and went ashore to put in a call to Ingersley.

Ruth answered. 'You have only just docked, darling?' She sounded pleased to hear him, and his mood lightened.

'I'll be home the day after tomorrow,' he said. 'Can't take my leave in the first wave.'

'No. Stay where you are. I'll be with you as soon as I can. I'll book into an hotel in Inverness.'

'Will you really? That's very good of you.' She must have missed him badly. 'I'll expect to hear from you tomorrow evening then.' Bemused, he put the receiver down.

Now, the following morning, with dawn breaking across the water, Gordon looked out from the bridge and saw that crew, sailors and half the company of Royal Marines the *Rutland* carried were crowded on deck, waiting at the rails for the bells to be piped before they could pour off the ship and make for the railway station, going home for three blessed days to family, wives and girlfriends. Only he, their captain, knew that they would be sailing for the Mediterranean as soon as the repairs were done. They would be gone for months. How many of them would see their loved ones again? The naval losses, conveyed to him with the sailing orders by coded wireless telegraphy message from the Admiralty, were grim. Three months into the war 114 ships had been sunk by U-boats.

Then, as he stood watching the men, he found himself staring in astonishment. Ruth was being escorted up the gangway by one of the senior officers. He blinked, then closed his eyes for a moment in case he was imagining it. He opened them. It *was* Ruth – Ruth, wearing a coat of jade green in the new wide-shoulder, swing-back style, over a matching costume, and both trimmed with black velvet at the stand-up collar and pockets. A black Cossack-style hat set off her golden hair, which swung with every movement and brought appreciative smiles and looks of admiration from the sailors and the Lieutenant-Commander who escorted her to him.

'How on earth did you get here so soon?' he asked once they were alone together in his cabin and he had given her a warm kiss. Then, smiling, 'You look wonderful.' It was good to have a wife waiting for him. He felt a surge of gratitude seeing her here before him. 'Let me look at you.'

149

Jade-green boots of suede with black fur cuffs could not conceal her long, slender legs that swished, silk on silk, as she returned his kiss. She did it lightly, brushing her lips gently across his before she took out a lace handkerchief to dab away traces of scarlet lipstick. Her arm was bandaged. He said, 'Your wrist? What have you done?'

'Nothing much. A slight sprain. It hasn't prevented me from driving.'

'You drove the Armstrong Siddeley all this way – to be with me?' He could scarcely believe it. His earlier gloomy mood was changing to one of gratitude and delight. 'You drove through the night, in this bitterly cold weather?'

'There was no snow. Patches of ice – but I was desperate for you, darling,' she said. He felt the familiar thrill of arousal and tried to draw her close but laughing she said, 'The Armstrong Siddeley is on the quay. Drive me to the hotel in Inverness. I can't wait ...'

'Give me an hour.' He wanted her now. Ruth knew the power of her sex appeal – he dared not imagine the pleasures to come or he would not be able to do his work. 'Have something to eat while I do what has to be done.'

Two hours later, with the hotel bedroom door locked and the 'Do Not Disturb' notice hanging from the handle, he took her in his arms and found her so gentle and loving and eager for his caresses that he could forget the war for a few minutes and forgive the demanding side of her nature – the side that had always wanted to dominate and have power over him. He needed her body.

Afterwards he lay with an arm protectively around her while she rested her head over his heart, her injured arm loose across her stomach. He had told her all he could tell – that he was going to be away from her for months, possibly as long as a year – and she had cried a little and clung to him and whispered words of undying love. He was grateful and glad to be loved. He smiled when she begged him to flee from the enemy, not put himself in any danger. He traced his finger over her face, along the clean lines of her jaw, to her delicate ear, and then ran his hand through the fair tousled hair. He said, 'Ruth, why can't we always be like this? You make me so very, very happy ...'

She smiled back at him, then eased herself into a sitting position so that he lay flat and she could look down at him. 'Gordon ...?'

'What?' He stretched contentedly and tried to pull her down on top of him. 'Come here ...'

'I didn't want to tell you before. I wasn't sure. I didn't want to disappoint you.'

'What are you talking about?'

'I'm having a baby. It was conceived on the last night you were ...'

His head lifted quickly, startled. 'Are you sure?' His face paled. 'Have you seen the doctor? Had it confirmed?'

'There's no need. I'm as certain as anyone, even a doctor, can be.'

He sat up. 'Oh, Ruth!' A flush of excitement and pride spread across his face even as he knew enormous fear – for Ruth, for his baby. He could not marshal his thoughts. He was going to be a father. After all this time, he was going to be a father. He held her close and kissed her gently, on the forehead, the cheeks, the throat. 'Should we have made love? Won't it disturb the baby?'

She pushed him back a little way, reached for her nightgown and carefully slipped it on. 'It won't do any harm at this stage.' She smiled and added, 'Besides, if I were not already pregnant, I would certainly be after this morning.'

'No. No. Don't!' He hated it when she spoke that way. It was coarse.

'I was teasing,' she assured him. 'But in another couple of weeks I shall have to take care.' She swung her legs over the side of the bed and felt for her bedroom slippers with a long, delicate foot while he watched, fascinated. She turned and said gently, 'I didn't tell you before because I needed your love. Just as much as you needed me.'

Gordon kissed her then started to dress as elation lifted through him. He had fathered a child. A son, perhaps – but what did it matter? A girl or a boy. His girl or boy. He turned to Ruth, who was now fully dressed and looked as chic and calm as any mannequin. He said, 'There are no signs. You are sure?'

'I am very healthy, darling. It is only the size of ...' She made a small space between her left thumb and forefinger and smiled at him.

He must not get over-anxious or excited. He'd been down this path before. He said, 'You will take great care? Your sister—'

'Elizabeth lost all of hers. I'll be careful. Nanny will look after me.'

'Nanny! Oh, goodness. Have you told her?'

'No. I wanted you to be the first to know,' she said. 'Besides, I hardly see her these days. She delivers babies, drives an ambulance and has volunteered her services as relief district nurse,' Ruth said. 'But this gives us a reason to keep the Armstrong Siddeley. We also get a bigger petrol ration.'

'We'll tell Nanny when we get home.' He would not have been able to contain himself if he'd been Ruth. But perhaps Ruth was a little afraid. He said, 'You will see a new side to Nanny once she has a baby to care for. She will overrule everyone.' He smiled, remembering Nanny, overprotective, like a mother hen. 'The baby always comes first with Nanny. Will you mind?'

'I'll probably be glad,' she laughed.

'Where will you go for the birth?' She must not take any risks. She should go to a cottage hospital in the Borders.

'Nanny will deliver it at Ingersley. I'll be perfectly all right there,' she said. 'It has been the birthplace of the Campbell family for generations.'

Gordon could barely keep still. He wanted to pace the room, to run outside and shout it from the rooftops. 'We can stay here overnight. I'll drive you back to Ingersley tomorrow and return the day after.'

'Darling?' She came towards him with arms outstretched. 'I want to stay with you here until you sail.'

This was so unlike her normal demanding behaviour that Gordon was taken aback. 'But the drive? You hate driving. And in your condition ...'

She put an arm around his waist, clutched tight and whispered in her new, passive manner, 'I won't go home, Gordon. I am perfectly capable of driving myself back when you are gone. I shall take the journey slowly.'

He placed his hands on her shoulders and buried his face in her hair. 'Oh, Ruth ... Oh, Ruth!'

What once he had thought of as a calculating expression in the back of her eyes today he saw as concern for him as she asked, 'You won't miss Ingersley if you don't see it this leave?'

'No. Not with you here.'

'You promise you won't think of selling? You will want your son to have an inheritance?'

He felt tears pricking the back of his eyes. 'Of course I do. I shall work hard to save the estate.' He felt her relax, with a great outrush of breath like a sigh of contentment. He was so lucky. So very lucky. He said, 'Speaking of Ingersley, darling, young Andrew Stewart is going to officer training at Portsmouth. He's done us all proud.'

He felt her stiffen then suddenly pull away to say, 'How long for? Where is he now?' in a hard, shrill voice.

'Aren't you proud of him?' he asked, and when she repeated her question, 'The course normally lasts six months. These days it could be as short as five weeks—'

She interrupted him. 'But where is he?'

'I saw him on deck when you arrived. He has a weekend leave, forty-eight hours, then he has to report to Portsmouth.'

'So he won't be coming back to the *Rutland*?'

'No. He will be given another posting. They don't return new officers to ships where their old shipmates are still serving as lower ranks.' He smiled. She did not normally show any interest in the boy he had guided. 'His mother will be as proud of him as I am.'

'I delivered a letter for Andrew,' she said. 'I left it at the office. It will be given to him? Do they ever make mistakes?'

He pulled her close and kissed her again. 'You are becoming very maternal, dear. Worrying about young Andrew Stewart. He'd have been given his mail when he collected his rail warrants. He's a brave and courageous sailor. He will make a fine officer.'

The 9.30 train, crowded with sailors, had taken five hours to travel from Inverness to Edinburgh with delays all along the way. But at last it was pulling in to the capital. 'See any signs of battle?' Andrew asked Greg as he dragged his kit bag off the luggage rack.

Greg opened the compartment door and went ahead into the

corridor. 'No. Auld Reekie's just the same as every place we've passed through,' he called over his shoulder. 'No wonder they call it the Phoney War.'

'It's all happening at sea, then.' Andrew came to stand beside Greg as the train entered the tunnel. 'And you'll be back in the thick of it ...'

Greg hauled his kit bag up on to his shoulder. 'Staying the night at my place?'

'Yes. I'll come up with you now, to dump this.' Andrew lifted his case. His fore and aft peaked cap tipped forward. He grinned and put it straight. At Invergordon he'd been kitted out in petty officer's uniform and given a green ATB bag for his luggage. He had what was left of today free. Tomorrow he would travel down to Portsmouth to join the course, which started on Monday morning. 'I'll be late back tonight,' he said as the train came to a stop at Waverley station.

Greg leaned out of the window and unlatched the door. 'So will I,' he laughed. 'But I have three nights. You've only one.'

Andrew followed him down the platform. And now they saw the difference. It was still light outside but here, where the glass roof that covered the great station had been covered and protected, it was almost dark, lit only by flickering lamps which created a pool of light here and there, briefly revealing the faces of those who searched for friends or family in the steamy, sooty gloom. There was a bank of sandbags in front of the waiting room and ticket office. Greg went striding ahead with only the round naval cap to distinguish him from the crowd. The station clock was lit and showed the time to be 2.30.

Greg stopped and said, 'I'll take your kit. Meet me in the Black Bull at nine o'clock tonight.' He slapped Andrew hard on the shoulder. 'Make the most of it. You might not see her again for a while.'

Andrew returned the comradely punch, waved Greg off then found his way to the WVS canteen, where uniformed lady volunteers served the servicemen and women who were joshing and hailing complete strangers like long-lost friends. He queued for tea, which he took to a corner table, and there, ignoring the sailors who shared the table with him, he took out the only letter that had been waiting for him at the regulating office in Invergordon. He opened it, flattened it on the table and saw that it had been written by, of all people, the woman he so disliked, the new Lady Campbell. He read: *Please inform Leading Stoker Andrew Stewart that his mother is at present a patient in the Morningside Nursing Home.* After this came the address and, *Mrs Stewart will be convalescing for the next few weeks after a severe attack of influenza. Please inform Leading Stoker Andrew Stewart that it is unnecessary for him to make the journey to Ingersley.*

This last sentence was both odd and superfluous; Ingersley was the last place he'd want to be unless Ma was there. He drank the tea quickly and went out to the telephone kiosk, where he put in a call to Mr Davidson's house. He had been unable to get through at nine o'clock this morning. Now he drummed his fingers on the black metal coin box while he waited. There was no reply. He pressed button B, got his money back and tried again. Still no reply.

'Blast!' he said under his breath to cover his anxiety with anger. 'Where are they?' They could be at some church thing, or rehearsing. But why had she not written?

He left the gloomy station and stepped out into daylight and the freezing air of a January day. He ran up the ancient stone steps that led, wide and steep, to Princes Street, where he caught a tram to the Morningside convalescent hospital. There, he found Ma in a three-bedded ward on the third floor, sitting propped up, tucking into a plate of ham and chips. She looked thin and pale, but was full of good humour.

'Andrew!' she cried in delight. 'You're an officer.'

'Not yet, Ma.' He kissed her. 'Acting petty officer. But I'm going for a commission!' and while he stole chips and bread and butter from her tray he told her all about the forthcoming months in Portsmouth. 'I'll probably get a week's leave when it's over,' he said as he swilled down a cup of tea. A nurse appeared bringing another tea tray, for himself.

'Ta!' He smiled at her and saw a pink blush come to her face. Then he said to his ma, 'So. Tell me all about it. How long have you been here in all this luxury?'

'Three days,' she said. 'It *is* luxury.'

'Who's paying for it?'

'Lady Campbell.'

'She's had a change of heart then,' he said. Ruth Bickerstaffe had never done a good deed in her life, in Andrew's opinion. There must be a reason for this uncharacteristic act. 'When do you go back?' he asked, and followed it quickly with, 'I don't want you to go back. Leave Ingersley if it's making you ill.'

'Lady Campbell came down to the ward to see me.'

'Ward?'

'At Ingersley. It's a hospital.'

'Right. I remember.' He said, 'You must have been very ill.'

Ma had gone even paler. She closed her eyes for a few seconds then leaned back against the pillows to get her second wind before continuing: 'Lady Campbell came down to see me in the ward – ten beds – that used to be the drawing room. She said, "Mrs Stewart, influenza is a serious illness, ye ken." I said, "But wee Bessie's gone doon. How can ye manage?" She said, "Your health is mair important, Mrs Stewart! Besides, we are at war. We all have to go short of something, ye ken."'

Andrew grinned at Ma's attempt at a cut-glass accent but said, 'Some hope of her going without anything.'

Ma's face was all alive, remembering. She told him not to be so cynical, then she was off again, retelling what she saw as her moment of glory. 'It was a surprise. She said, "I've been forced out of my ain hame, Mrs Stewart. I must needs look after myself under vairry cramped conditions. You ken that ladies with no children will be obliged to work? We cannae justify having servants when the country needs all the workers it can get."' Here Ma heaved herself up high against the pillows. '"We must make sacrifices. I must do for myself." I said, "What do you want me to sacrifice, Lady Campbell?" And she said, "I shall find you a position, Mrs Stewart. Until the war is over. I know many places that are looking for lady cooks – and paying vairry good wages, too. I shall make certain that your conditions and accommodation are equal to Ingersley."'

Andrew gave a dry laugh. 'They'll have to be a damn sight better, Ma – or I'll see her and tell her ...'

'You'll do nae such thing,' Ma said, and went on, 'She said, "I will close the South Lodge. Your home will be waiting for you

156

when this terrible war is over."' Ma smiled. 'She's on the billet-ing committee. She'll keep our house off the list, I'm sure of it.' A look of worry crossed her face briefly. 'What do you think?'

'She's up to something. I'm sure it's nothing trivial,' Andrew said.

'She's going to visit me here when she has something fixed up. And Andrew ...?'

'What?'

There was a look of pride on Ma's face as she waited a few seconds before announcing, 'She paid me off handsomely. A hundred pounds, cash – and I'll be getting twice as much in wages. Four pounds seventeen and six a week if I get into one of the good army billets.'

Andrew dared not upset her. 'She's up to no good, Ma. But it can't affect us and I'm glad you're getting out of it. Take no notice of what she suggests. I want you to find a good house. I'll pay the rent. Expense no object.' He implored her, 'Don't use your own money. I'll be on twenty-four pounds a month. And on my next leave, Flora and I are getting married!'

Ma's face split into an enormous smile. 'Did she say yes?'

'Aye.' He picked up her hand and whispered so only she could hear, 'We both want children and a happy home. We want you to live with us, in Edinburgh.'

'Och! Not many lasses want their mother-in-law—'

'Flora hasn't got anyone else in the world but you and me, Ma,' he said. 'I need to know you are looking after one another – and waiting for me to come home.'

He gave her his new address in Portsmouth and left the hospital to take a tram to Portobello. It was growing dark by 4.30, and the buses and trams ground slowly up Lothian Road. Andrew felt a quick thrill of recognition sweep through him when he made out the frozen white branches of the weeping tree in the graveyard under the castle. The tram turned the corner and the dynamo picked up pitch and speed as they went faster towards the East End of Princes Street. He pressed his face to the window to see where they were, but the monuments on Princes Street had either been taken down or sandbagged into neutrality, for he could not pick out one recognisable feature as they trundled on, leaving Princes Street for the pitch blackness of the road to Portobello. It seemed odd, not seeing

157

people about. Houses and shop windows were blacked out. Here and there he saw a faint flicker of light where a lone pedestrian flashed a pencil torch beam for a few seconds while he crossed a road or turned into a close. It was, as Flora had told him in her letters, dangerous to be out at night. The tram's speed could not have been more than fifteen miles per hour, for it was not until an hour later, at nearly six o'clock, that he got off at the power station in Portobello.

He walked along the deathly cold esplanade, where there was reflected light from the moon over the water. Then he was there – and knocking anxiously at Mr Davidson's door.

There was no sound – no reply to his knock. His anxiety grew. He tried the back gate. It was bolted. He climbed the wall and dropped six feet down into the back yard. The house was still. He put a bare hand on the window pane to melt the ice, and when he had cleared a patch he saw that the blackout curtains were not pulled and no fire glowed in the kitchen.

Alarmed, he climbed the wall again and headed towards St Philip's church. That, too, was closed but he could hear someone moving in the church hall. He rattled the door. A man who must be the old verger drew back the bolt and ushered him inside quickly so as not to show a chink of light. The place was deserted. Andrew asked, 'Do you know where I'll find the organist, Mr Davidson?'

'He was not at church last week,' the verger said. 'We are having to make do with the Sunday school pianist.'

'What about Flora? The girl who keeps house?'

'Nobody's seen her. They say she's left. That's why he can't get to church.'

Left? How could she just leave? Where had she gone? She had nobody. Worry was gnawing at him as he went back to the house. Stamping his feet, clapping his hands together to warm them, he waited – but not for another half-hour did he remember Flora's mentioning the woman next door, who took an inordinate interest in her movements.

In the blackout it was impossible to know if anyone was at home, but smoke was drifting thinly from the next door's chimney. He knocked hard before opening the letter-box flap and peering in. He saw an elderly woman coming towards the door.

'Who is it?' came her harsh voice.

'Andrew Stewart. I'm looking for Mr Davidson.'

The bolt was drawn. The door opened a little way and he rushed to say, 'I'm looking for Flora – my sister. She's nowhere to be found.'

She opened the door further and allowed him into the hall, then pulled a curtain across the door he'd come through and switched on a light, which showed her to be considerably older than Mr Davidson. A bad-tempered look was etched on her thin, lined face. 'You may well ask where Mr Davidson is,' she said. 'That sister of yours let him down, badly. Going around with a painted face.'

'That's enough!' Andrew said. He would not stand and listen to this. 'Flora would not upset Mr Davidson.'

'Then why wouldn't she let him know where she'd gone?' the woman snapped back. 'The first thing he knew was that she'd fallen on the ice and had been taken to hospital. A nurse came round. Then a different woman came by the next day to collect her belongings.'

'She fell? Which hospital?' He'd wasted all this time. He could have gone to half a dozen hospitals.

'I don't know. The woman didn't say.'

'Who was this woman? A nurse, you say?'

'I never saw her. She told Mr Davidson that Flora wasn't badly hurt, but the poor man was worried sick. And he was in a dreadful state the next day when the other woman came and asked for the girl's clothes and said she wouldn't be back.'

'How long ago?'

'About ten days.'

Flora had not written for at least three weeks.

'No explanation! The poor man has gone to live with his sister in Kelso. He'll not be back, I shouldn't wonder.'

Andrew was wasting his time talking to her. There was nothing for it – he'd have to ask Greg to spend a day of his leave making enquiries in every hospital in the area, as well as the shops and munitions factory here in Portobello. Meanwhile he must hope she'd written to him. The Royal Navy would send mail on wherever he was. His service number, not the name of the ship, ensured it.

Chapter Nine

In the attic room she had not left since she came to Ingersley, Flora was in bed when she heard, from outside, the slam of the door of the Armstrong Siddeley. It was early evening and Lady Campbell had told Nanny by telephone yesterday that she would leave Invergordon early so as to arrive back at Ingersley before dark. She had made it.

Flora's mouth went dry while she waited for news of Andrew. Lady Campbell was not a woman to beat about the bush, as Flora had learned on her second day here, when Lady Campbell reported back to her Mrs Stewart's horror at being told about Andrew's wrongdoing. It made no difference that Flora cried and protested that she was as much to blame as Andrew. Lady Campbell replied, 'You were an under-age child. Andrew Stewart was committing a criminal offence. No court in the country would believe that he was not aware of it.'

When Flora tearfully repeated that Andrew had told her to go to his ma if she needed anything, Lady Campbell said, 'Mrs Stewart has been transferred to a convalescent home. But she says she will not return here where she and her son are under a cloud of shame.'

Now, Flora thought, Lady Campbell would want to rest and eat before she came to her, and she jumped when, barely five minutes later, Lady Campbell came in, still wearing her driving coat and scarf.

Flora heaved herself up the bed and blurted out, 'Did you see Andrew? Did you give him my letter?'

Lady Campbell dropped on to the side of the bed and gripped Flora's hand. 'Did Andrew come to see you?' she asked eagerly, as if her life depended upon it. Her eyes were bright.

'No,' Flora replied, hesitantly.

'You have had no word – no contact?'

'No.' Flora held her breath.

'My dear.' Lady Campbell's face grew calm. She bit her lip, looked away for a second, then, 'I don't know how to tell you this.'

Flora knew her own face was pale because her mouth was stiff and numb and she could barely speak. 'You gave him my letter?'

'I left it at the office. He would have got it before he left the ship.' Lady Campbell stood up and took off her sheepskin coat. 'What did you say in the letter?'

For ever afterwards Flora would associate the thick, sweet smell of sheepskin with the helplessness and vulnerability she felt as she waited a few moments before finding the strength to say, in a voice that was little more than a whisper, 'I told him about the baby – begged him to come.'

Lady Campbell dropped on to the bed. 'He knew where to find you. And I left your new address with Mr Davidson.' She pursed her lips and frowned. 'I'm sorry, Flora. Andrew Stewart has left you to your fate.'

Flora let herself fall back against the pillows as the awful truth swept over her and Lady Campbell continued to spell out to her how dire was the trouble she was in.

After a few moments spent observing her, Lady Campbell said, 'I had to tell my husband, the Commander. You do realise that I had to do this?'

Flora pulled herself upright again, jumping with the pain that grew worse by the day. 'What did he say?'

'I don't think he believed it of Andrew. Andrew has been sent on an officer training scheme on my husband's recommendation. He would certainly not have promoted a man who had any civil action pending.'

'Where is Andrew?'

'I don't know. He is no longer a member of the *Rutland*'s crew. I don't have his new address. I have no way of contacting him.' Lady Campbell put a hand to her brow, gave a slight shake of the head and said, 'I'm sorry, my dear. I have left no stone unturned. I asked the regulating officer to tell him that you needed to see him. I said it was urgent, that you were injured.' Here Lady Campbell's pretty brows drew together. Again she took Flora's hand and held it fast in hers. 'I will leave you alone if you like.'

'No. Don't go.' Flora was all alone now – there was nowhere for her to go. She had to force out her words: 'What can I do?'

'I have been thinking of little else these last few days. I could send you away, far away, to have your baby, and when it is all over and the child has been put up for adoption you could return and make a new life for yourself.' Ruth affected a troubled look as she met Flora's stricken gaze. She pressed Flora's hand and said softly, 'You are not the first young woman to be betrayed, you know. It happens every day and to girls of all classes.' She hesitated, saw the girl's eyes fill with tears and went on, 'Their babies, if healthy and from respectable stock, will be found good homes. The girls then return and put the whole affair behind them. Nobody need know.'

Ruth waited for a few seconds for a reply, but Flora had closed her eyes, and as the desperation of her position sank in, her tears dried on her pale cheeks.

Ruth patted her hand. 'I'll help you through it.' It was best to leave it at this. Soon the girl would clutch at any suggestion that offered a ray of hope. She tiptoed out of the room and went in search of Nanny.

Nanny was in the kitchenette, stirring a pot of soup that was simmering on the solid electric plate of the new modern cooker. Ruth came to stand beside her, looked over Nanny's shoulder and sniffed appreciatively. 'Did you make it yourself, Nanny?' she asked. 'I didn't know you could cook.'

'Just simple dishes. Soups and stews – nursery food.' Nanny pulled off the half-apron she wore over her grey dress. She tied the strings and hung it over the towel hook. 'Leek, potato and celery. Afterwards a beef stew with dumplings and carrots. It's what that poor girl needs to get her strength up – or she won't be on her feet before the baby's born.'

So, Flora had told Nanny everything while she was in Invergordon. Ruth said, 'You know all about it, then?'

'Yes. I think it's wonderful that you are looking after the

162

poor lass.' Nanny fetched a tray from inside the new kitchen cabinet, which had little sections for everything a cook might need. She placed the tray on the pull-down flap and set it with a cloth and cutlery and the small silver salt and pepper pots. 'I've lost all regard for Mrs Stewart. She should have taken the girl in.'

'Mrs Stewart has gone to a convalescent home,' Ruth said as she went to warm herself at the two-bar electric fire that the hospital had lent to them.

Nanny was indignant. 'And by hired car. She didn't even wait for the ambulance. She isn't coming back. Flora told me.'

Ruth allowed Nanny to work herself up into a state of indignation about Mrs Stewart whilst she set the table. Ruth had to do this every day now that Mrs Stewart was no longer here and Bessie was ill. But it was an enjoyable task. The white enamel-top table had been a gift from either the Ministry or the hospital itself. Laid with a velvet undercover and then an embroidered cloth it made an acceptable dining table for one or two and gave Ruth a taste of the simple pleasures of the poor, who had the blessings of a life without servants.

While Nanny set Flora's tray to her satisfaction and went into her mother hen routine, practically clucking over the dish of stew she had taken from the oven, Ruth said, 'I want to talk to you about Flora, Nanny.'

'Yes ...' Nanny set the dish on the top of the stove, peered inside, stirred it and put it back in the oven before coming to sit at the table.

'Gordon and I have come to a decision about the baby.'

'You have told Gordon? Was that wise? We don't want to give him home worries as well as—' Nanny's eyebrows shot up.

'Nanny. Listen!' Ruth tapped slowly on the cloth with the handle of a table knife. 'We all know that there is no help for a girl like Flora. She has nobody to turn to, and though there are places other than the workhouse hospitals, her child will have to be adopted or spend a lifetime in a home.'

'Exactly. That's why I'd like to see Mrs Stewart. Tell her a few home truths.'

'Nanny!' Ruth stopped her before she could say more. 'Gordon and I are willing to adopt the child.'

There was a long silence. Nanny looked at first disbelieving then puzzled, but she watched and listened carefully as Ruth said slowly and calmly, 'We are going to adopt the baby with the utmost secrecy. We all know that it is best for an adopted child never to learn the truth. Such children suffer dreadfully, knowing their true parentage – that their mothers were deserted, unmarried women of feeble morals.'

At this Nanny rose to Flora's defence. 'There are unfortunates, Ruth. Flora is not one of those children of low moral fibre ...' she said.

They had evidently established a rapport in Ruth's absence. Ruth must choose her words with care. 'Precisely. Gordon and I – and you, Nanny – will know where the child came from; the stock! We will have no fears that the child could turn out to be a thief or an imbecile. This is more than most adoptive parents can know—'

Nanny came in fast, interrupting her. 'A child is a child. An adoptive one is no less likely to turn out badly if it has a good home.' She was incredulous. 'You say Gordon suggested this? As soon as he heard about it?'

'Of course.' Ruth looked away. Nanny had an uncanny knack of ferreting out the truth.

Nanny said, 'But they are on the same ship. They docked at the same time and received their mail when they arrived. How could Gordon have known that Andrew would not immediately come home to Flora and shoulder his responsibilities?'

Ruth had not foreseen this. Blood rushed to her head before the quick clarity of thought that always came to her rescue. 'Gordon does not confide *everything* in me, Nanny. He is a man of decision. When I gave him the news he told me to leave the ship for a couple of hours to rest and to eat – I'd driven all that way ...'

'Did he ask Andrew for an explanation when you were gone?' Nanny asked.

Ruth paused for a second or two, then, 'I can only assume so. And I can only assume that Andrew denied it and Gordon believed him.'

Nanny's face fell. 'So, who to believe – Flora or Andrew?' she said. 'But if Gordon had any doubt, I can't think why he'd suggest a secret adoption.'

'I can,' Ruth said quietly. 'Gordon has always wanted a child. A child is something to live for, especially in times of danger.' She stood up, went to the corner cupboard and took out a bottle of claret which she had placed there earlier. She brought it to the table and put it front of Nanny. 'Can you uncork it, Nanny?' she said and a Machiavellian excitement thrilled the pit of her stomach as she saw the relief on Nanny's face. 'I think we both need a little sustenance.' She gave a small, tight smile to cover the growing sense of her own power of control. Once Nanny was sure she was doing it for Gordon, it would be easy.

Nanny fished a corkscrew out of the drawer and expertly withdrew the cork as she said, 'But even if Flora agrees, how are you going to conceal it? It is not easy to hide a young pregnant woman.' She quickly found two wine glasses and poured.

Ruth smiled, watching her. She would only have a sip or two of wine and Nanny would finish the bottle. If Nanny went to Flora this evening certain that this was the best course for everyone, then the first hurdle was crossed. Ruth sipped her wine and put the glass down. 'It will all depend upon Flora's co-operation,' she said. 'She must be convinced that this is her best course of action.'

'How and where—?' Nanny took a long draught from her glass.

Ruth looked down at her hands for a second, then up with a pleading look at Nanny. 'Nanny, dear, it's a lot to ask of you ...' She took a deep breath and bit her lip. '... but would you take Flora in until the birth? Deliver the baby at Ivy Lodge?'

'Yes. But ...'

'Keep your apartments here, of course. Go back and forth as normal. I will take Bessie on as nursemaid and you can teach her ...'

'You don't want to keep Flora here?' Nanny sounded doubtful. Ruth came back firmly, 'No. As soon as she can be moved you will drive her to Ivy Lodge. It would be too distressing for all of us if she were to remain here.'

Nanny said lamely, 'Ivy Lodge is off the beaten track. There is no public transport. Flora will be house-bound.'

Ruth was safe now. 'Nanny! Flora is not going to be fit to go anywhere. The doctor says she will be unable to walk far, in fact bed-ridden very soon. Far better for her to be under your wing. An expectant mother needs rest, peace and quiet.'

'I know, but . . .' Nanny said.

'You will deliver the baby at Ivy Lodge. As soon as the child is born, you will bring it to me.'

Nanny looked puzzled. She took a quick sip of wine. 'How will you explain the arrival of an adopted baby in the dead of night?'

Ruth sighed. 'Gordon and I are not going to explain. We will accept the child as ours from the moment of its birth.'

'How?'

'If all goes smoothly, then a few weeks before the birth I shall let it be known that I am expecting a child. I will say that I was not even aware of my condition.'

Nanny's eyes flew wide open. 'You are going to feign a pregnancy to deceive the staff? But the doctor—?'

'I'm perfectly healthy. You are a qualified nurse and midwife.'

Nanny said as she topped up her glass, 'I will do anything for Gordon, but I'm amazed he's asked you to do this when you are newly married and with every prospect of having your own children.'

Ruth snapped, 'Nanny! What impertinence!' then, to mollify her, 'Gordon will have the child he's always hoped for – and nobody will know it is not his own. We have to keep it secret – I'm sure you can understand that.'

'What about registering the birth?'

Ruth sighed. 'I will register the baby as my own, Nanny.'

Nanny said, 'What about Flora?'

'As soon as the baby is handed over she will be given a hundred pounds to leave the estate and make a fresh start. A long, long way from here. She cannot come back to this area,' Ruth said.

'But . . .'

'But nothing!' Ruth snapped. 'If she has money she will be able to put it all behind her. She may marry in a few years' time. Her husband need never know. It happens all the time, you know that. How many unmarried women have you delivered? Some of the most respectable women you will ever meet have their little secrets.'

166

'I was going to say that Gordon is a magistrate. He must know that he is breaking the law in giving false information on the birth certificate. That's all.' Nanny drained her glass and put it down. 'I'd better see if the potatoes are done,' she said. She put on her apron, went to the stove, opened the door and took out a tray of golden-brown crispy roast potatoes. 'Done to perfection,' she said. 'I'll take Flora's tray up before I put ours out.'

'Don't say anything of this to Flora until you are sure yourself, Nanny,' Ruth said. 'We don't want to give her false hope. For unless it is done this way – then it is simply not going to happen.'

'I'll speak to her later,' Nanny replied, glancing at the half-empty bottle of claret as she took Flora's tray over to the stove and began to ladle soup into her bowl. 'I'll mull it over, over dinner.'

'Anything I can do?' Ruth asked, as if she had not given another thought to Flora. She was hungry after all the effort of the last few days, when she had barely touched food. 'Do you think we could manage another bottle between us, Nanny? Or perhaps a small brandy?'

Five weeks had passed since Flora had moved in to Ivy Lodge with Nanny, and there, the arrangement was working well. There was only one other delivery scheduled for Ivy Lodge. It was for next week and the girl would be company for Flora. Nanny slept at Ivy Lodge and spent her days doing her nursing rounds, or, as today, at Ingersley, where she was busy turning one of the attic rooms into a nursery.

Ruth was obliged to show willing and offer help, and when Nanny said, 'When I first came the whole attic floor was the nursery wing,' she replied, 'Yes, Nanny. And it looks as if everything – clothes, toys, cots, furniture – has been stored up here.' She glanced idly round the box room. 'This top floor can hardly be classed as an attic, though.' There were seven small rooms, each with its own box room, as well as a bathroom, landing and four large, sloping-ceilinged bedrooms for the family's use.

Nanny opened the cupboard and took out crib bedding and frilled white drapery which every spring had been laundered, wrapped in tissue paper and put away again, waiting for the first Campbell baby since Gordon to use them. She held them to her cheek and buried her nose in the folds of linen. 'I'm sure I can still trace the scent of Gordon, dear,' she said.

Ruth turned her back and went to the window, raising alarm signals in Nanny, who had been trying for weeks to get Ruth involved in the preparations. It was not the first time that Ruth had turned her back, and Nanny was becoming worried. Ruth had not yet been to see Flora. Now she said sharply, 'I'm worried about your commitment to this adoption, Ruth. I do wish you would show more interest.'

Ruth still had her back to Nanny as she replied in a bored voice, 'I am interested. I have started to mention heartburn and sickness to everyone. I've seen a knowing look on Lucy Hamilton's face. It's a wonder she hasn't said anything to you.' She stood on tiptoe the better to see something outside.

She obviously wanted to leave to Nanny all the counting and sorting of the mounting piles of small garments. Ruth had not done a single stitch whereas Nanny, in such spare moments as she had, cut out, sewed and embroidered Viyella nightdresses and fine linen pillowcases and sleep suits. It was as if Ruth found the whole business of motherhood a bore.

Ruth continued, 'Everyone will have guessed by now. In fact I intend to announce it very soon. We can't hide all these preparations from servants. But when – what exactly shall I say? When is the baby due?'

Nanny was losing patience. She said, 'We can't be sure of the birth date. Babies come when they please.'

'All right,' Ruth drawled. 'I'll try to contain myself until I have the child in my possession.'

Now Nanny warned her: 'You are expecting a lot of Flora. Many girls change their minds at the last minute.'

At last Ruth turned round. Her face had gone pale with fury. 'Is this what she says? How dare she threaten me ...?'

Nanny would not be intimidated. 'It's not what she says. But I know young mothers well enough to say that Flora *may* change her mind.' Nanny had seen in Flora nothing but gratitude, but she had a growing sense of the wrongness of the arrangement that had seemed expedient a few weeks before. Now she said, 'Why don't you visit her? Assure her that her child will be better off as a Campbell.'

Ruth seemed to think that because she willed it, Flora would fall in with her plans. But she changed her tone, softened and said, 'You know I can't risk that. And I can't have her here. It would be impossible.' She picked up a small heap of vests and, handling them carefully, took them to the nursery cupboard. 'I'm so wound up, Nanny. I'll probably go into labour before Flora does.'

Nanny said gently, 'I think we should have a contingency plan for when the baby is born.'

But Ruth was not going to give an inch. 'The contingency plan is that Flora will be given a hundred pounds and told to leave the area. What more could she expect?'

'Adoption societies by law must give a mother six weeks to decide.'

'Once the baby is mine, there is no proof that Flora ever had a child and I did not,' Ruth said. 'I would deny everything, Nanny.'

'There are certain physical changes,' Nanny reminded her.

'All right! I don't want to listen to the gory details of child-bearing. How soon after the birth would a woman be fit to travel?'

When Ruth was in this mood, there was no point in talking things over. Nanny said, 'Two weeks if everything runs smoothly.'

'Tch! Chinese women have them in the paddy fields and carry on with their work,' Ruth said. 'I'll give her two days.'

'What?'

'Or there will be no money. And I will have her turned off the estate.'

'I hope you are joking,' Nanny said.

'Then make sure she goes far, far away, Nanny,' Ruth said as she walked out of the little attic room.

Nanny put on the nursery table the little heap of clothes she would inspect carefully for any broken threads or missing ribbons or buttons. She prayed that Ruth was behaving in this manner because she was in a high state of nerves about the whole business – and she tried to convince herself that many a mother did not experience the deep bond between herself and her baby until it was born.

In the middle of her reverie, before she could begin to

inspect the baby clothes, there came the now-familiar sounds of the aeroplanes from the 602 Spitfire squadron at Drem, flying overhead. There must be another German attack on shipping and the docks on the Forth. Nanny was not blasé, but the attacks were a daily occurrence and her heart no longer came up into her throat at the sound. These were much louder than usual, though – lower and fast approaching. She went to the window and now her heart did leap into her throat. In that freezing February weather a German Heinkel 111 was coming towards the house, roaring above the park, the sunlight flashing off the windscreen, thick smoke pouring from a port engine. It was only a few yards above the winter-bare branches of the elms, heading straight for Ingersley. The noise was deafening. Above and behind it, pursuing it to the death, shooting flaming tracers of fire, came a Spitfire, its powerful engine whine recognisable – as familiar now to everyone in the area as were the sounds of the Brent geese that were taking to the air in a clumsy panic ahead of the fighter planes. Nanny instinctively ducked and put her arms over her head. The Heinkel cleared the roof. Nanny ran across to her own bedroom and saw the enemy plane going down in the direction of Ivy Lodge on the farthest reach of Ingersley land. Then both hunter and hunted disappeared from view. There was no explosion.

The nursery preparations could wait – Flora's baby was not due until mid-May. But she was a mere child of sixteen who had to live in hiding, and it was not right. Nanny flew like a youngster down the stairs to their living floor, put on her outdoor things and went down again to the hospital's casualty area. She was needed.

A nursing sister said, 'The ambulance has gone. A doctor and two nurses are with them. There's no need for you to turn out.'

Nanny said, 'Thank you. But I'm going that way anyway. If they need extra help, I'll offer.' Flora needed her. Though she was improving under Nanny's supervision, she still suffered pain in her back from the pressure of her enlarging abdomen. Nanny would have called in a doctor but Ruth said, 'No! Not unless she is really ill. Then I'll have her sent to one of the big maternity hospitals in Edinburgh.'

Nanny hurried to the front of the house, where the

Armstrong Siddeley stood. The frozen gravel crunched like broken glass under her sensible Gibson shoes. She reached the car, pushed down the icy door handle and climbed in. Then she surprised herself by calling out, 'Dash it!' when the motor coughed wearily and refused to turn. 'Dash again!' she said as she got out, dragging the starting handle from behind the seat. She rammed it into place under the radiator. She was used to it now – a hard down-stroke, keeping her thumb curled alongside her fingers, then let go as the handle swung up. The engine started at once. Nanny withdrew the handle and climbed back in, slammed the door and headed off towards the north entrance.

Lucy Hamilton was at the farmhouse gate, staring down the road. She was carrying her pregnancy well. Only a slight thickening at her waist and a widening of her hips and bottom showed her five months. Looking neat and fit in her maternity wear, she waved Nanny down and called out, 'I want to see what's going on. Can I come with you, Nanny?'

Nanny had not realised when this secret adoption was first put to her just how many lies she would have to tell, but Lucy was not to know – nobody was to know – anything at all about the connection between the Campbells and Flora. Nanny was always out and about in the area, with ten expectant mothers to attend to. Professional etiquette and a patient's confidentiality forbade her from talking about her patients so she wound down the window and said to Lucy, 'I'm afraid not, dear ...' and with a quick wave of her hand drove off at speed through the gates, to the road and the four-mile journey to the cottage.

A mile further on, two cars were stopped at a police post. Nanny crept slowly forward until she was level with the official – a man she had not seen before. An army of new officials had been brought in since East Lothian was designated an exclusion zone because of the number of operational airfields, camps and military installations.

'Identity card?' the officer said.

She handed it over. He scrutinised it. 'Where are you going?'

'I'm a nurse,' she said. 'I have patients to see. Do you need any more details?'

He said, 'No. We're only stopping people from crowding

into the area. The police are up there already, and the air force are on their way.'

She covered the last two miles quickly while pondering the problem of whisking the baby up to Ingersley if the country lanes as well as main roads were to have road blocks and inquisitive officials. So far they had been allowed to move around freely within the zone. Leaving the area was no problem – it was the incoming people who were checked.

Nanny drove down the rough road to Ivy Lodge, a two-storey house built of local sandstone and set well back from a road so narrow and deeply rutted it was impossible to travel by horse and cart. It was even difficult on foot, for it was a mile from the nearest paved road. Nanny knew every inch of it, though, and her wheels went spinning over the frozen puddles without once skidding off the track.

She found the house unusually quiet. Often she would hear Flora singing now that her difficult pregnancy was being carefully managed. She had a beautiful voice and would sit at the piano for hours, singing and trying to learn the accompaniment. Flora was a sweet and good girl.

In the kitchen the fire was lit in the cottage range, a spark guard was in place and a kettle simmered at the back of the stove. Nanny went out again and, shading her eyes against the glare as she scanned the fields, saw Flora being guided painfully slowly down the hillside by a man who was himself leaning on a stick. Flora raised her arm in recognition but so feebly that Nanny ran towards them and was out of breath when she finally got there. The old man was Davey Hamilton – Mike Hamilton's father – an outspoken, blunt countryman of Nanny's age, a man wrapped well for the weather in boots and gaiters, tweeds and a hat.

'Yon lass needs medical attention, Nurse!' he said. 'Winter clothes. A warm bed. Hot food. She cannae stand.' He was supporting Flora, who, wearing a lightweight coat that would not fasten round her, no hat and thin leather shoes, was obviously all-in, too weak and cold to talk. No doubt Davey Hamilton had spotted her as, unknowingly, she trespassed on his land. There was no law of trespass but this farmer investigated every roaming pair of feet that crossed his land. He was well known for pointing out to any walker whom he found

172

there the nearest public footpaths, and for exaggerating the dangers of not sticking to them.

He made no mention of Flora's condition, nor did he ask any questions on the last few yards to the cottage. He had no need to ask. He was as shrewd a judge of human and animal behaviour as could be found in a week's march of his farm. He was a silent man who had never been known to gossip, but all the same, Nanny would not tell Ruth. She thanked him and said, 'Will you stay for a cup of tea?' because she could not think of anything else she might do.

'No,' he answered dourly. Then, to Flora, whom they had laid on the chintz cushions of the drop-end settee. 'Next time the Luftwaffe falls oot the sky, don't try climbing yon hill to watch 'em, lassie.'

When he'd gone, though Flora protested that she only wanted to sleep, Nanny made her drink steaming tea. There was a bathroom upstairs but it took for ever to heat enough water to fill the tub, and today there was no time. While Flora took her tea, Nanny fetched the zinc bath and placed it before the fire, then filled it with jugs of hot water from the tap over the range and cold from the kitchen. 'You are chilled through,' she said, 'and I'm not leaving until I see you fed and warmed.'

She had not seen Flora undressed for a few weeks and now she hid her alarm at the network of stretch marks that streaked down the girl's body. They went from below her heavy breasts almost to Flora's knees. Her upper arms, too, from armpit to elbow were stretched – purple striae which would never fade completely.

Flora stepped into the tub and sat down. 'I didn't want to see the crashed aeroplane. I was making for the main road.'

'What?' Nanny said, shocked.

'I want to get away from here,' she said quietly and firmly.

'Why?'

'I'm trapped. I'm here because I have nowhere else to go.'

'You're not a prisoner.' Nanny was hurt at being likened to a jailer.

Flora picked up a flannel and held it to her face with shaking fingers, through which she whispered, 'It's not your fault. But if I told Lady Campbell, I couldn't stay here. My baby is kicking. I've started to love it and think I'm doing the wrong thing.'

So Nanny was right. Mother love was coming into the equation. She said, 'But how could you keep a baby, lass? You've no home.'

'But it's all wrong, Nanny. Don't you see? These choices shouldn't be forced on people.'

'Flora, dear, what choice have you?'

Tears were streaming down Flora's face now. 'Animals don't have to pay for their dens or nests like we do. They defend their homes and their young to the death. They don't give up their babies because they can't afford a roof over their heads and food to eat. All God's creatures have a right to forage for food and build a shelter. Why isn't it my right? It shouldn't be in any government's power to deny them to anyone. Why am I less important than a fox or a bird?'

'It's the way things are organised, I suppose.' There was a hard lump in Nanny's throat. 'What were you going to do if you found a way out of here?'

'I'd stay with my friend Jessie. She'd have me and the baby and she'd keep me till I got on my feet.' Flora's confidence was returning as warmth seeped into her.

'Think of the bairn. It will have a better life at Ingersley.' Nanny believed this to be true, otherwise she would never have gone along with this illegal adoption. Even now, she could take Flora to her friend Jessie's home. Ruth would lose face, of course, and Gordon would have to be told that the adoption had fallen through. But what kind of life would that be for this precious unborn baby? What sort of life would they have if Flora, penniless, had only temporary shelter in Leith, the city dock area? Nanny said gently, 'Your child will have the best of everything at Ingersley. You could never give it all that.'

'I know,' Flora cried softly as she squeezed the flannel and watched the water run over her swollen abdomen. 'I'd be cheating Lady Campbell if I take all her kindness and refuse to hand the baby over ...' She raised pleading eyes and said, 'But it doesn't stop me wanting to keep it. Can I come and visit?'

'No, Flora.' It came as a sudden cold certainty to Nanny that Ruth would stop at nothing if Flora ever came looking for her child. It sent a shiver down her arms, though she was up to her elbows in warm water as she soaped Flora. 'Go far away. Never come back.'

174

'Where could I go?'

'How would you like to go to my sister in Canada?' Nanny asked. Since the beginning of the war, from the Dominions and the USA, offers to take children had come pouring in. Nanny had received three letters from her younger sister in Canada, each more urgent than the last, in which Dorothy begged her to return, saying, 'We are registered as your host family. Secure a passage. No need to write. Telephone when you land. We are waiting for you.'

Nanny saw a look of hope on Flora's face, then watched it fade as she said, 'I'd need a lot of money.'

'A hundred pounds is enough. I have a little as well.' Nanny knew it would be the best solution for them all if Flora went far, far away. 'I'll see the emigration people in Glasgow and set the wheels in motion.'

'If I take the money, accept the passage – what will happen to me?'

'You have to put it behind you,' Nanny said with a shake of her head. 'There's no other way. You are young. You can make a fresh start.'

'And then I marry – and my husband need never be told?' Flora looked down at the purple stretch marks, then up at Nanny, who need not voice what they both knew. It would be impossible for Flora ever to hide from a future husband that she had already been through the mill of childbearing. Flora gave her a bleak smile. 'I want my baby. I don't want another man.'

Nanny said, 'You still love Andrew?'

Flora drew herself up in the water, her eyes flashing. 'I can't stop loving him – you can't help your feelings, Nanny!' Then she said, 'But I despise what he's done. He deserted me – disowned me and my ...' she spread her hands across her swollen body, '... and his baby!' Then, shaken by her own vehemence, she said more softly, 'I put my trust in Andrew and he's broken his promises. He wanted promotion and success more than he wanted me.' She looked down at her swollen body again. 'I'm sixteen! That's all. I feel like a woman of thirty-six.' Then, anxiously, 'I'm going to be all right, aren't I? My mother died having me. I was a very big baby.'

Nanny went on soaping and sponging until the warmth of the water seeped into Flora, warming her through. She said, 'You'll be all right. You are a big, strong girl, you know. And I'll be with you.' But she was worried. Women who carried as much water as Flora was carrying – for her ankles and fingers were twice their normal size – were in danger of heart failure, soaring blood pressure and thrombosis. 'From now on, lass, you will have to spend the rest of your time in bed. You must not put your feet to the floor.'

'But I have to . . .' Flora protested.

'No you don't! I'll pop back to the house twice a day when I'm working to give you your meals in bed. It won't be for long.' Nanny did not expect her to go until the middle of June, the date Flora said the baby was due. And if there were serious signs of complications, then her first duty was to her patient and the laws of her profession. A doctor would be called. Flora would be sent to hospital and Gordon and Ruth would have to make arrangements to adopt the baby in a proper, legal manner.

Six weeks later at Ivy Lodge, on a soft spring morning in April, Flora crawled out of bed as the ever-present pain in her back stabbed through her. She could only make it from the bedroom to the kitchen on her hands and knees. She dropped to the floor and between gritted teeth vowed, 'I will never, never again be dependent on anyone for anything when I am over this.' The coconut matting grazed her knees and shins as she crawled across the kitchen. She hauled herself up at the back door and caught sight of her reflection in the little mirror. 'But will I ever be over this?' she said out loud to her reflection. Her red face was bloated and shiny. Her eyelids were puffy. She could barely see her eyes. The abundance of flaming hair hung in lank strings.

Then, 'Yes, I will! I will get over it. I may be only sixteen but I am no longer a child. I'll be a mother and I'm going to keep my baby.' She remembered the last talk she and Gran had had – and Gran saying that it was a rare female who could love another's child. Nobody could ever love her baby the way Flora would. She had hidden a sharp knife under her pillow. 'I'll force Nanny to help me get away.' She had her ticket and a letter offering refuge in Canada. Nanny had given her more than enough for board and lodging until the boat sailed. She would not take the money from Lady Campbell but would escape with her baby to Canada, where Nanny's sister Dorothy and brother-in-law John were expecting her.

Outside the back door the world smelled of new grass and fresh-turned earth – of new life that had burst free of winter. Flora was barefooted and there, not more than six inches from her toes, a proud stand of daffodils nodded, brave and clean in the spring air that washed over her. She put up her arms to lift her lank hair to the breeze and at once knew a lightening of her load. The heaviness had gone. A welcome tightening was happening, low down, where something warm and wet flowed, unstoppable, down the insides of her thighs.

She looked down, startled. Her waters were breaking. She closed the door, grabbed a towel and a clean sheet that hung from the kitchen pulley. She was not afraid, but oddly excited, as she found she could now walk back to her bed and climb in. With the folded sheet beneath her, she waited for Nanny to arrive.

When Nanny popped back to Ivy Lodge to give Flora her lunch, she found that the labour was in the early stages. Flora was comfortable and Nanny drove straight back to Ingersley to tell Ruth to be prepared. She did not voice her worries – but this was a premature delivery. The baby might need an incubator or prove not to be strong enough to take from its mother.

And Nanny was having grave doubts about the adoption. The passage to Canada had been paid for by Ruth, and Nanny had given Flora money to tide her over, but with the birth being early – six weeks before the boat sailed – Flora could easily change her mind and come back demanding her baby. Also, Gordon would surely never have contemplated adopting the child if he'd seen such a lack of maternal feeling in Ruth.

At this moment, though, Nanny was angry. Ruth was coming down the stone steps dressed for riding. Nanny had forbidden the riding a month ago and told Ruth that an expectant mother would not ride during the last three months. Now, standing three steps below her on the flight at the front entrance, Nanny, her face set and determined, said, 'You are going nowhere today! Cancel all your arrangements. The baby will be born before midnight.'

'That leaves plenty of time. I can be home by mid-afternoon.'

Nanny took a step towards her. 'I don't think you can have heard me. I said, you will go nowhere!'

Ruth glowered but did not attempt to pass Nanny. She said, 'Are you threatening me?'

Nanny was losing the semblance of patience she had so far shown. She said, 'Go inside. At once!'

Reluctantly, Ruth obeyed, leaving the great oak door wide open. Nanny closed it and followed Ruth up the staircase, where sunlight slanted in at the glass cupola, revealing tiny agitated dust motes that danced above the threadbare edges of the carpet as Ruth's booted heels disturbed them on her furious way. The moment she realised that Bessie the housemaid was nowhere to be seen, she turned on Nanny and hissed in temper, 'Are you threatening me?'

Nanny, short of breath, after the climb, was not going to allow her any more leeway. 'If that is how you see it, then yes.'

Ruth changed her attitude instantly, as only Ruth could. She shook back her hair and removed her tweed jacket. The riding clothes still fitted her perfectly. The only concession she had made to the appearance of pregnancy was to wear two very thick jumpers one on top of the other and to leave her jacket buttons undone. She said, 'Then will you please call in at the farm on your way to Ivy Lodge. Tell the Hamiltons I'm not well.'

Nanny's hands were itching to give her a smart slapping. But she said in the same controlled voice, 'Light a fire in the nursery to make it warm. Place a hot-water bottle in the crib. Sterilise the feeding bottles and be prepared.' She added, 'You will give Bessie the afternoon off while you do all this. That is, if you are still bent on keeping this adoption a secret?'

Ruth smiled now, disarmingly. 'What time do you think the baby will be born?' she asked, as if she were awaiting a delivery of oats. She had not once concerned herself with Flora except to give Nanny, at Nanny's insistence, the hundred pounds in notes which she said was not to be handed over until the baby was in its crib here at Ingersley.

Nanny said, 'You must wait. You must go to bed and wait – just as a real mother does.' With that she went to her room and collected the baby clothes and the Moses basket for the return journey to Ivy Lodge.

Though the success of her encounter with Ruth had buoyed her up, on the drive back Nanny was in turmoil. She went by the main road, passing on the hill sheep with baby lambs at foot, and in the fields farmers and field workers planting cabbage under a great wide, clean-washed sky. It was Nanny's favourite time of year. She used to push Gordon out every afternoon in his pram along these lanes. She could recall every expression on her darling's little face, and a cold hand clutched at her heart every time she thought about the danger he was in. She whispered his name out loud now – 'Gordon, you don't know what you're asking of me' – for though she loved him as a son, Nanny knew that her first duty was to the mother she would deliver and the baby soon to be born. If Flora wanted to keep the baby, then, regardless of everyone's feelings, it was Nanny's bounden duty to help her.

Tears came to Nanny's eyes as she turned on to the rough lane – tears for Flora, who might only know the pains of child-birth and not the joys of motherhood; and tears for herself, for if Flora could not part with it, then Nanny would never again have a baby to call her own.

Flora managed to raise herself high on the pillow, despite the pains that were coming fast and strong. It was dark outside and in the dim light from the lamp she could just see the comfort-ing figure of Nanny setting out her things: a kidney dish covered with gauze, containing antiseptic lotion; string to tie off the cord, and sharp scissors. Everything – padding, cotton, binders and a heap of muslin squares – had been there for hours.

She managed to say, before falling back into the pillows as another pain took her, 'What's the time?'

Nanny turned round. She was wearing a large white apron over her grey dress, and over her face and mouth a gauze mask. The birth must be imminent. Flora groaned, tried to hold her breath, then breathe deeply. Nothing worked. The pains grew stronger. Sweat broke out on her brow.

'It's nearly midnight. Soon be here!' Nanny assured her, and came to sit beside her to mop her forehead with cologne-soaked cotton waste. 'Hold on to my arm when the next one comes.'

'It's – it's – here – it's – oh!' Flora's face contorted into a grimace as she grabbed Nanny's arm on the edge of the scream as the last pain overwhelmed her. Then the pulling and stretching pain ceased and suddenly it was as if a train were rushing through her and she found herself bearing down, grunting, sweating, gasping for breath.

'Good girl! Keep going!' Nanny encouraged, but Flora was beyond obeying Nanny now. Every last ounce of strength and energy was going into this impossible struggle to push her baby out.

'Stop pushing!' Nanny ordered. 'The head is nearly out. Now clamp your teeth together while breathing through your mouth.'

Orders and pains were coming together relentlessly, until with a cry of, 'I can't – but I can't!' and one enormous, sustained effort, it came slithering, sliding out into the world, into Nanny's hands.

'It's a boy – a beautiful boy!' Nanny said, and she held him up so that Flora could see and hear his first cry of surprise as his little lungs filled with air.

Flora lay limp and exhausted while Nanny tied off the cord, washing the squealing infant, wrapped him, then weighed him on a hand-held brass scale and put him into her arms, saying, 'He's only four and a half pounds, but he's perfect. Listen to that cry.'

Flora gazed down in wonder on the tiny crumpled face of her son, felt the solid little body moving under the shawl – then, before she could speak, another pain came, violent and short. She thrust the infant towards Nanny. 'Oh, God! Oh, help!' she cried as the pains came faster and faster.

'It's the afterbirth,' Nanny said, but she quickly laid the new-born infant at the foot of the bed and returned her attention to Flora.

'It's not!' Another pain came, stronger than before. Flora drew up her legs, held on to her knees, gave an almighty cry and bore down with all her might.

'Oh my!' Nanny cried as the second baby appeared, a larger baby, crying lustily the second its head emerged. 'Another boy!' The afterbirth slithered out. Flora closed her eyes, then opened them to watch Nanny, so calm, wrapping and tying a second cord, wiping the baby, swaddling him in one of the muslin squares then placing him in the crook of Flora's arm. 'Eight pounds, lass. No wonder you were so big. Identical twins. They shared a placenta.'

He was the most beautiful thing Flora had ever set eyes upon. She put her right arm out for the other baby and gently, tenderly held both sleeping, snuffling new-born boys, a beatific smile on her face. 'Don't take my babies, Nanny,' she whispered as she looked from one to the other. Then she smiled to see Nanny gather the smaller babe into her own arms and sit upon the edge of the bed, the infant held to her bosom, her eyes bright with tears which began to roll down her cheeks as she gazed from Flora to the baby she was holding and then back to the one she would for ever afterwards think of as her own.

'I must. I must take one, my child,' Nanny said. 'I'll take this little one. The bigger baby will be able to stand the long journey to Canada.'

'Nanny ...?'

'Yes?'

'You will love him? And when he's old enough – tell him I loved him, too.'

Tears were streaming down Nanny's face as, still cradling the baby in her arms, she leaned over and kissed Flora's troubled brow. 'I'll be the next best thing to a mother to him. But we must never tell anyone there were two. Nobody must know. Only you and me.'

Flora was drifting off to sleep, her baby tucked up in bed beside her and Nanny's voice a soothing background. She was saying she would drive her to North Berwick in two days' time to register the baby – what would Flora call him?

'Alexander Andrew,' Flora managed to say.

'Rest now,' Nanny said. 'I will have to get you out of here in two days' time.'

'Nanny – you come too. We could all go to Canada ...' but Flora's eyes were closing in deep, relaxing sleep. She woke again for only a few moments to see Nanny tenderly wrapping her first-born son in a fine wool shawl and placing the sleeping baby into the padded Moses basket. Nanny put her finger to her lips and whispered, 'Get some sleep. I'll be back.'

Flora thought about the knife under her pillow. She had no need of it. There was nothing she could do. It would be hard to flee with one baby; with two impossible. She kissed the head of the dark-haired infant beside her, who slept on peacefully. 'Forgive me, son,' she said. 'I hope you find your brother one day.'

Chapter Ten

The approach to their home port, Greenock, was along one of the fairest sea gateways in the world, and after seventeen days at sea Andrew felt a great weight lifting from them as they rounded the Mull of Kintyre and sailed past the gaunt rock of Ailsa Craig. His second trip as temporary probationer sub-lieutenant on Atlantic convoy escort was over.

Four hours ago he'd come, sodden wet, off watch and gone down to the mean slit of a two-berth cabin that three officers shared. It was June and hot on land, but out there, even in summer, Atlantic gales sent waves crashing over the bridge, soaking the top layer of clothing of the watch-keeper. On night watches he wore two of everything – oilskins, gloves, clumping sea boots, balaclavas – and still water found its way everywhere, filling the boots, pouring down the neck of his jerseys.

Along with such miserable discomfort, of course, was the ever-present danger from U-boats. In five days' time they would be back at sea and he would be pulling men aboard – burnt men from blazing oil tankers who would not live; maimed and half-drowned sailors from the merchant ships that were the U-boats' targets.

His officer training course had taken only six weeks and his posting to the *Iris* had begun on 14 May. Only two days earlier, after the British débâcle in Norway and Hitler's invasion of the Low Countries, Mr Chamberlain had lost the vote of confidence and resigned and Winston Churchill, the First Lord of the Admiralty, had become Prime Minister. Andrew heard their new leader's broadcast: 'I have nothing to offer but blood, toil, tears and sweat.' All who listened breathed a sigh of relief, and Andrew echoed in his heart the Prime Minister's confident certainty of victory. Churchill's unshakeable faith in himself was a beacon in a frightened world.

Now, standing at the rails with the comforting scents of land and home assailing him, Andrew watched the navy-blue bow waves break in frills of white as they set course for the Great and Little Cumbraes, Rothesay and the passage northwards along the spectacular Clyde coastline under a golden sun and a high drift of misty white clouds. Cloud shadows raced across the hills and banks of the pastureland and darkened the patches of pine and birch and oaks that towered over little ferry jetties and tiny stone cottages.

It was peaceful along this stretch of safe water and hard to believe that four hundred miles south-east of here thousands of British fighting men were under fire as they were brought home by an armada of small boats from the shores of Dunkirk.

From his aft station Lieutenant Sergeant Verne called out to him, 'We're going in. We'll have a few days ashore.'

Andrew grinned. 'Good,' he said. He needed leave. It was those few precious hours of normality that they all lived for – for wives, girlfriends and family. They would be going alongside in a couple of hours, for their anchorage was a mile offshore at the Tail of the Bank. On previous trips they had waited there, swinging on the anchor cable, served by supply boats and taken off for only a few hours' leave by liberty boats. He was longing to get home to Edinburgh, hoping against hope to find a letter from Flora waiting for him at Greenock.

Downstream from them as they neared Greenock was a vast pool of convoy shipping. The ships – liners and merchant vessels which were all under the Royal Navy's control now – would be there one night, gone the next morning and replenished with scarcely a day's delay as sea traffic ebbed and flowed. Andrew's heart went out to the mothers, teachers and children – the Bundles from Britain – who had to run the gauntlet of U-boats and torpedoes before they reached the welcome of their hosts in Canada and America.

From the window of the flat she had found in his absence, Ma was looking out for him as Andrew strode across The Meadows in the heart of the city. He waved and she came down the stairs to meet him at the main door, wearing a blue linen costume. The new way of life and her improved status obviously suited her. She was thrilled to see him and to show off their new home. 'Eh! I'm fair away wi' myself,' she said as he kissed her and wrapped an arm about her. 'You look braw in your uniform. I'm that proud of ye!'

He lifted her off her feet. 'I'm proud too, Ma! Proud to be an officer.' He smiled, put her down and said, 'I don't know much more than before, but I've learned how to handle men who I once saw as my mates, how to salute and how a naval officer responds to the loyal toast.'

'How long have you got?' Ma asked as he followed her up the stone staircase of the close.

'Three days. Then I have to be back in Greenock to join the corvette.'

She laughed. 'A corvette? What kind of boat is that?'

'They are broad-beamed, low in the water – built like the old whalers,' he said. 'But they are Clyde-built and as sound as a bell.'

'How big? How many of a crew?' She opened the door of the second-floor flat and stood back to let him go first into their new home.

'She's two hundred and three feet long, nine hundred tons. A crew of eighty men. It's crowded and cramped, wet and noisy and ...' he was grinning from ear to ear as he looked around him, '... she pitches and rolls and swings in the least breeze.' He was astonished at the size of the flat he was paying for.

May proudly showed him the bathroom. He marvelled at that to please her while she said, 'You are in charge of this boat?'

'No, Ma. I'm the lowest commissioned rank. I do normal duties during the day and at night I keep watch.' He followed her to the big square kitchen where a range gleamed from Ma's vigorous applications of black lead. Curtains billowed in the little breeze wafting through the great sash window that overlooked greens and, beyond, the Edinburgh Royal Infirmary. He would not tell Ma that night station watch-keeping was an endurance test when he stood for four hours, clamped to a wing of the open bridge, concentrating in the darkness on a blurred image or a beam of light which had to be the ship they were shadowing. There was always the dread that he had lost sight of it, a collision was about to happen and what he was seeing was water on his binoculars.

He had left his bag in the bedroom that was to be his, and now they stood in the large drawing room. It had a high ceiling with ornate plasterwork and a gas-fired centre light that you lowered on a fancy chain. Ma had done well to find the flat. He was supporting her, sending £12 a month home out of his £24 monthly pay.

'Where d'you get all this?' he asked, looking in astonishment at the big Axminster carpet, the plush drop-end sofa and the chairs with lacy antimacassars draped over their high backs. 'It's good stuff.'

'You won't believe me, son,' Ma said, a look of satisfaction on her face. 'Lady Campbell had it sent over on a lorry. She said that it was just sitting there in storage and I was welcome to it.'

'And the desk – and the piano,' he said. 'They're from Ingersley. From the servants' hall.'

Ma busied herself laying the table for supper. The table was the only thing as far as Andrew could see that had come from their old home at the South Lodge. He said, 'She was good to you, then?'

'She was very good. She's in charge of all the billeting. All those empty cottages are filled with evacuees.'

'They were damp. Falling down.'

'Better than nothing for they poor souls who were bombed out.'

'They were mostly empty,' Andrew reminded her. 'Did she have to furnish them as well?'

'She'd get an allowance and lots of government stuff was sent to Ingersley for the hospital – beds and drawers, cupboards and tables and ...'

'She gave you all this?' said Andrew, grinning. 'She must have had a guilty conscience.'

'She got me the job at the hospital,' Ma said. 'I'm grateful to her.'

'You know you don't have to work.'

'Everyone has to. There's no getting out of it. The government's passed the Emergency Powers Act. They can send you anywhere – men and women – unless you are the mother of small children.' Her face lit up with pleasure as she added, 'And what do you think? Lady Campbell's had a baby. A boy.'

'That will please Sir Gordon,' Andrew said, 'though it will probably be talking before he gets home.'

Ma went on excitedly, 'I went down to the house on my day off – to see Bessie. I must have gone the day after the baby was born. He had taken them all by surprise. Lady Campbell only found out she was expecting a few weeks before.' Then the happy smile went from her face as she said, 'But I felt as if I wasn't welcome. I felt as if Lady Campbell had said, "Tell her to go away." I never saw the baby. Bessie came to the door because she couldn't ask me in.'

'How did that make you feel?' Andrew asked. He felt his gorge rising, imagining his ma being shown the door – cold-shouldered after all those years of service to the Campbells.

Ma had taken it in her stride, though. She said, 'Oh. I told Bessie to come and see me when she gets a Sunday off. Then I went to the South Lodge – to have a last look.'

'And?' Ma used to love her little palace.

'They are using it as a store for the hospital.' She smiled. 'Do you know something? I wouldn't want to go back.'

'I'm glad. Don't talk about Ingersley. It's in the past.' Then, tentatively, for he already knew the answer, 'You've not looked for Flora?'

Ma looked crestfallen. 'I haven't had time, son.' She saw disappointment on Andrew's face and asked quickly, 'What about Greg? Did he find out anything?'

'Not much.' Greg had gone to the munitions factory and asked after Flora there. They'd told him that one day she'd come in limping badly and had made an appointment with the doctor. Greg did not ask to see him; there was no point, for they already knew about the fall on the ice. Now Andrew said to Ma, 'I have to find out what happened to her. I'll go to the police tomorrow. Flora wouldn't just stop writing. She'd tell me, whatever it was.'

'She had done it before, though, son. Run away,' Ma said. 'She ran away from Guthrie's. That's what you told me.'

'But that was before she ...' He gave a small smile. 'We made promises to one another. We both took them seriously.'

'I am sorry.'

'It's all right.' There was no point in going on about it, upsetting Ma. He'd look for a motorbike tomorrow and start searching. His first port of call would be Kelso, to find Mr Davidson.

The following morning his luck was in. It was hard to come by cars or motorcycles; particularly motorcycles, because of petrol rationing. But he found a Norton for sale and paid too much for it. It had a tiny engine with a chain drive and it would be just the thing to leave at the dock – or on the corvette if he were allowed. It would get him back to Edinburgh faster and more cheaply than by rail. He wouldn't waste any time in the port of Greenock – a dismal, dingy little town. He'd spend his leave searching for Flora. He put the cycle to good use immediately, driving down to Kelso.

He arrived at 2.15 p.m. and went straight to the town hall, where they gave him Mr Davidson's address. He was living with his sighted brother and family in a pleasant bungalow tucked into the hills – so far from the war that only rationing and the wireless brought the brutal facts home to them. They showed him into a front parlour that bristled with knick-knacks, embroidered crinoline ladies and aspidistras. Tea and scones were served as Andrew faced Mr Davidson over the wooden tea trolley. 'You say a nurse came round?'

'Yes. An elderly woman.'

'How would you know?' Andrew asked sharply, by now having lost all sensitivity and oppressed by the sense of time slipping away.

'Losing one's sight does not mean losing one's faculties, Andrew.'

'I'm sorry,' Andrew said. Then, quietly, 'The following day, another woman came?'

'Yes. A woman of importance. A WVS woman, I'd say. English.'

'How d'you know?' He'd done it again; been rude. He had the grace to say, 'I'm sorry.'

'She was used to giving orders – being obeyed.'

'Like a hospital almoner? A woman in authority?' Andrew leaned forward on the edge of his chair. 'What did she say?'

'She said that it would take some time but Flora was being

188

taken care of. She didn't say where. She said Flora would not be back and she took away all her belongings.' Mr Davidson's eyes flicked backwards and forwards as they did when he was agitated. 'But surely you know this, Andrew? You are her brother.'

It had been a wasted afternoon. He was no nearer finding her. The following day he went to Portobello police station but they paid scant attention to him. He stood his ground, made them take down a description of Flora, and finally they passed him on to an ageing sergeant who said kindly, 'It happens every day, sir. Girls meet someone else – civvies, Canadians. She maybe wanted to let you down lightly. Look in the bars.'

Andrew bit back an angry reply and said in a controlled voice, 'My girl would not be found in a bar. Now tell me, which hospitals have nurses who work outside the hospital?'

The sergeant said, 'You are looking for a private nurse?' Andrew shook his head impatiently and the sergeant added, 'I see. The nurse who went to see the blind man? A Red Cross nurse then. They work outside.'

'So – how do I find out? Have you got a list of Red Cross nurses?'

The sergeant was losing patience. He stood up. 'We have important work to do. Looking for eighteen-year-old girls who have dropped their boyfriends is not our priority.'

'Don't talk to me as if I were any old idiot.' Andrew banged his hand on the desk. It was a foolish gesture and it got him nowhere, but he needed to do it. He'd had enough of civilians telling those to whom they owed their lives how to behave. He said, 'I won't give up. Damn it!'

The sergeant sighed. 'We'll add her to the missing persons list. It will be circulated to the hospitals.'

'Will her details go to every police force in the country? Where will you start the search?' Andrew demanded.

'We won't search. If she turns up, we'll inform you.'

Andrew went to the door. 'Make sure you keep her name on the list,' he said before, angry and frustrated, he left the station, promising himself that when the war was over, he would join the police force. He liked service life, uniform and a hierarchy built on endeavour. And he'd have access to information and files and secret lists of missing persons. They would not be able to block his search then.

Tomorrow night he must return to Greenock. All he'd discovered was that a nurse and an Englishwoman of authority knew where Flora was. Edinburgh must be full of nurses fitting that description.

In the nursery at Ingersley, Nanny removed the teat from the drowsy infant's lips, placed the feeding bottle on a footstool, leaned back in the rocking chair and cradled six-week-old Robert close to her bosom. She gazed down at the dark wavy hair that crowned his tiny head. 'Mummy will be here in a minute, my darling,' she crooned. 'Baby Robert is going to have his first airing. Nanny will get the pram ready and take it down in the lift. Oh! He's a lucky boy.'

She looked up at the clock. Two o'clock. This was Bessie's afternoon off. Where was Ruth? Surely she had not forgotten that Nanny had maternity and post-natal patients to see this afternoon?

That Ruth might forget was the least of Nanny's fears. She could not wipe from her memory the events of the day she had delivered baby Robert to Ruth.

On the night the twins were born, Nanny left Flora and the stronger baby sleeping at Ivy Lodge then drove through the pitch-black night to Ingersley with the baby snug and warm in his basket. Night driving was dangerous since their headlights wore black cardboard covers that had only narrow slits to let through a small beam. But she made it safely and whisked the baby inside and up the stairs to Ruth, who, she'd have thought, would be pacing the floor in an agony of suspense.

Ruth was asleep, though it was only an hour past midnight. She shrugged away Nanny's hand on her shoulder. Nanny gave her a few seconds' grace then whispered, 'Look, Ruth! It's a boy – your adopted son is here.'

Ruth groaned, turned over, opened her eyes slowly and then sat up. She pushed her hair off her face, blinked and said, 'Did you *have* to wake me?' She looked at the baby, wrinkled her nose in disgust and said, 'My God! What an ugly infant. He's the image of his father.' Then, lying down and turning her back, 'Let me sleep. Everything is ready in the nursery.'

Nanny settled the infant and gave him his first feed. Her own room, part of the nursery suite, had been made ready and she tried to snatch an hour's sleep before she must return to Flora. She awoke at six, fed the baby again and took him to Ruth. This time she was in no mood to put up with Ruth's petulance. 'Wake up, Ruth!' she said. 'You must look after the baby. I am going back to Flora. I will drop in at the cottage, tell Bessie that the baby is born and ask her to come to you.'

'But ...'

'But nothing! You will put on a dressing gown – and look as if you have at least had a disturbed night – you wait for the arrival of Bessie and the doctor and you give the doctor the impression at least of post-partum tiredness. Do not let him examine you.'

All was well at Ivy Lodge. Flora was bathed and dressed. She said, 'Look, Nanny. Weeks ago I altered this dress. I let out the seams while I was lying in bed. It fits me!' She unfastened the front opening, picked up the baby and said shyly, 'He knows how to feed.'

Nanny stayed with her, watching as Flora contentedly nursed her baby. She would not stay too long, for she herself now had all the new-mother instincts, chief of which was never to let her infant out of her sight. Flora appeared to have accepted the fact that she could only keep the one baby. The heartbreak had not happened for her yet. But watching her, Nanny knew with a sinking, sick feeling that it was all going too much according to plan. Would the apple cart soon come crashing to the ground and bring them all down with it? Nanny was not cut out for deceit.

She returned to Ingersley towards midday to discover that Ruth was nowhere to be seen. To Nanny's relief, Bessie came to the door of the nursery, the sleeping babe in her arms and a big, broad smile on her face. She said, 'The doctor came, Nanny.'

'What did he say?'

'He checked the baby. He said, "What a surprise!" and he offered to check Lady Campbell over.'

'Oh?'

Bessie giggled. 'She gave him a good ticking-off!'

Relieved, Nanny took charge of the baby. 'Where is Lady Campbell?'

'In the drawing room – making telephone calls,' Bessie said. 'I'll go and make something to eat.'

'Don't get anything for me. I'll have a rest and listen out for the baby,' Nanny said. She settled the infant in his crib then went to her own bedroom and lay down, but she left the door slightly ajar so that she would hear the baby's cries. Her eyes were closed but sleep would not come because of the powerful feelings she now had for a child who was not her own. It was totally unprofessional to allow herself the natural mother's bond with the baby. Her stomach churned. It could all go disastrously wrong. There was a bottle of whisky in the cupboard – for medicinal use – and she got up and poured a large measure, sipped it and sat by the open dormer window, from where she would hear every little sound from the adjoining nursery.

After a few moments she must have drifted off but was pulled back into alert consciousness with a start when from the next room she heard a man's voice. 'I came straight up. You all right?'

Then came Ruth's reply. 'Perfectly. Why shouldn't I be?'

'It was so quick. And you've only known for two months.'

Ruth laughed. 'It was painless.'

Footsteps crossed the nursery and Nanny heard the creak of the cradle on its spring, then Mike Hamilton's voice – for she recognised it now – saying, 'Who's the father?'

Nanny's hand shook. She put down the glass.

Ruth said, 'Who do you imagine?'

A coppery taste came into Nanny's mouth and a sinking sensation to her stomach. Mike Hamilton's voice was thickening. He said, 'It is nine months exactly since you and I ...'

And Ruth, on a triumphant note, replied, 'So! You will never know – is it yours, born on time, or Gordon's, born early?'

Nanny was shaking from head to foot. What was Ruth saying? Why lying? Why laughing? This was no laughing matter.

'Christ, woman! He even looks like me. Gordon will never believe that you and he produced a dark-haired son.'

'Gordon *will* believe it's his. I gave birth two months early. Gordon will be as pleased as Punch.'

Strangled sounds came to Nanny's ears. Mike Hamilton, who had surprised everyone by fussing over Lucy's condition, protective and proud, was crying. Deep, throaty sobs were shaking that great frame as he cried, '*My son! My son!*' Ruth was hushing him, telling him to stop crying, and Nanny herself was cold to the marrow and shaking with fear and distrust. Ruth had duped her. But, far worse, Gordon had not only married a faithless woman but was to be deceived into fatherhood.

She tiptoed to the door and closed it so as not to alert them, then crept quietly back to bed, closed her eyes and pretended to be asleep. Why, oh why had she not foreseen this? She had questioned Ruth's insistence on secrecy, she had condoned all the lies, but never once had it occurred to her that she was implicated in a plot to cheat her beloved Gordon. A dozen questions came one after the other. Had Ruth given Andrew the letter from Flora? Did Andrew know nothing at all? Had Mrs Stewart's departure from the estate been engineered by Ruth? Surely Ruth was not so wicked as to plan all this, was she?

Nanny told herself to stop thinking this way. She tried to look at it from a different viewpoint and understand how such a terrible thing might have come about. When Ruth and Hamilton 'fell from grace' war was coming and two young people, thrown together for company when Gordon was away, had done something they would later regret. There could be no more to it than that. Nanny had to believe it, for if she did not she'd have to take the baby right back to Flora. Now.

But that was impossible. The baby was here. Her angel had been seen by the staff and the doctor. And where could they go? There was not another berth to be had on the boat to Canada. Nanny had pulled strings, pulled rank, cajoled and paid money to get a berth for Flora, and while nobody would turn away a passenger with a new-born infant, they would not accept a mother with twins. There was nothing she could do. They had all been delivered into Ruth's hands, exactly as she had intended.

*

193

Six weeks later, in the nursery, with the baby sound asleep in her arms, Nanny's fears had not subsided; rather they had grown with the awareness that Ruth actively disliked Robert. She looked again at the clock. It was ten minutes past two. Where was Ruth?

All at once the door was flung open and Ruth came into the room in a noisy flurry of, 'Oh, Nanny – I forgot!' The baby began to cry and the crying became a scream as Ruth, annoyed, bent over him, saying, 'Stop that noise at once!' followed by, 'Put it in its cot, Nanny. I can't think.'

Nanny settled him into his cot. 'He's six weeks old. Today you can take him out in the pram.'

Ruth looked into the cot. 'He'll be asleep soon. I have brought a book.'

'Baby needs fresh air. Every day from now on, rain or shine,' Nanny told her, 'Bessie or you or I will—'

Ruth interrupted her with a coarse laugh. 'I certainly won't be taking him for walks in the rain.'

Nanny cringed at her harshness and brought the pram forward. She had made it ready with a frilly pillow and an embroidered eiderdown. Ruth would change her mind – would want to push the baby out when she saw how adorable he looked. Nanny picked up Robert and handed him and his woollen coat to Ruth, and then winced to see how roughly Ruth handled the infant, who began to cry lustily again. It was a terrible thing for Nanny not to trust the baby's mother, but she dared not leave Ruth in sole charge of him. Only when Bessie was on duty did Nanny have peace of mind. Bessie – promoted to nurserymaid – had a cheerful disposition and the simple goodness of a country girl. Ruth had a cruel streak that led her to tease and almost to torment a defenceless baby whose birthright was the care and safety of a loving mother's arms.

Ruth held Robert at arm's length on the edge of her knees. 'Let us go down to the farm,' she said in the shrill voice that set the baby screaming in terror. 'We'll see Lucy Hamilton. We'll see if she is receiving yet, shall we?' Ruth had also acquired the habit of speaking to Nanny through the baby. She said, 'That is, if Nanny thinks that a week is long enough?'

Lucy's baby girl had been born a week earlier than expected

after three days of labour that had left her weak and probably unable to have more children.

'I expect Lucy has already scrubbed every floor in the house.' Ruth laughed. 'If we can't see Lucy then we'll show you off to Mike. Here, Nanny. Put it in the pram. I'm ready.'

When they had gone Nanny passed a hand over her eyes. What could she do? She dared not tell Gordon the truth – for if Gordon rejected the baby he would also reject Ruth, and, most certainly and with justification, herself as well. And the baby? What was his future? He had no protection, except that which Nanny could provide. She would give him her undivided love and attention and would not allow him to suffer.

The Canadian Pacific Steamship Company's *White Empress* slipped out of Greenock at night. When Flora awoke the following morning, she fed Alexander and went up on deck. Yesterday, she and Joan Almond, the friend she'd made, had been given a four-berth cabin and at this moment Joan and her eight-year-old daughter Mary were minding Alexander for her. The cabin was small and they had agreed that the only way to have privacy would be if, when Alex awoke at six o'clock, Flora fed him and left the cabin. Joan and Mary would then pull back the curtains on their bunks and wash themselves whilst watching Alex. It was a good arrangement, and so Flora found herself on deck at 7 a.m.

It was already warm and there was no swell on the sea. High in the clear blue sky above them an RAF flying boat circled lazily. On the horizon Flora could make out the smoke of the distant convoy they were to join, and behind, though too far away to recognise anybody standing on the decks, a corvette shadowed their progress.

She knew it was a corvette because two nights ago a group of four sailors – two of them from the corvette – had come into the bar of the small, seedy hotel where Flora had been living for the last five weeks. It was there that she'd met Joan, the young Scottish wife of a Canadian pilot. Joan and her daughter were going to stay for the duration of war with her husband's family in Montreal.

The four sailors were young, harmless boys who wanted to enjoy their last night before putting to sea again. One of them played the piano, and when he called out for a singer, a barmaid who had heard Flora singing, ran upstairs to ask her if she would oblige. With the baby sound asleep and the barmaid's assurance that she'd listen out for him, Flora went down to the room behind the public bar. It would be her last evening in Scotland until heaven only knew when. She may as well savour and remember it.

Enjoy it she did, for the requests came thick and fast, at first for the latest dancing tunes, 'Dancing with my Shadow', 'Begin the Beguine', 'Tea for Two'. Soon the place was full. People crowded into the spaces between tables and around the piano and Joan, who played the fiddle, was persuaded to join in. They sang the rousing patriotic songs that were currently on everyone's lips, the community songs that everyone knew – and ended with the old Scottish songs, 'Over the Sea to Skye', 'Westering Home' and 'It's Oh But I'm Longin' for my Ain Folk'. The evening ended with the sailors buying port and lemonade for Flora and Joan, promising to wave from the deck of their corvette should it come near enough to the *White Empress* and urging the two girls to go on the stage.

In Flora's room later, she and Joan talked far into the night. Joan said, 'If it doesn't work out for you, Flora – with your relatives in Ontario – come to Montreal, will you?'

Flora said, 'I'll keep some money aside, in case.' Nanny's sister Dorothy and her husband John, had two sons. One had joined the Royal Canadian Air Force at the outbreak of war, the other was studying to be a doctor. They kept a general store not far from Bancroft, a small town in northern Ontario where Flora would find a safe haven for the present. Then, seeing a shadow of disappointment cross Joan's face, she added, 'I won't stay indefinitely. I have to make a life and a home for myself and Alexander. I shall find work.'

'You are so brave,' Joan said. 'You and Alexander will fare well, I know you will. You are so confident.'

Flora would long remember this evening, when she'd stood in a bar with four sailors and sung her heart out for strangers, but she had not realised until Joan said the words that at last she had lost her shyness. With a baby to protect she was transformed. She said, 'You are my dear friend, Joan. I can't tell you how much it means to me to know you.'

When Joan went to her own room, Flora did the remainder of her packing, humming softly to herself as she pushed her belongings tight into the tin trunk which, with Alexander's little Rexine folding pram and a small suitcase for him, was all the luggage she was allowed to take aboard. Then she went to the window to have a last look at her country, for they would embark in the morning and wait for orders to sail. Outside, she saw and heard a sailor on a Norton motorcycle. He came tearing through the town, as he'd done on the last couple of nights. Tonight, though he could not possibly have seen her, something about him made her wave and wonder if he too would be on one of the escort ships that would protect them on their dangerous journey across the Atlantic.

When she had finished her packing, Flora knelt by her bed and said her prayers. She recited to herself the words she had heard in St Philip's church in Portobello. She said the prayers she loved, the prayers she had always said for Gran's soul. Though she'd told Nanny that she despised Andrew, it was not true. God knew the secrets of everyone's heart and she begged Him fervently to love and bring Andrew home safely. Last of all she prayed, as she had from the very hour they were born, for her two babies. 'Dear God. Keep my babies safe. Watch over the one who will never know me. Make him good and strong and true. And, please God, if ever he finds out what I have done and blames me for denying him his brother, let him know I loved him and help him forgive me.'

Then, quietened and comforted, she took Alexander into bed beside her where she could feed him and hold him close and feel his little heart beating against her breast. And in the dark emptiness of the night she knew there would never be a day of her life when she would not long for the missing son who had been conceived in love under a weeping tree.

Now, standing on the deck of the *White Empress* in the early morning, with her baby being minded by Joan, Flora told herself that she must put the past behind her. She and Alexander were taking their first steps into the unknown and yet she was not afraid. She had been told at the emigration office that they would be part of an eight-lane, ten-mile-long convoy, threatened by U-boats which, someone said, scored at the rate of four ships sunk on every crossing. The *White*

Empress carried four hundred unaccompanied children, many mothers with young babies and as many other adults, old and young.

She looked up. The sky was clear and empty. The aeroplane had gone. Some distance behind was the comforting presence of their escort.

Half a mile astern of the *White Empress*, Andrew stood at watch, binoculars to hand but not needed. The tail of the convoy was well within sight. They would collect more ships off the Irish coast, then, heading due west, would shadow them until the halfway point, where Canadian boats would take over. The *Iris* meanwhile would escort the eastbound convoy back to Britain.

He lifted the binoculars to keep station on the ship in front – a CPSS he recognised as the *White Empress*. He did not know how many ships would join the convoy at Dublin – nor the names of any of them – though the captain would. Throughout the trip they would be in constant contact by wireless and light signals with the other RN ships' commands. The crew, however, was never told anything until they were underway. The RN ships' names had been painted out and sailors' hat bands were blank. Secrecy was all, for the docks were natural feeding grounds for spies.

Only this morning Andrew had had to put on orders two sailors from the *Iris*. They'd returned late last night after spending the evening in an hotel bar at Greenock. Quite an evening by the sound of things. Two women who were going west on the *White Empress*, to sit out the war with relatives, had joined in the fun, one singing, one playing the fiddle.

Andrew had come down hard on the sailors, saying, 'You knew it was an offence. The night before we sail is not the time to get loose-tongued with cheap women in a bar on the docks. Explain yourselves.'

'Sir. We said nothing. I played the piano. My oppo sang. The women – Joan Almond and Flora Macdonald – were decent types – one a married woman, the other a young widow – going out to Canada with their children.'

Andrew's heart leaped. Then he pulled himself together. Flora Macdonald was a much more common name than he'd have believed – as he was discovering in his search. There were at least four in Edinburgh including an old lady of ninety, an actress, a younger girl and his own Flora. He said, 'You told them that you were sailing on a corvette, escorting the convoy?'

'Yes.'

'You will be reported.'

He had let them off lightly. They would probably lose two days' pay – but it was an eleventh-hour offence such as he might have made had he been in their shoes, enjoying the company of women, forgetting for one night what might lie ahead for all of them.

As the *White Empress* drew closer to Canada, tempers on board were becoming frayed. Everyone, the children included, was quieter than at the start of the trip. Bored now with the long journey under the cramped conditions of the cabin, Flora and Joan were starting to snap at one another, then, as quickly, apologising. Over the last week, so as not to aggravate a fraught situation, Flora had spent as much time as possible on deck, no longer keeping a lookout for the grey blobs in the distance that were the other ships in the convoy but instead allowing feelings of homesickness and doubt to assail her. Was she running away again? Should she have fought to keep both her babies? She could never go back unless the biggest deception of all came to light – the existence of the baby she had left behind. The questions went round and round in her head as she gazed back over a swirling, zigzagging wake.

Then, early in the morning of 1 July, as soon as she went on deck she noticed a change in the air. It was warmer and there, ahead, was the first sight of land in three weeks.

It was a wonderful, welcome sight and the negative mood of the last week evaporated in an instant. She ran back down the stairs and passageways to their cabin, where Joan was dressing young Mary, and said, 'Joan – quick! Come up on deck! Land ahoy!'

Joan grinned. She had done this trip before. 'Go ahead,' she said. 'We'll bring Alex up. Don't miss any of it.'

'I was beginning to think we'd sail on for ever,' Flora said. 'How long before we dock?'

'Hours yet. Let's get breakfast.'

Excitement was building in Flora as she washed Alexander, changed him and put him in the little pram which she must now remember to call a buggy. They made their way to the dining room for what would be their penultimate breakfast and listened carefully to the loudspeaker system and the repeated announcements that 'We will dock at midday. Will those passengers who disembark today please have their trunks packed. Those who wish to remain on board until tomorrow are requested not to block the passageways and stairs with their luggage. There will be ample time when today's passengers have left.'

Four hours later, fluttering with excitement, Flora stood at the rails amid churning propellers and the welcome hooting and tooting of tugs. She watched the berthing of the *White Empress* in the deep harbour that was right in the centre of the old town of Halifax. From the approach she had seen that Halifax was built on three hills. The houses appeared to be constructed in tiers, plentifully dotted with church spires, and towering over all, on top of the highest hill, was a citadel. 'No wonder the first explorers called this land Nova Scotia,' she'd said to Joan as they drew nearer.

All at once she had a shiver of what she could only liken to stage fright, such as she'd experienced in the ship's chapel when they asked her to sing the anthem last Sunday. Suppose the Murrays, Dorothy and John, did not like her – or she them? Would they resent her arrival when their own elder son was a Spitfire pilot in England, fighting the war? The younger son was at medical school at the University of Toronto.

'I am going ashore, Joan,' she said. 'Look after Alex. I have to ring Aunt Dorothy to let them know I'm here.'

She must also write to Nanny to let her know of her safe arrival. Just the one letter, Nanny had said. After that all the information she would receive would come through Dorothy.

'Go on then,' Joan said with a laugh in her voice. 'You're nervous, aren't you? I told you – you can always stay with me in Montreal.'

Flora found a phone box and soon she was speaking to a soft-voiced woman who made every sentence sound like a question because of the upward inflection of her Canadian accent.

'Glad you've arrived,' said Aunt Dorothy.

'Yes, I am,' Flora replied. 'I mean – thank you.'

'We'll meet you in Montreal.'

'No. No thank you,' Flora gabbled on. 'I'll stay with a friend for a few days.'

The slow drawl came back, 'Gee. You have no idea how worried we were about you, Flora. Now I can tell Uncle John that you'll soon be here. We'll see you in Bancroft, honey. Just as soon as you like.'

'Did you get the letter? The one telling you that I have a baby with me?' Flora asked. Suppose they could not accept both her and Alex?

'Yes, honey. My sister told us all about it – you being a young widow with a new-born baby. You are both wanted and welcome here.'

'Thank you. Thank you so much ...'

Later she began her letter to Nanny on the few sheets of headed *White Empress* notepaper she had saved.

Dear Nanny,

The voyage was uneventful and the *White Empress* comfortable but crowded. Our cabin companions were my new friend Joan and her daughter Mary. It made a difference having Joan. We shared the children though she could not feed Alexander. He is thriving – a really bonny bouncing baby. He weighs 12 pounds and has been no trouble at all. He is such a contented child.

We left Halifax by rail on the CPR to Montreal, setting off at 10.30 a.m. Joan and I had separate sleepers and we arrived in Montreal the next day at 10.30 a.m. We travelled through deeply forested country with high rolling hills and a wide, slow-flowing river that Joan says is used to transport lumber in the spring.

I loved Montreal but found it a disadvantage that I don't speak French. Joan is fluent. She said, 'Good job you aren't going to Quebec.'

Left Montreal at 9.30 and reached Belleville at 4 p.m. then changed trains for Bancroft. Thirteen little whistle-stops and four hours later we arrived in Bancroft.

Aunt Dorothy and Uncle John met us and drove us home.

They are wonderful people. I thank you from my heart for everything. Alexander is being thoroughly spoiled by Aunt Dorothy who says it's nice to have a baby in the house again after all these years.

The letter was not sent for another week, until Flora was settled, temporarily she thought, in the home of the kindest people she had ever known.

Chapter Eleven

Flora threw herself with enthusiasm into the life of the family. Aunt Dorothy, small and slim, with blue eyes like Nanny's and Nanny's quiet strength, was an immediate success with Alexander, who kicked his heels in delight whenever she approached.

It was odd that Flora had expected to find houses built of stone and brick, made to last for centuries. Here, wood gave the houses and the town a temporary feel, which was liberating to Flora, though the small, tight cabin on the *White Empress* had at last cured her of her fear of closed-in spaces. She asked why, with so much stone and rock, they used wood. They said that speed was the big factor. Timber was always to hand and houses, hospitals, schools, shops and factories could be built before the snows came. But she was warned of the ever-present danger of fire – and told heartbreaking tales of the loss of settlers' homes and businesses.

The Murrays' home was not as fancy as those of the rich lumber barons but they lived in comfort in a house that had a sitting room and parlour and a large dining room. There was a pantry and kitchen and a small summer kitchen, all on the ground floor, with upstairs five bedrooms and a bathroom. All wooden and shiny and no need for paint. Flora loved the clean lines of beds and painted cabinets, the maple floors, and even the squirrels that leaped and chased about in the branches of the trees and raced across the roof over the bedroom she shared with Alexander.

Aunt Dorothy was thrilled with Flora's pleasure in all things domestic. 'Wait till you see this,' she'd say, before showing her one of the latest delights. 'You've never seen one of these ...' of the big American washing machine with its huge rubber mangle rollers that were worked by electricity, on top of its shiny cream and chrome lid.

'Oh! May I use it?' Flora asked in a hushed, respectful whisper. Already she was astonished at the laundry – the huge furnace and the indoor airing lines where she could dry Alexander's diapers in no time at all. 'Imagine! All this space. The whole cellar for a laundry.'

'Not the whole of it,' Aunt Dorothy said. 'We have the furnace down here too, and storage space – and a big games room. But it's essential in this climate of cold winters and hot summers that the foundations of the houses go deep below the frost line.'

Around three sides of the house was a veranda – the deck – where Flora could put Alexander in the big baby carriage that Aunt Dorothy had saved from her own sons' babyhood for 'The grandbabies we hope to have one day.'

Uncle John Murray was a big burly man in his fifties with a weatherbeaten face, kind eyes and a shock of grey hair. Tough and cheerful, he was the eldest of five sons of an Irish farmer who had come to Canada as an immigrant to find that the virgin land he'd been given was uncleared forest with thin rocky soil. John had helped him work the land and build their home in the summer months; then he and his brothers had gone, with their father, as many young men did, to the winter logging camps in Algonquin Park in northern Ontario.

The family had prospered, and now Uncle John had a sawmill at Bird's Creek, handy for the York River and only a mile or two from Bancroft. The general store at Bird's Creek sold everything – from kerosene and finished planks from the sawmill to ladies' corsets, butter, eggs and cheese. The store was run by Aunt Dorothy, who told Flora she'd have peace of mind knowing Flora was minding the house for her. Flora said enthusiastically, 'I'd really love to.'

In the evenings, Flora sat and knitted balaclava helmets for sailors, glad to be a part of this happy family, while Aunt Dorothy served supper. And all the while, Uncle John told tales of old logging winters; of how sixty men living in one huge wooden hut never changed their clothes, but worked and slept in them the whole winter. He laughed at Flora's horrified outburst of 'Oh! How could they?'

'There was no choice,' he replied with a hearty chuckle. 'No running hot water. They'd wash their socks and string them up to dry in the smoke from the big central stove that was used for cooking and heating.'

He told of horses dragging 120-foot logs on sledges and slides down to the frozen rivers and lakes, there to await the spring thaw, when they would begin their slow journey down the rivers – the Ottawa, Petawawa and Madawaska further north, and the York River that ran right through Bancroft and Hastings county. And he told of the dangers of the drives downstream – for log jams were a fact of life on river drives and he'd seen brave men venture out on to a mountain of logs that sometimes were backed up for miles behind the jam. They had to find and saw through the key logs that were holding the others back. A missed footing or a sudden release of logs and these men did not make it back to the banks but slipped underwater as the logs closed above their heads.

Flora was horrified and enthralled. 'Will I see the logs?' she asked. 'Do they send them downriver now?'

'You'll see some. They send logs down the York as far as Baptiste for the electricity poles and railway sleeper ties. But not like the old days,' Uncle John replied. 'Now they have the railways they don't need to send them by river.' He said, 'Would you like me to take you around – show you the lakes and forest?'

'What about Alexander?' she said.

'Dorothy will be in seventh heaven if you'd leave him with her for a day,' he said. 'It's only a half-day's drive to Algonquin. And would you like to see the sawmill?'

'Yes.' She would. She would like nothing better than to be accepted, to be useful to this big, cheerful family of uncles and aunts and cousins who had all been to visit and welcome her into their midst, making her feel she belonged, giving her a chance. 'But,' she said, 'I intend to work for my living wherever I can have Alexander with me. I have sworn that never in my life will I be homeless or penniless again.'

'What are you trained for?' asked Aunt Dorothy.

Flora looked downcast. 'Domestic work's about it, I

suppose. I can cook and sew and wash and iron. I worked as housekeeper to a blind man ...' Then she added wistfully, 'I loved that job.'

'That was before you married?' Aunt Dorothy asked.

It had been the very last lie she'd told – and this one at Nanny's insistence. She had travelled as the young widow of a seaman. Now, Flora did not want her new life to start on the basis of lies, though the biggest secret of all could never be admitted. She knew she was blushing, and felt her cheeks go fiery as she said, 'Would it make you think badly of me if I told you that I was never officially married?'

Aunt Dorothy's eyes filled quickly with tears. 'Of course not. Thank you for telling us. I won't mention it again.'

Uncle John could not stand 'tears and talk', as he described women's secrets. 'If we are not too small a start for you, you can work in the store as soon as you are ready,' he said. 'I'll pay you the going wage and you can live here and help Dorothy in return for your board and lodgings. Dorothy goes into the store every day and we need another pair of hands. Take the baby with you. Two of you can manage the work and a baby. We are getting busy now the depression's over. Pity it took a war.'

'I'm ready now.' Flora wanted to work, to be useful, to do her bit.

She finished the letter to Nanny:

I have said that I will not stay without paying my way, and since they refuse to take the money (I still have nearly £100 left – or rather, $440 – and when you consider that a working wage is $18 a week that makes me rich), I shall make myself useful around the store and house.

I hear the news and read the papers. We get a few British papers though they come weeks late. And I am afraid for you living with the bombs and Blitz and rationing when I am living in luxury in a land of plenty. I wish you were here, Nanny, out of harm's way. I owe you such a debt of gratitude. It was not until we sailed that I began to appreciate all you have done for Alexander and me. Joan Almond, my friend, told me that there were 210,000 applications for a place on the *White Empress* and that ugly questions were asked in Parliament, where the organisers were accused of giving places to 'the moneyed classes' while the working class languished.

Mr Churchill did not approve of the evacuation – he deprecates what he calls a stampede from Britain – but there was really not much that I could have done to help. Alexander and I would just be another two mouths to feed.

Now I am here I am going to do whatever I can to help the war effort, as well as praying every night for you all.

Love, Flora.

She dared not ask of Nanny the question she so desperately wanted to: did Nanny think Robert really was better off with a title and as heir to an estate than with his own flesh and blood?

She remembered Gran's words – 'it's a rare female of any species that will adopt a suckling' – and hoped that Ruth never had cause to regret adopting Robert. If Ruth were to have a child of her own, wouldn't she love it more than she ever could Robert?

She sealed the envelope and on the little rounded flap point, though it would mean nothing to Nanny, drew a weeping tree for Robert.

1944

Ruth came to in a bleak private ward with a tearing pain across her belly and an unbearable thirst for water. Two nurses were holding her. 'I'm going to—' she said, before she was violently sick. 'Oh, no! No!' she managed to moan before another bout of projectile vomiting jerked her upright again.

'It's all right. Don't panic,' the senior nurse said briskly, while the younger one mopped Ruth's face with some kind of disinfectant-laden gauze. 'It's all over. You had a son – a fine seven-pound boy.'

Ruth's whole body from the waist down was on fire. Another spasm overtook her and she clutched at the young nurse's arm. 'Drink of water,' she demanded.

'No water for you. I'll bring the baby to you,' said the older nurse in her bossy, no-nonsense way.

'Don't you dare!' Ruth tried to shout but her voice sounded squeaky. It would be the chloroform – it was coming back to her now. She had demanded hospital and this Caesarean operation though the doctors had tried to dissuade her. How dared these women order her about? Yesterday she'd read in the papers about the free health service the country was to get when the war was finally over. Once that was imposed it would make little tyrants of the doctors and nurses. The patients would become supplicants. Well, it had not happened yet and here and now they should be reminded of who was paying whom. She said, 'I am paying for this! Don't tell me what I will or won't do.'

'All right, mother,' the nurse said, but the hectoring tone had gone. She turned on the junior instead. 'Bring Lady Campbell a feeding cup with two fluid ounces of water. Be quick.' Then, to Ruth, as she laid her back against the pillows, 'Try to sleep, Lady Campbell. You can have your baby when you are rested.'

Ruth fell back against the pillows, closed her eyes for a second or two then said, 'Before you go, Nurse, something for the pain, please.'

Five minutes later she felt the spout of the china drinking cup on her lips and this time obeyed the order: 'Take it slowly, Lady Campbell, or you'll bring it all back.' The old nurse added, 'Your husband and son are here. I told them you must not be disturbed until you are ready. They are with the baby.' Then she gave her an injection at the top of her thigh. Funny, Ruth thought as she drifted off, funny thinking of the nurse as old – she might even be younger than I am.

Ruth was thirty-four and considered herself too old for this child-bearing nonsense. She remembered as she drifted into the limbo between sleep and wakefulness that her age was the reason she'd given to the team of specialists and surgeons that they cut it out of her. She would not, could not, contemplate the ruin of her body that a normal delivery would entail.

So Gordon was here at the Simpson Maternity Hospital and had the other brat with him? He would be satisfied now, she hoped – and she hoped too for his speedy recall to naval duties. She put her hand down to her middle, wanting to feel the old flatness, but pulled away fast as an agonising pain shot through her. Her body had been bound with tight bandages – at her own insistence. Losing one's figure was to be expected, Gordon had said – and had added, 'As long as you and the baby are all right, my dear.'

She would be all right and the baby was a healthy weight, so her duty was done. Thank the Lord. At Ingersley a new, younger nurse had been engaged. Between the new girl, Bessie and Nanny, who had closed Ivy Lodge and moved back into the house to look after the brat, they should be able to cope with two children. Ruth had no interest whatever in either of them. All she wanted to do was to get back to normal, to the riding and the civic duties which to her surprise she enjoyed. She'd taken to the work of JP as the proverbial duck to water.

One nurse would be enough for the baby. Besides, it was all the estate could afford. The evacuees had gone and plans were afoot to build estates of council houses and prefabricated houses using German and Italian prisoner-of-war labour. Nobody wanted to live in hamlets and villages and isolated farm cottages. Ruth's income had already dropped. The Great War had started the decline in their fortunes, and Elizabeth's legacy had revived them for a time, but half of Ruth's own money was now gone. The war, changing attitudes and the obscene wages that labouring people now expected had drained all the big estates. Ingersley and the Campbells were not alone. Any number of landed families were in worse trouble than they were. When it was over and everyone counted the cost, many estates would go to the wall. Many – but not hers. Ruth would not budge.

There was a commotion outside her room when Ruth came to and looked at the clock: 3 p.m. She had been asleep for an hour and could have slept for longer. She looked down at herself. They had put her own pink silk nightgown on her and the angora-trimmed bed-jacket was draped prettily across her shoulders.

She heard Gordon's voice and the brat, Robert, clattering his feet on the polished floor outside her room, tapping at her door. 'Come in,' she said in a faint voice, and slid lower in the bed.

Gordon had evidently seen the baby, for he came to her misty-eyed, with arms outstretched. 'Darling! How was it?'

'Hell,' she replied, closing her eyes and turning her face away from his lips so that they brushed her ear. 'There will be no more.' She meant it – and he'd know now that his married life was over.

She had already told him that a woman of her age had no interest in married love – and that if he wished he could take a young mistress. Gordon had been horrified at the suggestion, saying that he would abide by her decision but that he hoped she would change her mind once the baby was here. She would not. She could no longer bear his lovemaking, the timid fumblings and his gratitude when he was so quickly and easily satisfied.

Today he wore uniform, which made him appear authoritative and handsome. Behind him stood two nurses, one of them with a bundle in her arms. Gordon quickly lifted Robert, who held a bunch of carnations, on to the bed, saying, 'You wanted to come and see your mummy and baby brother, didn't you?'

Ruth screeched, 'Get him off me. My God – my stitches!' as Gordon set down the frightened child, who began to cry loudly: 'Don't whip me, Mummy. I'm sorry – sorry – sorry!'

'Robert didn't know—' Gordon began, but at that moment one of the nurses came forward quickly to help Ruth into a sitting position, while the other held out the bundle, saying, 'Can you manage, Lady Campbell, or shall I hold baby?'

She must get it over with. Gordon was displeased by her outburst against the brat – the apple of his eye. She made a half-hearted attempt at a smile. The nurse gently placed the bundle into her arms and Ruth looked with polite curiosity for a moment at the tiny face of her baby.

She knew they were all waiting for her to say something – but she could not, for as she looked at the baby, the room seemed to fade about her. There came a terrible pain in her throat and her heart, then a sudden, searing surge of emotion that immobilised her in the stillness of the room. Tightening her arm around him to hold him secure, and with the piercing and heady scent of carnations filling the space around her, Ruth gently pulled back the shawl so that she could better see this tiny, blond, pink and perfect creature. Never in her life until now had she felt this powerful, protective force. Never had she seen a child so beautiful. Love for him overwhelmed her as she looked up, starry-eyed, at Gordon. 'He's your living image. He's beautiful, Gordon,' she whispered. 'Thank you.'

Gordon came to sit at her side, embarrassed now. 'No need to thank me, darling,' he joked. 'You did it all, you know.'

Robert came clambering on to Gordon's lap. He put a restraining arm around the child but said, 'Have another look at your brother, Robert.'

Ruth watched, horrified, as the brat poked his great ugly head into the baby's face. She shouted, 'Get your head out of the way!' and pushed her open hand hard against Robert's face to send him toppling backwards on to Gordon's lap.

'Steady on!' Gordon said as he held Robert close and comforted him. The child cried harder. Gordon had seen enough. 'Come on, my boy. Let us leave Mummy and baby to rest a while.' He stood and held fast to Robert's hand. 'Where do you want to go?' he asked, smiling, rumpling his son's dark curls affectionately. 'You are still my first-born, my son and heir. You will always be number one to me, Robert,' he said.

When they had gone, Ruth put the angelic bundle on to the bed. The baby cried. Ruth picked him up and he stopped crying at once. Smiling, she put him down again. Again he started to cry. The nurse was still in the room and Ruth turned to her. 'Bring a cradle in here, Nurse,' she said. 'I have changed my mind. I'll keep him beside me, day and night.'

She gazed down at her baby. He was so fair, sweet and content. To think she had given life to this – this wonder. He was her; he was herself but new and shiny. She would mould him to be herself but better. He was Napoleon. He was Jesus Christ. There had never been such a child. All else faded into insignificance as the nursing sister came back, wheeling the cradle, took the sleeping baby from Ruth and wrapped him firmly in the shawl.

She placed him in the crib and left the room while Ruth lay, watching her miracle – Edward, she would call him – snuffling, his tiny, delicate hand waving in front of his face. All her pains had gone. She reached over and placed her little finger in his hand. The infant grabbed it with surprising strength. She smiled and whispered, 'You, Edward, are the real son and heir. The rightful son and heir of Ingersley. It will be yours. I have been keeping it for you. Nobody shall threaten you, my lovely, my darling.'

13 May 1945
Suddenly it was all over. After almost six years, the war was

over. In London, 50,000 people went wild with joy, shaking hands, kissing and hugging strangers, dancing in the streets and gathering around Queen Victoria's statue at the Palace, demanding 'We want the King!' until eight times the Royal Family came on to the balcony, waving in shy astonishment at the joyful people celebrating their victory below.

In the North Atlantic on that day, the frigate on which Andrew, now first lieutenant, was on duty as officer of the watch slowly circled on the flat, calm sea, waiting for the word. He could do nothing but watch the horizon around them, the dull sky overhead, the blank radar screen, as they turned ninety degrees to port every half-hour, obeying orders, waiting, waiting. They had been steaming for two days and two nights at a steady ten knots, getting nowhere; keyed up in case there were any last-minute attacks.

At ten o'clock the signal came: *Hostilities terminated. All U-boats have been ordered to surrender. The signal is a large black flag.* There were no U-boats in the waters around them, Andrew was certain. U-boat attacks were sporadic now.

Then the beaten foe emerged. All over the Atlantic, where they had been lying or hiding, they surfaced. Some, he later learned, scuttled themselves. Most, like the two he now saw before him, rose dripping and silent on the horizon, their hard shapes topping the grey sea level.

The captain ordered them to sail towards the foe in a swaying, corkscrew pattern. There would be no last-minute desperate torpedoes for their ship. When they drew near Andrew could see that the two U-boats were side by side, stationary, with the black flags drooping at the mast-head. The decks were crowded with men, as their own decks were.

Their war was ended. Andrew would enjoy the victory – the parades, the recognition, the homecoming – and then what?

Three months later, he went home for a blessed leave. He followed up every slender lead he had in the search for his Flora. He'd discovered that she was the elder of the two young Flora Macdonalds in Edinburgh. A younger Flora Macdonald than his had been issued with a ration book. His own darling Flora had worked at the munitions factory in Portobello until she injured her back and left. He checked the registers at every hospital where she could have been taken. There was no Flora Macdonald on any of their lists. It seemed that both Flora Macdonalds had vanished. But then, hundreds of people passed through Edinburgh during the war and disappeared from the records. He would not, could not stop searching.

A week before he returned to his ship, Andrew and Ma received an invitation from Sir Gordon Campbell to join the VJ Day celebrations at Ingersley on Saturday 18 August. Andrew would not be demobbed for another year and Sir Gordon was going to continue until he retired, but the victory in August, when Japan surrendered after Hiroshima, had been celebrated with street parties up and down the land. Ingersley was going to do it in style and Andrew would be able to put aside his search for the day.

He wore his best uniform and Ma decked herself out in an apple-green dress of crêpe de Chine with a picture hat in fine white straw. Bessie's occasional visits to the flat meant that Ma had 'kept up', as she put it, with the goings-on at Ingersley and in the East Lothian area, and now she regaled Andrew with second-hand stories.

Bessie had told her of the excitement when a Heinkel was brought down over Davey Hamilton's land. She told of the prisoner-of-war camps at Gosford where 3,000 Germans were held and the overcrowding there which meant that other camps had to be opened in Haddington. They were still there, Ma said, but she doubted if they'd be allowed to go and look around.

Andrew said, 'Why would I go and stare at German POWs?'

'You know Ingersley stopped being a hospital, don't you?'

'Really?' he said, to please her.

'Aye. They requisitioned a bigger place, outside the danger zone. Ingersley couldn't hold enough patients so it was used for administration instead until a month ago. Now it's the family home of the Campbells again. As long as Lady Campbell doesn't ask for the furniture back,' she added, as they set off for the VJ party.

'Too bad,' Andrew said. 'She got rid of you cheaply.'

'Don't, Andrew. You don't still feel bad about them, do you?'

'No. I'm grateful to Sir Gordon. He made me pull my socks

213

up and join the navy. He treated us well. But you don't owe anything to Lady Campbell, Ma,' he said.

'She's a cruel woman. Bessie says so.'

It was not like Ma to speak unkindly and Andrew raised his eyebrows in enquiry and asked what she meant.

'She was cruel from the start to wee Robert. Never took to him. I expect because she didn't know she was having a baby. I don't think she ever really wanted one. It didn't matter so much that she was cold-hearted, though, for Bessie and Nanny doted on him. But when Edward was born it all changed. Lady Campbell thinks the sun shines out of his bottom, Bessie says. She favours him all the time over Robert, who's a poor weakling of a lad. And no wonder. He doesn't get enough to eat. Bessie bakes treats for him and sneaks food up the stairs to him at nights.'

Andrew felt his hackles rise. What sort of a woman would be cruel to her own flesh and blood? He said, 'Then Miss Taylor and Bessie had better do right by him. Sir Gordon can't know about it.'

Ma said, 'Lady Campbell's going to send the poor little thing away to a boarding school when he's seven.'

'That's the way they are – the upper classes,' Andrew said. 'They don't have any real feelings.'

'Bessie's going to leave when they send him away. She says Nanny Taylor goes the other way to make up, keeping the wee lad from his mother as best she can.'

It sounded like mere servants' gossip to Andrew. 'Don't listen, Ma,' he said. 'Come on – are you ready?'

There had been many changes since Andrew had last seen it, but that day Ingersley looked good. The sun shone and they could hear children's happy laughter ringing out as they went through the wooden gates beside their old South Lodge home. The house was still unoccupied, though the Campbells had engaged a new cook from the village. The smell of cut grass was sweet in the golden afternoon sun as they walked on the mown lawn, where little folding tables had been set for the adults. In the centre was a long trestle table for the children of the villages and estate. The trestle table was laid, Ma noticed, with hospital plates and beakers. Volunteers were needed. Ma was one of the first to offer, and soon she had shanghaied a team of women into carrying out ashets laden with sand-wiches, jellies, cakes and trifles to the children, who could barely contain their excitement.

Sir Gordon Campbell and his wife mingled with the guests, shaking hands with all. 'Pleased to see so many friends,' said Sir Gordon when they reached Andrew and Ma.

Lady Campbell had not changed. She was still pretty and looked good in a pleated silk frock of patriotic red, white and blue, and a small, whining child clung to her hand, taking most of her attention. She gave Andrew the impression that she was pretending indifference whilst watching him closely, yet she managed to look down her nose at him as she held out a limp hand. 'Andrew,' she drawled. 'So you made it unscathed, too. How nice to see you.'

Sir Gordon asked if Andrew would continue in the Royal Navy.

'No, sir. The police are recruiting. I thought I'd join.'

'And leave the sea?' Sir Gordon's eyebrows lifted in amused astonishment.

'I can't bring myself to cut all ties,' Andrew smiled. 'I shall buy a small boat and join a sailing club.'

Sir Gordon could not linger for too long with any one guest. He had just started to say, 'You will stay for the dancing and the evening entertainment – you and your mother. We'll have a talk then ...' when a skinny little livewire of about five years old came tearing across the grass, laughing and shouting, 'Daddy! Daddy! Here I am!' His dark curls fell across his eyes, blinding him as he launched himself at Sir Gordon's legs and, as he did so, knocked to the grass his baby brother, who started to cry.

It was ordinary childish high spirits and did not warrant the violent reaction of Lady Campbell. Andrew had never seen anyone roused so quickly from passiveness to fury. It was shocking to him and must have terrified the child. Her eyes were wild. 'You wicked boy!' she snarled. She snatched the child from Sir Gordon's legs with fingers like talons, roughly enough to bruise the arm of the young boy, whose face was suddenly white with terror as his mother said, through clenched teeth, 'You will go to your room. No tea. No party for you. I will deal with you later!' Ignoring the shaking child's sobs, Lady Campbell called out for Nanny, who came racing to protect the heartbroken child from his mother and take him away. The punishment was harsh and excessive and Andrew found himself fighting back the urge to defend the little lad.

Sir Gordon picked up his younger son and remonstrated with his wife. 'No punishment today, Mummy,' he said firmly. 'My son, Robert, meant no harm.'

Andrew silently noted the phrase, *My son, Robert*, and wondered what Sir Gordon had meant by it. Was it a slip of the tongue? Whatever it was, the Commander must have made his point, for Robert was included in the tea party and Andrew felt enormously relieved – almost as if he himself were the child's protector.

Later there was another incident. Ma was talking to Lucy Hamilton, who had her child, Phoebe, by the hand, when little Robert, without adult supervision, came up to them and slipped his hand into Andrew's. He stuck his other thumb in his mouth and regarded Andrew solemnly. Andrew smiled and bent down to talk to him. He was a dear little chap.

The child took his thumb out but still held fast to Andrew's hand. 'You're a sailor,' he said. 'Sandy's daddy is a sailor.'

'Is he?' Andrew, puzzled, smiled at him.

Lucy Hamilton laughingly explained, 'Sandy is Robert's imaginary friend. Nobody has ever seen him ...'

'I have,' said Robert, still with his hand in Andrew's, but at that moment Nanny Taylor, displaying the energy of a young girl, came haring across the grass again to take the child away. It was as if the boy were Nanny's own.

'It's all right,' Andrew said, as Nanny lifted Robert off his feet and held him fast. 'We were having a nice little talk – weren't we?' but Nanny looked at him with eyes wide with alarm, as if he were about to kidnap her precious child. She did not say a word but turned and scorched across the grass to the house, the boy laughing in her arms and waving back at Andrew.

All in all, though, he and Ma agreed on the train home, it had been a good day of celebration. The old drawing room – cleared of desks and equipment but not yet restored to its former elegance – made a fine place for dancing. A band had

216

been hired and in the smoky, dusty room that had once been so grand, masters and servants, with social barriers gone, danced to the eightsome reel, the Dashing White Sergeant and the energetic Scottish country dances.

On the train home Ma said, 'I shouldn't say this, son – but did you see Lady Campbell dancing the Gay Gordons with Mike Hamilton?' She giggled. 'She looked as if she was swooning in his arms. She must have had a drop to drink.' Then she added, 'I don't think Sir Gordon noticed.'

'No,' Andrew said. 'People never see what's under their noses.' And he sat back to think about the day and to wonder whether the favoured son was Mike Hamilton's.

By 1946 it should have been easy to forget and consign to the past the lies and the fear of being found out. But never a day passed when Flora did not ache for her lost son, though her working and home life was secure and happy.

Aunt Dorothy and Uncle John loved her like a daughter, and Alexander, who would start school soon, was their 'little big guy' who followed Uncle John everywhere. Alexander was a delight; a happy, contented and outgoing child who was easy to please and devoted to the man in his life, Uncle John. He was six years old, tall and strong, and had an enormous, healthy appetite. He had dark wavy hair like Andrew's and eyes that everyone said were like Flora's own; large and round and liquid green. Alexander could read a few words, talk like an angel and pick out a tune on the cottage piano. He was not allowed to go up to the sawmill with Uncle John for safety reasons, but he'd come flying across the yard or along the deck whenever he heard the engine of the Dodge arriving, and always he'd yell, 'I'm here – I am here, Uncle John. Wait for me and Campbell.'

Flora would startle every time he said it. It was common for lonely children to have imaginary friends, but there was more to it with Alexander. Flora's own guilt and pain came to taunt her day and night. Alexander had probably got the name Campbell from the letters from Nanny that Dorothy read out to them – news of Robert and the Campbell family, once even a photograph of Nanny and Robert but taken from so far away that it was impossible to make out their features or Robert's

217

shape, though he looked smaller and thinner than Alexander. But then Robert's birth weight had only been half Alexander's, and rationing was still severe at home – and Flora told herself not to worry because you couldn't tell a thing from a photo.

However, Campbell was not a childish phase. Campbell had been there from the start – from infancy, when Alexander would reach out and cry when he found that his arms were empty. When Flora avidly read the British newspapers that were sent to Bancroft – the Edinburgh *Evening News* amongst them – Alexander would sit, thumb in mouth, watching, once making her heart almost stop by pronouncing solemnly as Flora scrutinised a newspaper photograph of a group of naval officers, 'Campbell's daddy is a sailor. Like my daddy was – wasn't he, Mommy?'

Flora asked, 'Where does Campbell live?'

Alexander took his thumb from his mouth and replied solemnly, 'Stockland. Silly.'

Flora had to set an extra place at table for Campbell. Alexander would shout, 'Don't close the door. Campbell's not in yet,' or, 'Hold Campbell's hand too, Mommy.' It was an obsession.

When she forgot, for a few hours, her anxiety for Robert and her guilt over both boys, Flora was happy and lucky, she believed. She went down on her knees every night to thank God for delivering her into the Murray family, who now declared themselves fearful that she might leave them to find something better. She worked hard in the store and was keen to learn the lumber business. And she was well liked in the town she had come to love for its friendliness, its wooden homes and shops and wide, straight streets, and its crystal-clear air scented with pine that was clean, healthy and energising. She loved the space and the sense of belonging to a small community that had put down roots and tamed a land of few people but a wealth of natural resources. She thrilled to the feeling of kinship she shared with the Scottish society. She became a leading light in both the amateur operatic society and the church, where she sang in the choir. She was also one of the prettiest girls in a town that was famed for them. Aunt Dorothy said she was a little too thin, but her green eyes were clear and bright and the long red hair which she wore in the American style of a ponytail, or at shoulder length, was thick and wavy.

Soon after she settled in, she met Jake Murray, who came home on leave from the RCAF. He had miraculously survived a crash, suffering only surface burns on his feet, and was flown home for two months' leave. Jake was tall and burly like his brother Peter, whom she already knew well. Both the Murray sons had blue eyes and curly fair hair, as their father's had been. The only cloud on this particular front was the brothers' rivalry for her attention. Flora felt badly about it, though Aunt Dorothy laughed and said, 'They have always competed, Flora. But once you choose, the other will back off.'

All the same, Flora did not want to choose between the brothers, though she found herself drawn to Jake – the raffish one, the daredevil who made her laugh and, in the four November weeks he was home, taught her to ski and skate despite his own injuries. Jake wanted to follow in his father's footsteps after the war – take over the sawmill, run the store, buy timber limits, mines, for there were gems and minerals and precious metals to be dug from the ground. He even got Flora on to a ranger's flight over some of the thousands of small lakes of northern Ontario and up to see the great remote forest of Algonquin Park. Before he returned to England they went to Toronto to stay with relatives for a weekend, and there Jake took her to a romantic dinner and dance where he kissed her and said, 'I'll make you the richest woman in Canada, honey. You will never regret it.'

Flora laughed at his joking and said, 'I hope you are not proposing, Jake.'

Then she saw that he was serious for he said, 'I have nothing to offer yet.' He laughed, held her tight, whirled her around the dance floor and said, 'When the war is over, you and I will set the place alight.'

She would not, could not, say to a man who needed hope of a bright future whilst in mortal danger that she had never felt for any man the love she still had for Andrew and, unless she could feel that way again, she would never marry. And she was glad that she had not turned him down, because barely six months before the end of the war, in late 1944 when the war

219

news was good – when the tide had turned against Hitler, when hope sprang in everyone's heart at the news from England, when Aunt Dorothy and Uncle John were confident that Jake would soon be home – the blow fell.

Jake's Spitfire went down over the Channel. Jake was dead and the Murrays could not recover from their loss. Aunt Dorothy's hair went white in the space of three weeks and Uncle John came to a halt. He lost his energy and drive and would sit by the fire or in the stock room at the store, saying little, refusing to go to church, even when Flora was singing.

He did not pull himself out of it for months – until his misery started to affect Alexander, who followed him around and was always there like a faithful puppy. That year, Alexander began bursting into uncontrollable hysterical sobbing that had no apparent cause. When Flora asked what was the trouble, the child cried harder and said, 'Campbell's mommy hurts him. She hurts him real bad. I want Campbell.'

Flora went cold to her heart. But Alexander's obsession with Campbell was to last until, at the age of twelve, he stopped telling his mom about Campbell, who needed someone like Alex to stand up for him, help him fight the enemy that was ranged against him.

Chapter Twelve

1952

Nanny Taylor regarded herself in the nursery mirror. She was still a fine looking woman and she was seventy-two years of age. Her white hair was thick and plentiful and she wore it pulled back into a bun at the nape of her neck. She had never been vain but was glad that all the nonsense of youth was behind her, even though her duties were not. Robert was away at boarding school and her most onerous task should have been. She should be living out her retirement in Ivy Lodge. As it was, eight-year-old Edward could be a bit of a handful and she was often needed at Ingersley House.

Ruth had come to motherhood and maternal feelings late and was hypercritical of anyone, other than Nanny, who had charge of Edward. Nurses came and went with unsettling regularity and Nanny had to stand in for them, between times.

She still had plentiful energy and could have managed the occasional duties from Ivy Lodge had it not been for Ruth's overpowering hatred for the child Nanny loved above all – loved, in fact, above all who had ever come within a mile of her. She had cared for Robert from months before he was even born. Her instincts were as strong as they would have been had she herself given birth to him. Robert was hers. And she must protect him against Ruth's savage and vengeful authority.

Nanny had always been in a unique position with Gordon. Now she was in the same position with Robert. Ruth must let Nanny have her way because Nanny could not be dismissed. She knew too much. Nanny wished with all her heart that she did not, for knowing was a burden that had grown with the years, just as the dread of Gordon's ever finding out that he had been cheated had never gone. The longer she kept the secret, the deeper her miserable involvement. But she could never tell.

Twice Nanny had postponed her long-planned trip to Canada because she could neither leave Robert to the mercy of Ruth nor take him with her if the secret were to be kept. She must wait until Gordon retired. Gordon was Robert's best safeguard against Ruth's cruelty.

Today Ruth had sent for her to discuss Robert's latest wrongdoing. Nanny descended to the drawing-room floor from her apartments in the attic to find Ruth, wearing the severely tailored suit she used for magisterial work, in a fury, pacing the drawing room, fuming. 'You will have to go for him, Nanny. It is impossible for me. The wretched child!'

'What is it?' Nanny said. 'Please stop pacing, Ruth.' She spoke to Ruth as if she, Nanny, were the senior authority figure. It evened things up a little.

'It's Robert. I had a phone call from the school. He ran away.'

Ruth spoke harshly and, Nanny noticed, high spots of colour had come into her cheeks. There were times when Ruth seemed certifiably deranged, to Nanny's mind. 'Why?'

'He's wicked. He just ran away again.'

Nanny's heart skipped a beat. Robert had not 'bolted' as Ruth termed his escapes, for a couple of years. It used to frighten her to death – his going missing for days and her not being allowed to report it. She used to have to keep it quiet because he only did it when Gordon was away at sea, and Ruth would not go to the police and have the family name dragged through the mire. Ruth used to say, 'He'll turn up when he's hungry enough. I'll make sure he won't do it again.'

Now, in the drawing room, Nanny looked at Ruth and asked, 'Why? Where? Do you know?'

'No!'

Robert's school was as far from home as it was possible to be, on the outskirts of London. Ruth said it was one of the most distinguished prep schools in Britain. Robert detested it and referred to it as Colditz. Nanny had never seen it though Gordon described it to her as 'a toughening-up establishment'.

In Nanny's opinion 'a toughening-up establishment' was the last thing Robert needed.

Robert was a weakling – there was no doubt about it. But how could a child flourish in a home where he was in fear of his mother's temper and the whippings she gave him? And how could a boy grow straight and strong if he were not given good nourishment? To insist that he was not to be given second helpings was cruel; the latest order, given to the kitchen staff and not to Nanny on his last end-of-term holiday, that Robert was to eat meat only twice a week, was quite wrong. Tuberculosis and infantile paralysis were the scourge of children, and Nanny was going to countermand all such orders. If it happened again she would tell Gordon about it. Anyone would imagine that Ruth was trying to enfeeble Robert.

Now she looked Ruth in the eye. 'Don't you think it's your duty to go to the school since Gordon can't do it?'

'No!' Ruth snapped open her crocodile handbag and fished out a vanity case and a wallet. 'There's a train at ten,' she took four five-pound notes out and put them on the overmantel. 'That's for your fare and the hotel bill,' she said. 'You have full authority to take any action in this matter, no matter how severe. And you are much more likely to get to the truth than I. Frankly I won't waste my time listening to Robert's excuses.'

She sat down, opened the vanity case and pursed her lips as she inspected her eyebrows and hair. 'I have so little time these days.' She applied a small powder puff to her nose and then took out a large gold-plated lipstick and made swooping vermilion curves on her full, small mouth.

Nanny watched, disgusted. She did not approve of cosmetics and saw no reason for Ruth to use them, especially as the intimate side of her marriage was evidently over. She and Gordon had separate bedrooms. And though Nanny suspected that Gordon would have preferred it otherwise, she knew that some women could not continue a physical relationship at Ruth's age. Ruth showed no interest whatever in the opposite sex and Nanny sometimes wondered if she had imagined that conversation with Mike Hamilton in the nursery. She said now in reply to Ruth, 'It would mean a great deal to Robert if you went. I'm sure Gordon would want you to.'

Ruth looked up from the mirror and raised one expressive

223

eyebrow. 'I said I have so little time, Nanny. So little time for Gordon. I have *no* time for Robert.'

So it was that by eleven o'clock Nanny found herself travelling in a third-class carriage speeding towards London, unable to concentrate on anything but her darling Robert. What on earth had happened? What was so awful that her darling Robert, at only twelve years old, would run away to London? And what action could she take but soothe the righteous anger of the school's headmaster and ask him not to be too hard on her angel?

Robert limped out of the headmaster's study after receiving six of the best. He would not blub, especially in front of Whitmore and Cutler and their six stinking, rotten cowards who were spread out down the corridor about ten feet apart, ready to trip him or jeer if he stumbled or showed any sign of weakness.

His knees felt like jelly, and the red-hot, searing pain in his buttocks and his back was agonising. His skin must be broken, for he could feel the pull of his underwear against sticky, drying blood. He would probably be marked for life, he thought bitterly. The last whiplash scarring had not faded.

The headmaster, Thomas Barber, to whom Robert had given the deserved secret nickname the Barbarian, was a crashing snob who made his preferences for his several young lordling pupils very plain. He made plainer his predilection for delivering ferocious beatings to young boys who had no protection.

If Robert had had Cutler's money or Whitmore's foothold in the English aristocracy he'd no doubt be one of the Barbarian's blue-eyed boys. Now he drew level with Whitmore who, at thirteen, was six months older than himself, but a head taller and twice as broad.

'Och, the noo. He's crying,' Whitmore jeered. 'Smacked bottoms for the wee laddie, was it?'

Robert put a hand to his forehead to push back the wavy dark hair from his eyes. It was stuck, damp with the sweat of fear, not tears. He was halfway down the panelled corridor. If he could keep going, if his legs would carry him steady, he'd make it to the sick bay. It wasn't cowardice – he was short of breath again, the tight feeling was in his chest and all the signs were there for another attack of coughing and wheezing.

'Puny little thing! Eh, what?' said Cutler, sticking out one foot, hoping to trip him. Robert avoided the foot but only by taking two steps in quick succession and nearly stumbling. This made the bullies laugh and, following Cutler's lead, cry, 'Do it again!'

'Do the Highland fling!'

'I'll bet he looks sweet in his kilt, dancing to the bagpipes.'

They would close in at any moment and make threats. Robert was at the end of his tether with it. Now he summoned up the courage to mutter, 'Shuddup!' before, to his relief, one of the masters came through the door at the end of the corridor. He was safe for the moment, although masters never intervened in bullying, which for Robert confirmed that it was deliberately encouraged by the Barbarian.

The master was Robert's music teacher, a crusty old fellow whose only sanction over these bullies would be to give detentions for loitering in the corridor. 'What are you doing here?' he demanded of Whitmore. Whitmore had no musical ability; piano playing was seen as sissy by the mob.

'Nothing, sir,' said Whitmore.

'Then do something,' said the master curtly. Four order marks and the boy would have to do an hour's drill before breakfast as well as having a half-hour added to prep for each order mark.

The toughs moved on, the mob followed and the master watched them go.

Robert ran up the stairs to the sick room. He was gasping for breath when he reached the school nurse's domain. She was not motherly, but being the only female in the place, apart from the masters' wives, was more like an elderly aunt. She was, at least, dutiful.

'Ah! They brought you back. What a state you are in. Come here!'

Robert leaned his shoulder against the closed door. His whole body was trembling uncontrollably now but he dared not let his backside touch anything. His underpants and grey flannels felt as if they were made of hair cord on the hot, tender area. He closed his eyes and put his hands on to the door to steady himself before he drew in several rapid, shallow breaths. Now he was afraid. The air in his lungs could not be released fast enough. He could not speak. His face was suffused with blood. His head was spinning as, clutching his knees, he bent forwards, struggling to breathe, unable to speak. A few seconds later he slid to the shiny linoleum and lay, semi-conscious, at the nurse's feet.

He dreamed – and yet he knew that he was dreaming, because only half of his dream had really happened. He had run away after a night of terror in the dormitory where, because he was the smallest and weediest, they had soaked his mattress with water. He had to sleep on it, knowing that if he complained to the dormitory duty master he wouldn't be believed, but that not to complain was an implicit admission of bed-wetting. He'd lain there, cold, hungry and afraid until dawn.

Dawn came early in May, and this morning, in the cool grey light, he had dressed in flannels and a shirt. He did not put on the stiff collar that would give the game away. He took with him a jersey and a few things from his locker, and unseen he climbed out of the window and dropped to the balcony of the woodwork room. There he hung by his hands before dropping to the grass and running like the devil for the wall.

Once over it, he picked himself up and ran. A mile from school he reached the main road and cadged a lift from a lorry driver.

Jack, for that was the driver's name, was an ex-naval type who was about to stop for breakfast at a transport café. Robert asked if he might eat too. Jack said, 'I hope you're telling the truth. You're on your way to Scotland. You have a train ticket but you lost your money for the bus?'

'Yes,' Robert lied, then added, 'I'll give you the money back when the post offices open. I have my book with me,' and was soon tucking into the best breakfast he'd had in his entire life.

Jack bought him a huge plate of bacon, sausages, two eggs, mushroom, tomato and fried bread. This he ate with three bread rolls and a steaming mug of strong tea with all the sugar he wanted, though sugar was still rationed, seven years after the war had ended. And all this in a smoky place with laughter and jokes and the Wurlitzer playing Guy Mitchell's 'She Had a Dark and Roving Eye'. Robert would never forget it.

Jack wanted to talk about the war. 'Your father's in the navy?'

226

'Yes. Soon be out though. He's finishing at fifty-five.'
Robert was full and happy. He didn't want to show off to Jack,
who had been an able seaman throughout the war. 'He was on
the *Rutland*.'

'A mate of mine was on the *Rutland*,' said Jack. 'Had some
hairy near misses in the Med. Said if they'd not had the
captain they did, he'd be on the bottom by now.' He began to
regale Robert and the two others at the table with stories of his
wartime experiences in Coastal Command. He said, 'Can you
manage more?' to Robert, seeing him wiping with his bread
every last streak of egg from the plate.

'Would you mind awfully if I did?' Robert said. He never had
enough to eat. School meals were foul. Earwigs crawling out of
the salad were commonplace. Once he'd found white maggots –
live ones – under his one slice of cold meat. Even at home
Mother said he was greedy and must not be over-fed. She kept
strict watch over his voracious appetite, saying he must have
worms or some other noxious sickness. The only times he'd
ever not been hungry were when he went out on the boat with
Father – those wonderful days, few and far between, when
Father was home and they'd take a picnic hamper stuffed with
good food, and even sometimes pull in at Dunbar harbour and
dine out. There, fish and chip suppers could be had at any hour
of the day.

Jack shouted, 'Another breakfast for me cock-sparrer,' to the
man at the counter, who came at once to place a second plate
before Robert, saying, 'Got hollow legs, boys this age.'

'How old are you?' asked Jack.

'Fourteen.' Robert's twelfth birthday had come a month ago.
He'd had no presents. Two cards only had arrived for him –
one from Nanny, containing three pounds, and one from
Mother and Edward combined, containing a ten-shilling note.
It was more than enough to buy his ticket home. And he'd have
time to wander around London – look at the Egyptian mummy
in the British Museum, go to Lyon's Corner House.

The best part of the dream, though, was getting on to the
train and having enough money to buy a four-course lunch,
and later getting out at York to buy food on the platform to see
him through until Edinburgh.

The dream became particularly fanciful after that, because

instead of the cold-shouldering and fierce fury of Mother and the reasoned bafflement of Father, he'd been welcomed home like the prodigal son and told he need never return to the place he'd remember for the rest of his life for its terrors, the humbug of its headmaster and the unchecked bullying that made every minute there a nightmare.

In fact the real-life adventure had ended there, in Trafalgar Square, where, emerging from Lyon's Corner House, he'd walked straight into two policemen and been driven back to school to be punished by the Barbarian.

He was floating up, up out of the dream. A cool breeze was stirring the starched curtain at the sick-room window. There was a smell of iodine and he saw beside his bed the inhalator bowl that the nurse always spiced with friar's balsam. He must have had a severe attack of asthma – so severe he couldn't remember a thing about it. His eyes began to focus. There was a new doctor, stethoscope dangling, standing over him and there, behind the doctor, the nurse. Beside the nurse was the headmaster – and wonderfully there, beside the Barbarian, was Nanny.

He blinked and checked. He was awake and Nanny was talking in her most severe voice to the Barbarian. 'What do you mean – you do not allow a pupil to be examined by his own doctor?'

The Barbarian answered testily: 'He has been seen by the school doctor.'

'And?' said Nanny.

The Barbarian replied, 'There is nothing wrong with him. It was an attack of asthma. He has had treatment and a sedative.'

Nanny said, 'I am here as Sir Gordon Campbell's representative. I demand a second opinion.' She nodded to the doctor. 'Go ahead, please.'

The Barbarian could do nothing to stop him. Robert was being stripped of his clothes; he flinched and winced as the doctor, with Nanny's help, peeled the bloodied vest and underpants away from his skin. The doctor drew in breath sharply when he saw the bruising, the weals and open wounds. Then Robert felt the cold metal of the stethoscope on his chest and back, while Nanny turned and held him with gentle hands.

Finally the doctor looked towards the headmaster and said, 'You realise that if I were dealing with a poor boy at a state school I should be duty-bound to report this to the Schools Inspectorate?'

'We are the seedbed for Eton and the best public schools in England. We inculcate qualities of leadership, bravery and endeavour,' the Barbarian blustered.

'I am going to remove him to hospital,' the doctor said. 'He is underweight and unclean. Not even basic health care has been given to this boy.' With one index finger he lifted Robert's chin to reveal the grime on his neck. Helpfully, Robert tipped his head back.

The doctor evidently could see what nobody else had noticed. The school regime was squalid; the facilities minimal. They were allowed only two tepid, shallow baths in a communal bathroom every week, with no adult supervision and the mob in attendance.

'He has been severely beaten,' the doctor said. 'Beaten to the point of collapse. I must have an explanation.'

Robert began to enjoy himself. The Barbarian would not admit to having inflicted the injuries and Robert himself would not dare to tell who had administered the beating or it would be the worse for him, but it was gratifying to lie there listening to the Barbarian's explanations and excuses. Maybe he'd spend a couple of days in the sick room or hospital. It would be a welcome respite.

Nanny spoke up. 'Robert will not be taken to hospital. Nor will he remain here. I am taking him home.'

Robert opened his eyes and smiled at her. She was standing beside the bed, pulling the sheet over his exposed behind. He adored Nanny. She was old; in fact, she was ancient. She had been Nanny to Father and Father was over fifty. But she was a powerful presence and theirs was a mutual affection. She said, 'Can you stand, Robert?'

He swung his legs off the bed. He was in pain but he would not give the Barbarian the satisfaction of seeing his agony. 'Yes,' he said.

'Pack your case. Bring only personal things. The school will send the rest.'

Gingerly he pulled on his flannels and left the room while

Nanny made clear her own feelings to the assembled official-dom.

His small case was found for him by the groundsman who kept the box-room keys, and when this was done Robert made for the dorm. Whitmore was there, alone. He was seldom alone and never brave without his mob around him. But he looked down his nose at Robert and said, 'In a funk now, are we? Sent for Nanny?'

Robert knew he'd not be coming back. He had seen as much in Nanny's face. He would never again have the opportunity to stand up to Whitmore, man to man. It was going to be his first serious fight. He'd scrapped before – to save himself – but had never started a fight. He could not know that from now on he would never wait until his enemies struck first. He simply knew it was now or never.

He was small for twelve, but wiry and angry and hungry – all the things Whitmore was not. He dropped his case and squared up to the bigger boy. 'Say that again, Whitmore,' he snarled.

Whitmore, to buy time and save face, ignored him. Robert went in close. 'Say it again!'

'Don't be a fool, wee Scot—' Whitmore sneered, but he did not finish the sentence. Robert hadn't known his own strength or fury or whatever it was that drove his right fist into Whitmore's face as his left caught him in the chest.

Whitmore put up his own fists, but far too slowly. Robert hit him under the jaw and saw his eyes bulge with fear. Whitmore's arms flailed wildly. He staggered back with Robert going after him like a terrier, landing every blow to his enemy's body, to his face, his head. Whitmore fell to the floor as the door opened and Cutler and the mob came in.

Robert turned on them. 'Who's next?' he demanded in a voice that had suddenly decided to stick at the lower register it had been dropping to over the last months. 'You, Cutler?'

Whitmore got to his feet, his hands to his head, tears streaming down his face, mingling with the blood from his nose. He went backwards, to his bed, saying nothing. Robert ignored him and went for Cutler. But one crack was all Cutler needed to turn tail and fly for the door, slightly ahead of the mob, who scrambled to get out before him.

Robert stood tall. 'That felt good!' he said. Then, to himself, because he never spoke aloud these days about the imaginary friend – the other half who had never gone from his imagination – he murmured, 'What about that, Sandy? How am I doing?' Sandy had always been the dauntless one.

1957

'Sandy. Are you ready?' Uncle John strode down through the clearing to the jetty on the lake, where Alexander was stowing the outboard motor on the boat.

Alexander, Sandy now to Uncle John, waved, uncurled his six-foot-two scrawny, strong frame and hopped on to the jetty. He tied the boat fast to the ring and called, 'I'm coming. We have four trucks to unload today. Can you spare a couple of hands from the sawmill?'

Alexander loved it all – especially the weekends and holidays spent here at the cottage on Lake Paudash. Paudash was eight miles long and one mile wide – and, the locals boasted, had a hundred miles of shoreline, counting all the bays and inlets. Thousands of lakes joined one another in a lacework of rivers and lakes and forest and grassland that stretched from almost the Arctic Circle to the Great Lakes, which separated what Alexander thought of as his homeland from the Rocky Mountains and America.

Alexander spent Monday to Fridays at school, living in the house at Bancroft with Aunt Dorothy and Uncle John. Aunt Dorothy still ran the Bird's Creek store and the house at Bancroft while Mom, treated as a partner in the business as well as the daughter of the family, helped Uncle John run the sawmill from her cottage here on Lake Paudash.

'Cottage' was a misleading name for the sprawling timber lodge set in fifty acres of forest on a raised site overlooking the lake. The house had four bedrooms, three living rooms, kitchen, bathroom and basement. Uncle John had built it for Mom – had given it to her in appreciation of all the work Mom did for them.

Lake Paudash had been popular since the twenties with people who could afford to work in the towns and along the York River and buy a weekend place where in summer they sailed, swam and fished and in winter, when the lakes froze solid for four months, skated, tobagganed and skied.

Alexander stood up as Uncle John reached the jetty and called out, 'The Polanski brothers will unload.' The mill employed thirty Poles who had stayed on after the war. Many of them had Canadian wives.

'Good,' Alexander said. The Poles were hard workers.

'Were you hoping to go out in the boat?' John asked as they went towards the Dodge and the fifteen-mile journey to the sawmill at Bird's Creek. 'I haven't messed up your day, have I? Your Aunt Dorothy will have a meal ready for us all at midday at the store if the work takes longer than a morning.' The mill workers' week finished at twelve o'clock on Sundays.

'OK.' Alexander grinned. 'I'm just checking the engine for Peter.' Peter Murray, Uncle John's son, a paediatrician at Toronto General Hospital, was staying with them at the cottage for the weekend.

'He arrived?' Uncle John put the Dodge into first gear and drove slowly and carefully over the rough forest tracks towards the main road. 'A whole weekend! He's not usually here for more than a day.'

'Well, it's not every weekend you call a family conference,' Alex replied. 'Gonna tell me what it's about?'

Uncle John ignored his question and started to sing to himself. At this point Alexander switched off. He was too much of a musician to be able to concentrate on anything while listening to Uncle John singing out of tune, out of time and the wrong words. He looked at his uncle – the shock of curly white hair, the ruddy face, strong hands on the wheel – and wished as he did every day of his life that Uncle John had been his real father instead of simply the man who had taken him and his Mom in and whom both of them loved and honoured for the decent good man he was. He said, 'Does Peter know what it's all about?'

Uncle John grinned and sang louder. Alexander smiled, but it was difficult to look convincing. Alexander's latest love was the guitar, though he could play every musical instrument he'd ever tried. He didn't boast: he was simply a musician.

'Have you made up your mind?' Uncle John broke off from singing.

'About university? Yes. I'm not going.' Mom had some bee

232

in her bonnet about his not falling behind, as if he were in some unspecified competition with a contemporary. 'I'll tell Mom soon.'

'Sure you are making the right decision – to go into the sawmill?'

'Sure I am.' Alexander loved it all – he loved everything about the life Uncle John led: the pace, the independence of knowing you stood or fell by your own efforts. Even if he were to find what he had always sought – the perfect partner for music, singing and playing, becoming stars of the music scene – he'd always need the touchstone, the security of home. He said, 'Mom, too. She's never been happier than she is now with her own place. It was real generous of you.'

'Nonsense. Your mom does the books, the buying and selling, the wages and the hiring and firing. The sawmill did only half as much before she took charge.'

So the family conference was not about the sawmill. Uncle John began to sing again. He loved to keep things from them – keep them guessing, as he put it.

Alexander hated secrets. He couldn't say so to Uncle John but it drove him crazy at times when he got to wondering and asking, pestering Mom for answers. He'd say, 'Who was my dad?' for he thought Mom was lying when she said that she and his dad had married under a weeping tree, exchanging vows which they both swore were for ever, and that Alexander must not think he was illegitimate, because in Scotland your word was your bond and—

'I don't care about illegitimacy,' he said. 'It happens all the time in Canada. Men in the outback couldn't get away from their farms or logging limits for a religious ceremony. They wanted brides to sew and keep house and they chose them or had them chosen by the guardians at the orphanages. They would marry them when they had the time. No, it's not that. But how do you know my father died at sea? You won't even tell me his name. Did he desert us, Mom?' If his father had deserted him and Mom then he would find out who and where this man was and make him sorry. That he would. Make no mistake.

Uncle John stopped singing as he swung the Dodge into the yard where men were working, adding to the great stacks of cut timber that half filled the place. He said, 'Don't worry about a thing, Sandy. I'll put in a word for you tonight with your mom. You don't have to go to university if that's what you've decided.'

Flora came up the forest track from her swim in the lake, her wet hair like bronze ropes hanging down over her lightly tanned shoulders almost to the waist of her navy-blue swim-suit. There was something about the air here, or the sunlight that came filtering, green and honey-soft, through the trees, turning her skin a pale sandy colour with none of the freckles that had plagued her childhood.

She saw Peter, tall and fair and ridiculously boyish in appearance, though he was thirty-seven, standing on the deck, leaning over, watching her.

She waved and called to him: 'Lazybones. I thought you wanted to swim.' She reached the cottage and stood looking up at him before climbing the steps to the side entrance, for the house was built on two levels on the hillside. Peter was bare-foot, wearing shorts and a sloppy joe. The fair hairs on his arms shone golden in the morning sunshine.

He said, 'I've made coffee. Want some?'

'Yes.' She ran up the steps, slipped into the bathrobe she kept in the bathroom by the door and went into the kitchen. Peter had made a big breakfast of fruit, scrambled eggs on toast and waffles with maple syrup. He'd set a place for her and she sat, sipping piping-hot coffee while he served her. 'This is a treat,' she said. 'You know what? It might be a good idea to marry you after all.'

He laughed. 'Well, I don't know what this conference is all about, but I'll bet a dollar to a piece of toast that Dad and Mother will suggest it.'

'As if the idea had only just occurred to them!' Flora laughed too. This urging of them to marry had been going on year after year. They liked one another a lot but neither Peter nor she felt that liking was strong enough to base marriage upon.

Peter became serious. 'Flora, you still love the man you left behind in Scotland. I've never fallen wildly in love in my life. But we are both single and getting on in years. I'm thirty-

234

seven. You're thirty-three. We'll have to take the plunge some time, you know.'

Peter went to the boat while Flora cleared the dishes then went to the bathroom to shower and change into her jeans and T-shirt. She thought about marriage to the serious, work-centred Peter and she knew she would have to tell Peter everything if she were to marry him. Flora could not tell anyone, ever, about Robert.

Alexander was the living image of his father, though not yet as broad and strong. She never need wonder what Robert looked like, she reflected, though she was starved of news of her son. Nanny had never been able to send photos of him for obvious reasons, and for the last few years had written little about him, except to say that they had ambitions for him that included Fettes College and university.

Much later, after supper, they all sat around the pine tables on the deck, watching the boats bobbing on the water by the jetty, while around them tiny moths fluttered about the lanterns on the deck's rail. Tied up for their use was Peter's canoe, the little sailing dinghy and the Dispro, the motor boat with a disappearing propeller that Flora used to cross the lake for gas and kerosene and boat supplies. They knew something serious was afoot when Uncle John brought from the trunk of the Dodge sherry for the ladies and a bottle of Glenfiddich whisky for himself and Peter, and even whisky well watered with soda for Alexander. Respectable women did not allow their menfolk to drink in their presence.

'Now then, you guys,' Uncle John began. Peter and Flora exchanged smiles. Uncle John poured, then sat, then stood, and finally, leaning against the rail of the veranda, with fire-flies dancing about his shock of white hair, said, 'I'm sixty-seven. It's time to retire. Dorothy and I want to see a few places before we die. While we are fit. Now, any suggestions?'

'You mean – where will you travel?' Flora asked.

'No. We'll travel in America for six months. Then Dot's old country.' Aunt Dorothy had been born in Edinburgh. Flora felt her face go pale. Suppose they turned up to see Nanny at Ingersley when Robert was there? It would be a terrible shock for them. She must write to Nanny and tell her to visit them here, in Canada. If she did, then there would be no need for Aunt Dorothy and Uncle John to go to Ingersley.

'We can't carry on doing this work for ever,' Aunt Dorothy said while she handed round marzipan fruits. 'And we could not have done half of this if it were not for Flora. She's the backbone of the family.' She added nervously, while giving a wistful look towards Flora, 'If Flora and Peter were married—'

Peter grinned and Flora gave him a quick wink and smiled.

Alexander said, 'Well, I am ready to leave school. Any time.'

'No!' said Flora. 'I want you to go to university.'

'I've made up my mind, Mom. There's nothing I want to do that I'd need a degree for.' Alexander looked at Uncle John for support. 'Mom and I could run the store and the sawmill.'

Flora said, 'We've talked round the subject for months. I think Alexander should have an education. What do you all think?'

Uncle John said, 'There was no choice in my day. It was work or starve,' and, taking a sip of whisky and looking side-long at Alexander as if to confirm that he was indeed being helpful, 'I remember when the logs for Bancroft Hydro came out of Bruton Swamp in Haliburton County. At Sandy's age I was navigating the chain of lakes above Baptiste, overseeing our logs being bagged in huge chained-together boomsticks and towed to the High Falls dam. At Baptiste's foot they were channelled down a man-made chute ...' He took a quick sip of whisky and before anyone could stop him went on fast: 'Past Crooked Rapids and Flat Rapids it was smooth sailing on the York until we reached the hydro mill just north of Bancroft ...'

'Yes, Dad!' Peter said finally. 'But this is now. And you made sure that Jake and I had an education.'

'I don't want it!' Alexander got to his feet and went to stand beside his hero. 'I want to work. I want to work in the lumber business, like Uncle John.'

Flora knew that nothing would shift him. He was a young man of decision and he'd made up his mind. She made one last stab. 'If you don't want university, then how about music school?' Alexander was talented – more talented than she was. He could play almost every instrument – not to concert standard, but well enough to be first violin in the school orchestra and the accompanist at her own music society rehearsals. He played at the Scottish nights, and when he got up there on stage or at the centre of the gathering his face was a study in out-of-this-world enjoyment. It was as if he were lit from within.

Now he did not even smile as he replied, 'Mom, I'm never going to be Hank Williams. And unless I find someone as good at singing as I am at playing – unless I find a partner – I'll play for my own enjoyment.'

'And ours,' said Aunt Dorothy loyally.

'Of course.' Now he smiled. 'Once we've thrashed this out, I'll play for you, Aunt Dorothy.'

'I give in,' Flora said. She stood up. 'Carry on. You know my views. I'm going to put out the food for the racoons.'

She had nailed a little platform to one of the trees – one where the light from the house glowed, slanting in the moonlight, into the forest. On the platform she now put the remainder of the supper: meat and cheese, biscuits and apples. Alexander's words had struck her like a knife wound. Nanny had told her that Robert had a lovely singing voice. She went back into the house and waited, watching through the glass the pointed, striped face of the heavy racoon who lowered himself slowly down the tree to the platform, where he sat, gnawing the food which he held in one little paw.

She could hear every word they spoke on the deck. They were becoming voluble now. How could she and Alexander manage the mill? Should they sell the store and keep the mill because Alexander wanted it? Would Peter need the nest egg that a sale would bring? And Peter, laughing and saying that it was the parents who needed money and how about this ... they keep the house, sell the store and leave the sawmill in the capable hands of the holy three – the mill manager, Flora and Alexander – for the next two years to see how it all panned out.

Flora watched the racoon, who seemed unconcerned that he was spilling food from his platform. Suddenly and at great speed he climbed the tree – and was out of sight within seconds.

She turned. Peter was behind her. He said, 'Come out on the lake with me tomorrow?'

'Yes.' She smiled and gave him a quick, friendly kiss on the cheek. 'Thank you. I'd like that.'

The following afternoon Peter took her out on the lake in his sailing dinghy as they had done dozens of times before, sometimes staying ashore in one of the bays, watching the wildlife – the beavers, chickadees and deer – and listening to the loons whose eerie cries, like wild laughter, echoed across the water.

There were a dozen other boats on the lake, and the trees were aflame, bronze, orange, yellow and red among the dark green pines. At lunchtime, Peter tied up in one of the dozens of little coves and helped her ashore. They sat and made their picnic and watched a colony of beavers that at first set up a din, banging their tails on the water to let the others know that humans were there, before they returned to gnawing through tree branches, harvesting little pieces of trees before the frosts of late November. 'They store small pieces to eat in winter,' Peter told her when she said that their den looked like a muddled pile of brushwood. 'It's hollow inside above the water line. Their exit is underwater.'

Flora thought she had seen everything. Now, suddenly, she caught hold of Peter's arm and froze. 'Turn very slowly,' she said. High above them on the crest of the forested hill, looking down on them as if they were nothing more than water rats, were two bears; one an adult, the other a youngster. Peter had not brought his gun, but the boat was only feet away and the forest was silent.

'It won't come down to us,' he said calmly. He was right, and when the bears had lumbered away, as silently as they had appeared, Peter kept his arm about her and pulled her close.

She looked up at him and saw that his eyes were shining very brightly. He was nervous, for the hands that were holding her were shaking. He bent his head down to hers and kissed her gently, without passion but with tenderness and affection.

Flora moved away a little. She would not let him think that she was any nearer to falling in love with him. She knew he had kissed her for all the old-fashioned reasons – they were a man and a woman, without attachments, in a remote and beautiful place, and the urge to make something more than a mere picnic of the day had overcome him. But she was certain that he felt no more than that for her.

As for herself, it was crazy ... illogical ... but she still dreamed that one day, like the proverbial prince of fairy stories, Andrew would find her. He would unravel the mystery of her disappearance. He would discover that he was the father of Robert – and of Alex. He would forgive her and come to Canada to claim her as his wife. But this fanciful idea was no use to her now. She said, 'Haven't you fallen in love yet, Peter?'

There were many pretty nurses at the hospital. Flora had seen them when Peter took her round the children's department. She had noticed nurses go soft and compliant and shining-eyed when he asked anything of them.

'I don't think so,' he said thoughtfully. Then, apologetically, 'I don't mean to sound cold, Flora.'

'I know you are not,' she said kindly. But he was doing it again – proposing a marriage without love, based only on kindness and consideration.

Peter was saying, 'I'm so fond of you. I have never met a girl like you. Couldn't you consider ...?'

'Don't!' She knew she must turn the talk around, make light of it. 'I'll tell you what – if neither of us meets anyone else, if we don't fall in love, we'll reconsider in a year's time. How's that?'

Chapter Thirteen

Andrew had risen to the rank of detective sergeant. He now had an interview room on Edinburgh's Royal Terrace and a spectacular view over Queen's Park, where on that October afternoon the weather was glorious. The leaves in the city's parks and gardens were falling, lying golden and bronze, thick on the grass, drifting around the tree trunks and the footpaths in the light breeze. If this weather continued, it would be perfect for sailing. He had a week's leave starting the next day. His days were long and the mountain of work grew steadily.

A week's sailing holiday, away from the station, was what he needed. If he got a move on, he could be out of the office in fifteen minutes' time. He began to clear his desk, then, because thoughts of Flora were never far from his mind, even after sixteen years, he rang for his cadet lad and told him to bring the missing persons files.

The cadet was young, fresh-faced and eager to make a good impression. He brought in the heavy box of folders and set them down on the desk. Andrew could not resist saying, 'Thought you were going to have an easy week, did you, Brodie?'

Brodie blushed. 'No, Sergeant! I want to do a proper, useful job.'

Andrew took out everything he had accumulated on the Flora Macdonald case and said, 'I want you to go through this file. See if there is anything we might have missed. Not much hope. But it's good practice.'

Brodie said, 'Do I give it priority?'

'No,' Andrew replied before he dismissed him. 'Fit it in

240

with your normal duties. Go through it carefully. Read the report. Make enquiries if you find anything worth following up.' Not that Andrew thought there was anything left to find, but a new eye – a different slant – might come up with a lead. Years ago he had found Jessie Fairbairn, Flora's friend from Guthrie's, but Jessie was sure that Flora was dead. In his heart, though, where it mattered, he knew she was not. If he had believed she was dead he would have given up the search years ago.

He had gone through the missing persons lists of every police department in Scotland, and though there had been many losses during the war there were few unidentified bodies. He had also tried to get hold of the lists of patients in all the hospitals in the Edinburgh area. This had not been so easy. Until the National Health Service came into being, hospital records were scanty. Yet the fact that Flora had injured her back and gone to hospital was the only clear lead he'd ever had. After that, she disappeared. He had a card system – a private matter – where every mention and record of the name of Flora Macdonald, no matter how bizarre, was noted.

He was left with only two Flora Macdonalds. One of them was his Flora; the other was a girl almost three years younger who had been issued with an identity card in Edinburgh in 1940 and then she too disappeared from the records. It was possible that this younger girl had joined the forces when she reached eighteen – or had married outside Edinburgh. He knew neither she nor Flora had married in Edinburgh. He'd been through the Edinburgh registers of marriage since 1940 and not found a single Flora Macdonald.

He would keep at it until he was forty. Then he'd give up the search and start to look seriously for a wife. He had three years to go.

Carelessly he brushed his hand through his thick, dark hair while he dealt with the heap of files on his desk, then he smiled to himself, thinking of Flora's singing and the huge chorus that the amateur operatic society would need when rehearsals for *Oklahoma!* began at the end of the year. They pulled his leg on the station about the romantic leads he played, though not seriously, because he helped produce the annual police show, *Off the Beat*, a stage production of songs

241

and sketches and variety acts which ran at the Empire for three weeks every year. Many of the men from this station would be coerced into taking part, just as most of them would come to *Oklahoma!* to see Andrew singing the part of Curly.

Now, to amuse himself, and knowing the remarks they'd be making outside in the hall, he ran his hands through his own curly hair and began to sing in his fine tenor voice, 'There's a bright golden haze on the meadow ...' However, he had not expected so fast a reaction, for just before, 'The corn is as high as an elephant's eye ...', the door opened and the duty officer entered.

'Sir Gordon Campbell to see you, Sergeant,' he said, somehow managing to keep his face straight.

Andrew flattened his hair quickly and put the remaining papers in a neat pile. 'Show him in.'

Sir Gordon was retired from the sea now. Andrew saw him at yacht club dinners, for the Commander was an honorary member of Andrew's club. He was also a local hero, and highly respected. Andrew held the door open for his old captain and said, 'Good afternoon, Sir Gordon.' He was not on such familiar terms that he'd call him anything but sir.

Sir Gordon looked as impressive in tweeds and brogues as he used to do in uniform. At fifty-seven he had an upright bearing, thick silver hair and eyes that shone with friendliness as he held out a hand.

Andrew shook it. 'Sit down, sir,' he said and when the usual enquiries – about the boat and Sir Gordon's own North Berwick sailing club – brought forth no new confidences, he ordered that coffee be brought to the office. This would give Sir Gordon time to get around to the real purpose of his visit.

Over the years Sir Gordon had had trouble with his elder son, Robert, who, between the ages of six and ten, used to go missing for days on end when his father was at sea. Lady Campbell never reported her son's disappearance. Not until the boy was found sleeping on a park bench or at a harbour, curled up on the fishing nets, were the police involved, and then the lad would be brought in and questioned carefully. It was a fairly routine matter, returning runaway children to their home, and Andrew prided himself on never taking it for granted that a child would run away without reason. He always pursued a few enquiries and time and again had been able to press charges for child neglect or cruelty against feckless or neglectful parents or guardians. But never in Robert Campbell's case. He was always examined by a doctor, no bruises were ever found and he'd be pronounced fit and healthy. Andrew knew that coldness and tongue-lashing left no visible marks. His father only got to hear of these 'escapes' when Nanny reported them to him. Then he would come along to whichever station had found the boy, thank them profusely and assure them that it was a family matter that had been dealt with.

When the coffee had been brought and the door closed again Andrew said, 'Anything I can do in my official capacity, sir?'

'I'm not here on official business,' said Sir Gordon. 'I'm going to ask you a personal favour, Andrew.'

'Anything at all,' Andrew said.

'I want your advice about my son,' he said quietly.

'I'm flattered. But I don't know if my advice will be worth taking.'

'You know how it feels to be a young hot-head like Robert.'

Andrew had last seen Robert a year ago, crewing for his father at a regatta. He assumed that the boy was now over the runaway phase. Sir Gordon said, 'Robert reminds me very much of you, Andrew. He is like you were at sixteen.'

Andrew smiled. He knew that it could only be in minor ways that they were alike and that there the resemblance ended, for young Robert had had a very different upbringing from his own. Where Andrew himself had had no father but a loving mother, Robert had a loving but absent father and a mother whose neglect of her elder son was the talk of, if not East Lothian, certainly both the Lothians and Borders police forces.

A deep frown creased Sir Gordon's brow. 'He's musical. Gifted. Before I had sons I used to say that it was a father's duty to guide and help them. I haven't been much of a father to him.'

'I'm sure you have,' Andrew said. At all their earlier meetings Sir Gordon had talked with unashamed pride about young Robert.

'I told you that he was never top of the class or anything?'

243

'That's not the end of the world.'

'What I didn't tell you was that Robert fights. The school ...' Robert went to an Edinburgh public school, '... the school is only going to give him one more chance. If he does anything – anything at all – he'll be expelled.'

Andrew tried not to smile. 'What does he fight about? Girls?'

'No. Nothing like that. When he was young he was under-weight, asthmatic – an easy target for bullies. We sent him away to school but he had a rough time and eventually ran away.' He looked Andrew straight in the eye. 'You knew that he used to run away when he was small?'

'I did know. We often found him and took him home,' Andrew said. Sir Gordon was not to know that every police station kept files of all missing children in case they went missing again. 'He was found quickly when he ran away from his school?' he asked.

'Yes. And with Nanny's care and good food, and of course, the fresh air and sailing, he flourished. He's grown six inches in the last year. He's a big boy now – not powerful, but tall and strong—'

Andrew stopped him. 'And now he gets into fights?'

'They are not his fault,' Sir Gordon said defensively. 'Robert can't stand by and watch someone taking the punishment he suffered. Lady Campbell thinks that every boy should learn to stand up for himself and that Robert should not interfere in other boys' troubles.'

Sir Gordon paused for a few moments, then continued in a rueful voice, 'I'm afraid that my wife and I don't see eye to eye on the matter of our sons – or, rather, their upbringing. I feel we are taking the right action, but with the wrong sons. Edward is the boy who should have had the strict school and firmer hand but we have indulged him to the point where he can appear arrogant and rude. Robert has had a much rougher time.'

'Why?'

'I don't know. I was away a lot in Robert's early years. But there is a special bond between a father and his first-born.' He seemed to be contemplating what to say, then suddenly confided, 'Lady Campbell sets great store by inheritance –

much more than I ever have. She feels we should make Edward successor to the title and estate.'

Andrew was taken aback by this confidence. He ought to choose his words carefully but found himself critical of the family and protective of Robert. He said hotly, 'Then you have your answer to Robert's behaviour. He can't be expected to give up his position without a fight.'

Sir Gordon said, 'Land isn't an asset – a privilege – any more. The men who will make their mark in this world will be the inventors, the industrialists. The landed gentleman's days are over!'

'All the same, you cannot go against traditions,' said Andrew.

'I agree,' Sir Gordon said. 'And Nanny takes exactly the same view as you, Andrew. You remember Miss Taylor?'

'I remember her well.'

'She is devoted to Robert, and he to her. Probably because she delivered him under trying circumstances when we were at war. Robert was a sickly, premature baby. Nanny took charge of him from birth. She drove an ambulance as well as caring for mothers and babies from one end of the county to the other.' He smiled with pride as he went on, 'Nanny was amazing. Ingersley House was a hospital – and bang in the middle of an exclusion zone that was teeming with evacuated families. The area was full of prisoner-of-war camps and airfields. You had to show your identity card at every turn because everything was so tightly controlled. Nanny coped with all this aggravation as well as her work, *and* she took care of Robert.'

Andrew smiled back. Sir Gordon was clearly still devoted to the old lady. He said, 'She must be getting on in years ...?'

'She's seventy-six. Doesn't look it. She's living in Ivy Lodge now, in retirement. I want her to retire completely and visit her sister in Canada before it's too late. I've told her I'll pay her fare. But she won't go she says, until Robert doesn't need her.'

'How can I help?' Andrew said.

'Would you return the favour I did you when you were a very young man? Would you tell Robert that the Royal Navy is a grand career? I want him to work hard and apply to Dartmouth.'

'I have never forgotten my debt to you, sir,' Andrew said. He was glad to be able to do something in return though he added, 'But, unless Robert himself wants to follow in your footsteps, I don't see—'

Sir Gordon said quickly, 'Yes. Yes. But you will put it to him?'

'I will,' Andrew assured him. 'I won't wave the big stick. I'm on holiday next week. Send Robert to see me when I'm back. Any time.'

'Thank you, Andrew.'

Andrew saw Sir Gordon to his car before returning to the office and calling for Brodie again. 'There's one line I didn't explore, Brodie,' he said. 'It occurred to me only recently.' In fact it had occurred to him only five minutes ago when he'd been reminded of the wartime travel restrictions. 'If there are any, I want you to track down all records of movements in the Edinburgh and Lothians exclusion zone. See if you can find Flora Macdonald.'

'Yes, Sergeant.'

But it was time he laid this search to rest and listened to Ma. Ma had long since become exasperated with him and was for ever exhorting him to marry a nice girl and make her a grandmother. Ma kept house for him – they were still in the flat in The Meadows – and since his demob fifteen years ago she had not done any paid work. She declared that at last, she was a lady of leisure.

Ruth dressed herself carefully in her best hunting wear of cord jodhpurs, boots and black riding jacket, and picking up her riding crop, went to waken Edward, who slept in the bedroom next to hers. He was twelve years old – just the age when a young man needed a lot of rest.

She tiptoed in and found him fast asleep. 'Darling?' she cooed softly. 'Remember where we're going today. It's your first hunt.' Mike Hamilton had taken their horses down yesterday: Big Red, her own chestnut gelding; and Edward's light hunter – a thoroughbred bay that had cost Ruth a small fortune. Mike would be waiting for her and Edward in Coldstream this morning.

She went to the window, pulled the curtains back quietly and saw him sit up, dazed. She said, 'Come along. It's half past seven. You'll need some breakfast.'

He smiled at her, bleary-eyed. He was such a handsome young man – fair and tall like his father, yet a bold and fearless horseman. She loved to show him off. He said, 'You look wonderful, Mummy.' Then, wistfully, because he adored his father, 'I wish Father hunted.'

'He won't,' Ruth replied. 'Your father doesn't approve of field sports. Can you dress and be ready in fifteen minutes?'

'Yes.' He leaped out of bed. 'But not with you watching, Mummy.'

She laughed. 'Sorry, darling. I'll go and wake Robert.'

She left Edward's bedroom and ran up the attic stairs. Since he'd been sent down from his prep school in disgrace, Robert had refused to budge from the attic nursery floor, saying he needed privacy. The very thought of Robert altered her mood and she was in a fair paddy by the time she burst unannounced into his bedroom.

'Get up!' she ordered. 'I told you last night that Edward and I were riding out with the Border hunt.' She went to the window, drew back the curtains and flung open the casement, before turning to see the rumpled heap of a bed.

'You lazy oaf!' she stormed while Robert buried his head deeper under the covers. He was the bane of her life. Why had she ever adopted him in the first place? Just to save the girl, Flora, from disgrace – that was all it was. Her own generous nature had led her into it.

She glanced round the room and now saw the state it was in. Clothes were strewn on the floor. There were empty lemonade bottles on the chair and that dreadful guitar was propped against the fireplace. At the sight of it all Ruth completely lost her head; she leaned over Robert and said, 'If you are not out of bed, dressed and ready to give a hand at the farm in ten minutes, I'll tell your father.'

She heard Edward's boots pounding up the attic stairs and turned to see him standing in the doorway, looking divine in his hunt wear. She shook Robert violently. 'I mean it!' she snarled into his ear.

Mike was expecting Robert to supervise the transfer of milk to the Milk Marketing Board's tanker. A sample had to be taken and the details recorded. Lucy and the dairyman could do it, of course, but that was not the point. The point was that Robert must learn that money was not easily come by. Gordon was notoriously mean – questioning every bill and purchase, claiming that they would soon be wiped out. Gordon did not make personal allowances to either Robert or Edward. But Edward was too young to work. Robert must earn his spending money and was being paid to lend a hand every day over the half-term holiday. Ruth gritted her teeth. All this palaver because Mike Hamilton still believed that Robert was his own son. He pointed out Robert's likeness to himself and said he very well understood why she would deny it. She had not denied it strenuously. It could be useful one day – and it was another hold over Mike Hamilton.

Robert rolled over and poked his head into the light. 'Can't you leave me alone?' he said. 'You are always going on at me.' He opened his eyes and, seeing his mother's wild eyes glittering with menace, added, 'I am not going to work on the farm today.'

'You certainly are. Mr Hamilton's expecting you.'

'Then Mr Hamilton's losing his marbles.' Robert threw back the covers and uncurled the six foot two inches of thin, wiry body. He said, 'I told him yesterday that I should not be in today.'

He slept naked, Ruth knew, to annoy her. She quickly averted her eyes and went to the door to put an arm around Edward's shoulders. 'You did what?' She could feel anger rising in her. 'Why?'

'He's a cruel swine,' Robert answered, pulling on his underpants, his back to them. 'And if I see him drag another new-born calf out of a cow and leave it to die because it is weak and not a heifer, I'll give him the hiding of his life!'

He meant it. He could not stand cruelty – and neither could Father. If Father knew the half of it, he'd foreclose on Hamilton's lease. And if Father had seen Edward ratting with Hamilton – going after the rats they had smoked out of the drains with spades and shovels, and yelling, Hamilton with delight, Edward with fear, when they smashed the squealing creatures into a pulp – then he would have felt as revolted as Robert himself. There was no need to be cruel, even to vermin. Mike Hamilton had his ratting dogs who could tear a rat to pieces in a split second if they caught it. Mother kept strychnine to poison them.

'What nonsense you talk!' Mother said. 'You have a typical townsman's view. You think that country life is all about picking flowers ...' She turned to Edward. 'You'd gladly help Mr Hamilton, wouldn't you?' but did not wait for a reply before adding, 'Were it not for the fact that the hunt is a man short—'

'A man?' Robert went to the bed, rummaged, unearthed a jersey and pulled it over his skinny ribs. 'Edward's thirteen. About the same age as the fox, I suppose.'

Robert was sick of it all – sick of Mother and, though he loved his brother, sick of Edward, who was pampered and indulged by both Mother and Father. He was also heartily sick of Hamilton, who blew hot and cold; one day crawling and ingratiating because he knew Robert would inherit the estate, the next off-hand if he thought Robert was spending too much time with Lucy and Phoebe. This was hurtful to Robert, whose only haven of peace and normality – whose only experience of home life – had been found in the company of the Hamilton womenfolk. He could walk into their house, into their kitchen as if it were his own and always they were pleased to see him. Hamilton was seldom there; he was inclined to eat on the run and expected Lucy to provide a hot meal whenever he wanted one.

Now Robert said to Mother, 'On your way out, give my apologies to Mrs Hamilton and Phoebe,' knowing she would do that. Mother spent a lot of time supervising, bossing Hamilton and his family. If Robert were a farmer he wouldn't tolerate it – the owner's wife coming round every day to see that he was running the farm properly and consult him about every little thing.

'You can afford a week with no pay, then?' Mother said. Mike Hamilton gave him three pounds a week for thirty-six hours' work. 'And what shall I say has kept you from your work?'

In the old days, before he grew six inches in a year, she'd have taken her riding whip to him for what he said next. He was pulling on his flannel trousers, fastening them as he said,

'You can tell Hamilton to stuff his job where the monkeys stuff their nuts.'

Mother was outraged. She said to Edward, 'I don't want you to listen to this, darling—'

'I'm old enough. And Robert's right, Mummy—' Edward began, but seeing her expression, 'All right. I'll wait in the car,' and turned tail and fled back down the attic stairs.

Mother came to stand over Robert now that he was dressed, seated and tying his shoelaces. She liked to encourage him, to challenge him to retaliate so that she could go to Father and demand that Robert be punished or sent away – anything to discredit him in Father's eyes. What she was really aiming for was for Father to disown him and make Edward heir to the estate. This amused Robert. There would be nothing left to inherit, the way things were going. Father had confided in him that the farm would soon have to be sold to the Hamiltons who, with Lucy's own fortune and Davey Hamilton's farm coming to Mike one day, were better off than the Campbells would ever be. The remaining Ingersley land would have to be sold to developers and builders. Estates of council and private developments were growing apace – right to the walls of Ingersley. Father said that they could not hold out much longer. There never had been enough money to maintain the house. The grass-cutting and gardening was contracted out to a local company and the house employed only a housemaid and cook – and these because they were old retainers who could not afford to leave their tied cottages. Mother made sure of that.

Now, standing over him, Mother put her hands on her hips, planted her feet apart and, scathing, said, 'If I had suspected when you were born that you were going to turn out to be a rude, lazy good-for-nothing—'

Robert looked up from his task and gave a wry grin. 'What would you have done? Drowned me – or fed me that poisonous medicine with which you cure all ills?' This in reference to her sedative tonic – a contradiction if he'd ever heard one – which, she had ruled, he was to take three times a day to cool his violent temper and improve his stamina, because it was full of iron, which gave it its bitter taste.

She ignored his rudeness for once. 'I said, what are you doing that is more important than your job at the farm?'

250

'Father wants to take me to Edinburgh. To see Andrew Stewart, the detective sergeant.'

'Andrew Stewart?' Her voice went high and querulous. Robert looked at her quickly. She was very pale, though he didn't think she was afraid of anyone. She, like Edward, was strong-willed and reckless, but she was definitely ruffled as she said, 'I didn't think your father had anything to do with the Stewarts.'

'You don't really know much then, do you, Mother?' he replied. She had split the family by the old divide-and-rule method she had perfected, pitting Father and himself against her and Edward so that the two halves of the family led almost separate lives. They only came together in the evening for supper at seven, and that was conducted with the hideous, false politeness that could take away the appetite of anyone who had less hunger than he. And it was all to no avail. The odd man out was not himself or Edward or even Father. Father and his two sons had respect and love for one another. It was Mother who wreaked havoc on the family. He said, 'Father's very fond of Andrew Stewart. I like him too. I have met him several times – at regattas.'

'Nanny won't like this,' Mother said.

'What has Nanny to do with it?'

'Nanny won't approve of your father allowing you to mix with the lower orders,' was all she could come up with.

Robert laughed drily. Nanny was the least snobbish person he had ever met. 'What's the matter? It's not Nanny. It's you who doesn't approve of Father and me going to see a detective.' Then, to rekindle her fury, he said, 'Not trying to kill us, are you?'

Mother composed herself, drew in her breath then exhaled fast, as if nauseated. 'You really are a nasty piece of work!' she said. 'Perhaps a sleuth could throw a little light on your behaviour.'

With that, she left him alone to wonder what Father and Andrew Stewart had in mind for him. Andrew had no doubt been recruited to supply back-up for Father and Nanny.

He went to the window and watched Mother and Edward roar off through the South Gate in the big shooting-brake that Mother drove fast and furiously. And though he asked himself

251

what sort of a man he was that he couldn't stop himself from being rude to his mother, he knew, he had always known, that she hated him. And he knew as well that he hated himself for what he had become. Four years ago, when he first stood up to a bully, he had been proud. But what sort of person was he now?

He was aggressive, though not in his own defence; he was not particularly clever, and, were it not for the father he admired and loved and knew would miss him, he'd up sticks and disappear out of their lives at the first opportunity. He could make a living, he was sure, doing as they did in America, bumming around, picking up casual work, singing and playing his way across the country until he found a partner. It would be a quarter of a century before his hale and hearty father would come to the end of his life and expect Robert to carry on in his place. In fact Father had said to him on more than one occasion, 'It's all for you, Robert. I've held on to it for you but you can see how little is left. When your time comes, boy, sell up. Give your brother his share but don't saddle yourself with keeping up an old property that has had its day.'

Robert took a drink of water then sat down, picked up his guitar and tuned it, tightening, plucking and strumming. The only talents he had were perfect pitch, a facility for learning any musical instrument and a singing voice that he knew would take him far, given the opportunity.

Now he began to play, at first desultorily and then with feeling, the American country and western songs that had evolved from old Scottish and European folk songs a couple of centuries ago. He sang along as he played 'The Red River Valley' and his rich tenor voice carried out through the open window and gladdened the heart of Nanny, who had come over to see him and was in the dining room two storeys beneath him. And since nobody else was about, Nanny went to the window, opened it a little way the better to hear her darling boy, and sang along in a thin, reedy voice, substituting her own words for the traditional ones:

From this valley they say you are going,
I will miss your bright eyes and sweet smile,

They say you are taking the sunshine,
That brightened our pathway a while ...
Come sit by my side if you love me,
Do not hasten to bid me adieu
But remember the Red River Valley
And your Nanny who loved you so true.

Then, unaccountably, remembering Flora and Alexander, she
began to cry.

Sir Gordon Campbell dropped Robert off at Royal Terrace.
Andrew went down to the front desk to greet him and was
jolted to see the change in Robert. He was tall – almost as tall
as Andrew himself – with dark wavy hair and the greeny-blue
eyes that normally went with red hair. Eyes of that colour and
shape always brought thoughts of Flora back to him – like a
scent, such things went straight to the part of the brain that
conjured up sweet memories. But practice had taught him to
dismiss such thoughts and concentrate on the job in hand. He
had been drawn to the boy every time they had met and now he
put out his hand. 'Shall we go up to my office, Robert?'

'Yes, sir,' said the boy in a rich, deep voice. He shook
Andrew's hand then stood back to let Andrew go first. He had
impeccable manners, acquired no doubt from his father and the
expensive schools that had also made him reserved and, by his
father's account, quietly aggressive.

Andrew told him to be seated, then, following Sir Gordon's
request, began to talk to him in a fatherly way, pointing out the
advantages of the Royal Navy and the Dartmouth training
course, as Sir Gordon had requested. He said, 'Your father was
– still is – a heroic figure. Not only to me, though I have
everything to thank him for. He is one of the most loved and
respected men in Scotland today.'

Robert looked thoughtful and worried by turns as they
talked, and as he responded Andrew found himself again
drawn to the boy who was in many ways like himself – born
and brought up on the Ingersley estate; a good-looking boy,
musically gifted, whose perfect manners hid a rebellious,
uncompromising nature that struck a chord with Andrew.

'I agree,' Robert said. His dark eyebrows were drawn

253

together and his wide, generous mouth was held firm as if he were restraining himself. 'Nobody could have a better father than I. If it were not for him, I'd clear off.' He smiled. 'I haven't forgotten your talking to me like a Dutch uncle when I ran away.'

'You were very young then,' Andrew said. 'But now – you ought to pull your socks up. You are the elder son. You will come into the title and the estate in your time. Shouldn't you prepare for it? Follow in your father's footsteps?'

'I don't have much interest in the title – though I love the land and estate,' Robert said. Then he added bitterly, 'In that respect, I am more like my mother.' He'd tried to sound matter-of-fact, and had failed. His feelings for his mother, then, were the root of the problem.

Andrew said, 'What about the Royal Navy?'

Robert looked down at his hands. He seemed to be withdrawing from the exchange. Andrew waited, then said, 'Well?'

'I won't join the Royal Navy,' said Robert. Then, as if he had decided he could trust Andrew, it all came tumbling out. 'I enjoy the sea and sailing but if I went into the Royal Navy it would have to be a career. It couldn't be anything less, with Father to live up to. If I get through the medical – and it's doubtful because I have asthma – I shall have to do my National Service but I'll do it in the Merchant Navy. I don't want to have authority over anyone but myself. And since I'll never be allowed to make decisions, I don't want to live at home ... Does that make sense?'

'Yes.' It made perfect sense to Andrew. There was no point in pursuing that line. 'You are musically talented, your father tells me?'

'Well, I play the piano. And the guitar. I write songs.' He laughed. 'I sing. And all that sounds like boasting.'

'Not at all. What do you want to do with all this talent?' Andrew was smiling broadly. He said, 'Do you like opera, musical comedy, or – who's that American singer who plays guitars and sings?'

'Elvis Presley. The blues singer. Yes, I do,' Robert said. 'And what I'd really love to do is go to America – to Nashville, Tennessee – and take my chances—'

'Blues?' Andrew said. 'I thought that was Bing Crosby ...?'

Robert laughed a big, hearty laugh. 'No, he is a crooner.'

'Why Nashville?' Andrew wanted to know. All this was foreign to him, but he was enjoying himself.

'The radio is the big thing there. Music stations all day long. Almost anybody can get on the air – country folks, some with little talent and no formal training, go to Nashville to get on the radio, and it has made some very big stars.'

'So you are not snobbish about music, Robert?'

'No, I like all music,' he said, and his face lit up with enthusiasm. 'Have you heard of Ernie Ford, Johnny Cash, Hawkshaw Hawkins, Hank Snow, Hank Williams ...?'

Andrew laughed out loud. 'No. Stop! Never heard of them. But if you want a chance to sing, you could join the operatic society. I'm a member. They are a good crowd. And always short of male singers.' He was letting his enthusiasm for singing become infectious. Singing was a great way to wind down, to get one's mind completely off the daily troubles and problems of a policeman's life. Police work hardened a man. He said, 'It's a good way, for me, to let off steam, Robert. To realise that there is a world of art and imagination out there. But I imagine you are well aware of all that?'

Robert's face was still lit up. Music, then, was the key. He said, 'There's a lot going on in Edinburgh. Have you heard of The Place?'

'On Victoria Street, below the Central Library?'

'Yes. You go down steps, floor after floor. Musicians of all kinds play there. Folk and popular music. Ever heard of the Corries?' He smiled and relaxed.

'Er, no,' Andrew said. Young Robert knew more about the Edinburgh music scene than he did.

'I'm saving a bit of money. If I get to university there's plenty going on – dancing and jazz clubs, pop music, folk, trad ...'

'Oh. You'll get there. And have a wonderful time,' Andrew said. 'And you'll be pleasing your father.'

'I'll join your operatic society. I might find a singing partner.'

'You very well might,' said Andrew. 'I look forward to introducing you to the crowd.'

With that he shook Robert's hand and saw him to the door,

thinking, wistfully, that Sir Gordon Campbell was blessed in his elder son.

From that interview on they met frequently and Andrew saw Robert begin to blossom, ease up and enjoy himself. Occasionally he asked the boy to crew for him and there, on the ketch, crossing the water or sailing from Granton to Dunbar, a closeness grew between them that worried Andrew. He was becoming very protective of Robert, concerned if he didn't hear from him for a few weeks, then arranging meetings and sailings so he'd have the boy's company. He was pleased out of all proportion when Robert dropped into the station to see him and sat on the end of the desk telling him all the boyish irrelevancies that young men have on their minds: girls, food, an illicit beer and girls again, for it appeared that Robert had struck up a friendship that was not yet a romance with Phoebe Hamilton and was troubled by the fact that the Hamiltons were not encouraging, though they had welcomed him into their home for years. Andrew was glad that Robert was enjoying life but was worried that this one young man was bringing him such pleasure.

He told Ma about it and she said, 'It's time you got married and had sons of your ain.' She did not understand.

There was one occasion that afterwards haunted Andrew because he felt he had let Robert down. They had sailed down to Dunbar on a cold autumn morning, tied up and gone into a harbourside bar for a beer. A welcoming coal fire blazed in the public bar, and they were sitting warming themselves, talking seriously about Robert's chances of passing his Highers, the passport to university, when Robert suddenly said, 'Do you ever feel as if part of you is missing – that you don't really belong?'

'As a matter of fact, yes,' Andrew replied. It was the way he'd felt when he realised that he had lost Flora.

'I have this feeling – I have always had it – that out there—' he waved an arm towards the sea – 'is my other half.'

Andrew said, 'You mean the girl for you?'

'No. Though it could be that, I suppose.' His brows drew together as he frowned into his beer. 'When I was a kid, I used to have this imaginary friend, Sandy. Sandy was as real to me as if he were my brother.' He seemed to be searching for the right words. 'Have you ever loved anyone more than you love yourself or your family?'

Andrew would treat the question as seriously as it was meant. 'Yes, I have. I loved a girl very much. I lost her early in the war. All my searches came to nothing ...'

He reflected, as they sipped their beer companionably, how he'd asked Brodie to check the records of exclusion zone entries. Then, on his week's holiday, while Brodie was retracing Andrew's own earlier steps, he had gone to Dr Guthrie's to check their old registers. He wanted to be sure that he and Brodie were following up the same Flora Macdonald. And this had been his first break, for from that simple search had come the startling fact that there *was* only one Flora Macdonald, not two as he'd believed. His own Flora had lied to him about her age. It had made him want to both laugh and cry – and at the same time it infuriated him that he had not thought of it earlier. The combined movements of what he'd once thought were two girls started to make sense. He'd discovered years ago during the war that a Flora Macdonald had sailed the Atlantic to Canada on the *White Empress* when he was on convoy duty, but he could not discover how these passages were allocated. The addresses of applicants had been lost and the girl who sailed to Canada could have come from anywhere in Scotland. His Flora would never have fled. She had no relatives or connections in Canada.

Then, Brodie had found the lists of evacuees to East Lothian, and to his astonishment Andrew discovered that Miss Flora Macdonald's name appeared on a list of names taken at North Berwick station on the very day she had disappeared from Portobello. And again he drew a blank, for her name did not appear on the list of evacuees for whom Lady Campbell's billeting committee had responsibility.

Now, to answer Robert, he went on. 'But I know she isn't dead. And I believe that one day I'll find her.' He waved his arm towards the open sea and said, 'Somewhere out there.'

'Have you ever looked at your family and known, just known that you don't belong to them – that you have nothing of them in you?'

'No,' Andrew said. 'I have not.' And again he was troubled because this sounded like disloyalty. Andrew saw himself in this boy and was growing fond of him – loving him like the son he might never have.

'I have more in common with you than I ever had with my family.' Robert smiled shyly at Andrew. 'I look at my mother and I don't need to be told that she hates me. She adores my brother Edward. I suppose it's because they are so alike. Both of them like fast horses and danger. Father and I don't come up to standard but at the same time she does not like to see us together. I want Father to be proud of me but I don't think I'm doing very well.'

'You're doing very well, Robert,' Andrew said. 'Your father is proud of you. He has told me so.' He decided to end the conversation there by suggesting that they went into the little town to find a fish and chip shop before they sailed back. He did not want Robert to say anything he might later regret; did not want to encourage introspective ramblings that the boy may later be embarrassed about. Andrew would not make comparisons, take sides.

After that, he drew back a little but couldn't help but think he had failed the boy in some way.

Robert duly took his Highers, but then, when everyone thought he was ready to go to university, he disappeared. This time, Sir Gordon reported his disappearance immediately to Andrew and told him that Hamilton's daughter Phoebe had also gone from the estate. It was not suggested that they had run away together. Phoebe was found a couple of miles away, at her grandfather's farm. It looked more like a lovers' tiff, which had seriously upset the Hamiltons.

Three days later a dirty, dishevelled Robert was brought to the police station by the Leith harbourmaster. He had tried to stow away on a ship which was sailing from Leith Docks to San Francisco. He was alone and was plainly surprised to hear that Phoebe, too, had been missing. Andrew questioned him. Robert's only explanation, given reluctantly, was a tight-lipped remark about learning something that had made his position intolerable.

It was a minor offence, and after questioning him, relieved that he was safe, Andrew took him home, expecting a welcome for both Robert and himself at Ingersley. But he was again shocked by Lady Campbell's fury. In the backlash of her temper, far from being relieved at her son's reappearance, she turned on Robert. 'I wash my hands of you!' she said. 'I never want to speak to you again.' There was no forgiveness in her.

Andrew felt a surge of protective emotion for Robert, who had simply to stand there, head bowed, and take it all. He wanted to speak out in Robert's defence but it was not his place to do so.

Sir Gordon asked Andrew to come into the study while he dealt with Robert. Now Andrew could feel his own anger rising. Why were his parents not questioning the boy? Why weren't they asking what it was that made his position intolerable? Or what Phoebe Hamilton had to do with it? As far as stowing away went, Robert had committed no real crime. The boat had not sailed and that side of it could have been resolved quietly. But again, Andrew could not interfere between father and son and must stand by, impotent with rage at the injustice being done to Robert.

Sir Gordon said, 'I am angry and disappointed. You have disgraced me, Robert. You would not join the Royal Navy—'

'No, sir.'

'Yet you try to run away to sea. Have you anything to say?'

'No, sir. I want to get away.'

Sir Gordon Campbell was clearly at a loss, but he pulled himself together as if reminding himself that he was once in authority over hundreds of men and why shouldn't he be able to deal with his own much-loved son? He said, 'I don't want to see you unhappy but you can't go on like this. You have to make some decisions about your future. You have three choices – university, National Service or the Merchant Navy.'

'I'll take the latter.'

Sir Gordon winced, then, 'Very well. I will take you to Leith to see someone I know. Initially you will be a lowly deck hand but you will be independent and it will make a man of you.' Then he added, and there was a terrible air of sad resignation about him as he spoke, 'I'm glad Nanny is not here to see this sorry day. Thank goodness she is having a happy time in Canada at that family wedding.'

Robert lifted his eyes to his father and in a choking voice said, 'I take it you will give me until tomorrow to pack my things?'

259

Sir Gordon's voice was sorrowful. 'Tomorrow. Nine thirty. We'll go to Leith and see if that same boat will take you on. They sail to San Francisco regularly with a cargo of Drambuie. It means that you will be returning to your home port after every trip. This way I can keep my eye on you.'

'Thank you, sir.' Robert, grim-faced, nodded to Andrew and left the room.

Chapter Fourteen

When he reached his own room Robert closed the door and threw himself on to the bed, there to lie, miserable and lost and on the brink of tears. He couldn't have told them anything. How could he have said a word in his own defence?

Last Friday, Phoebe Hamilton had invited him over and, ever sensitive to change, Robert wondered why *invite* him especially? He still worked on the farm at weekends and holidays; his pay was three shillings an hour plus lunch and supper, which he took with the family on Saturdays and Sundays. But he saw Phoebe most days and Lucy Hamilton always asked him to eat with them. Robert loved the informality of eating in the kitchen with Lucy and Phoebe. Nourished by Lucy's motherly interest in him, he thrived on the welcome smiles that always greeted his arrival. But it had seemed to him lately that the Hamiltons thought that he and Phoebe were being 'thrown together', as they called it. They were clearly afraid of a romantic attachment developing between them.

They were worrying unnecessarily. Once he was at university, he'd be gone from the estate during term-time. Both he and Phoebe were too young to be serious, or hope for marriage. Father would fund his lodgings in Edinburgh but Robert must earn his spending money, and this was all going to plan on Robert's side. Not so Phoebe's. The Hamiltons wanted their daughter to go to college to train to be a teacher, but Phoebe wanted to stay at home with her mother. She wished for nothing but to marry and live an identical life to Lucy's, preferably near at hand.

Now Robert asked himself whether Phoebe had alarmed her

parents by sharing with her mother the secret of their stolen kisses. When nobody was in the room with them it would not be long before Phoebe, like a kitten testing out its claws, would preen and tease to tempt him until he couldn't help but succumb and kiss her. Last week he'd even found her waiting outside the picture house in North Berwick. When he'd turned up, alone, to see *Around the World in Eighty Days*, she'd said, 'I didn't know you'd be here.' She did. He'd told her so the day before. 'Can we sit together? I've bought my ticket?' she said. He'd laughed and they'd held hands and he'd slipped an arm around her until the lights went up. She had made a point of leaving first, because her father was meeting her and she did not want him to see them together.

So it looked to Robert as if he and Phoebe were going to be lectured after supper tonight about being too young to make any promises.

He arrived at 6.30 to find Lucy Hamilton in the kitchen, stout and comfortable and energetic – the perfect mother figure. Two cleaning ladies came every Monday and Friday morning but the rest – cooking, shopping and laundry – was done by Lucy, even though she could afford all the servants she wanted. This evening, however, she did not give Robert the usual words of greeting, or even smile with her normal warmth.

'Where's Phoebe?' he asked.

'In the drawing room. Go and talk to her,' she said.

He went into the warm, cosy and comfortable sitting room where cretonne-covered chairs were set by the fire and plush *chaise-longues* and tub chairs were placed in the window bays. On the low pedestal tables bowls of flowers and silver-framed photographs fought for space, whilst the walls were all but invisible under the dozens of watercolour landscapes and old family oil portraits. It was June, very light, and Phoebe was sitting in the window that overlooked the rose garden.

'You all right?' he asked. She did not turn her head, so he went to the window and put his hands on her shoulders, expecting her to smile at him with those starry blue eyes that were so full of fun.

Her dark hair had been cut in what she declared was the gamine look – a soft-fringed, urchin style – and when she did

262

not respond to his hands on her shoulders, he ran his fingers through the wispy ends at the back of her neck. She turned. 'Stop it!' she said in a closed-in, hurt voice she had never used before.

He squeezed his lanky frame into the small tub chair facing her. 'What's wrong?'

She looked as if she were about to cry as she drummed her fingers on the chintz-covered arm of the chair. 'I don't know how to tell you.'

'What?'

'We can't see one another any more.'

Her eyes were brimming with tears, and though he wanted to hold and comfort her, he felt protest rising in him just as it did when he saw someone being picked upon for no reason. 'It's your father, isn't it?' he said. 'Who does he think he is? He can't tell me—'

'Yes he can!' Her blue eyes flashed behind the tears. 'He has every right.'

'How come?'

'Because – because—' She hesitated, then blurted out, 'He's not only my father! He's your father too, Robert Campbell!'

He wanted to laugh but Phoebe looked so serious and upset that what he said was, 'You been drinking or something?'

She got to her feet and flounced, as he thought it, to the middle of the room. Then she folded her arms and with tears streaming down her face stared back at him. 'If you don't believe me, ask Mummy. She'll tell you the truth.'

'Ask what?'

'Ask is it true that my father and your mother are lovers. Ask is it true that you, Robert Campbell, are my father's child.'

He was incredulous. 'Are you trying to say I'm not my own father's son? How can you believe such nonsense?'

'I am saying that,' she said, 'so even if you asked me, I couldn't marry my own brother.' She began to weep noisily. 'I'm going away. I can't live here any more. I can't bear it.' With that she fled from the room. He heard her running up the stairs, heard the bedroom door slam.

He had gone cold, for all it was a warm June night and outside, beyond the garden, he could see men, Mike Hamilton among them, stripped to the waist hauling bales of hay into stacks in the meadow so they could be loaded on to the trailer. They would be working until nearly midnight. He would go and ask Lucy if she knew what had got into Phoebe.

Lucy was washing dishes at the big white sink. She looked round when he came into the room. Her face was pale. 'Has she told you?'

'It isn't true. It can't be ...' he said. 'You don't believe it, do you?'

Lucy Hamilton, normally so calm, pulled her hands out of the water, wiped them hastily on a towel and said, 'I'm sorry. It's true.' Then she too burst into tears. 'I'll go to Phoebe. Wait.' She fled from him.

It was half an hour before she came back, and the longer he waited and thought about it, the more the accusations seemed both ridiculous and spiteful. Robert had seen Mother and Hamilton together, many times – almost daily – but Mother's attitude was always condescending and Hamilton's the very opposite of loving.

Lately it had become an embarrassment. Robert could feel the hostile tension between them when Mother demanded that Hamilton help with her horse – Mother's wishes always taking precedence over the work on the land – and Hamilton muttering that she must surely be going out of her mind.

No, Phoebe had some bee in her bonnet, but even as he thought this way, cold warning waves ran down his spine when he realised that Lucy Hamilton would never have said such a thing unless ... He went to the door that opened on to the hallway and heard Phoebe crying hysterically.

He shuddered and went into the sitting room, leaving the door ajar so Lucy would see him when she came downstairs, as she did five minutes later when Phoebe's cries had settled down to a low, sobbing sound.

Lucy closed the door and came to stand beside him. 'She won't come down. She won't listen to me.'

Robert's eyes were clouded. 'Just tell me.'

'What did she say to you?' She indicated to him to be seated.

Robert clenched his left hand into a fist and said, 'Phoebe told me that her father and mine are one and the same.'

There was a long silence. He looked up to see that Lucy had

264

a handkerchief to her face. She blew her nose, pressed her lips together, then spoke. 'I wish Phoebe had not told you. It can't do any good. Do you want me to say it isn't true? Are you and Phoebe becoming fond of one another?'

'Tell me everything. Please,' he said.

'All right.' Then, softly, so that Robert knew he must not interrupt her, she began to speak. 'I'm a little older than Mike, but since I was a girl I have been attracted to him. I was thirty. I'd had one or two proposals but had not found anyone else. Sir Gordon Campbell and your mother had just caused a sensation on the estate by marrying and it was not until then that Mike started calling at our farm, night after night. It was as if marriage were catching. War was coming and lots of couples were all at once desperate to get married. I knew that Mike wanted marriage too and I was so happy that at last he had chosen me.'

Robert nodded and said nothing as she continued: 'So you can imagine how shocked I was when he came to me – it would be about this time of the year, haymaking – and told me that he and Ruth had been lovers until she married, when their affair ceased. Then he said, "It *had* ceased. Until tonight."' Lucy looked at him, to see how he was taking it. Robert's face was stony, but he nodded his head for her to continue.

'That very night. The night he proposed to me – only an hour before he asked me to marry him, he had been with her. He wanted to confess. He wanted to get it off his chest and start marriage to me with a clean slate.' She paused. 'I had my pride. I refused him. He cried and pleaded and said he wished he had not told me for then I'd have said yes. So ... I felt sorry for him. I said I wanted to think it over as I could not marry a man who was in love with somebody else. However, he cried again and said he did not love Ruth. It was a kind of animal instinct that had led him on, but now the affair was over. He would never mention her again. I wavered. He pleaded, begged me to marry him. This was in the July before the war started in September.'

'Well, there you are,' Robert cut in. 'Perhaps it was just one of those things – a little pre-marital experience.'

She put a finger to her lips to stop him. 'He promised it would never happen again. I forgave him and we married the day before war was declared. We were happy. I think – I have always believed that he truly loved me. Then, in the April, nine months after he and Ruth—'

'I know. I was born.'

'And on the day you were born Mike was in a dreadful state. He dashed up to Ingersley to see you when you were hours old. Ruth would not admit that you were his child but Mike was convinced.'

'And you chose to believe Mike?' He could still not believe it.

She took a deep breath to control herself. 'I was seven months gone with Phoebe. How do you think I felt, seeing my husband crying over another woman's child? Don't you think I wanted to believe Ruth? Wanted to believe that you were not Mike's?'

He wanted to tell her to stop but he dared not. It was his life they were talking about as well as hers. He said, 'But – Mother was married to Father. So what's to say . . . ?'

Lucy's teeth sank into her bottom lip. 'The Commander was at sea when you were conceived.'

'Only if I was born on time. I've always been told I arrived early. Surprised everyone.'

'Mike was told that, by Ruth, but he said, "You don't breed a black colt from two palominos. Especially with the palomino stallion a thousand miles away."'

'I must be Father's son.' Father would have suspected, Robert thought.

'Sir Gordon was at sea, at war, when you were born. He'd be told that you were premature.' She stood up and patted him on the shoulder. 'I'm sorry you had to find out like this.'

'I still think it may not be true,' Robert said. 'It's all circumstantial evidence. Your husband and my mother had a brief fling before they were married. It can't have amounted to much. They both married soon after.'

Lucy looked immensely sad. Her face was drained of expression and feelings as she added quietly, 'The affair still continues . . . Phoebe—'

'What about Phoebe?'

'Three days ago, late in the evening, Mike went down to the stables to move the last row of hay bales, before the new lot was stacked in the loft. Phoebe wanted to ask her dad something. She said it couldn't wait. She would go and find him.'

'And—?'

'She came home in tears. She'd gone up to the hayloft.'

The hayloft could only be entered from the outside stone stairway. Robert repeated, 'And?'

'They were there in the stable below. Your mother and Mike. Phoebe couldn't give away her presence. She just had to lie there, listening to their talk. As well as the other ...'

'Meaning ...?'

'Yes. It frightened Phoebe – seeing them. She wouldn't give me the details and I didn't want to hear them. I was as upset for Phoebe as I was for myself.'

Robert put his hands to his face. 'Oh, no ...'

Lucy continued. 'When they had – had finished, Mike said, "And will my son be helping me tomorrow?" and Ruth replied; "I don't know. He's getting out of hand." Then she said, "I wish there were some way to tell Robert that Gordon is not his father."'

Robert had a painful lump in his throat. 'I'm sorry.' He was sorry – sorry for Lucy and Phoebe, who believed it to be true. Mother would enjoy having a hold over Hamilton – and Mother had absolutely no scruples or sense of fair play.

Lucy was crying. 'I'm more sorry than you are, Robert.'

'Who are you going to tell?' He was not afraid for himself but for Father, who loved him.

'Nobody.' She blew her nose again and gave him a watery smile. 'There's nothing to be gained.'

'Will you leave?'

'No. I have to stay here.'

'You won't tell? Why?'

She pressed her lips together to stop herself from crying hard. 'You don't live with a person for eighteen years and feel nothing for them. I love him.'

Robert hung his head. His world was falling around his ears. He'd have to leave before Father found out any of this.

The following day, he had tried to stow away.

Now, sitting in his room, Robert could still not believe that he was Mike Hamilton's son – but then he had always had the feeling that he was not even his mother's son. All at once he wanted Nanny. Nanny would have told him all she knew.

He found himself walking through the estate towards Ivy Lodge. There was a key to Nanny's house hidden underneath a stack of plant pots in the potting shed. He would let himself in and leave his farewells in a note to her. And as he walked through the fading summer twilight he realised that he did not know when Nanny might be home. She had gone out to Canada two weeks ago, to a family wedding. She had sailed and might even still be en route. If he found himself on the same continent, as well he might, he would try to contact her. Nanny had a stack of letters from her sister, going back years, in an attaché case under her bed. He would look for the address and telephone number of her sister and surprise Nanny by calling her from San Francisco.

At ten o'clock in the morning, in Bancroft, Nanny put John's jacket on a hanger and held it out for Flora's inspection. 'It still smells of mothballs,' she said. 'Where shall I hang it?'

'On the deck in the fresh air.' Flora put the finishing creases in Uncle John's suit trousers. She laughed. 'For the rest of the day, I should think. When did it last go to a wedding?' Tomorrow, Peter was marrying Valerie, the love of his life, whom he had met, courted and proposed to within the space of a week. The family were driving down to Toronto later that afternoon. There was a mountain of work to get through first.

Nanny handed the jacket over and said, 'Probably the last time the suit saw the light of day was at his own wedding. What are you wearing?'

'A yellow silk outfit. It has an A-line dress and a matching hat.' Flora took the suit out on to the veranda to hang it from the roof support. 'Let's sit out here with our coffee, Nanny,' she called over her shoulder. 'It's not too hot. We've finished pressing.'

Nanny came out on to the deck and leaned over the rail. 'Shall I make the coffee?' she asked. It was wonderful being here, seeing Flora looking so well and confident and – Nanny glanced at her again – so beautiful. Flora still had the delicate features, fragile skin and tall, willowy figure that Nanny remembered, but now, underneath the surface, she was all strength and capability.

'I'll do it. Sit down,' said Flora.

'Thank you, dear.' Nanny sat for a moment, content. Everything was coming right for all of them. It was a delight being with Alex, so like Robert in looks and yet supremely confident in himself and his abilities. He ran the sawmill for John, and though Flora did the books, Alex was perfectly capable of doing it all. Unlike Robert he was a decision-maker; he learned fast and was light years ahead of Robert in maturity. Lacking a father, he had modelled himself on John, adopting his mannerisms and authority.

Peter was about to return to Bancroft to take up a position in the local hospital, and his bride was willing to learn the lumbering business. That was, Nanny speculated, between babies. But they were a united family. There would be no squabbles in the Murray clan. It was all so very different from Ingersley where, since Ruth had come into the Campbell family, they fought to the death for every crumb of individual advantage.

Flora went about her daily round with practised ease, and now Nanny saw her through the open door, making coffee in the kitchen. The telephone rang in the living room and Flora smiled as she went to answer it. Nanny heard her say, 'Yes. It is. Yes – she is—' Her voice died away, making Nanny look up quickly at her white face as she said, 'Who shall I say—? Just a moment ...'

Flora came out on to the veranda, all colour gone from her face. 'It's for you, Nanny,' she said in a small, childishly hurt voice as she dropped into a deckchair. 'It's Robert.'

Nanny could not feel her own limbs. All strength went from them as she went back to where the telephone dangled from its cord. 'Robert?'

'Yes! Nanny, it's me.'

It was good hearing his voice, but terrifying. This was the last thing she had expected. 'Where are you?'

'San Francisco. I have jumped ship.'

Nanny's legs went from under her. She dropped on to the telephone seat, the hand set clutched between the nerveless fingers of both hands. 'You've done what? Why? What are you doing here?'

'I did it again. Three weeks ago. Ran away. Father's patience snapped. He got me into the Merchant Navy on a Drambuie boat.'

'You are docked in San Francisco?' she whispered.

'No. I told you. I jumped ship.'

'How did you find me?'

'Sorry, Nanny. I knew where you kept your letters. I stole the one on top. I didn't pry. I took the top one. It had the name and address on it. It was a simple matter to find the phone number. I'll post it back to you when you return.'

On top of the pile she had always kept Flora's first letter, the one with the funny little drawing of a weeping willow tree on the back of the envelope. It was as well that Robert had taken that one. Later letters from Dorothy had occasionally contained photographs of Flora and Alexander. Robert did not know the truth.

Nanny did not know how she was going to appear normal, but she must, for Flora knew nothing of Robert's chequered past. She had to keep on talking until she regained her composure. 'It doesn't matter. Keep the letter until you come home.' There was a silence at the other end and she knew he did not intend to return. He could not lie to her. She said, 'You can't come here ...'

'I don't want to. I can't expect to run to you, darling Nanny, every time I get myself into a mess. But ... Nanny ...?'

Nanny's strength was reasserting itself. 'You will have to return to the ship, Robert. What will your father say?'

Robert said, 'I had to get away. Phoebe told me something that made it impossible for me to stay any longer.'

'What did Phoebe tell you?' The new-found strength left Nanny. Her arms began to tremble. She pressed them to her sides. There was nothing that Phoebe could know. Phoebe couldn't have discovered that, before she and Robert were born, Ruth and Mike Hamilton had once 'fallen from grace'. It had all happened years and years ago. Nanny had remained quiet about it and had seen nothing to make her think that the day she had overheard that dreadful conversation in the nursery had been anything but a bad dream.

Again there was a pause before he said, 'I can't come back, Nanny. I can't tell you why. I have to think things over. I'll write to you at Ivy Lodge. Tell Father I'm all right. I don't want him to worry about me and I don't want him or anyone to come looking for me.'

Nanny said in a weak, croaking voice, 'What about money?'

'I have enough for six months. After that I'm going to earn my living singing and playing. I'll work my way around America.' He laughed. 'I won't have a permanent address for a bit. Hey! Nanny! Start listening to the radio. Country and western and blues. I'll call myself Rabbie Campbell and I'll come for you when I am famous.'

When Nanny put the phone back, she sat for a few moments in silence. Flora was at her side, standing with one arm about her shoulder. 'You all right?' she asked. She dropped to her knees in front of Nanny. 'Nanny,' she said softly. 'I heard you say he's in San Francisco. I feel I should go to him – find him, bring him here to Alexander, come clean ... I can't tell you how I've wanted this moment.'

Tears coursed down Nanny's cheeks. 'No, no! It would be quite the wrong thing. Robert and Gordon would be harmed. They must never know. Oh dear! I'm sorry! Nobody but you and I know that there are two boys. Nobody else knows the whole story.'

1961

Three years had passed since Robert had disappeared. There had been no word from him and Ruth was confident that he was dead – certainly he would never return. Nanny and Gordon exchanged knowing smiles whenever his name was mentioned, but in the only amicable agreement Ruth and Gordon had come to during the last few years, his will had been changed. Gordon had worded it precisely. As it now stood, in the event of Gordon's death Ruth would have sole charge of the estate until the 'rightful heir', as Gordon put it, reached the age of twenty-one.

Everything was going right for Ruth. Nanny was living happily in Ivy Lodge, visited daily by both herself and Gordon. Edward was growing up, and Ruth was busy as a Justice of the Peace. She still ran the estate and did it far better than Gordon ever could or would. It was true that they had financial worries, but they had come to a workable arrangement. Gordon and she led separate lives, Gordon spending all his time sailing and she ... In spite of the headaches and insomnia that now plagued her, she had always had her special way of relaxing.

It was June again – her favourite time of the year, when the nights were at their longest and you could read a newspaper, if you had a mind to, at eleven o'clock at night. From nine o'clock on there came a magical twilight when the sky faded from the spectacle of sunset to the misty, silent and pearly evening light. Then, the water of the Forth estuary would be platinum and silver and the tides mild and freshly crunching across sands of palest gold. The sky became mother-of-pearl and the air itself like champagne, cool, fresh and invigorating. Standing at the water's edge on such a night, it was impossible to feel older than sixteen.

On such a night, with the hay not ready for cutting, there was little for Mike to do. Ruth went to the paddock carrying her saddle and bridle. She tacked up Big Red and led him through the gate, which she closed after elbowing Mike's horse out of the way. 'OK,' she said to Major – another Major – 'I expect you will be joining us down on the beach later.'

She mounted and they went at a slow walk to the stables, where she found Mike brushing out the hayloft, opening the slatted shutters wide to let the pure, fresh air through. She stopped in the yard and called to him, 'I'm going down to the beach. Want to come along for the ride? We'll only be about half an hour.'

Mike came to stand on the top step, his eyes alight with anticipation, though he merely said casually, in case anyone were about, that he would try to join her later. Ruth waved and walked on, smiling to herself, knowing that Mike would be there. They were getting older, she fifty-two, Mike fifty-seven, and these days she liked to keep him guessing. It had been at least three weeks since the last time but the excitement was in her tonight, the midsummer madness upon her – the adrenalin rush an afternoon in court gave to her.

She smoked a Senior Service cigarette as she trotted Big Red down the beach, aware that the animal did not get enough hard riding. She threw the stub away at the old slipway and rode back listening to the hastening beat of her heart, feeling the silkiness between her legs and the unmistakable tightening inside at the prospect of their coming together. It was a magical night, the sky silvery and the light ethereal. She slowed to a walk through the remaining area of soft sand and into the secluded bay below the buckthorn. 'Whoa!' She tightened the bit, drawing Big Red to a halt, seeing, less than half an hour after she had spoken to him, Mike Hamilton on Major coming down through the buckthorn to her.

He halted before her and said, 'I thought we'd swim ... first?'

She laughed. It was she who demanded; she who must be humoured. 'It won't be dark for—' she looked at her watch – 'an hour.'

'There's nobody about,' he said. Ruth fell into line beside him as they trotted side by side down the silent beach.

'Where's Phoebe?' Ruth said.

'Still with my dad,' he said. 'Dad's place is more convenient for her work.' Phoebe was a counter clerk at the Royal Bank of Scotland. 'She's never home these days. Where's Edward?'

Ruth's present to Edward on his seventeenth birthday had been a red MG. Both she and Gordon had tried to dissuade him, for he drove as recklessly as he rode, as if he needed something to fight against. She smiled to think that there was no denying Edward's heart's desire. 'He'll not be back until the early hours. It's a different girl every night since I bought him the car.'

'That won't suit you,' Mike Hamilton laughed. 'Chip off the old block, eh? Where's Gordon?'

'Went out on the tide. He makes a night of it in good weather.'

'So we have the place to ourselves and all night to enjoy it.'

They turned at the slipway and cantered back along the water's foaming edge. There was no breath in them now for talking. Not until they halted did Ruth say, 'Want to have me out here in the open?'

'You need ask?'

'I have a feeling that tonight ...' she began, but he was off his horse, helping her down, fastening the horses on a long lead to the buckthorn behind the rocks. The rocks below the tide line were rounded, flat-topped and smooth; those above it, where the horses were tethered, jagged.

The tide was going out. They tore off their clothes and ran, hand in hand, plunging through the cool shock of the waves into deeper, calmer water. The breeze was light in this sheltered bay and it blew across Ruth's shoulders, raising goosebumps, making her nipples stand out hard and firm. After a few minutes of his noisy puffing and blowing, Mike came wading towards her. He put his arm about her shoulder, then stooped and bent to suck on her breasts and tease with his fingers under the water where she stood with her feet planted wide apart. She was being lifted from the sea bed by the swell of the water, supported by its strength until her feet rose in front of her and she was wildly aware of the hard fingers that were inside her, straight and firm, moving in and out with a motion that drove her lustful body crazy.

'You devil,' Mike whispered. 'You're daring us to be seen. Gordon could come round those rocks any minute.' The arm of the bay hid from view any sailing craft, but they could appear suddenly.

'Gordon will be in Fife – tied up in Crail harbour by now.' She could barely speak for the heat that was blinding her while she thrilled to his probing fingers. 'Quick, Mike,' she gasped. 'Not in the water. Let's get out. Take me fast and hard ... oh, please ...' Her voice had become husky with need of him. 'I want you ...'

He needed no second telling or encouragement. He had the body and desires of a young man with twice a young man's stamina. In fun he dragged her from the water and made her run towards the flat, dry sand between two smooth, sea-washed rocks. 'Over the rock,' he said, easing her down to lie on her back. He spread her arms wide while he grasped her ankles and pulled her legs apart, lifting them to rest upon his shoulders until she locked her sandy feet behind his neck. With few preliminaries, for he knew that she liked him to use force, he pressed forward into her, forcing her knees apart until his face was inches from her hot centre and she was gasping and pleading with him to take her. 'Now ... Mike ... now!'

He held her fast at the hips with his large, horny hands. She could not move, though he was going slow and deep into her. She liked the feel of rough, hard stone on her skin as she lay on the rock, head back, wet hair chilling, groaning and thrashing in her ecstasy and having to stifle the urge to cry out lest she attract the attention of anyone on the water.

She put a salty hand to her mouth and bit hard on it. She would make no sound while Mike tightened his hold on her with hard, calloused hands and thrust harder and faster and made his own grunting noises as she came, over the top, in a great tightening wave of pleasure and pain. It was always fast with them the first time. He was an expert. Later he would take his time, teasing her until she felt she might die of passion. But for now it was over. He sat beside her on the smooth black stone, saying, 'Into the water – then we'll dry off.' He laughed and said, 'We are worse than we were twenty years ago.'

Ruth said, 'Into the water, then.' She stood up and put on her French knickers and the wispy net brassière.

'What on earth ...?' Mike said, watching her.

'Put your underwear on,' she laughed, 'if you are afraid we'll be seen from the water. Nobody can see us from the land without binoculars.'

They swam and made love again in the way she liked it, with Mike behind and on top of her while she clung to the rock like a cat on a wall. Then, when they had done and dressed, she sent him ahead, following twenty minutes later to find him waiting at the stable to take Big Red from her.

He said, 'Gordon's back.'

'Gordon? Did you see him?'

'No. I saw his car in front of the house.'

'I wonder why he turned back?'

She had no premonition of disaster as she returned to Ingersley. She was merely surprised not to find him in the drawing room, watching the news on the big television set. She went to the study and tapped. 'Darling? Are you there?'

He came out, his face thunderous. 'Into the dining room, please.'

'Whatever is it?' She went ahead of him.

He closed the door carefully, then spoke to her as she had never heard him address even an inferior. 'Don't sit down!' he ordered ominously. 'What I have to say won't take long.' His head was held slightly back as he looked down at her. 'You may have a strong drink if you need it.'

'You know I never touch it. What's going on?' Her voice was high and querulous. She was not accustomed to being spoken to like this.

'Very well.' He poured a large whisky for himself before turning to face her, then, looking at her as if she were the lowest creature he had ever dealt with, dropped the bombshell. 'I was at the old boathouse tonight. I saw it all. You have a choice. Leave the estate quietly or I shall divorce you and cite Hamilton.'

Her knees went weak. A metallic taste was in her mouth but she stood her ground. 'What the devil were you doing at the boathouse?'

'Never mind what I was doing – and don't even think of concocting a story. I saw everything. So did my companion, the harbourmaster. Luckily he did not recognise either the horses or riders.'

What could she say? He had seen them. There was no point in denying it – she could only limit the damage. She said, 'I'll tell you ...'

'You won't,' he said brusquely. 'I am not in the mood for lies.'

'I wouldn't ...'

'I have been taken for a fool by Hamilton.' He put up his hand to indicate that he would not let her finish. 'But as for you! You disgust me. If you are not gone one week from today, I will consult my lawyers.'

At the speed of lightning her mood changed. She decided that attack was the best option. Her voice was as shrill as nails being wrenched from wood. 'You can't do that. You can't force me to leave my own home.'

He looked contemptuous. 'I don't suppose I am the first man to dispose of an adulterous wife who is an encumbrance.'

'I'm the mother of your children.'

He laughed drily. 'You have driven one son away and the other is driving himself fast into trouble.'

'So! Not content with attacking your wife, you are turning against Edward for what is nothing more than an adolescent prank.'

'Dangerous driving is not a prank. Edward is not an adolescent. He will soon be in very hot water. I do not intend to let that happen.'

'How dare you lay down the law down like this?' she blazed. 'How could you stop him?'

'By removing you. Edward will make a reliable, steady man if he does not have to show off to earn your approval. He will pass his entrance examination to Dartmouth. His honour and future depend upon it. I will set my son on the right path.' Gordon drained the last of his whisky.

'*Your* son?' she said in mock enquiry.

'You are implying that I am not Edward's father?'

'Of course not.'

'After what I saw tonight, my dear, the only thing I can be certain of is that you are his mother,' he said, disdain in every inflection of his voice. 'It doesn't matter. I have two sons. I love them both.'

'Do you know something I don't?' she demanded. 'Is Robert alive?'

'Do you care?' He gave her a withering look and lowered his voice. 'I would die rather than let my sons witness what I saw tonight. Their own mother . . . !'

'I will not be turned out. I am not going!' she said finally.

'You are. And so is Hamilton. His lease will not be renewed in September. I am going to sell up. One week is all you have.'

She ranted and raved, threatened and pleaded, but Gordon would not budge. It was him or her. She would find a way. She would never, never admit defeat. How dare he threaten her?

Chapter Fifteen

1961

The Zephyr purred as Andrew drove alongside the sparkling waters of the Firth of Forth towards the mortuary at Musselburgh, glancing again at last week's newspaper that lay on the passenger seat beside him. He read the first page again.

> The sea search for Sir Gordon Campbell of Ingersley has been called off. Sir Gordon sailed out of North Berwick harbour at high tide on 15 June in perfect sailing conditions. His empty yacht drifted ashore the following day but there have been no sightings and there is little hope now of finding the wartime naval captain alive.

This first paragraph contained reporting errors, but then the local papers were staffed by writers, not investigators. It probably sounded more dramatic to say 'his empty yacht drifted' when really, *The Lizzie* – for Sir Gordon had given the same name to every yacht he'd owned since the first – had inched towards the shore, sails lowered and stowed, dragging her anchor chain, with masthead, stern and navigation lights lit.

Sir Gordon had obviously dropped anchor somewhere, intent on sleeping aboard rather than sailing all night, but had not had time to hoist an anchor light on the forestay before he'd gone overboard. But where? And why? There had been a dozen boats out on the Forth that night but nobody had seen *The Lizzie*. Andrew couldn't make even a calculated guess as to where he'd dropped anchor. If he could have guessed, the police would have dived or dredged for the anchor light and anything else that might have gone over.

He glanced again at the paper.

Lady Campbell, well-known local figure, JP and school governor, told reporters that her husband was being treated for depression. He had never recovered from the loss at sea of his son Robert, who went missing, presumed drowned off the coast of San Francisco three years ago. It is looking increasingly likely that our foremost local family has once again been struck by tragedy.

He was only a mile from Musselburgh now. The waters of the Forth were on his left as he approached the harbour at Fisherrow. He slowed and watched half a dozen small sailing boats heading for the harbour, and for once had no feeling of envy. He did not wish to be on the water. His duty now was to Sir Gordon Campbell – to view the body and then to speak to his widow. Routine cases of accidental death by drowning were dealt with by junior ranks, but Andrew knew that Sir Gordon would have wanted him to handle the preliminary stages of the investigation. He had made it known in the force that he was taking personal charge of the Commander's case.

Why had Lady Campbell talked to the newspapers of depression and in doing so implied suicide? Money had always been a problem for the estate. Sir Gordon would have had some life insurance and that would not be paid if the insured died by his own hand. Lady Campbell had also repeated another contradiction in her statement to the paper. Far from not recovering from the loss of Robert, Sir Gordon had steadfastly refused to believe that his son was dead.

Andrew turned the Zephyr into the little alleyway beside Musselburgh police station and steeling himself for a sight of the body, went inside.

The mortuary was a small, dark cell separate from the police station, and there, upon the four-foot-high white porcelain slab, lay Sir Gordon Campbell's mortal remains. Dr Evans was there; the police pathologist had evidently just finished his examination. His remit was to examine the body and send his report to the procurator fiscal's office for the death certificate to be issued if he considered that there were no unusual circumstances.

The stench was appalling. Andrew took out his handkerchief and held it to his face, though he ought to be used to it by now. He had dragged oil-soaked, burning men from the sea when there was nothing he could do but watch them die. He had smelled the vile cocktail of blood and oil seeping out of the body bags as their bodies were returned to the water. He had faced this and the long toll of civil accident and murder victims over the years with horror and pity. These feelings should be overwhelming him now – instead of the slow-burning, stomach-cramping anger that he felt at the loss of his hero. He said, 'Have Photography been?'

'Been and gone.' Dr Evans was an experienced man who normally kept up a jolly banter whilst tackling the most gruesome investigations. Today his face was grim as he looked at Andrew.

Andrew's anger rose as he approached the slab. The body's clothing and its build and hair made it recognisable as Sir Gordon Campbell, but otherwise it was barely recognisable as human. The face was all but gone, pecked away by sea birds, though the back of the head was intact. Foul water ran from the body in a dirty stream into the drain hole. The Commander's fingers were eaten down to the bones. What flesh clung to the skull was clay-coloured. Andrew felt his stomach contents coming up and turned to cough into his handkerchief while he said, 'Surely this was no accidental drowning?'

The doctor said, 'I am not satisfied. Nor is the fiscal depute. The body will be sent for forensic tests.' He pulled off his rubber gloves, dropped them into a bucket and began to scrub his hands before drying them on the greying but clean roller towel. He pulled down his shirt sleeves. 'Sir Gordon Campbell would not have fallen overboard. He was too good a sailor.'

'Any ideas?' Andrew steeled himself to look again at the body. 'He was a fine man.'

'I know. I am a member of the same yacht club,' Dr Evans said.

'How long since you last saw him?' Andrew demanded. It was

automatic, no matter how revulsed he was, to clock up the little details until he had a hazy picture in his mind. It was a year since he had spoken to Sir Gordon at a Naval Association dinner. They had exchanged only a few words but his old captain had appeared calm and relaxed.

'I was down at the harbour when he sailed out, only hours before he went missing. He was in good form. He joked that in those conditions – they were perfect – he could sail around the world and might bump into young Robert, whom he reckoned would be sunning himself on a tropical island. He never believed his son was dead.'

These were not the observations of a suicidal man. Andrew said, 'What about the other boy, Edward? Was he causing trouble?'

'Edward's doing the family proud. He's been accepted for Dartmouth and is all set to follow in his father's footsteps.'

'Have the pathology report sent to me personally. It should only take three or four days,' Andrew said. 'Suspect anything?'

Dr Evans looked stern. 'I don't make guesses.' He put his jacket on and they both left the mortuary.

Andrew went straight into the station and spoke to the sergeant. He said, 'Has anyone gone to Ingersley to tell his wife?'

'No, sir. I'd have sent someone, but you said you—'

'Yes. I'm on my way. She must identify the body,' Andrew said. He left the station to drive the final fifteen miles to Ingersley, anger rising and suspicions gathering as he went. He'd learn nothing from Lady Campbell, so why had he insisted on driving to Ingersley to break the news himself? He recognised it now, of course; as a bloodhound sniffs the air to scent its prey, Andrew sensed intrigue. There were two separate stories here. On the one hand a wife who had no love for her husband letting it be known that he was suicidal; on the other, a husband who plainly was not.

Why would a cold wife prefer the world to think that her husband had committed suicide than that he had drowned accidentally – except as a cover story if the body were found and the cause of death established? Lady Campbell was a JP who nurtured her image as a heavy-handed magistrate. She was swift and ruthless and gave no second chances. Such a woman would value this reputation. No matter how little blame could be attached to her, the widow of a man driven to suicide was often and unfairly the subject of conjecture. Then he thought back to the day when, at seventeen, he had overheard Ruth Bickerstaffe and Mike Hamilton in action. It had changed his own life, for the better as it turned out, and now he asked himself whether Sir Gordon's death could have had anything to do with Hamilton. No. The affair must have ended years ago.

Seven miles away, at Ingersley, Ruth raced along the sands of the private beach – not as recklessly as when she was young, but fast. The sun was sinking behind the hills of Fife across the water, setting fire to the clouds in a blaze of copper and blood red, under a sky that was deep indigo overhead and shaded through blue, green and palest yellow to silvery white. Underfoot on the private beach the sand was pale biscuit; the tide was about to turn and Ruth rode along the water's edge, urging her horse: 'Come on, Big Red!'

There was a strange, ominous air about the beach for all that the evening was calm and still, but Ruth reminded herself that these were early days; only four weeks since Gordon had disappeared. Edward was the cause of her present unease. She had not expected him to take the death of his father so badly. He had moved out into what must be a student 'squat'. Nobody would pay to live under the conditions her darling boy was enduring.

She reached the slipway and there pulled to a halt. And now her worries fell away and she wanted to shout for joy. She looked up at the boathouse halfway down the cliff. It took agility to reach it from the cliff top, as the steps were rotted away. Gordon must have been determined – must have harboured suspicions and grudges against her to have searched for her that night. He'd come down here, binoculars to hand, to spy upon her. He had even brought the harbourmaster as a witness. She had no regrets – except for making that one mistake in telling the reporters that Gordon had been treated for depression. The police had taken samples of her sedative tonic. If the body were found they might even connect Gordon's death with that of Elizabeth, who had only taken enough sedative medicine to disorient her. Vengeful feelings boiled in Ruth at the very thought of all that had happened, and then, just as quickly, for this was the way she functioned nowadays, revenge evaporated into euphoria ...

Gordon's body had not been found – and after all this time probably would not be. All that remained was for Robert to be legally declared missing, presumed dead. Neither Robert in the flesh nor Robert's body had been found, but Ruth was certain that he would never return. He had been gone too long. She was free. The estate was in her control for the next four years until Edward was twenty-one. Edward would recover his good spirits and come home. He would forget his father and this Royal Navy nonsense.

She dismounted and took from her pocket a packet of cigarettes. She had started smoking openly as soon as Gordon went missing. It calmed her nerves. She had never dared to smoke when he was alive. He'd expressed disgust at seeing women with cigarettes in their mouths. When she'd finished, she ground the cigarette butt into the sand, mounted and rode back from the beach alone. Mike Hamilton worked late into the long summer nights. She would find him in the barn moving hay bales. He always did this two or three weeks after the hay was in, restacking from one long side to the other; leaving spaces between the bales to make sure that heat did not build. He was a good farmer. They had never lost their hay through spontaneous combustion. She untacked Big Red and put him out to graze in the paddock with Major before she went to look for Mike.

He did not see her at once, and she stood for a full two minutes enjoying the sight of him, tanned and stripped to the waist, his chest hair gone grey while that on his back was still dark. His movements were youthful and easy and she found herself stirring inside, wanting him. She spoke at last and smiled to see him startle. 'When you've finished ...'

He came to stand by her. 'I can leave it,' he said. 'At the stables? Later?'

'Come to the house.' They had never used the house before and he raised his eyebrows in question. She said, 'Tell Lucy that you are dropping by to sign next year's lease.'

He said, 'Don't you think you ought to leave it until Gordon's ...'

'Oh! For heaven's sake. You won't be signing. We can't renew the lease until my powers are recognised.'

He stared at her. 'You are a hard woman, Ruth. You know your husband must be dead. You haven't shed a tear.'

Perhaps she was hard. There was a certain recklessness about her now that surprised her. She had been rude to Nanny, telling her to take her last remaining items of furniture and clothing to Ivy Lodge since she was no longer needed in the house. When Nanny asked whether she was sure, and wouldn't it be better to have a companion at such a time, Ruth had told her sharply to mind her own business.

She must not let her mood of elation show. Now she touched Mike's arm and spoke in a soft, appealing voice. 'I have to be strong. Everything falls on to my shoulders.'

'All right. I'll come about half past eight.'

She left the barn, fizzing with excitement. She would have time to bathe and scent herself. They would not be disturbed. The cleaners came in daily and only the cook and a housemaid were in residence. She would let them know that she did not need their services this evening.

At eight o'clock she was waiting for him, bathed and dressed in a revealing but simple shirtwaist dress made from double layers of fine black georgette, under which she wore nothing but buttoned French knickers. Since Gordon's disappearance she had discovered a great well of passion in herself – she was much more needful – at the same time as Mike's lust seemed to be waning. She would make him wild with desire tonight.

It was warm in the house. She went to the drawing-room window to open it wide and enjoy the sight of her land, her park, her estate. And as she watched, a metallic-gold Ford Zephyr came gliding through the gates at the South Lodge to arrive smoothly on the gravel below.

'Damn!' she muttered as she left the drawing-room. 'Who on earth would call at this time in the evening, without an invitation?' She went quickly down the stairs before the doorbell could ring and a servant go to answer it. She flung open the inner door just as heavy footsteps reached the top of the stone steps and a man stepped into the tiled entrance lobby. It was Andrew Stewart. He could only be here on official business.

They must have found Gordon. Well, at least she'd be given administrative powers earlier. Just as long as the procurator fiscal's office issued the death certificate without question.

'Lady Campbell,' Andrew said, 'may I come in and speak to you privately?'

'Of course. Follow me.' She went ahead of him in a cloud of scent; up the stairs to hold open the door to the drawing room, which Andrew had not seen for a few years. The smell of fresh paint was evident and the aristocratic, shabby look had gone. He knew at once that Sir Gordon had not had a say in this décor. It was the fashion now, in the houses that were being built all over the land, as well as the boxy little council offices, to have two different wall coverings – as contrast, it was said – to give an optical illusion of height, depth or width. But this room had perfect proportions and now was decked out in orange hessian, which covered the fireplace wall, and a striped wallpaper with overblown flowers of indefinable species around the other three. The ceiling had been painted a lighter shade of orange and the plasterwork was multicoloured, gilt-trimmed and ghastly. There was also displayed a silver-framed photograph of Sir Gordon Campbell and his wife outside Buckingham Palace, Sir Gordon looking at his uniformed best and Ruth Campbell a wilting tulip on his arm. Seeing it, Andrew's anger flared.

Watching her carefully, he said, 'I am sorry to have to break the news, Lady Campbell. Your husband's body has been found.'

She showed no feeling whatever. 'How – how dreadful. Where?'

'The River Esk.' He waited. There was not a flicker of emotion on her face. She must be expecting company, dressed as she was for entertaining. He said, 'I realise that this cannot be a shock. But please sit down and let me get something for you.'

'I don't drink,' she said. She sat down. 'What do I do now?'

'You have to come to the mortuary to identify your husband.' She would know this – she had enough experience of courts and legal matters. 'I'll drive you to Musselburgh,' he said as coolly as he could.

'No. It must wait until morning,' she said with an impatient wave of a perfectly manicured hand. 'I ... I can't face it. Not tonight.'

'Ah, but you have to.' Andrew stood up. 'I will bring you back as soon as it is done.' And as he watched her, a cold certainty grew with every word, every flicker of an eyelash. Ruth Campbell was behind her husband's death. She knew a death certificate would not be issued unless the procurator fiscal was satisfied that the cause of death had been established and that there were no suspicious circumstances. She had not even asked if a doctor had viewed the body. He said, 'I must ask you for any medicines your husband may have been taking, for further forensic tests. I'm sure you know the form, Lady Campbell.'

'Let me know when we can have the funeral,' she replied. 'It will be a very quiet family affair. Under the circumstances.'

The circumstances she spoke of was the question of the death certificate. Until it was given, the funeral could only go ahead with the restriction that burial, not cremation, was chosen. She seemed to realise this for she said, 'It will be a burial. I quite understand that you have your job to do, Constable.'

'Inspector.'

'I will take the medicine with me to Musselburgh.' She gave Andrew a calculating look and then, in one of her remarkable lightning changes of mood, took a handkerchief from her pocket and began to dab at her eyes and hunch her shoulders forward. 'Oh dear. Poor Gordon. I ...' She looked up. 'It seems as if the Campbells are destined to die tragically, unexpectedly ...'

Andrew wore a noncommittal facial expression as he replied, 'They certainly don't die peacefully, do they? And what about the Bickerstaffes?'

'Bickerstaffes?' She looked up, startled. Andrew was certain of her guilt. It had been sheer impertinence on his part to say what he'd said. She would be justified in making a complaint. Instead she said, 'My sister's death was an unfortunate accident, Constable.'

'Inspector,' he corrected her again.

She dropped her eyes, 'I would rather not go to identify the body unaccompanied. I will ring my farm manager and ask him to take me.' She stood up. 'Please excuse me,' and went from the room to the study across the hallway.

Andrew moved to the door on the pretext of looking at the pictures in the hallway, though his heart was thumping as he strained to listen to what she was saying. He heard her say, 'No. Now,' without even a catch in her voice.

The phone slammed down and a few moments later she came back into the drawing room, dabbing her eyes as if distressed, to find him standing by the open window, looking towards the South Lodge. Andrew said, 'Would you like me to tell Miss Taylor for you?'

She was alarmed. The crying ceased. 'No!' she said. Then, 'Nanny Taylor is very old. And rapidly becoming senile. I will tell her in my own way, tomorrow.'

'Would you like me to make international enquiries about Robert, Lady Campbell?' he now asked coolly. 'He is heir to the estate.'

A dark flush rose on her face. 'I must ask you to leave the Campbell family's business to me,' she said.

And that might have been as far as it went that evening. Andrew had clocked up several lines of investigation – to check up on Elizabeth Campbell's death, to look in on Miss Taylor since Ruth wished him not to, and to make international enquiries about Robert – but now Mike Hamilton appeared, well dressed and shaved, to drive Lady Campbell to Musselburgh.

Hamilton had not done all this in five minutes. At this time of the year, as Andrew knew full well, a farmer rarely finished work until the sun went down. He had not simply jumped at his owner's command. He had been getting ready for something, and by the look of her – scented and wearing next to nothing – the affair was still going on.

Lady Campbell did not waste a minute in explanation either to Andrew or Hamilton. She went towards the door, clearly at ease with Hamilton, then turned to Andrew to dismiss him.

'I can see myself out,' he said, pre-empting her.

He drove to North Berwick, parked on Quality Street, bought an *Evening News* and walked down to the harbour to watch the boats. He knew that much of what he was thinking was intuition and guesswork, but never before had there been a case closer to his heart than this one, which he was coming to think of as Campbell versus Campbell.

At the harbour, he sat on the steps that descended into the water, glanced at the boats for a few minutes then unfolded the paper. The stop press section read: *Body of Sir Gordon Campbell recovered from the Esk*.

It would make the headlines in tomorrow's daily papers. Reading it in the newspaper was no way for Sir Gordon Campbell's old nanny to find out. Ivy Lodge, Nanny Taylor's home, was right on the edge of Ingersley land, abutting Davey Hamilton's farm and not too far from the main road.

Andrew would go back to Edinburgh on the A1, first taking the country road and enjoying the sight of the sun going down, red and orange, blazing over the cornfields, lighting the scarlet faces of the poppies that dappled and drifted in clouds across the fields of waist-high golden corn. The unanswered questions that teemed in him proved a distraction from the beauty of the countryside. The gold Zephyr, like the wind it was named after, whispered by hedgerows of hawthorn and birch that seemed to come forward, dark green and silver, to meet him. There was the scent of the sea in his nostrils, and inside himself on this rare, tranquil night, as the sun dropped low, a host of questions, overlaid with seething anger.

He reached the A1, turned left and drove the three miles to the turn-off for Ivy Lodge. The track to the lodge had never been given a good surface, so he parked the Zephyr on the grass verge and walked the quarter of a mile to the house.

Nanny Taylor was in her garden, talking to an old man and a young girl. As Andrew drew near he saw that the man was Davey Hamilton, Mike Hamilton's father, and the girl his granddaughter Phoebe, whom Andrew recognised from photos young Robert had shown him.

'Miss Taylor?' he called from the gate.

Nanny looked up at once, put up a steady hand to shade her eyes. 'Who is it?'

He opened the gate and went towards them. 'Andrew Stewart. You may remember me?'

She was flustered. Her hand, which had been steady, shook as she held it out to him. Why was he having this effect? She said, 'Of course I remember you. It must be about three years since we met at Ingersley. You came to take Robert sailing.'

'That's right.' He shook hands then turned. 'Mr Hamilton. I don't suppose you will remember me?'

The old man, still sprightly and upright said, 'Are you the one who went to sea? Your mother used to be the cook?'

'That's me,' he said. 'And this must be Phoebe. Robert talked a lot about you.'

She smiled, shook hands then went quiet as Davey Hamilton continued, 'We've come to break the news to Miss Taylor before she hears it on the radio or in the paper. I take it that's why you are here.'

'I'm sorry, Miss Taylor,' Andrew said. 'Though I am sure you were expecting something like this.'

Now Nanny Taylor pulled herself up and set her shoulders back. 'Gordon would never have committed suicide! He would not do a dishonourable act.'

'We don't know the cause of death,' Andrew started to say, but here she interrupted him.

'Never. Never. No matter what Lady Campbell said to the papers. Depression? Nonsense!' She spoke vehemently and Andrew noticed the flushing round her eyes and her darting glances at Davey Hamilton.

She had been drinking. He tried to keep his face straight, and decided to probe a little. 'You don't think that Sir Gordon was depressed about losing Robert?'

Indignation made the reddening even more noticeable as she replied, 'How could he be? Robert is a very successful singer and song-writer in America. Sir Gordon and I talked about him all the time.' Here she stopped and put a hand to her mouth as if realising that she'd let the cat out of the bag. In a much softer voice she said now, 'Excuse me. I'm tired.' She nodded quickly as if to dismiss them all, then slowly went back into her house.

Davey Hamilton said to Andrew, 'We'll walk down the lane with you.'

So, Nanny Taylor knew that Robert was alive and well. She also knew that Ruth Campbell was lying. Andrew turned this over in his mind, and so engrossed was he in his own thoughts that he barely listened to Davey Hamilton's wartime reminiscences. He did notice that Phoebe had evidently heard them all before, for it was her voice that finally brought him out of his ruminations as she said, 'Yes, Grandpa. You captured the pilot of the German plane that came down ...'

Davey laughed at her. 'No. Of course not,' he said.

Andrew roused himself to ask, 'Did it come down on your land?'

'No. Over the far side of the A1. Not my land.' Davey Hamilton smiled. 'It's this lassie o' mine. She likes to tease.'

'It must have been exciting. I'll bet it brought out the crowds?'

'Aye. They came from miles away. It gave the police a hard time, I can tell you. Keeping away souvenir-hunters,' Davey said. 'I never even got there on the day. I had to help one of Miss Taylor's patients back to Ivy Lodge. Got all the way over the fields she had – and her on the brink of giving birth.' He went on, reminiscing, 'Bonny young lass. Tall, with flaming red hair ...'

Andrew all at once was brought up with a start. 'Who was she?'

'Och! There were a dozen or more bairns born that first year. Miss Taylor was running around the area like a scalded hen. You never knew who any of them were, though they mostly came from the city. Here one day – had their babies – then moved on into permanent accommodation somewhere.' Davey Hamilton scratched his head and a frown creased his brow. 'I believe that girl went to Canada with her baby.'

Andrew's heart came shuddering almost to a stop but he managed to ask calmly, 'So Miss Taylor opened Ivy Lodge as a nursing home?'

'Yes. Delivered all the babies around here. Phoebe, Robert ...' Davey Hamilton, suddenly tired, stopped walking, leaned on Phoebe's arm and said, 'Well, this is as far as I'm going for a few more minutes. Here we are.' He put out his hand to Andrew.

Andrew's car was only fifty yards ahead. He shook Davey Hamilton's hand. 'It was nice to meet you again,' he said.

Davey said, 'Remember me to your mother.'

'I will,' Andrew replied, then strode off back to his car, his mind spinning. He must find somewhere quiet. He headed for the monument to the Napoleonic Wars victory. It stood on top of Garleton Hill about five miles from where he was. It would provide a quiet place to think, without distraction.

All the little coincidences had begun to fall into place. Discovering that Flora had concealed her age had been the first real breakthrough after all these years. This had brought the revelation that there was only one Flora Macdonald. Now at last he felt in his bones that he was on the right track. Suppose his search through hospital records for a girl who had injured her back had been another false lead? Suppose that she had not fallen on the ice at all? Suppose that their one act of love, under the weeping tree, had resulted in Flora's pregnancy? What then for Flora? She would lie to Mr Davidson and go to Ingersley to find Ma. Had Ma left Ingersley by then? And as he realised that Ma's last days at Ingersley could have been Flora's first, he knew the second gut-churning certainty of the evening.

He parked at the foot of the monument and ran up the hill to the tall tower. He opened the door and climbed the steps to the narrow platform at the top, from where he could see a splendid panorama – Edinburgh and the Lothians and down to the Borders and across the water to the distant hills, with everything bathed in magical golden light. Even as he drank in the peaceful scene, the questions and train of thought that a chance remark of Davey Hamilton's had brought took his mind racing. Was he looking at an impossible scenario? If the pregnant girl with flaming red hair was his Flora, then why had she not told him? Hardest of all to equate with this line of thought was the question: could Flora have become Nanny Taylor's patient without either Nanny or Lady Campbell being aware that he, Andrew Stewart, the son of their cook, was the father of her unborn child?

He leaned his elbows on the narrow parapet and tried to be rational, but he knew this gut-churning sensation well. It came to him when he was on the right track. Who was it who said of detection that if you took all the evidence and eliminated the impossible, then what you were left with, however far-fetched, had to be the probable? He was now left with the probability that Flora gave birth at Ivy Lodge, then fled to Canada with their child. He had no idea why she would do this, and, until he found her – and find her he would – no clue as to why she would have wanted to cut him out of her life when she most needed him.

He descended the steps and sat on the grass at the foot of the monument for another few minutes. Shivers ran up and down his spine, for all the heat of the July night. And as he sat, his hands around his head, there swept over him an almost spiritual sensation; one he would never recapture. It was as if were looking, humbly, on the face of God. His child – the unique person that was half himself and half Flora – somewhere walked the face of the earth today, living and breathing and knowing nothing of his, or her, father.

The sky above him was cobalt blue now and he saw through his teary, misty eyes the clouds ablaze, copper and bronze and flaming red behind the distant dusky hills of Fife, and as a great lump came into his throat, his feelings turned from humility to desperation. He would not rest until he discovered the truth of what had gone on at Ingersley in 1940. He would not rest until he saw and touched his own child who was conceived under the weeping tree.

He sped back to Edinburgh to question Ma without upsetting her; careful not to hint that Flora's disappearance was on his mind. 'Do you remember the exact day you left Ingersley?' he asked casually, knowing the date that was one day after Flora Macdonald left Mr Davidson's house in Portobello and signed on as an evacuee at North Berwick station.

Ma remembered and the date fitted. He asked, 'Tell me again, Ma. How did it happen?'

She told him of being visited in the old drawing room of Ingersley House – then a hospital ward – by Lady Campbell, who said she was to be removed to a convalescent home. Ma finished with, 'I never went back, you remember. She found me my first good job—'

Andrew remembered. 'And she gave you furniture – and money.' Lady Campbell had deliberately sent Ma away. But why? She was no philanthropist, no giver of charity. She had never acted except in self-interest in her life.

'Yes. She was good to me. She was having problems of her own. All those evacuees to find homes for. And her expecting her first baby.'

If Flora, pregnant and desperate, had gone to Ingersley

looking for Ma, why was Ma never told? Who had kept it from her? Why? It still did not add up. He could be on the wrong track – the girl may not have been Flora. He'd need a few more facts before he tackled Nanny Taylor.

The following morning at the office, as soon as he had drunk a cup of coffee and read his post, he sent for Brodie and asked him to check the register of births in North Berwick between the date the Heinkel was shot down and the end of July. Next, and thinking about the investigation in hand, he put in a transatlantic call to New York. There was a reciprocal agreement through Interpol and soon he found himself speaking to his American counterpart. 'I want you to trace a Robert Campbell,' he said. 'He landed in June, nineteen fifty eight and has become a successful singer and song-writer over there.'

'Who?'

'Robert Campbell.'

'Never heard of the guy.'

Andrew believed him. It would be Nanny Taylor's exaggeration. He laughed. 'Try Nashville, Tennessee. He wanted to go there.'

'How old?'

In front of Andrew was Robert's file, from his running-away days. 'He was born on the fifteenth of April, nineteen forty. He'll be twenty-one.'

'Description?'

'Scottish accent. Tall. Dark haired.'

'Worn long?'

'Oh, I expect so, by now.'

'What's it about?'

'Tell him his father is dead. He must come home.'

'You'll pay for his ticket?'

'Yes. Give him enough for the ticket and a couple of nights in hotels en route. And tell him to call me as soon as he lands. I want to put him in the picture.'

Andrew put the phone down. It rang immediately and he picked it up. It was Brodie, who said, 'I found it, sir. Flora Macdonald gave birth to a boy. Alexander Andrew Macdonald. On the fifteenth of April, nineteen forty.'

The hairs on Andrew's arms stood on end as his stomach

lurched. He was a father. He fought back the tears and the lump that came into his throat as he put his hands up to his face and realised that Flora had had her baby – his own baby son – in Ivy Lodge on the very day that Lady Campbell gave birth to Robert at Ingersley. And slowly the feeling of tearful elation was being replaced with a simmering anger. How could Lady Campbell not have known that Nanny Taylor had delivered a baby on the same day as herself? They lived only four miles apart.

Chapter Sixteen

Robert did not have enough luggage to put in the hold. He took his guitar case on board. A sweet Scottish air hostess smiled and allowed him through, seeing that the guitar case was larger than the small haversack he carried. The sack only contained two worn-out pairs of jeans, four shirts that had seen better days and the jacket he'd retrieved from pawn with the money the cops gave him.

The air hostess showed him to a single seat by the emergency exit. 'You'll be comfortable here,' she said. 'More leg room. If we are not full I'll let you into first class later. That is, if you will give us a tune.'

'Sure thing,' he said as he stretched his long legs out. 'It's going to be a long flight.' He closed his eyes as soon as she retreated. The flight would be a luxury after the last six months of sharing a room with four others in a flop-house in steaming-hot Nashville.

A smile crossed his face quickly as he thought about the bare light bulbs, the broken furniture, the bugs and the noise all night long from drunks, trucks, whores, occasional gunshots and fighting couples. The four of them were too poor to buy what they needed. When they needed guitar strings they could not afford the coin laundry but had to do their washing in the bathroom and drape the wet clothes over the backs of chairs.

Although the four of them – all player/song-writer hopefuls like himself – shared the one room, they were seldom all home together. Robert had found a job for the last six months waiting-on in a hotel, where at least he was fed when on duty –

one meal a day when he'd stuff himself full so he could last out until the next. Meals otherwise were nonexistent. Breakfast was a cigarette and coffee, lunch half a sandwich with cigarettes and coffee, supper the other half of the sandwich.

Two of the other guys worked at a soda fountain and Tex, the luckiest of the four, as a box-office clerk at the Grand Ole Opry. It was Tex who'd slip them in to watch the stars performing and Tex who kept them all going, assuring them that their songs would be sung all over the world; Tex who told them that the acts at the Grand Ole Opry were not half as good as theirs and that they were all gonna make it big.

The safety-belt lights were on now and his girl was back, fastening his belt for him. Robert kept his eyes closed, enjoying the feel of her little hands going down his chest to pull the thing tight across his lap. When he heard the snap of the buckle, he opened his eyes and winked at her.

She pulled his hair – he wore it shoulder length and curly now – and said, 'You can move up to first class when we are in the air.'

He grinned, the lopsided, engaging grin that some girls, he thought gratefully, found irresistible.

Later, after he'd been moved up to the front when they were flying through the black night, he told Cathy – for that was the hostess's name – all about his years in America and how he would not be returning to Nashville. The climate didn't suit him. With the humidity, ninety degrees Fahrenheit felt like two hundred. 'So I'm going home,' he said. 'My father's dead. I have come into the estate and the title.' There were folk-singing groups in Edinburgh. Singing and writing songs would have to be his recreation. He had given it a fair go – but he hadn't made it, and unless he found a partner, he never would.

'A title?' she smiled. 'So you're rich and famous?'

He laughed. 'Neither. I won't use the title.' He had long ago stopped wondering if he were Father's legitimate heir; stopped asking himself if he really were entitled to the estate, reasoning that if he were Mike Hamilton's offspring then Edward probably was too. The important thing was that Father had never been told the truth of Mother's adultery and that he had trusted Robert to come back, take on the estate and look after Mother and Edward. Robert wanted it too – wanted to run the estate and the farm in the interests of all of them. But he'd never imagined it coming to him this way, through his father's premature death. He had not given Nanny his last address, so could not have known about this tragedy. The cops had given him the newspaper with a four-week-old report of Father's going missing. They'd also given him the most recent report, a two-day old *Scotsman* which had his own photograph emblazoned across the front page beside Father's.

He was hurt by the newspaper story that Father was depressed and had never recovered from the loss of his elder son. Nanny had told Father from the beginning, that he was safe. She had even reported back to him Father's hopes for his success.

He opened the locker and got out his guitar case. The *Scotsman* was zipped inside with his songs and music. He read the front page of the newspaper and again felt anger rising in him. Father would never commit suicide. There were questions to be answered – and to think that, without Andrew Stewart's intervention, he might never have known.

Afterwards, Alex realised, he might never have known the truth had he not dropped by at the library on his way to the rehearsal. It was pouring with rain – a summer shower and the worse for being unseasonal for it was mid July and he was dressed in jeans and a thin shirt. However, he was wearing a tie to impress Jean, the new library assistant, who was tall and red-haired like Mom.

He parked Mom's Studebaker in front of Kelusky's in the only parking spot he could find. He stood looking in the window at the sale goods, wondering if he should buy the rubber knee boots that were reduced to $1.95. He decided against it and took his chances, and ran fast, so as not to get too wet, to the library on Flint Street. In the porch he ran his fingers through the hair he wore longer than the family approved. He liked the feel of it against his neck and the look of the dark curls that bounced over his ears and fell forward over the greeny-grey eyes that were so like his mother's.

Pushing open the door, he saw that Jean was there, and went over to her where she worked behind the high maplewood desk. 'Hi!' he said.

297

'Hi!' she replied shyly, looking up at him and down to her books very quickly. 'Have you read them all? It's only two days ...'

'I was looking for something – er – exciting,' he said, and grinned to see the blush that spread at great speed, poppy red, on her cheeks. Girls with Mom and Jean's colouring could never hide their blushes.

Her straight hair was cut to chin length and it fell slanting across her face as, flirtatious now, she smiled back at him and said, 'You mean the books?'

Alex looked around. There were only four people in the hushed library apart from themselves. The others wouldn't hear if he kept his voice down. 'I mean what time do you finish? Do you have a date?'

'I don't have a date. But ...' she glanced at him again, 'but you have a reputation.'

'For what?' he whispered, smothering the ready laugh. He'd had a few girlfriends but nothing serious, until Jean came to town and he fell in love – or whatever one called this urge to see her, speak to her, only be happy in her presence and to fret if she were not at work every day.

'For being a Don Juan – a lady-killer.'

'That's all right then,' he said. 'I prefer you alive.'

She laughed, and it was a sweet sound like water burbling over mountain stones. She said, 'All right. Eight o'clock.' She looked up at the big wall clock. 'It's only five. You don't want to wait around here.'

'I have to go to Mom's rehearsal.' He leaned over the counter the better to see her small hands riffling through the pages of returned books as she looked for damage. 'She's in *The Mikado*.'

Mom was singing the part of Yum Yum in the production that was to be staged next month in Bancroft. Alex played the piano at rehearsals.

'She's good. I never miss the operatic society productions.'

'Shall I meet you here?' he said. 'We could go for a drive ...'

She smiled the secret smile he could not fathom. 'We'll go to the coffee bar,' she said softly.

He was about to leave when she added, 'By the way – go and look at the newspapers.' There was a large table in the far corner of the room. On it were placed the dailies, local and national, and in a large rack against the wall the monthlies and international news.

'What for?' he said.

'Look at last week's *Scotsman*. Front page. He looks like you.'

'Who does?' Alex grinned at her but went obediently to the empty table and took a few old copies of *The Scotsman* from the rack. He placed them on the table, opened the top one out and felt his face growing pale. There, right in the middle of the front page, was a picture of a man in naval uniform – next to one of himself. It was himself yet not himself. He had never had this particular picture taken and the photograph was of a young man with shorter, neatly cut hair such as Brits wore.

The stark headline read: *Naval Hero Found Drowned.* Underneath the article continued:

The body of Sir Gordon Campbell of Ingersley has been found. Sir Gordon sailed out of North Berwick harbour at high tide on 15 June in perfect sailing conditions. His empty yacht drifted ashore the following day but until today there had been no sightings. The cause of death has not yet been established but the police are treating the case as non-accidental drowning. The procurator fiscal has announced an inquiry.

Lady Campbell, well-known local figure, JP and school governor, told reporters that her husband was being treated for depression. He had never recovered from the loss at sea of his son Robert (right, above), who went missing, presumed drowned, off the coast of San Francisco three years ago.

But it was not the report that held Alex's horrified attention. It was the photograph of Robert Campbell. Alex stared again at the photograph of himself – himself but not quite. Underneath he read: *Robert Campbell, son of the late Sir Gordon Campbell. Born North Berwick, 15 April 1940.* Alex looked round at Jean, who had come to stand beside him and was saying, 'Don't you think you and he are alike?'

He said, 'Not only alike. He was born on the same day as

me. In the same place. But how ...?' His hands were trembling. Robert Campbell was the boy Aunt Dorothy's sister wrote about. Robert Campbell had been his own other half – his imaginary friend – all his life. 'Can I take the paper?' Alex said to Jean. 'It's really important.'

'OK. Nobody will even notice, I expect,' she said.

'And would you mind if I broke our date? The first and last time?'

'Not at all,' she said. 'I'll see you whenever,' but he had gone and was running back to the Studebaker, ramming it into gear and going hell for leather for the rehearsal hall.

Normally he enjoyed rehearsals and often stayed on after time, but now his mind and concentration were not on the music. He hardly knew how he got through it.

He seated himself at the piano where the score was opened at page sixty-four. The trio. He didn't need the music but it pleased Mom to have someone stand by the piano and turn the pages for him. Mom was talking to the other two Little Maids, Peep Bo and Pitti Sing. He watched her, unobserved, for a few moments. He had always known that there was a mystery around his birth, but how could any mother – how could his own, adored, wonderful Mom – hide from her son the fact that she had given away his identical twin – his 'missing presumed drowned' twin, for that was the only answer.

The producer called, 'All right, ladies,' and a hush came over the cast who were all assembled now in the area around the piano. The Three Little Maids stood in line. Alex caught the producer's eye and began the introduction, *allegretto grazioso*, and the women came in without faltering, exactly on cue, with Mom singing as if this were the only challenge she had ever faced in her life.

Two hours later, with Mom in the Studebaker beside him, Alex pulled up fifty yards short of the house, switched off the engine and said, 'Stop chattering, Mom. You have some explaining to do.'

'What?' she said, and there was the little catch in her voice that always afflicted her when she knew that awkward questions were coming.

He reached over to the back seat and presented the paper to her. Then he watched the colour drain from her face, saw her hands start to shake and finally saw the frightened look in her eyes. He said, 'The game's up, Mom. You have to tell.'

When she had finished reading, she looked at him with a world of pain in her tearful eyes. 'Robert? He isn't dead! He must never have let them know he's alive!' she said.

'Tell me. Please, Mom.'

She started slowly, and he listened, appalled, to the tale of her abandonment by the father of her babies, the frightening pregnancy of a girl of sixteen who had nobody in the world, the offer of shelter from a woman whose price for help was the child Mom was bearing. She told him how she loved him and how she had lived with her burden of guilt for abandoning Robert. She said, 'Nanny said that Robert would have a better life with the Campbells than with us and I knew it was true. One of my boys at least would have security. Robert would have a title and an estate. I was not to worry about him. I would never have left you behind, Alex.'

She looked exhausted when she had finished, and now he put his arm about her and said, 'It doesn't matter about me, Mom. But it sure as hell matters.'

He stared out at the rain that was hammering on the windscreen and running in rivulets down the side windows. He said, 'So Lady Campbell never knew there were two of us?'

'No. Nanny never told her. Nanny wouldn't tell her.'

'And nobody – not even Nanny – knows what has since happened to my natural father?'

'Nanny has never mentioned him. I was never to ask, she said. It was best that way. If there were anything to tell, Nanny would have said so in the letters to Aunt Dorothy. I was to put it behind me and start afresh.'

'And you did!'

She started to cry. 'No. I have never forgotten, not for one hour. And I never lost the feeling that I was doing wrong – for all I was told was that Robert was well and content.'

'So my natural father may be married. He may have other children – and he does not know I exist?' he demanded.

'Yes.'

'We are going back, Mom. We have to find Robert.'

She twisted her handkerchief between tense fingers, as if she were on the edge of breaking down. 'He's not there. Three

301

years ago he rang from San Francisco. He'd jumped ship. He wanted to be a singer and was heading for Nashville.'

'I wish you had told me.'

'I wanted to go find him, tell him the truth and bring him to you.'

His voice was cold now. His emotions were confused. He could not comfort Mom. 'Why didn't you?'

'Nanny said that both Robert and Sir Gordon Campbell would be broken-hearted if they discovered that Robert was not his son.'

'We are going to find him.'

'In America?'

'No. I know him, Mom. Don't ask how. I just know. He is me. He will go back home when he discovers that his father is dead. His Nanny is still alive. She'll find him. He'll take over the estate – won't he?'

She wept. She couldn't control herself any longer. Her face was red and blotchy and her breath was coming in great lurching gasps. 'I can't, Alex! I can't go with you. I have carried it for all these years – the guilt. I couldn't face it. What if Robert doesn't want to know the truth at a time like this? He's lost his father and now he has to take the title ...' Her shoulders heaved as she said, 'I couldn't bear it if he turned against me.'

Mom might not be able to bear rejection but Alex knew that his identical twin would feel exactly the same as he did. 'He will want to know his brother. He will want to know the truth,' he told her. 'I won't just go barging into his home and demand to see him, or anything like that. I'll be discreet.' But he could see that it would be difficult for Mom.

'How will you do it?'

'I don't know yet. It will come to me when I get to Edinburgh.' He put an arm about her and pulled her close. 'Mom, I love you. Leave it to me. I'll send for you but only if it all turns out right.' He was not nearly as sure of success as he sounded. But he had determination and he had the strength to help Mom and spare her agony. He said, 'I'll see if there is a flight tomorrow. Now let's go and confess to the family.'

It was three days before the order to investigate the death of Sir Gordon Campbell arrived from the procurator fiscal's

302

department. Traces of strychnine had been found in the form of small crystals in his spine. The report that landed on Andrew's desk from the forensic men gave only these details and noted the fact that the medicine Sir Gordon Campbell had taken was known to contain the poison but in such small quantities as would make an accidental overdose impossible. Pure strychnine, probably in the form of rat poison, had been administered, or self-administered.

Anger flared in Andrew as he read the report. His hero had died an agonising death. His wife – for he was certain it was she – had chosen the ugliest method of poisoning. He went to the bookcase, took down the reference work and read:

Strychnine: A colourless, crystalline powder with a bitter taste. The substance occurs naturally in some seeds and plants, in particular the seeds of Strychnos nux vomica.
Effects: Strychnine attacks the central nervous system. It causes exaggerated reflex effects when all the muscles contract at the same time.
Symptoms: The victim's neck and face become stiff. Arms and legs go into spasm. The spasms become increasingly severe until the victim is almost continuously in the arched-back position with the head and feet on the floor or other surface. Rigor mortis sets in immediately upon death, leaving the body in the convulsed position with eyes wide open and extreme facial grimace. Death from strychnine poisoning results from paralysis of the brain's respiratory centre rather than from convulsions. Strychnine is frequently used as a poison for rats and vermin.

He would get her for this. No poison had been found in her sister's body when she died, but these violent deaths – of her mother and Elizabeth and now her husband – were more than coincidence. Ruth Campbell had to have put rat poison into food or drink that Sir Gordon had taken on board. Andrew would start by having *The Lizzie*, which was impounded at North Berwick, examined for traces of the poison.

The funeral was being held on the day after the report came through to him. It was scheduled for 11 a.m. in the little grave-yard on the Ingersley estate. Lady Campbell had requested that only immediate family and estate people attend, but Andrew would go and she could not stop him. Under such circumstances a police representative would normally be there.

However, Andrew had loved and admired Sir Gordon Campbell, who would not have wanted him to attend his burial as a representative of the police or cause distress to the family. They would all be questioned in due course, so he would play down his own presence and pay his personal last respects while keeping his eyes open.

On the morning of the funeral, Andrew, wearing a dark grey suit and black tie, was about to leave for the office when the phone rang. It would probably be for him, he thought, and waited until Ma came into the living room, her round face pink, cheerful and surprised. 'It's Robert,' she said. 'Robert Campbell. He's at the airport.'

'Tell him to wait there. Beside the main door. I'll pick him up,' Andrew said. 'Then ring the office to say I'll be in later this afternoon.'

He drove to the airport fast and spotted Robert from a good hundred yards or so. The boy had grown. He was broader, taller, and his hair – Andrew grinned as he shook hands – made him look like a pop star.

'Good to see you, Robert.'

'You too. All in black?'

'Yes.' Andrew opened the boot of the Zephyr for Robert's guitar. 'It's your father's funeral this morning. Eleven o'clock.'

Robert got in the front, beside him. 'I can't go like this,' he said, indicating the worn jeans, the open-necked cheesecloth shirt, the unshaven face. 'Should I hold back, do you think?'

Andrew wanted to see Ruth Campbell's reaction to Robert's return. He said, 'Of course you must go.' He looked Robert up and down. 'You're about my size. I'll lend you a dark suit and shoes. We'll go to my place and drive down to Ingersley together.'

'I hope old Nanny doesn't die of shock,' Robert said. Then, 'Do you know how my father died?'

'Afraid so,' Andrew said. 'I'll give you details on the way.'

Two hours later, at 10.50, the Zephyr rolled in at the South Lodge gate. Robert looked immaculate in his borrowed clothes. He was lucky, he thought. He and Andrew were very alike – almost like brothers, or father and son – and Andrew's clothes fitted him. Robert was narrower but they were exactly the same height and leg length. Even his shoes were a perfect fit. Andrew had also been considerate and professional in giving the forensic details and questioning him on Father's habits. Robert now knew that poison had been administered and that Mother was under suspicion.

He tried not to think about it as they got out of the car and walked the two hundred yards to the cemetery, cutting through the parkland of the estate, which, he realised, he had missed. Already he felt more alert, invigorated and alive. The air was cool by Tennessee standards – it reminded him of the very best in air-conditioning, clean and clear. On the breeze could be smelled the sea. And in his heart Robert knew that there lurked under the loss of a great man something unseen and rotten. He had told Andrew that he had been certain for a long time that his mother had periods of madness, of old-fashioned lunacy. They often coincided with certain times of the year. He told him that he had come to expect them without ever admitting as much to himself. He could be sure of erratic behaviour and wildness in Mother in midsummer, with its long, light nights'.

Andrew said, 'Convenient. It won't stand as a defence. However, we have no proof – nothing to suggest anyone other than your father himself administered the poison.' Then Andrew suggested that they get today's funeral over with before police investigations commenced.

They reached the little graveyard where, around the family, hiding them from view, was a crowd of estate staff, maids, farm workers and their relatives. Local tradesmen too were there to pay their respects, so it was not until they were within a few yards of the grave that they were seen by the family.

Robert saw his darling Nanny, looking old and unsteady, leaning on a stick, her back as straight as ever. Her silver hair was drawn tightly down into the nape of her neck and a black velour hat was pulled down firmly, almost to her eyebrows. She looked across and saw him, smiled broadly and tugged at Mother's black-clad sleeve.

Ruth looked up over the gash in the earth where Father's coffin lay. Her face drained of colour as she recognised him. It was clearly, a shock to her. She mouthed the word 'Robert' to Edward, who had his back to them. Edward turned, looked across at them and gave a small, tight smile. Robert and Andrew approached the graveside and stood still, next to Edward, as the priest intoned, 'Ashes to ashes . . .'

When the crowd of mourners started off back to the house, Ruth turned to him. 'So. You're back! Why?'

Robert towered above her. He was a head taller than Edward, who kept giving him grateful glances as if to say, *I'm glad you're home!*

'To claim my inheritance. To run my estate,' he said grimly.

'Then you are on a wild-goose chase.' She had recovered her temper fast. 'There's nothing left of it and nobody can claim a thing until Gordon's case has satisfied the procurator fiscal.' She looked at Andrew. 'You have the report by now, I expect?'

'Yes,' Andrew replied.

'You will want to talk to me?' she said. 'I can spare an hour, tomorrow afternoon.'

'We won't discuss it now.' Andrew saw, for the first time, a frightened look at the back of her shrewd blue eyes.

'Two o'clock tomorrow, then.'

Andrew nodded in agreement and fell behind to have a few words with the farm workers he had not seen for so many years.

Robert, too, dropped back to wait for Nanny, after saying in the cultured, deep Scottish voice that proclaimed his good manners, 'Excuse me, Mother.' Nanny was walking behind them, and now she took his hands eagerly and held on to him.

'You aren't going back, are you, darling?' she said. 'We need you here, you know.'

She had shrunk a little and he had to bend right down to kiss her old cheeks. 'I won't leave again, Nanny. I'm back now – to look after you and Edward.'

He gave her his arm and escorted her into the house, where Mother had ordered a paltry cold spread – tiny sandwiches, biscuits and tea. There, everyone came up to him to say they were glad he was home. Edward particularly would not leave his side and seemed grateful to him that he had returned to take over responsibilities that he'd been afraid would fall to him. Only Mother looked as if she'd prefer it if this were his funeral instead.

Robert asked Phoebe if he could call later and then he saw them off – old man Davey Hamilton, Phoebe and Nanny – since Andrew had offered to drop them off at their homes, four miles away.

Outside, Andrew helped Miss Taylor into the front seat while Phoebe and Davey Hamilton climbed into the back.

He'd drop Miss Taylor off last and spring the surprise question on her when the others were gone. He said, to comfort her as they drove away, 'Today must be a strain for you, Miss Taylor. To see Sir Gordon Campbell laid to rest and to have Robert return.'

'I can't believe it,' she said. 'He never gave me his last address.'

'No.' Andrew smiled. 'I found him.'

'I can't believe it.'

Phoebe said, 'Lady Campbell didn't look too pleased to see Robert. She wants the estate for Edward.'

Andrew listened carefully. He'd noticed a lot – that Mike Hamilton and Ruth Campbell were at daggers drawn; that Phoebe too had little respect for her father but saved her iciest manner for Lady Campbell. It was plain now, from her tone of voice, that Phoebe detested Ruth.

'Tut tut,' Miss Taylor said. 'Lady Campbell always thought Edward would make the better landowner.' Nanny looked annoyed. She did not regain her composure for some minutes until Andrew turned off towards the A1 and Davey Hamilton's land.

'Those days are gone,' said Davey Hamilton. 'The old estates were doomed long ago. If his sons have his common sense they will sell up—'

Phoebe said, 'We make a profit.'

Her grandfather came back with, 'For how long? The lease expires soon. Young Robert may not renew it. Anything could happen. He could sell it for building, for caravan parks.'

'I don't think Robert will turn us off the land we've farmed for so long,' Phoebe said. Then wistfully, 'Unless he marries ...'

Davey Hamilton leaned forward. He tapped Andrew's shoulder. 'Over there,' he said pointing towards Traprain Law.

307

'What?' said Andrew.

'Where the Heinkel came down.'

'It must have been exciting all the same,' Andrew acknowledged before pulling up at a farmhouse with a neat, well-kept garden. Davey Hamilton thanked him and with Phoebe's assistance made it safely to his front door.

Andrew waved to them and drove Miss Taylor homewards. When they had gone a little way and she was relaxed, leaning back into the upholstery and off her guard, Andrew said, 'Do you remember all your patients – your clients, Miss Taylor?'

She looked at him quickly, unaware that he could see her every flicker of expression from the corner of his eye, and said, 'Many of them, yes.'

'Do you remember a Flora Macdonald?'

He saw her hands tremble as she put them nervously to her throat and said, 'No. I can't say that I do.'

'She was tall. Red haired. She had a baby which you delivered.'

'No. No. I can't recall a girl of that name,' she protested, but her voice was feeble, her face was pale and Andrew knew she was lying.

He said, as they bumped along the stony path to her door, 'She had a boy on the fifteenth of April, nineteen forty. Fifteenth of April, nineteen forty. The birth was registered in North Berwick on the very day Robert was born.' He pulled up and looked at her. She had gone chalk white and he knew she would tell him no more.

He was much nearer to the truth now; not on a false trail this time. It was not until he returned home later in the evening that he realised that Robert's guitar was still in the boot. He carried it into the flat, rang Ingersley and asked to speak to Robert.

'He's not here,' said Lady Campbell. 'Try Hamilton's farm.' But after a moment's pause, in a voice that had lost its didactic ring so that she sounded now as if she might crack, 'Why can't you leave us alone? I refuse to speak to you! I can't answer any more of your questions.'

'They are necessary, Lady Campbell. And you know they are.' But she had slammed down the phone.

Andrew rang the farm and spoke to Robert. 'You left your guitar,' he said. 'I have it here. It's safe.'

'I don't need the guitar,' said Robert. 'But I need some things that are zipped inside the pocket: my wallet, passport and stuff.'

'I'm coming to Ingersley to – to interview your mother. I'll bring it tomorrow,' said Andrew.

'I have to go to Edinburgh to see the lawyer in the morning,' said Robert. 'Could you possibly take the papers to your office? I'll collect them on my way there. You could drop off the guitar in the afternoon, or—' there was a moment's pause – 'could I ask for a lift back to Ingersley? I'd like to be there when you question everyone.'

Andrew said, 'Of course,' and put the phone down. He was not looking forward to tomorrow. He knew he would get enough evidence to charge Ruth Campbell, but what damage would this cause to Robert? He could be forced to sell and move away. Edward could lose his place at Dartmouth. And Nanny Taylor would lose all the people she loved.

He unfastened the guitar case, found the zipped pocket and withdrew all the papers it contained. He would find an old briefcase to hold the untidy sheets of music – he put these aside – the newspapers, wallet, passport and letters. Then – and it felt as if an electric current had shot through him – he came across an old letter in a parchment envelope and his heart came thundering into his throat. The writing was familiar.

He stared. His hands shook. It was Flora's handwriting, exactly as it was when she last wrote to him. Not all that distinctive, but so well known. He had all her letters still. He'd recognise her handwriting anywhere. He turned it over and there, drawn on the flap of the envelope, was her own signature – the little drawing of a weeping tree.

His fingers were trembling as he took out the pages of ship's notepaper and under the heading *White Empress* read:

Dear Nanny,
The voyage was uneventful and the *White Empress* comfortable but crowded. Our cabin companions were my new friend Joan and her daughter Mary. It made a difference

having Joan. We shared the children though she could not feed Alexander. He is thriving – a really bonny bouncing baby. He weighs 12 pounds and has been no trouble at all. He is such a contented child.

We left Halifax by rail on the CPR to Montreal, setting off at 10.30 a.m. Joan and I had separate sleepers and we arrived in Montreal the next day at 10.30 a.m. We travelled through deeply forested country with high rolling hills and a wide, slow-flowing river that Joan says is used to transport lumber in the spring.

I loved Montreal but found it a big disadvantage that I don't speak French. Joan is fluent. She said, 'Good job you aren't going to Quebec.'

Left Montreal at 9.30 and reached Belleville at 4 p.m. then changed trains for Bancroft. Thirteen little whistle-stops and four hours later we arrived in Bancroft.

Aunt Dorothy and Uncle John met us and drove us home. They are wonderful people and I thank you from my heart for everything. Alexander is being thoroughly spoiled by Aunt Dorothy who says it's nice to have a baby in the house again after all these years.

I have said that I will not stay without paying my way, and since they refuse to take the money (I still have nearly £100 left – or rather, $440 – and when you consider that a working wage is $18 a week that makes me rich), I shall make myself useful around the store and house.

I hear the news and read the papers. We got a few British papers though they come weeks late. And I am afraid for you living with the bombs and Blitz and rationing when I am living in luxury in a land of plenty. I wish you were here, Nanny, out of harm's way. I owe you such a debt of gratitude. It was not until we sailed that I began to appreciate all you have done for Alexander and me. Joan Almond, my friend, told me that there were 210,000 applications for a place on the *White Empress* and that ugly questions were asked in Parliament, where the organisers were accused of giving places to 'the moneyed classes' while the working class languished.

Mr Churchill did not approve of the evacuation – he deprecates what he calls a stampede from Britain – but there was really not much that I could have done to help. Alexander and I would just be another two mouths to feed.

Now I am here I am going to do whatever I can to help the war effort, as well as praying every night for you all.

Love, Flora.

'God Almighty!' Andrew breathed when he put the pages down with fingers that had lost all sensation. 'There is even an address – Bancroft – she might still be there.' Then, as he thought about the baby, Alexander, with the knowledge that this was his own, only son, his mouth went tight and his eyes filled with tears. He stood, running his fingers through his curly hair while pacing the room.

He could work out the sequence of events now. Nanny Taylor had delivered Flora's baby and, since they had nowhere to go, packed them off to Canada to live with her sister. It did not explain why Flora agreed to this, but now he saw how the connection had been kept up all these years – how Robert had come to be given the address when he went to San Francisco and Nanny Taylor was in Canada, having that long awaited holiday with her sister.

Had Robert met Flora and his, Andrew's, son? His Alex? He could not wait until tomorrow to find out. He rang the farm again and was told by a surly-sounding Hamilton that Robert and Phoebe had gone for a walk and he had no time to go to look for them because the hay had to be moved.

'All right,' Andrew said. He'd have to leave it until tomorrow to ask Robert. Well, he'd waited twenty-one years. A day more would make no difference. But right now he'd go and break the news, gently, to Ma, and tell her that as soon as this case was over, he'd take a holiday – he'd take her to Canada, to a place called Bancroft, in Hastings county, and they would try to trace her grandson.

Chapter Seventeen

'They are all turning against me,' Ruth muttered to herself as she put down the phone. 'That horrible man Andrew Stewart will be here tomorrow afternoon to question and pry and lie and accuse me.' The walls were closing in on her and nobody was here to support her.

'Edward!' she called as she ran up the stairs. 'Where are you?' She flung open his bedroom door. He was not there, but his suitcase was open on the bed, half packed. She ran to it, turned it upside down and scattered the contents on the floor. 'You will not leave it all to me,' she said to the empty room. 'I did it for you. Do you hear! Don't you dare turn against me.' She had seen the cold look in his eyes once too often.

It was all Robert's doing, of course. The two of them had had their heads together all day; changing the subject when she came near. Then she'd interrupted Robert as he'd tried to ring the doctor. They were going to convince the doctor that she had gone mad. They'd need two doctors for that. She knew the law. She'd signed enough warrants to certify and lock up mad people – in the middle of the night sometimes. They would not do this to her. She would triumph over them. She would show them.

She slammed Edward's door then went to her own room. 'My God!' she exclaimed. 'Ingratitude!' she raged and went to the mirror. She looked wild. Her hair was awful. Static electricity was making it stand up on top and lie flat to her temples. She changed out of her black dress, pulled on her jodhpurs over her bare skin and stuffed her arms into a clean white blouse which she fastened hastily. She would ride – and she'd make Mike

Hamilton ride with her. 'He won't get away with ignoring me!' she swore as she pulled on her riding hat and ankle boots.

She left the house, clattering noisily down the steps, making for the barn where she knew she would find him. 'How dare he ignore me?' He had barely spoken to her since the night they went to Musselburgh's mortuary to view Gordon's body. She'd been surprised to find how squeamish he was – running outside to be violently sick in the police yard.

She reached the barn and found him complacently moving bales from one side to the other. This time she did not hang around in the doorway. She went up to him. 'You have to do something for me,' she said loudly, not caring any longer about discretion.

He looked at her, his black eyes narrow and gleaming. 'What?' he said coldly. 'I told you, it's over, Ruth. I love my wife. I have promised Lucy – and Phoebe.'

'Damn Phoebe! Damn Lucy! You threaten me?'

He came and stood in front of her, holding her arms in an iron grip. 'I said, I'll have no more of you!'

'Mike – please – Mike. You have to!' She was all but screaming now, and he loosened his hold while she said, 'One last thing . . .'

'What is it?'

'They are coming tomorrow. To question me about Gordon.'

'Well?'

'He did it, you know. Not me. He must have put it in his brandy flask. I never touched his brandy flask!'

'What the hell are you on about?'

'Will you tell him? Andrew Stewart. Tell him Gordon came to you and asked you for it?'

'Asked for what, woman?' His voice was high and loud now. She had seen him before like this – close to losing control completely.

'Rat poison.'

He stared at her and now his eyes were hot and wild, but what she saw in them was hatred as well as rage. She backed away but he came towards her, spittle oozing out of the corners of his mouth, his voice gritty as he demanded, 'Gordon died from strychnine poisoning?'

'It wasn't me—'

313

'Gordon died like a rat?' He hit her. She fell back but managed to stay on her feet. The side of her face was dull with a numbness that would soon be excruciating pain. He came after her again. 'Gordon was poisoned by you? The man I respected and loved? He died like a rat?' he yelled, hitting her again, this time on the left side of her head.

She stumbled once more, but regained her balance and darted away from him, between the towering bales of hay. He'd left spaces, made steps, and now she climbed, chattering and crying, to the top as he came after her, snorting like an old horse.

She fell, dropping from sight behind the last row of bales, then looked up and saw his fierce face. He was going to pull down the bales to reach her. Already the top bale had gone.

His hairy arms were reaching down for her. One more row and he'd have her cornered like a rat.

Feverishly she felt in her pocket – surely it must be there. Her fingers closed about the petrol lighter. She slid it out of her pocket, put her hand behind her so he would not see it and laughed out loud. Click, it went. Click. Click.

'What the ...' he yelled as a sheet of crackling flames shot right up the wall of the bales, spitting and rasping. 'Ruth! Get out!'

'How dare you threaten me?' She would not get out.

The last she saw of him was his hands, those hairy-backed hands, frantically tearing at the flaming bales, throwing them out of the way, only to have them spread their fire ...

Andrew had spent a night of fitful sleep; dreaming first that he found Flora and his son and then, secondly, that he found them only to be spurned. Not since the war had he been so edgy and watchful; afraid even to sleep lest he missed some vital clue as to why Flora had run away. Last night, Ma had said, 'Be prepared. She may not want to know you now.' And, wistfully, 'I hope she does let me meet my grandson some day.'

This morning she had remonstrated with him as if he too were a young man; ticking him off because he didn't want breakfast.

He dressed carefully in a dark suit for his return to Ingersley with a detective sergeant and a constable, and as he did so he

314

tried to anticipate his interview with Nanny Taylor. His heart beat faster. She held the answer to everything. He would insist on knowing every last detail. While he would be talking to the old woman, Lady Campbell would be brought to the station for questioning and, possibly, charging. He would do the charging though he did not think for a second that she would confess or show any emotion whatever.

He went into the office early – an hour before the night shift left. It was they who reported to him that the fire brigade had been called to a fire in the barn at Ingersley.

'The hay.' He did not have any suspicion at this point but was concerned that this might delay his discovering the truth about Flora and her – no, *his* – son. And again came the tingling down his arms and the thrilling thought that he was a father. It was difficult to put it to the back of his mind while he dealt with unrelated police work.

He looked at his watch. It was eight o'clock. 'I'll be in my office,' he said, 'in about ten minutes.'

His stomach felt hollow, so he went out, bought a newspaper and a couple of morning rolls with bacon and returned to the office. He ran up the stairs, entered the room and found four recorded messages waiting for him. He turned on the machine and heard the first one. It was from Robert. 'I have to speak to Detective Chief Inspector Stewart.' There was the sound of the call being transferred to his machine, then Robert's anxious voice. 'Andrew! Mother is dead!' There was a break in his voice. 'Mike Hamilton too. They have just found the bodies – and a cigarette lighter. It looks as if Mother had gone to the barn first ...' His voice thickened, 'Can I talk to you today? This afternoon?'

Andrew switched off the machine. 'She beat me to it,' he whispered. 'She'd have known she was done for – but taking Hamilton with her ...? He could not go to Ingersley today, after this. It could be too much for the old woman. He dialled Ingersley. A maid answered and told him that Robert was at the Hamiltons. Andrew rang there and was soon reassuring Robert, 'It will be all right. Come and see me this afternoon.'

He switched the machine back on. The next two messages were unimportant reminders of scheduled meetings. He made notes and waited for the final message ...

The voice came clear, deep and slow with a rich Canadian accent. 'My name is Alexander Macdonald. I'd like to talk to whoever is in charge of the "death by drowning" case of Sir Gordon Campbell.' Andrew felt the blood leaving his face as the voice continued, 'I'll call by this morning, at eleven o'clock. Thank you.'

It was his son. Andrew did not know how many shocks a person could take before his heart failed. His hands were shaking violently as he played the message again and again. He found it hard to believe his ears. The boy plainly did not know who Andrew was. He tried to pour a coffee from the dispensing machine outside in the hallway but spilled the hot liquid and then burnt his mouth.

What would he say to Alexander – his son? How, to put it? How not to? He silently rehearsed several lines, '*Now, sit down, Alex. I have to tell you before we go any further. I am your father.*' No. '*Has your mother ever mentioned my name to you?*' No. '*Son. I have found you.*' No.

Oh God, it will come to me, he thought. I wonder if he looks like me, or Flora. Would I have recognised him if I'd passed him in the street?

He rang down to the desk. 'When an Alexander Macdonald arrives, please send him straight up. No! I'll come down!' Then he worked furiously for the next hour on the Campbell report to the procurator fiscal, wrapping the thing up, hoping they would be satisfied that there was now no murderer to charge, praying that it could be brought to, at least, a private end. He did not want Robert and Edward to suffer more than was necessary.

It was ten-forty-five when the call came. As quick as lightning he picked up the extension phone.

'Detective Chief Inspector? Your visitor, Alexander Macdonald, is in the hall.'

'I'll be down.' Andrew took a deep breath, flattened his hair, pulled in his stomach and went down the stairs to find Robert, dressed in jeans and checked shirt, waiting for him.

He was about to say, 'Robert, I wasn't expecting you yet ...' when the young man put his hand out and said in a deep Canadian voice, 'I'm Alexander Macdonald. I wonder if you can help me. I'm over here to find my twin brother, Robert Campbell.'

Andrew closed his eyes as his hand was squeezed in a firm shake. 'Your twin brother?' he said, in a voice that had become high and hesitant.

'You all right, sir?' the duty sergeant said. 'You're very white.'

'I'm all right.' Andrew inclined his head towards the desk. Robert's twin? But of course – it explained everything. Andrew opened his eyes, closed and opened them again, to be sure. His legs, hands, even his voice didn't seem right. 'I – I'll take you out, Alexander,' he said. And finally, 'I have a great deal to tell you.'

He turned to the desk where the sergeant, who had heard every word and seen everything, was grinning like a Cheshire cat. Andrew said quietly to him, 'Sergeant, by the time I return, you will have an even bigger smile on your face. If Robert-Campbell does come, will you please ask him to wait in my office, and say nothing.' Then to Alex, 'Ready? I'll take you to the Caledonian Hotel for lunch. But first, to the American Bar. We are going to need a large Scotch or two.'

And there, in the American Bar, over a couple of drams to ease the tension, they talked. Once Alexander knew that the Detective Chief Inspector knew Robert he relaxed, and when questioned, began to tell Andrew briefly, all about his child-hood.

Andrew watched and listened carefully, drinking in the sound and sight of his own son. It was astonishing to him that, brought up separately as Alexander and Robert had been, they had identical mannerisms; the traits that Andrew believed were learned behaviour; the laugh was identical as was the quick blink of the eyes before opening wide, then the resting position of their hands – even their choice of words. Andrew had had many a heart-to-heart with Robert. It was uncanny.

But he was going to tell Alex the truth and he must do it before they met Robert. Alex was saying, 'My wonderful Mom has been riven with guilt all these years for allowing her babies to be separated at birth. She has never gotten over it.'

'She wouldn't get over it,' Andrew remarked before asking the question that could destroy his dreams for ever. 'And has your mother re-married?'

'No.' Alex made the familiar blink before he opened his eyes wider and added, 'I don't think she has ever stopped loving our father.'

'Did she tell you anything about your father?' Andrew asked and his stomach heaved. 'Did she ever say anything about him?'

'He was a sailor. He deserted her.'

'No! He didn't.' Andrew's voice was gruff as he fought both tears and anger. 'It was she who deserted him. She took her baby and fled to Canada.'

'But Lady Campbell's price for taking care of her, seeing her through the birth, was that she handed over the baby. She never knew that there were two of us. Nanny would never tell her. And it was Nanny who got Mom away, to Canada, to her sister ... and told Mom that she must never again speak about my father, nor try to contact him. It was best for Robert, you see.'

Andrew put his head in his hands, there in the crowded American Bar where he had already nodded to several people he knew. He was beyond caring if anyone saw him in distress now.

Alex put a hand on his arm. 'You all right, sir?'

Andrew looked at him and unsprung tears were clouding his vision. 'It is me,' he said. 'I am Andrew Stewart. Your father ...' and then in answer to Alex's bewilderment, 'Come on! Let's get out of here. We have a lot of catching up to do – you and Robert and I.'

It was the last performance of *The Mikado* in Hasting's County Community Hall. Flora should have got over her nerves by now – the show had been running for a week, playing to packed houses. Tonight, though, she was on edge as never before.

There had been no word from Alex. Nothing at all. She had tried to contact Nanny but the phone rang and rang with no answer.

Tonight, her make-up done and her kimono fastened, she pulled on the black wig that was ready styled and adorned with what Alex laughingly called knitting needles. The other two Little Maids were chatting and laughing at their dressing tables. It was a big changing room so there was plenty of space if you wanted to think not talk, as she did.

318

She may have lost both her sons now. Why hadn't Alex phoned?

The intercom was on and she heard the orchestra tuning up – heard the footsteps and muffled talk of the audience as the hall filled. She took a sip of water then blotted her lips on a tissue.

Something was going on in the family, too. They were hiding things from her. She knew it. And their faces ... so serious. Yet they had taken the news well that she was the mother of Nanny's darling Robert. They had been dumbfounded at first. Then Aunt Dorothy had said, 'Alexander is right. He must find his twin.'

'I have always known him, you know,' Alex had said. 'He won't be a stranger to me.' He had gone, and he had not come back – and it was a month since she had last seen him.

The family were trying to make up for it. Tonight, Peter's wife Valerie, Aunt Dorothy and Uncle John would be here, sitting in the seats she had booked for them – centre seats, three rows back. Later they were having a party at the house – open house – for all the cast.

Nerves and worry were her constant companions. Somehow she couldn't stop shaking. Where was Alex?

'Overture and beginners, please,' was coming over the tannoy.

Pitti-Sing, her friend Maggie, said, 'Ready, Flora?'

'Yes.'

The three of them went backstage and stood in the wings, trying to get a glimpse of the hall before the lights went down. Then the overture began and then it was all excitement and dashing on- and off-stage, although there were no changes of costume for the three sisters whose songs came one after the other towards the end of Act One.

'I couldn't see a thing out there,' said Peep-Bo, coming from the wings at the interval. 'But they are enjoying it.'

'Not even my lot?' asked Flora plaintively, then laughed at herself for sounding so petty. It was the first time ever that Alex had missed her show. She so longed to set eyes on Alex.

Flora's second song, in Act Two, 'The sun, whose rays are all ablaze ...' brought the house down. But someone, somewhere in the darkened hall would not stop applauding. The rest joined in and she had to do an encore. She came off-stage, eyes sparkling, cheeks glowing through the white mask-like make-up.

'Wonderful!' breathed Jack as he passed her to go on-stage. Jack's character Nanki Poo was in love with Yum Yum – and Jack himself was half in love with Flora. Then the four of them sang, 'Brightly Dawns our Wedding Day' and again the audience called for an encore.

The mood of the audience was catching and the songs were lovely; and, silly as it was, some of the corniest made a lump come into Flora's throat, so that when Ko Ko sang, 'On a tree by a river, a little Tom-tit, sang willow, tit willow, tit willow ...' Flora could cry a little tear for Alex and not be teased.

Then it was the last chorus and they were all on stage and singing lustily, 'For ... he's going to marry Yum Yum, Yum Yum ...' and the rafters were ringing with joyful song.

The curtain fell. The applause was deafening. The curtain rose and fell and still they went on applauding. The cast went off-stage. The lights went up. The chorus went out and took their bows, stepped back and parted for the cast to come forward in reverse order of importance.

And suddenly it was her turn. Flora went to centre stage, lifted her hands in acknowledgement, then quickly cast her eyes towards the centre of the third row.

Her knees gave way and she had to make an effort to stand. Her skin prickled. Her eyes went swimmingly out of focus – then back.

They were there: Andrew, her Andrew, with, one either side, Alexander and Robert.

She stepped back, but could not take her eyes off them, her sons, with their father.

The Mikado took three curtain calls. Then the whole ensemble took three more.

The curtain was lowered and lifted for the last time. They were still there, still clapping, and now, slowly the applause ceased and the bouquets and little speeches of thanks began.

'To our producer ...' A bouquet was presented. 'The conductor ...' another bouquet. 'The Mikado ....' another.

Then the stage manager came forward to say, 'And tonight, ladies and gentlemen, we have some special guests with us. All

320

the way from Scotland to see our own Yum Yum – Flora Macdonald ...' he nodded to the third row, '... and to present her with a very special bouquet.'

And she was laughing and crying as Andrew climbed the stairs to the stage, Alex and Robert behind him.

He stood before her, a huge bouquet of roses in his arms, but it was the look in his eyes that told her more than flowers ever could.

She bobbed a little Japanese curtsey, and whispered through the hard, tight knot in her throat, 'Thank you! Oh, thank you Andrew!' and all to wild applause.

And as the final curtain came down she stood, arms open wide, with her sons, one held fast by each hand while she was held firmly in the arms of the husband she had married by habit and repute, under a weeping willow tree, so very long ago.

The end.

Wise Child
Audrey Reimann

Through War and Depression, an epic saga of three families

Everyone knows me as Isobel now. I have not used the name I was born with for years, yet within half an hour of arriving in Macclesfield I passed my old enemy and heard her say, "My God! It's Lily Stanway ..."

Silk mills and secrets. All of Lily's young life has been dominated by undercurrents among her elders that she could sense but not understand. The ties of business and love that bind the Stanways, Hammonds and Chancellors are never discussed, yet the younger generation are deeply aware of them. But when Lily grows up and falls for the very man she should not, *must* not marry, it looks as if the delicate façade of inheritance, both of blood and property, will collapse and draw the three families to ruin with it ...

A Better Love Next Time
Doreen Edwards

A Welsh saga in the best-selling tradition of Iris Gower

Swansea in the 1950s and Florence Philpotts is ahead of her time. Her parents and boyfriend Ken may see her as an impetuous dreamer, but surely there is more to life than the typing pool?

Defying everyone, Florence takes a job as an apprentice hairdresser. She knows she has talent and enthusiasm, but it isn't going to be plain sailing – she has to avoid the unwanted attentions of her boss, Mr Tony, for a start.

Then, in the midst of a glorious local scandal, the opportunity arises to take over the salon. But neither her parents nor the bank will take a slip of a girl seriously. And marriage to Tony's mysterious brother Cliff could be a step too far even for determined, impulsive, ambitious Florence Philpotts ...

Catch The Moment
Euanie MacDonald

A compelling Scottish saga

Annie Ramsay is fourteen when she travels to Ayrshire to work as a milkmaid on Clachan's farm. Annie's spirited nature immediately makes an impression on the farmer's only son, Ian – a match considered above her station.

Then she rescues Alexandra Cameron, the daughter of the Laird of Craigdrummond, and is swept away by her new friend to the Paris of the Belle Epoque. There, Alexandra's loyalty proves to be fickle and Annie is left to fend for herself in the exciting but depraved Café Society of Montmartre. As the new century approaches, Annie experiences great happiness and deep sorrow.

But, for all her willingness to catch the moment and use it well, fate is not done with Annie Ramsay yet...

Full Circle
Mary A. Larkin

All families have their secrets...

Annie has been happily married to Sean Devlin for several years when the telegram arrives: her sister, Rosaleen, is coming home to Belfast from Canada. Annie is full of misgivings about the reunion with her beautiful sister – for many years before Sean and Rosaleen had a brief affair with far-reaching consequences. Though their love kept Annie and Sean together, the affair nearly destroyed them.

And she is right to be wary of Rosaleen's visit. For Rosaleen finds herself as attracted to Sean as ever. But does he feel the same? And could either of them betray Annie again?

The Seaweed Gatherers
Jessica Blair

From the best-selling author of *The Red Shawl*

Newcastle, 1802. Lucy is beside her beloved father as he dies. His legacy is held in the mystery of his final words: "The de Northbys owe you".

Lucy learns that Richard de Northby is the wealthy owner of an alum works in Ravenscar. Headstrong, she decides to leave the security of her respectable family and, with her sister Alice, stows away on a ship delivering coal to Ravenscar. Once there, the sisters find employment as seaweed gatherers – and Lucy meets handsome army officer Mark Cossart. However, de Northby's spoilt daughter Zilpha regards him as her personal property. And so, as the sisters attempt to unravel a mystery of the past, a new dispute may be developing in the present...

The Jewel Streets
Una Horne

"A great novel of passion and family ties" *Woman's Realm*

When times grow hard in her Durham pit village, Hetty Pearson is forced into service at Hope Hall near Whitby. A humble skivvy, she soon strikes up an unexpected friendship with Richard, the younger son of the house. He sees her change from skinny child to lovely young woman – only to catch the eye of his brother Matthew, a spoilt and ruthless seducer who has Hetty thrown from the house when she rejects him.

Hetty seeks a change of fortune among the jewel-named streets of Saltburn-by-the-Sea, but work is hard to come by. Her situation is near desperate when Matthew turns up, swearing he truly loves her. Has she misjudged the Hope heir? And where, when she most needs his friendship, is Richard?

A stirring saga of passion, class conflict and intrigue by the author of *A Time To Heal* and *Under The Rowan Tree*.

For All the Bright Promise
Elizabeth Lord

A stunning saga of the East End at war

Maggie has been in love with the handsome and successful Matthew Ward since she was sixteen and she moved to the East End of London. The trouble is he sees her as the girl-next-door, just one of the crowd.

When war breaks out in 1939 Matthew leaves home and joins the army. Maggie disentangles herself from her clinging mother and decides to train as a nurse. And so, by chance, she discovers her vocation and, with the attentions of the doctors and soldiers she cares for, her confidence grows. Matthew will come back to find a very different girl.

Yet when Matthew returns on leave he drops his own bombshell: Mrs Susan Ward, his wife. But the times are unpredictable and, although there is heartache to come for Matt and Maggie, their story is far from over...

Like a Diamond
Malcolm Ross

A compelling Cornish saga

It is 1910 and Peter de Vivian, arriving at the new family home in Cornwall, is instantly smitten with the grace and beauty of Gemma Penhallow, the upper housemaid.

But Gemma, despite her attraction to Peter, wants to keep her distance. Her recent experience has taught her to be wary of all men outside her own class. Peter is determined to convince her of the sincerity of his feelings, but he has underestimated both the opposition of his family and the independence of his beloved.

The very best of Piatkus fiction is now available in paperback as well as hardcover. Piatkus paperbacks, where *every* book is special.

The prices shown above were correct at the time of going to press. However, Piatkus Books reserve the right to show new retail prices on covers which may differ from those previously advertised in the text or elsewhere.

Piatkus Books will be available from your bookshop or newsagent, or can be ordered from the following address:
Piatkus Paperbacks, PO Box 11, Falmouth, TR10 9EN
Alternatively you can fax your order to this address on 01326 374 888 or e-mail us at books@barni.avel.co.uk

Payments can be made as follows: Sterling cheque, Eurocheque, postal order (payable to Piatkus Books) or by credit card, Visa/Mastercard. Do not send cash or currency. UK and B.F.P.O. customers should allow £1.00 postage and packing for the first book, 50p for the second and 30p for each additional book ordered to a maximum of £3.00 (7 books plus).

Overseas customers, including Eire, allow £2.00 for postage and packing for the first book, plus £1.00 for the second and 50p for each subsequent title ordered.

NAME (block letters) _____

ADDRESS_____

_____

I enclose my remittance for £ _____

I wish to pay by Visa/Mastercard   Expiry Date:_____
